Rogue Agent: A Thriller

Sean Sweeney

Rogue Agent
Copyright © 2011 by Sean Sweeney

This book, an original publication, was registered with the United States Library of Congress Copyright Office in May 2011.

Cover art courtesy Chris DelVecchio
Cover designed by Trisha L. Reeves

ACKNOWLEDGEMENTS

The author would like to thank the following people for their help and support of this project:

Steven Savile, Helen Smith, Brian M. Logan, Dean M. Drinkel, Bruce Sarte, Kent Holloway, Imogen Rose, Susanne O'Leary, Mary McDonald, Naomi Kramer, Donna Fasano, William L.k., Stan Tremblay, Rob Cordiner, Jim C. Hines, Paul S. Kemp, D.G. Gass, Deborah Levinson and Jeanie Phelps. The Indie Author Mafia crew of David Dalglish, David McAfee, Daniel Arenson, Mike Crane, Rob DuPerre, Jason Letts, and Amanda Hocking, my brothers and sister in this writing game.

Special thanks go out to Rasina Tanvir and Al Kunz. To the folks on the Amazon Kindle and Nook fan pages on Facebook, as well as those who congregate on the Amazon.com messageboards and Twitter, I thank you for helping get the word out about MODEL AGENT.

I would be remiss if I did not thank Jackie Hazeldine, Doug Monson and Trudy Messingham in this space. Thanks for the inspiration!

And as always, mom and Estee were in my corner from conception to delivery.

DEDICATION
For Mark Ambrose and Diane Zeiner

The two high school English teachers who never gave up on me,
even to this day.
For that, I dedicate this novel to them.

Rogue Agent: A Thriller

Sean Sweeney

Hand in hand, father and son rode the escalator from the platform all the way up to the gate of the Wembley Park Tube station. The sun licked their faces, much as it had before they melded with the crowd and surged underground at Bond Street. Sweat covered their brows before they stepped back outside.

The father was in his mid 30s, with black hair on the road to receding. His rather long, hawkish nose was prominent on his face, one that would have made the late Robert Helpmann jealous: It was so much like the one Helpmann's most famous character, the Childcatcher, used to sniff out children in the old Disney movie *Chitty Chitty Bang Bang*. He wore a faded red Liverpool F.C. jersey with Fowler 9 printed on the back. He had pulled it on so much on the weekends and for midweek matches that he feared he would tear it on accident if the Reds came close to winning their 19th First Division title or their sixth European Cup.

Of course, like a true Liverpool supporter, he did not like to walk alone and never did when it came to football: His 8-year-old son, who loved Liverpool just as much as he did, was with him, the little boy's left hand firmly clenching his father's right. The son had looked forward to this Olympic football tournament match between their home country, the United States, and the Great Britain team, which, while it carried the moniker of the Home Nations, primarily consisted of Under-21s from England. His father told him that his hero, Steven Gerrard, would not play in the match. There was some disappointment to be sure, but the boy, holding onto his father's hand for dear life, shed his anger as soon as the glass northern side of Wembley Stadium came into view.

The boy was not old enough to realize that the stadium he looked at was not the original Wembley; that stadium came down some four years before he was born. But to him, this was a fabulous place to watch a match; it was so much better than Gillette Stadium back home in Massachusetts. Even though it was his first time in England, he had watched several matches online, and he was excited at the prospect of reaching out and touching the famous pitch. As it so happened, he wore a small, youth-sized England jersey his father bought him. It was unadorned with name or number, even though the father knew the son would not be happy unless Gerrard 4 was on the back.

"But daddy," the boy said when he opened the dirty parcel, "I wanted a Captain Fantastic shirt. That way, when he sees me, he can smile."

1

"I know, I know, but I have to tell you something: You're supposed to root for the badge," the father said with a smile of his own, pointing to the Three Lions crest that would cover his son's heart, "not the player wearing the badge. I think I've told you that before, especially after your uncle's obsession with Brett Favre."

The boy sighed in their living room and begrudgingly put the shirt on. Now, some five months later, with the greenery of Wembley Park sprawling to either side of him and the Home of Football approaching dead center, that conversation was dead within his past, the memory forgotten.

The son was wide-eyed, and to the father, who looked down every so often at his offspring, his son's happiness was truly all that mattered. He would give his life in exchange for his son's, and he sacrificed countless times to make sure that his son, while not spoiled, had anything his heart desired. Seeing his son's expression caused his heart to leap taller than the arch that soared high above Wembley. He had to admit it to himself, albeit quietly: He was looking forward to this match just as much as his son.

Even though it was warm, northwest London was somewhat free of the smog that usually covered the city. Father and son could take a deep breath without choking on bad air, even though they slowly walked with the sweat-stained crowd toward the pedestrian walkway. The father had made this walk before, when his New England Patriots demolished the Tampa Bay Buccaneers here in 2009. That was nearly three years ago, and he had flown to England on business; that same day, Liverpool played Manchester United at Anfield, and the Reds beat the Red Devils, 2-0, in a match that he had to watch at a nearby pub instead of on The Kop. The photos and the souvenirs he brought home to his son, coupled with his son's excitement, confirmed to him that he wanted to bring him over for the Summer Olympics.

They continued walking along the brick-lined Wembley Way.

"Daddy, I see the arch!" the boy exclaimed, pointing at the 133-meter tall structure the way all boys do when excited. His eyes were brighter than his father had ever seen them. "Can we climb it, daddy? Can we, can we, can we?"

The father chuckled, and so did the two small boys walking nearby with their own father. Their father shushed them and apologized.

"No, Tommy, we won't be able to climb it. It's not like the Arch in St. Louis. This arch is like one big Erector set, and I don't think the security team would like it if they found us hanging onto it."

The boy gave an "aww, shucks" in return, which reminded the father of the jersey incident. The father simply shook his head, smiling all the same.

"Let's get into the stadium and find our seats, okay?"

"Okay daddy."

Mere seconds after passing Currys, father and son walked up the walkway and came to the statue of Sir Bobby Moore, the defender who led England to its only World Cup win in 1966. The father made sure he got a picture of his son next to the statue, the souvenir of all souvenirs.

At the gate, both of them went through security, each given a cursory pat down and waved over with one of those electro-magnetic wands they had at Logan Airport before they hopped on the Emirates Airlines jet to Heathrow a few days before. The father wasn't concerned for himself, since he wasn't carrying a gun and had no reason to be detained. He was more concerned for his son, who had never gone through a pat down before.

He looked to his right and saw the security guard give his son a grape flavored lollipop after the wand passed over him.

"Daddy, why were they doing that with the stick?"

"It's security, Tommy. This is a big event. They don't want people coming in with stuff to hurt people, so they make sure that anyone who tries can't get inside. They had guns, and there are police officers nearby. Remember that the police are here to help people."

"Except when they give you a speeding ticket."

"You still haven't told your mother, right?"

"No daddy, I want a PlayStation 4. I'm keeping my mouth shut."

The father grinned, for some reason proud of the boy's deception.

I trained him well, he thought.

They bought two sodas and hot dogs at a concession stand — the son poured mustard all over the hot dog and nearly on his jersey, but the father caught him before he stained the lilywhite shirt — and then entered the stadium proper. The green pitch of Wembley, re-laid for what seemed like the one hundredth time after the FA Cup Final two months ago, met their eyes. Red seats unfurled like the Red Sox' 2004 World Championship banner and spread into every nook and cranny of the stadium's lower bowl. Aisles of golden tipped concrete broke the monotony. Other supporters were sitting, while over in the corner, a chorus of God Save The Queen broke out among those who stood.

While the father grinned, the son was just as wide-eyed as he had been a few minutes ago.

"Wow! It's so green!" he said.

"Yes it is. Just wait until I take you to Fenway in a few weeks. That will be a lot of green; green all over the place."

"That is a lot of green. Wait," the son replied after a moment. "We're going to Fenway?"

"Oh, I didn't tell you?" the father said with a touch of fatherly sarcasm. "It's Part 2 of your ninth birthday present. This is Part 1."

The grin on the son's face was brighter than the day. He launched himself into his father's waist.

"I love you, daddy!"

The father simply wrapped his arms around his son, who would turn 9 in two weeks' time. He took a deep breath. He knew these moments would grow few and far between as he got older.

"I love you too, Tommy. Let's go over here; we'll get to see the players come out for warm-ups soon."

Eager to watch the players come out onto the pitch, Tommy and his father walked over to the area behind the dugouts and waited. Security did not step in and intercede, which surprised the father — all he had heard about coming into this Olympics was how they would be safer and more security-conscious. It had been sixteen years since Atlanta and the bombing of the Centennial Olympic Park, and there were no incidents in Sydney, Athens or Beijing, nor in Nagano, Salt Lake City, Turin or Vancouver. It may have been a fool's hope that terrorists would spare London 2012, especially in this post-9/11 world, but organizers and the International Olympic Committee were taking no chances. Security was to be top-notch.

The father noticed that truly was not the case.

Once the game began, they took their seats behind the United States dugout, despite wearing jerseys of England and rooting for the young Great Britain stars they watched every Saturday and Sunday on Fox Soccer Channel, Fox Soccer Plus and ESPN2. The United States Under-23 team, many said, were lucky to qualify for these Olympics, despite the rather easy qualifying schedule of CONCACAF. Great Britain, however, were not the favorites of the tournament despite being the host nation: That fell to Italy, which was currently playing its final group stage match against Argentina at Old Trafford in Manchester.

Even though the players on the pitch were different, many were calling this match a rematch of the USA-England World Cup match from 2010, where the Three Lions drew the Yanks, 1-1, during their opening match in South Africa. Now, without the big stars of the English Premier League in the match, there was a level of anticipation on the other side of the Atlantic that the Americans could quite possibly upset the Britons. It led ESPN to break out and dust off the "Over There" commercials it had played during World Cup qualifying in 2009. Speculation on who would score first was heavy in Las Vegas. NBC, the American television rights holder of the Summer Olympics since 1988, showed the match live.

As it turned out, Great Britain scored first as young Donnie Rhodes, an Everton F.C. first teamer, scored on a blistering shot from distance in the right channel, easily beating the American keeper after 25 minutes.

A cacophony of verse rose from the English supporters' section:

He wears a Lion on his chest, Donnie, Donnie
We know he is the fucking best, Donnie, Donnie
He punched his bird, he burned his house
But we don't care, he fucking scouse
Donnie Rho-odes, Great Britain's Number 9

The father grinned as the faithful began jumping up and down, reminiscent of the Kop when the Liverpool supporters once serenaded Fernando Torres. The entire southern side of the stadium swayed while chants of "Nah nah, nah nah, nah-nah-nah-nah, nah-nah" echoed off Wembley's roof.

The Americans' resolve was great, though, and without prompting, they brought the match to level terms as Steve Membrino, a virtual unknown from Wake Forest, used his pace off the center kick and blazed and spun through the Brits' defense like Diego Maradona had in Mexico City 26 years earlier.

Tommy leaped to his feet, jumped on the seat cushion and applauded Membrino as his right-footed strike beat the English keeper on the right-hand side. He wanted to tear his shirt off and swing it over his head like Membrino did at the near corner flag along with a little two-step dance to match. The American supporters chanted the intro to Chelsea Dagger while the referee brandished a yellow card Membrino's way.

The noise inside Wembley was deafening, and although Tommy and his father were rooting for Great Britain at the beginning, the intensity shown by the American youngsters caused them and many of the others in attendance to rise to their feet and applaud the underdogs.

That's what the Olympics was about to them. The possibility of a huge upset was in the making — a tie would have sent the Americans through to the knockout stages and left the Great Britain team watching at home, scratching their heads — and they all felt an excitement not seen at Wembley since Blackpool were promoted to the Premier League following the 2009-10 season.

"Wow daddy, this is fantastic!" he said. "I really hope we win."

"A draw is as good as a win right now. Do you see what happens when you play attacking football? The hockey team did that in 1980, and look what happened? They beat the Soviets and they ended up winning the gold medal. That could happen if we end up beating or drawing with the Brits today."

The wonder in the son's eyes showed as the father explained the Miracle on Ice. This match, a Miracle on Grass, still had a long way to go, though.

And as they said on television, anything could happen in football.

Something *would* happen.

It just wouldn't be what anyone expected.

The West End, London, England

30 July 2012 — 20.10 GMT/3:10 p.m. ET

In the middle of his evening prayers — with the television on — the shouting BBC announcer distracted Jafar Abdullah Mohammed.

"And the Yanks have brought this Olympic group stage match to level terms! What a beautiful strike by Steve Membrino!"

Jafar's eyes flew open. He turned his head toward the television.

This is the sign, he thought.

Jafar felt the anticipation running through his skin as he lurched from his prayer cushion, his prayers incomplete. He stumbled slightly, but that was because his knees did not bend properly. He grimaced hard and bit back a Muslim curse.

"I am sorry, Allah. Forgive me for not finishing," he said, looking toward the ceiling. "I will offer you my blood in penance. But I must cleanse the world of infidel filth."

He sat down on his couch with his laptop in front of him. He intently watched the match and waited for just the right time. The minutes ticked off, and every second was unbearable as the last. Fear began to creep into Jafar's conscience.

What if the Brits reclaim the lead? The operation would be for naught, he thought.

He shook his head.

The operation can continue. The West is the West is the West. Just because the Americans are unsuccessful and the British win does not mean the months of planning go up in smoke. This is why we've had all those meetings and spent Allah's money on weapons and explosives. This one event is what it's all about! Great Britain is just as much an enemy to

6

us as the United States! We can deal a crippling blow to their morale with this act today. Allah has blessed our endeavor. I cannot waste this opportunity!

A smile crept along Jafar's lips as he thought about this, just as the Americans' defense dispossessed the Brits' striker as he surged into the penalty area. The cheer from the American fans was sickening, and it mirrored the groan coming from the British supporters.

Jafar wanted to vomit. The West places so much importance on sport, especially football and American football and — the thought made him gag — baseball.

Baseball is a children's game, like rounders, compared to our cricket, the game of men, he thought.

Jafar spat his disgust.

The West should care about things that are more important. Staying out of Middle Eastern affairs would be a good start. Allah will punish these non-believers for plundering our land and not letting our leaders command our people. If the criminal Bush hadn't stuck up for his daddy, mighty Saddam would still be in command of Iraq.

He looked at the television again and saw the Americans sprinting up the pitch, casually moving the ball between players, playing an incessant game of keep away from the Brits. Two touches later, the Americans were into the attacking third, looking for an opening in the home side's defense. Surely, the Americans wouldn't go with a shot from distance again.

They didn't.

The Americans pounded the ball right into the heart of the penalty area, a thumping volley by the right side midfielder. Jafar watched as the players closed in on Membrino, who stood near the penalty spot, staying onside. The tall American striker bent his knees, leaped and beat the Brits to the ball. Membrino nodded the ball low. The keeper dove.

The keeper pounded the grass with his gloved hand as the ball tickled the back of the onion bag.

Jafar looked to the upper left-hand corner of the screen and smiled maliciously as the score line now read GBR 1-2 USA.

There was still less than an hour to play, still time for the Brits to come up with an equalizer. Was time on their side? Jafar could not tell. They looked disjointed.

Jafar wiped the sweat away. Even though the sun was down, his flat continued baking. It was after 20.30 now, which meant he could eat; Jafar maintained the strict rules of Ramadan and fasted from sunrise to sunset, and would do so for the next 20 days.

Another thing for the infidels to pay for, Jafar thought. *The Olympics fall during our holy month, and they knew it would cause our Muslim athletes, those who follow the tenets of our religion to a tee, to fast during the day and put them at an extreme disadvantage against everyone else, their American and Canadian and British heroes. They must pay for this breach of etiquette!*

They do not care about Muslims. They do not care that our athletes will be shunned and crucified for this. Why can't the IOC be mindful of Muslims' needs?

No, they can't do that. The West wouldn't want to compete fairly — that would be too much of a stretch, even for them — much like they want to completely eradicate us from the face of the Earth. It is why we must fight back with vengeance at every opportunity! We must not let the West win!

Jafar seethed now, his anger palpable. His heart rate rose as the fist-sized muscle pounded against the inside of his breastbone. He did not care what the scoreline in the match was now. It was not an issue any longer. The Brits could win. The Yanks could win. It could have ended a draw. Jafar did not care.

It was time for him to carry out his plans, his turn to do his part in Allah's Grand Scheme.

He opened a browser window on his laptop. He punched in his commands, his fingers flying across the keyboard so quickly, they appeared to be a blur.

He pressed enter.

He turned his attention to the television screen, and kept another eye on the CCTV link on his laptop. It showed Wembley Stadium from the outside. There were some people in Wembley Park watching the match on large monitors, much like the ones that were in Trafalgar Square for the announcement of London's winning Olympics bid.

The CCTV view had no audio, so Jafar could not tell who was boisterously happy and who was glum. The wide-angle shot was perfectly serene.

For now.

***

Halftime approached. The atmosphere around the Yanks' dugout was of enthusiastic disbelief, the murmurs growing into cheers of celebration. It was like 1950 all over again.

"We are beating the Brits! We're going to advance in the Olympics! Clear a path!"

Then the chanting began:

"The Yanks are coming, the Yanks are coming, the drums rum-tumming everywhere! So prepare, say a prayer, send the word, send the word to be there! We'll be over, we're coming over, and we won't be back till it's over, over there!"

The son cheered along with the rest of the American supporters, Sam's Army, as the team walked off the pitch. The fans felt like they had Great Britain on the ropes and that young Membrino would score again in the second half to give the United States a healthy two-goal cushion. Some of them may have not been knowledgeable in the ways of European football and there wasn't a Tim McCarver-like presence to follow along with on television, but they did know that a two-goal lead in this sport was better than a one-goal lead.

The father, though, was cautious. He had seen dramatic implosions surrounding Team USA before. He recalled the Americans going ahead of Brazil in the Confederations Cup final in 2009 before the Brazilians came back and humbled their opponents with three second-half goals. He saw the same against the Italians in the group stages of the same competition. And being a Red Sox fan, he was used to September Swoons — until 2004, that is.

He took the safe road in thinking the British would have something to say about the scoreline in the second half, and he made sure that he told his son — and everyone else around him — that there were still 45 minutes left, and that anything could happen. That left the American fans, who noticed the father's Liverpool jersey and the son's England jersey as if for the first time, grumbling about Benedict Arnolds.

The son said, "Come on, daddy. You know we're going to beat the British. We beat them in 1776, we can beat them today." Tommy smiled so wide that the father couldn't deny his son.

"We'll see, buddy. We'll see. I'm going to use the bathroom. Do you want anything from the concession stand while I'm away?"

The boy's eyes lit up.

"Can you get me another soda and another hot dog? And one of those long horns that some people are blowing?"

The father laughed.

"A soda yes, a hot dog yes, a vuvuzela no. I don't think customs would let us bring one into the country when we get back home, Tommy. How about a foam finger instead?"

The boy's face fell.

"If you must. Spike will just eat it."

"Don't leave it lying around your room and he won't. Your mother and I have been telling you to keep an eye on your stuff so the dog doesn't get at it. Besides," the father said, "what do you think Spike would do if he got his jaws around a vuvuzela and tried to eat it?" He winked.

The son brought his finger to his jaw, as if thoughtful.

"His barks would sound better than they do now."

"And the idiot neighbors would call the cops again."

The son mocked shock. The father simply laughed again.

"I'll be back in a few minutes, okay? Don't go walking around the stadium." He kissed his son on the forehead.

The boy wiped it off.

The father squirted himself out of the row and jogged up the stairs that led all the way up to the Royal Box. He came upon a tall steward, standing at the ramp entrance. The man had his hands wrapped behind him, coming to a rest at the small of his back. He eyed the father warily.

"Excuse me, sir. I have to go use the bathroom. Would you mind keeping an eye on my son? He's right there in the England shirt." He pointed toward his son, a few rows away.

"Stewards aren't babysitters, sir," the steward replied pompously, giving the father a look of impatience. "We get paid to babysit this lot," he added, waving his arm about, indicating the crowd, "not your son."

The father dug money out of his pocket and peeled off a twenty-pound note. He grabbed the steward's arm, tore it away from his backside and thrust the bill into his hand.

"How about now?"

The steward looked down at the note with wide eyes. He usually received five-pound tips from helping people find their seats.

"Which one is your lad, sir? I'll make sure he doesn't get into no trouble at all," the steward replied, this time less haughtily and more with a Cockney accent.

The father smiled and patted him on the shoulder, then directed his gaze to his son.

"I'll only be a few minutes. Just a quick bathroom visit, a trip to a concession stand and I'll be back before the second half starts."

"No problem, sir. He won't move a muscle."

The father took one more look at his son before he turned and started to walk down the ramp, a smile on his face. His hands were in his pockets holding onto the notes.

The force of the blast changed that. Instead of staying on his feet, the father found himself thrown forward, as if the hand of God lifted him up from where he walked and tossed him twenty feet. The notes flew out of his hand and burned in the ensuing fireball. The father hit the cement hard, dislocating his shoulder and sending him rolling. His momentum finally stopped as soon as his body collided with a concession stand, causing his body to shudder even more; he didn't even feel his ribs snap. He didn't even register the severe amount of pain that he was in. Someone close by screamed, and his ears did not even register it as a scream of terror; his eardrums were concussed. It was only then that he smelled burning flesh.

It took him several more seconds to realize the burning flesh was his.

Someone smothered him with a woolen blanket, and soon the fire that had encompassed his backside was out. The screams continued, but he didn't hear a thing.

The father tried to get up from the concourse floor, but someone's weight kept him down. He could detect people rushing past him, toward the explosion. Thick black smoke began to fill the concourse as well as pour out from the stadium's wound.

Once more he tried to get up, and this time felt no resistance. His body screamed at him to stay down and not move, for movement caused his nerves extreme discomfort. He stood up and looked toward where he came from, expecting to see a wall with concessionaires near the ramp that led into the stadium proper.

All he saw was smoke, fire, and through it, the south side of the stadium.

It was at that moment that the father began to panic.

Disregarding the pain as he stumbled forward, the father said "No!" repeatedly, shouting it louder and louder until he thought he could hear himself. He began to run toward the ramp, but he tripped as soon as he got there. He fell on top of a burning woman lying face down on the cement.

She was dead.

He looked up toward the stadium and saw the ramp littered with bodies. Smoke poured off them. He even saw the broken body of his babysitting steward laying at a right angle — but not a right angle that would be natural for human beings.

The father vomited violently, his insides coming out of him with the speed of an unstoppable train. The stuff spilled atop the dead woman, splattering on her back and off it onto the concrete. The stench of vomit and burning flesh reeked, and soon the smell of acrid, black smoke would counter it.

He tried his best to avoid stepping on the bodies, but at that point, he did not care: His only thought was making sure his son was okay.

Yet as he walked up the ramp, tiptoeing through the bodies, he had an incredibly bad feeling he would not like what he saw when he emerged.

His breath caught in his throat as he surveyed the damage.

The scene was incredible.

The scene was horrific.

He could not believe his eyes.

As a Liverpool supporter, what he saw at that very moment reminded him of what happened at Hillsborough, the deadly crush that occurred during an FA Cup semifinal over 23 years ago. He had seen YouTube footage from the BBC of the event, and the scene had sickened him senseless. He recalled people rushing onto the pitch, using the advertising boards that ran around the playing surface as makeshift stretchers to carry the wounded and the dead away.

This was Hillsborough on a much greater scale, he thought. This was September 11, Hillsborough and any terror attack rolled into one.

The thought made him want to puke again.

The blast vaporized three entire sections of seats near the United States' dugout. Bodies were burning. He saw stewards from the southern side of the stadium running across the pitch to help, even though it would have been prudent to stay put and prevent the crowd from panicking. Fans, both British and American, also came across. Perhaps there were nurses, doctors, constables and firefighters on that side, but right now, they looked like Olympic sprinters.

He began to shout Tommy's name repeatedly, hoping his son would recognize his voice, pleading for the boy to come find his father.

The father couldn't see him. No one shorter than five feet came running toward him. His bottom lip began to tremble as his eyes searched the crowd on the pitch.

God, he prayed, *if you're listening, please bring Tommy back to me. It's his birthday soon. I need him to come home with me.*

The father did not hear silence in return, nor did he hear anything at all.

He began panicking, and it was almost like he wanted the dead steward to hand him his money back and to restrain him as he walked forward toward where he and his son sat during the first half. He couldn't find those seats, though.

He stumbled forward, his feet kicking up shards of concrete, metal and plastic, the debris left over from the blast. He was surprised it wasn't incinerated like the rest. He turned and looked up at the Royal Box and found it gone. Even up higher, the upper decks did not appear to exist.

He turned his head back toward the pitch and walked gingerly. People tried to stop him, but he shoved them aside, the pain still not registering. He got to what had been the Americans' dugout and he shouted his son's name again.

Once again, he received no answer.

He tried to climb the wall, but a wave of pain finally brought him to a halt. He finally noticed his hanging right arm and felt his back blistering from the flames. He leaned against the short wall.

He caught a glimpse of a white shirt upon a small child several yards away. The shirt had scorch marks, but the child's arms were askew in such a way that the father had no reason to doubt that the child's arms were broken.

The father dug deep and pushed himself up and over the wall, dropping down on his injured shoulder. He felt the pop knock his shoulder back into place. If he had anything left in his stomach, he would have thrown it back up. He pushed himself up to his knees and felt another wave of pain go through him. It would have knocked a lesser man to the ground, but he was a man possessed with finding his son. His son's safety was the only thing that mattered to him at that moment. He ignored the pain.

He got to his feet and walked toward the broken child. It was only a few feet away. He kept his eyes on the child's back the entire time and had a horrible feeling begin to sink into the pit of his stomach as he got closer. The child's hair was the same color of his son's. The shorts looked identical, though burned. The shirt, where blackened, had melted into the child's skin.

"Oh, Tommy," he said. "No, please don't be dead."

He hit his knees again and turned the child over.

It was Tommy. He looked like he was sleeping, but his mouth was slack. The father's eyes became wet, and heavy sobs rattled his frame. His heart broke, and he didn't care about a dislocated shoulder or broken ribs or that he had nearly been incinerated by the fireball. His son was dead because of that explosion, and he did not care about his own body. At that very moment, his world had ended.

He had no idea how he would tell his wife that her youngest child was dead.

The father grabbed his son in his own damaged arms and looked toward Heaven, crying, "Why, God? Why my son?" His eyes closed as tears cut rivulets into his face.

***

Jafar did not know if the explosion took place as planned. With the BBC on a commercial break, there was no way to know what happened. He looked to the CCTV monitor that showed the north side of Wembley Stadium as well as the area of Wembley Park surrounding the building.

At first, Jafar could not see anything different. Wembley's floodlights were on, but after about a minute or two, the lights at the top of the stadium began to cut out as smoke rose into the sky, blocking the light from the CCTV cameras. A minute later, the BBC came back to the studio:

"We're supposed to go back to Wembley for comment, but we have to shift gears as an explosion rocked the stadium just after the players left the pitch for halftime. These pictures tell the story," the studio host said.

Jafar held his breath.

The cameras inside Wembley told the tale. Black smoke rose into the air, dissipating slightly. Bodies littered the pitch, and people from the south side flooded it. The scenes were chaotic, and Jafar tuned out the pundits who tried describing what occurred.

Then they showed the explosion, taped and taken from the wide angle camera that followed the action during the first half. The loge level went first. A fireball lifted fans into the air, the rolling inferno swallowing bodies whole. A second explosion took the next deck. A third followed. The BBC, in a fit of stupidity, then added the audio.

The screams sent goose bumps running up Jafar's forearms and caused a smile to drift across his face. He heard the shock in the broadcasters' voices. He wanted to see that replay, the replay of Wembley's north side exploding, over and over and over again; he had heard that an American broadcaster, after seeing one of their space shuttles explode on replay so many times, demanded his producers stop showing it.

The terrorist could tell that many died from the blast he created, and with so many rushing to help, he knew those people would have nightmares until the day they died. He wanted to lord over that knowledge, the knowledge that he gave them those nightmares – payment for the nightmares that echoed in the ears of Afghani children, his young brothers and sisters in Allah, after the Americans struck his country in 2001. It was a vengeful slap, one that Jafar wished he could have seen live.

He prayed to Allah and asked for an announcement on the death toll soon, for he craved to know how many people perished.

He wanted to know before he took credit for what the world saw.

Chapter 2
Situation Room, White House, Washington, D.C.
30 July, 2012 — 23.00 GMT/6:00 p.m. ET

Eric Forrister, like many Americans, sat glued to his television during the first half of the Olympic soccer match. Forrister enjoyed watching the English game every weekend and, try as he may, he kept up with the midweek matches, as well. Certain things — like running the United States, for instance — got in the way of his fun.

The President of the United States saw the images broadcast by NBC and it sent his heart plummeting into his stomach. He saw the black smoke, saw the bodies sprawled upon the field, and knew there were deaths.

When Bob Costas explained that the explosion happened behind the American dugout, Forrister's heart sank even further. He did not dare move his feet for fear of shattering it.

Many American citizens died today, he thought. *I need to find out what happened.*

Forrister called the special number reserved for diplomats and heads of state. A busy signal met his ears. He set the receiver down and returned to the television, waiting for the flood of people to enter the Oval Office.

As if on cue, the door from his secretary's office opened.

"Mr. President," his secretary said, "the Prime Minister of the United Kingdom is on line three for you, sir. And Director Dupuis is waiting for you in the Situation Room."

That didn't take long, Forrister thought. *Alexandra doesn't surprise me, though. She probably had her driver run every red light to get here from Langley.*

"Thank you, Edna." Forrister waited until she left before picking up the phone. "Rich, what is happening over there?"

"We're scrambling to find things out for you, Eric," Richard Coe said. "We're just as shocked. They told us these Olympics would be safe. This attack on Wembley proves our Games are not. And right now, England is the laughing stock of the international community."

Forrister thought the Prime Minister was on the verge of collapse. The President felt his opposite had every right to be upset.

"Rich, listen to me. You're not the laughing stock; I can think of several other countries that can take that position from you very easily. The free world will stand by you and help you in any way they can. You have my word that if you request help from the United States, the United

States will send help. Those are our citizens lying dead on that field, and my people will want someone's blood for it.

"I am about to head into a meeting with Alex Dupuis, and I'll see what she says. In the meantime, try to get some sleep. The carnage will still be there in the morning."

"That's not very reassuring Eric, but I'm sure Alex has already been in contact with the Ministry of Defense and MI5. She probably has a better run-down than I have."

Forrister smiled. *Yes, she probably did*, he thought. *Then again, Rich really doesn't have a lot of favor with the Queen and the rest of Her Majesty's government any longer.*

"If there is anything we can give you, you know we'll be glad to help. Call me in the afternoon tomorrow and I'll let you know what's going on with our side."

He didn't wait for the Prime Minister to answer, instead hanging up the phone and grabbing his suit jacket. He walked out the door and past the Secret Service agents guarding the President's private office.

"Eagle is moving," Forrister heard the agent say into his cuff microphone as he passed.

Several minutes later, the President walked into the Situation Room, located in the basement of the West Wing. Television screens showed Wembley Stadium from several different angles. It was nighttime in London, which meant that the CCTV images were blurred. NBC, however, was in the middle, with the images showing rescue workers tending to the injured. The video of a man holding a dead child stood frozen on another screen. White sheets covered the dead.

From his view in the doorway, Forrister saw many white sheets. The green turf of Wembley was an eerie backdrop.

Several people inside the Situation Room stood as the President entered. The woman at the end of the table nearest the President's seat stayed in her chair, a secure phone looking like someone had surgically attached it to her ear and left shoulder.

"Take your seats, everyone. We'll wait for Alex to finish her call before we begin," Forrister said.

Dupuis put her hand over the receiver.

"I'll be right with you, Mr. President. I'm speaking with my opposite number in England."

Forrister let loose half a grin. *Coe was right*, he thought. *I'm glad I have her on my side.*

The President returned his gaze to the television monitors behind him. He saw Costas speaking to the camera, but with the sound down, he could not hear a word. He got the gist of Costas's message, though: Someone has attacked the Olympic Games, the magnitude not felt in sports in 40 years.

Forrister, a life-long sports fan, knew that to be very accurate. Terrorists left sports alone, while they attacked everyday life.

Another phone rang nearby. Forrister saw Dupuis put her hand to her ear to block out the buzzing. An aide picked it up, then turned to Forrister.

"Mr. President," the aide said, "the President of the International Olympic Committee is on the phone for you."

Forrister stood at this unexpected call. He grabbed the phone from the aide and thanked him with a nod.

"Mr. President, thank you for calling me during this dreadful time," he said.

"Indeed it is dreadful, Mr. President," the man said on the other end. The President of the IOC spoke with a crisp, Belgian accent. "I cannot say how sorry I am for the people of the United States and Great Britain. This is a terrible tragedy, and my people will find out what happened."

"Thank you for your diligence, Mr. President. I am sorry that this happened during the final Olympics of your tenure. I have already spoken with the Prime Minister of England, and my director of the CIA is on the phone as we speak with the Ministry of Defense and the head of MI5. I'm sure that our governments will work together to find the culprits involved in this heinous attack that is not only against our governments, but against the Olympic movement as a whole."

Forrister heard a sigh on the other end, and it sounded like the man was crying and trying to compose himself.

"Mr. President, are you okay?" Forrister asked.

Several seconds later, the President of the IOC answered, "Yes, Mr. President. I am fine. You just reminded me of my final Olympics. I was hoping, like President Samaranch before me, to declare the Games the best ever. Right now, though, that is looking grim."

"I hope that for the sake of the Olympic movement, we will find who did this and make sure they are held accountable." He paused for a moment before he added, "Mr. President, will you be addressing the media soon?"

"I was planning on a world-wide address tomorrow afternoon, at about 8 a.m. your time. I will tell the world that the Games must go on, much like they did in Atlanta, much like they did in Munich. I may have to quote your own President Brundage during my address."

"I will be sure to watch your address, then. I will have my secretary give me an early wake up call, and I will follow yours with an address to the American people and the world, as well."

"And I will be sure to watch yours, Mr. President. You are certainly a better friend to the Olympic movement than your predecessors, especially the one who wanted to keep Cuba out of your World Baseball Classic."

Forrister smiled at the IOC president's veiled attack against one of his Republican predecessors, several elections removed. Forrister remembered him shooting himself in the foot with his words — it wasn't the first time — and nearly costing America's inclusion in the Games.

With what happened today in London, Forrister thought, *maybe it would have been better if the United States weren't involved in the Olympics. It would have been another country attacked in the USA's place, though.*

Forrister grimaced at such a thought.

"We try to help our friends around the world, Mr. President, just as we would want to be helped. I'll be in contact with you soon."

"Thank you, Mr. President."

Forrister hung up the phone just as Dupuis ended her call.

"Sorry for that, Mr. President. That was David Willows from SIS."

"And what does the British Secret Intelligence Service have to say, Alex?"

"As of right now, the death toll is at one thousand and rising steadily."

The Situation Room became one long intense murmur until Forrister called for silence.

"That will be enough of that," he said, causing everyone to quiet down. At that moment, Dick Bennett, Forrister's White House Chief of Staff, entered the Situation Room. "Dick, how nice of you to join us."

"I'm sorry I'm late, Mr. President. The meeting I told you about with the majority leader did not go as well as planned." Bennett grabbed his seat at the end opposite the president.

Forrister held in his grimace.

I have matters that are more important on the table — one thousand-plus Americans died today, he thought. *Congress's bitching can wait.*

"You'll have to tell me about it after we handle this meeting and this situation. Have you heard about what happened in London earlier today, Dick?"

Bennett looked confused.

"No sir, I hadn't heard. The meetings went long, and they were closed to everyone who had nothing to offer to the conversation."

"So they let the Republicans in anyway?" said an aide off to the side, not missing a beat.

Even Forrister, a staunch member of the liberal left wing, had to laugh at that.

"Alright, let's be serious. Dick, the Olympics were attacked at Wembley Stadium."

Bennett's breath got caught in his throat.

"Wow. During the soccer match? What happened?" Bennett sounded as if he was in shock.

"There were several explosions," Forrister said plainly. "Many were killed. Right now, the British say they've counted one thousand dead, and that number will rise by the hour. This was a heinous attack, one that we cannot let go unpunished."

Forrister directed Bennett's attention to the monitors behind him, which Bennett did not see when he walked in. The president had the aide play the DVR for the chief of staff, going through what NBC had taped just as the teams were leaving the pitch at halftime. They watched as the camera went back to a regular position over the pitch. The first explosion occurred, then the second a level up, and then the third level blew. A large, gaping hole remained as soon as the smoke cleared. Once the people on the south side of the stadium began their surge across the field to help tend to the injured, the president stopped the recording.

"Wow," Bennett said once again. "I'm surprised there was anyone left alive by that blast."

"Luckily," Dupuis said, "what I have gathered from the British indicates that only that side of the stadium was affected. Within an hour, the stadium was evacuated in an orderly fashion."

"Imagine if there was another device somewhere in the stadium and they detonated it," Bennett interrupted. "Orderly fashion or not, there would have been more dead people, and the recovery efforts would be that much more difficult to accomplish."

"Which is why we're thankful there wasn't another bomb," Dupuis countered.

"Exactly," Forrister said. "Alex, have the British asked us to get involved on your end?"

"Yes they have, Mr. President. MI5 wants our best agent available to come and assist them, not take over their investigation. It's their jurisdiction, but because there are American deaths, they want us there so our ass is covered. They have the feeling that if we don't send someone, the people will be on our ass for letting dead American citizens be un-avenged."

"We can't have that now, can we?" Bennett said, slightly sarcastically, to the CIA leader.

Forrister silenced him with a look. He then turned back to Dupuis.

"Alex, by all means, call in your best agent immediately. Tell him that he is to —"

"Him, Mr. President?"

"Yes, him Alex. He's still available, isn't he?"

Alex looked at the president perplexed.

"No sir, the agent you're thinking of is off on another assignment in the Middle East; he's deep undercover and cannot be extracted. I was thinking more of a her than a him, Mr. President."

Forrister knew exactly who she meant. He had sent Jaclyn Johnson, the agent Alex referred to, on an assassination mission a week after his predecessor, Sarah Kendall, died during a selfless operation on the Quabbin Reservoir in Massachusetts.

"You're right. Call her in and tell her to get to London before anyone else is killed. Tell her that she is to assist MI5, not to do her own investigation."

"Yes, Mr. President."

"Mr. President," Bennett interrupted, "are you sure you want to have the CIA involved in something like this? We're talking about an international incident here. The CIA doesn't go in and assist other agencies. They go in and do their own investigations. The taxpayers would flip if they found out we spent their tax dollars on our operatives being second fiddles to SIS. No offense, Alex."

"None taken, Dick," Dupuis said. She did not like Bennett, and she knew — rather intimately, in fact — that Bennett did not like her or the CIA. She knew Bennett felt that the CIA overstepped its bounds during the War on Terror, torturing Islamic prisoners.

While the White House Chief of Staff did not like how the CIA did business, the president — while a liberal on most things; government spending, for one — liked to take a more aggressive approach to terrorism. It was one thing that the GOP liked about Forrister: his foreign policy was akin to Bush Junior's.

It was about as far as the similarities between the two went, though.

"Mr. President," Dupuis went on, "the CIA exists to protect American interests. This is an American interest."

"I know Alex, which is why I want Johnson called in," Forrister said. He directed it more to Bennett than to Dupuis, and the president's eyes meant it so.

An aide hurried into the Situation Room and grabbed the remote control before Bennett could say anything else.

"Mr. President, I think you need to see this," she said, turning the television to CNN.

"What's up, Stefanie?"

"Someone is taking credit for the attack. They emailed and routed a digital message to the BBC. They sent it to all of the American networks."

The Situation Room went deadly silent.

The television showed a man wearing a black wool balaclava over his face, hiding his identity from view. Only his eyes showed, and everyone in the room could feel the hatred burning inside them. He wore a white turban that came down and covered his ears. A Grand Boubou covered his body entirely, a flowing robe primarily worn in western Africa.

"Citizens of the world, especially the United States and the United Kingdom," the man said. He spoke with a clipped British accent. "My name is Kafil Abdul Mohammed, and I once lived amongst you all for a time. I am an al-Qaeda operative."

"Someone write that name down and get everything we can find on him," Forrister ordered. The masked man's pacing was such that Forrister blurted that sentence without missing a word of his message. The scratching sound of a pen on paper met the president's ears. Forrister kept his eyes on the television.

"The attack you all saw in London today was only the beginning of what will occur if you Americans and Brits do not pull out of the Middle East and leave us to our own affairs. Leave Israel to its fate! Leave Afghanistan alone! Let our great leader, Ayman al-Zawahiri, rule the Middle East as it should be ruled!"

"Fucking militant camel jockey," Bennett breathed. No one heard him.

"I picked the football match because it would be a perfect way to exploit both nations that so vigorously hate the great religion of Islam."

"Apparently this jackass doesn't realize we have freedom of religion here," the president said, not taking his eyes off the screen.

"I also picked it because of the United States' bastardization of football must be stopped; I watched many matches during my time in England, and you Americans refuse to see the greatness of the world's game. You Americans also bastardize the great sport of cricket by calling it baseball. You lower yourselves to your petty American football games on Sunday afternoons. Allah spits on your fat, useless, American selves."

"You mean to tell me that this guy attacked the Olympics because of soccer? Is he serious?" Bennett said, not believing what he just heard.

"Quiet, Dick," Forrister said.

"The next attack will come soon, United States and England. Prepare for Allah's coming, because only he will be able to save you! *Allahu Akbar!*"

The tape winked out, which then caused the CNN pundits to talk about what they and the rest of America just saw.

Forrister grabbed the remote and shut the power off.

"Alex," he said, staring at the television, "I want her to kill this bastard. I don't care what the British want; tell her to pretend she's following their lead. She has my permission to use all and any means necessary to achieve her objective."

"I'll call her right now," Dupuis said before she grabbed her phone and left the Situation Room.

***

As soon as Dupuis had the phone to her ear and walked out of the Situation Room, Bennett unloaded on the president.

"Damn it Eric! You could have spoken to me before you unleashed the dogs from the kennel. Hell, you should have called Homeland Security. They would have told you to leave it alone and let the British handle it; it's on their soil, their problem. Why didn't the SIS call Interpol? You know the CIA is going to screw this up; they've screwed so much up when terrorism is involved."

"What, like Christmas 2009? We put an end to that bullshit, Dick. When it comes to that stuff, I'm pulling the trigger against the terrorists. And when this nutjob," Forrister said, pointing at the television that showed the balaclava-wearing Muslim only a minute ago, "said he did it over soccer — something you even said was stupid, by your tone — he made himself an enemy of the United States and her people."

"Her people won't give a shit because it's soccer."

"That's enough. American citizens died today, Dick. The Brits are outraged; Downing Street is nearly catatonic that it happened during their grand celebration of sport. It's ridiculous, and this guy is going to pay with his own blood. And for the record, I happen to trust the CIA, especially after what happened with Sarah."

Bennett paused for a few moments in thought; he truly missed Sarah Kendall. He smiled before he rose from his seat.

"Greg, I know how you feel about the CIA, and I knew how Sarah felt. I'm just saying leaving this to them is dangerous. They won't follow any sort of protocol that the UN has approved when it comes to prisoners. This chick is just going to go in and shoot first and ask questions later; she did it in Boston. Congress will have a field day on your administration if they find out about this."

"Are you going to tell them, Dick?" Forrister asked, nearly flattening Bennett with a penetrating stare. Forrister may have been 60, but his stares were lethal, especially in the political arena.

Bennett stared back, disbelieving what Forrister accused him of possibly doing.

"No," he said once he recovered. "I'm telling you what would happen. It would be the end of your presidency. You'll be handing the White House to Jepson and the Republicans if you go through with this."

Forrister took a deep breath. Bennett had struck a nerve. The Democrats had not yet held their national convention. It was still a few weeks away, and Charlotte — Forrister's adopted hometown since he and his family moved there from New Hampshire when he was a boy — was gearing up for the biggest party ever held in that city. The Republicans held their convention a week earlier in Houston, and Texas Senator Randall Jepson won the nomination.

"Jepson doesn't have a chance, Dick. After the Republicans obstructed every piece of legislation we've put out and not offering a sensible counter in its place has led the public to not trust the GOP. We're going to win this election without a problem, and the CIA is going to stop this terrorist threat on the Olympics. I know this to be a fact. The British want our help. They called Alex and you heard her tell us that they want us to send our best agent —"

"Johnson is half-blind; she'll be lucky if she can sniff out a camel humper in London. Hell, that may be something she'll be good at, seeing as there's a huge Muslim population there."

"That's enough, Dick," Forrister said with finality. "I've heard your arguments against sending in the CIA to England. I happen to think you're wrong. Congress won't hear a word about this; they won't even know we're going to be involved."

Bennett sighed heavily.

"Okay, but I'm going to tell you that it's your presidency's funeral if this chick fucks up over there. You need to be ready to hang the CIA out to dry once and for all; I would suggest having deniability."

Forrister looked taken aback at Bennett's suggestion.

"That'll be the end of it." The president moved for the door. He grabbed the doorknob and turned to face his chief of staff. "If you have an issue with this, you may want to think about updating your resume."

Forrister left Bennett speechless, grabbing the back of his chair for support. The president's threat left him reeling.

***

Dupuis rattled off a list of orders for her secretary to accomplish in the next five minutes.

"Jeanine, get in touch with CTB and have them get Jaclyn on the line right away. Have them patch the call to my cell. I'm still in the White House, but I'm headed to the limo right now; I'll be on way back to Langley in moments." Dupuis could imagine her secretary's hand cramping up on her. "Once you're done with that, call the Andrews hanger and tell them to fetch Jaclyn; she's in New York, so have them go to LaGuardia. Call the service and have them put her stuff on the plane, and make sure she has her diplomatic pass so she can get that stuff into England without an issue from customs. I'm going to send a patch to her iPad so she can review the briefing before she lands at Heathrow. And Jeanine?"

"Yes, Madame Director?"

"When you're done that, go home to that husband of yours."

Dupuis could hear her smile through the phone.

"I will. Don't worry about a thing; I'm already calling CTB as we speak."

Confident that Jeanine would do as ordered — and not share a word of it with her other half — Dupuis hung up the phone and walked to the limo, parked in front of the White House.

***

Flash bulbs popped inside the New York studio where Jaclyn Johnson took part in a massive photo shoot for *Vogue*. Jaclyn's beauty was such that every magazine wanted her for their covers — *Sports Illustrated* even wanted her for the Swimsuit Issue, but she didn't even like posing for Victoria's Secret.

Wearing her trademark shades that had become the rage with teenage girls recently, Jaclyn posed with her arms crossed under her breasts, her

26

sunglasses lowered so that the camera could catch the pigment in her eyes — or what looked like the pigment in her eyes.

Jaclyn had been born partially blind, so much so that both natural and incandescent light affected her eyes. For most of her formative years, Jaclyn wore sunglasses constantly, much like she did on an everyday basis now, to protect her eyes. She could see shadows with her sunglasses, but that was pretty much the extent of her sight. She began counting on her other four senses, with touch, smell and hearing the most important of the four.

In her parents' Seattle home, the government installed prototype LED lights to spare Jaclyn the pain of regular light bulbs; her parents worked for the government, and the expense was of no concern. They made plenty of money and asked the government's top scientists to help their daughter to see. At the age of 12, Jaclyn began wearing specially made contact lenses that would give her the appearance of healthy-looking eyes, contact lenses that would refract light and deflect it aside so she would not live in such pain from day to day. They wouldn't help her see properly though, and instead of sunglasses, Jaclyn began wearing regular eyeglasses to augment her vision.

To Jaclyn's mind, it was freedom in every possible way imaginable.

But when she was 14, she wished she could return to the shadows so she could not see what she and the rest of the world saw on September 11, 2001.

Her parents were in Washington, D.C. that morning, having left Seattle-Tacoma International Airport the night before. They had important business at the Pentagon to conduct: her father was a retired general in the United States Army; her mother, his secretary. They went to speak in regards to the Middle East, and as they walked past a section of the building undergoing renovations, American Airlines Flight 77 flew into the building.

Jaclyn's parents perished that day.

The CIA sensed an opportunity, an opportunity to mold a fighter the world had never before seen. They took 14-year-old Jaclyn and educated her themselves, all at taxpayer expense. They trained her in combat, small arms weaponry and explosive detonation. She was rather prodigious at chemistry as well as close form fighting. They outfitted her with devices that would aid her in her endeavors, as well as a pair of Foster Grant sunglasses that were not what they seemed on the outside. To the world at large, Jaclyn's sunglasses were just that: a pair of regular sunglasses.

And when the government finally set her loose, she saved the city of Boston from a major disaster a year ago, stopping megalomaniac Grant Chillings from poisoning the Quabbin Reservoir, Boston's main water supply. She could not save Sarah Kendall, though. She had arrived half a moment too late.

It had been a blow to her, but she managed to recover from it. She had been on several missions since the Quabbin incident, which remained classified despite demands from Congress to inform them about her operations.

Jaclyn turned her body as her photographer asked, showing off her remarkable profile. She felt her calves tighten slightly as she moved. She pouted her lower lip, separating the pink entities by mere millimeters. The flash bulb went off again. Another pose, this time bringing her hand up to touch her cheek, then another flash.

The heads-up display in her sunglasses alerted her to a call coming in. The display showed her that it was not a call she could afford to let go unanswered.

"Charlie, hold on, I need to get this call," she said, walking off the set and leaving her photographer unsettled.

"What? I don't hear anything."

The sounds of a synthesized samba began to echo through the room. Charlie's face fell.

Jaclyn just smiled as she picked up the phone and pressed the accept call button.

"This is Jaclyn."

"Agent Snapshot, this is the CIA Counterterrorism Bureau calling. I'm to patch you through to Director Dupuis. Are you secure at the moment?"

Jaclyn slid her hand into her nylon MZ Wallace purse and pulled out what looked to be a small gray cube. She lowered the phone and turned to Charlie.

"I'll be back in a few minutes, Charlie. Family business to attend to, I'm afraid."

Without waiting for Charlie to answer, she turned on her heel and walked out of the room. She found a staircase and vaulted up the steps, finding her way to the roof of the building. She stepped outside and immediately depressed a button on the gray cube. A light thrumming emerged from the device, surrounding her and her phone with rays that would prevent anyone from eavesdropping upon an important government call.

"I'm all set."

"Patching the call through now; stand by, Snapshot."

Jaclyn began to shimmy her right foot as the phone beeped three times. She then heard the electronic ringing, a ringing that reminding her of the end of Pink Floyd's *Young Lust*, go through.

Dupuis answered on the third ring.

"Jaclyn?"

"Hey Chief, what's going on?"

"We have an international security situation," Dupuis said.

There's always a situation, Jaclyn thought. *An international security situation? That's a new one to me.*

"British Secret Intelligence Service is requesting our assistance in a sensitive matter. I'm sending you to London, Agent Snapshot."

"What's the situation?"

"Have you been watching the news the past few hours?"

"No Chief, I've been in a photo shoot since 3," Jaclyn replied. She bit her lip and tasted the pink lipstick they threw at her an hour before the shoot began. "I'm actually glad you interrupted, believe it or not."

"I'm going to have to pull you out of the shoot, Jaclyn. You're headed to Wembley Stadium in northwest London."

If I had a nickel for every time Alex pulled me out of a shoot, Jaclyn thought. *London? This is different.*

"What happened there that MI5 can't handle on their own? That's internal, and they usually don't call upon the CIA to help. Mossad wouldn't be calling us for help with something in Jerusalem."

Jaclyn bit her tongue as soon as she said it. How many times had she read missives of the Israelis calling upon American clandestine services to infiltrate Palestinian enclaves in the past two decades? She could not recall.

"The situation involves dead Americans. Wembley Stadium was the site of a terrorist attack a few hours ago. The death toll is at two thousand confirmed. It continues to rise."

Jaclyn felt the air leave her chest. She leaned against the building.

"Wow. What happened?"

"Three massive explosions. I've transmitted details and video to your iPad. I suggest you become familiar with the facts before you touch down at Heathrow."

"That's going to be a long flight and no sleep, Chief."

"The president feels that we cannot fall asleep on this, Snapshot." Jaclyn let the corner of her mouth turn upward for the briefest moment as Dupuis played on her agent's slightly sarcastic tone. "He feels that with the amount of people dead in this attack, and many of them being

American citizens, we must take a proactive role in finding the terrorist who senselessly murdered them."

"I'm sure Congress would think otherwise."

"Congress will know nothing of your involvement, as usual. The British are asking for your assistance, not for you to lead an investigation. That's the official request they have made of the president, and that is the president's official request to Langley."

Jaclyn rubbed her lips together.

"And what is President Forrister's unofficial request?" she said slowly.

Dupuis' response, as Jaclyn expected, was quick and to the point.

"Unofficially," she said, "the president wishes you to do what you do best and to use any and all methods necessary to bring this son of a bitch down. In other words, Snapshot: The president wishes you to put several caps in this terrorist's ass."

Jaclyn grinned.

"Tell the president that his wish is my command."

"I will when I return to Langley," Dupuis said. "I have a GPS fix on you. A car will be coming to pick you up and bring you to LaGuardia. The plane is on its way. You'll find clothes and the necessities are already on board. Nigel Messingham of MI5 will meet you at Heathrow. He'll be your lead while in London. Report in to me when you get to Wembley."

"Will do, Alex."

"Jaclyn?"

"Yeah?"

"Remember the time difference between London and Washington, please. And tell Nigel's driver to go slow on the M4; I don't want you waking me up at 2 freaking a.m. again."

Dupuis cut the connection. Jaclyn pressed the button on the cube again, cancelling the distortion waves. She leaned against the building, thinking about the pending flight across the Atlantic.

First a four-hour photo shoot, now a flight to London. This is already turning out to be a long day, she thought. *I better tell Charlie that Vogue is going to have to wait until I get back.*

She walked back toward the studio.

And since there are terrorists involved, I may not get back at all.

Chapter 3
The West End, London, England
31 July, 2012 — 05.00 GMT/12 a.m. ET

Jafar rolled over and saw the digital read-out indicate that it was 5 a.m. He went to bed shortly after 11 p.m., after he enjoyed watching BBC One describe what happened that evening at Wembley, as well as watching the commentators ramble on about his digital recording. He went to sleep praising Allah, thankful of his blessings and that the plans proceeded as Allah wanted.

The West fear Allah, he thought.

Swinging his legs off the side of the bed, sweat coated him. The flat's central air conditioning unit was on the fritz again, and he simply refused to open a window. It reminded him of home, though, and it drove and fueled his rage toward the technologically enhanced West.

If the West can come up with such a device, they should make it perfectly so it does not break down! he thought.

He groaned as he stood, his knees aching. He slept with his legs bent and never with some support or cushioning under them. That, too, fed his hatred. His Imam had taught him that pain can be used to spur one on, if focused properly.

Jafar followed loyally and blindly. *The Imam is never wrong,* he thought.

He raised his arms above his head and stretched, a deep, guttural moan escaping him as he felt the weariness of sleep do the same. He walked to his prayer window and looked outside.

The sun was only minutes away from breaking the plane of the eastern horizon. Morning's first light wanted to burst over London, bringing a new day and a new hope for the world; after yesterday, Britons and Americans both wanted to make sure yesterday was just a dream.

No, it wasn't a dream, Jafar thought. *It happened, and it will happen again, even before you blink.*

He thought back to six days ago, when he knelt at this window, facing Mecca. That day, July 25, had been Jafar's final meeting with his lieutenants, those in the know of the Wembley attack.

Jafar allowed a grin as the memory of the event flooded him.

***

"Gracious and merciful Allah," he had whispered, "guide me in this noble task."

He knelt at his window — the third of five times he would humbly visit this window today — facing toward the southeast in the general direction of Mecca. The man bowed his head, his hands clasped in front of him, his eyes closed, his lips moving silently. He sunk deep into prayer.

"*Allahu Akbar*," his prayer continued, "*Subhan Allah, Al-hamdu Lillah, La ilaha illa-llah.*" Allah is the greatest, Glory be to Allah, Praise be to Allah, There is no god but Allah. "*A'uzu billahi minashaitanir rajim.*" I seek refuge in Allah from the outcast Satan.

Jafar had tightened his eyes as he murmured his prayers. If he had opened them and looked out his window, he would see the breadth of London just north of the River Thames unfurling in front of him. The buildings in front of his Cavendish Square flat lined Oxford Street, and if he cared to look past them, he would see many people, disbelievers all, walking south along Regent Street as they ducked into the nearby Apple Store or even Hamleys a little further down the narrow way. The London College of Fashion stood tall and proud, immediately in front of his flat. How many times had he stared out the window and saw those burqa-less women walking in and out of its doors? It disgusted him that these women flaunted their exposed bodies, their tanned flesh, for the camera, for their men, and for the world to see. It was not right. It made him sick to his stomach.

Blasphemers, Jafar thought. *All of them were blasphemers. Slaves to the Western world and the Almighty Dollar, the Almighty Euro, the Almighty Pound. Being slaves to Western ways was not Allah's way.*

I will teach them all, he thought. *Oh yes, Allah will show me the way, and I will carry out his deeds. Allahu Akbar!*

He had allowed himself a smile, but it was only a brief one. He had cursed himself mightily and asked Allah for forgiveness. He did not mean for the wretched West to enter his thoughts during this solemn moment of his day, no matter how hard he tried to stem the flow. His hatred for the West, fueled by the teachings of his Imam and his Taliban handlers back home in Afghanistan, could not be undone, not even during his prayers.

Damn the West! he thought. He wished he had never heard of the United States, or the United Kingdom, their petty grievances against Allah's chosen ones, and their continued open defiance of him by supporting the blasted Israelis. He wished the Soviets — *more unbelievers, the godless Communists!* — had never forged that agreement with the People's Democratic Party of Afghanistan and had never entered

32

the country, for then the United States would not have come in to support the *mujahideen* even before his country's civil war began.

If the Soviets did not come, the United States would never have made a promise, a promise to help rebuild his country, one it never intended to keep.

Jafar had bit back a curse.

The Geneva Accords ruined everything! he thought. *We were going to be back on track! Our country was to be revitalized in a way that the Shah, Daoud, Taraki or Amin could never have dreamed of! But no, those infidel Americans saw no further use for us once Gorbechev and the Soviets left us to fight among ourselves. That scoundrel, that Bush, the father of the criminal, saw nothing but devastation and left us for dead!*

He had taken a deep, calming breath, but kept his eyes closed. His eyes burned with the memory of his parents, killed in the initial Soviet invasion. It had been 34 years, but he kept their memory alive during his prayers. He knew he wasn't supposed to cry for his ancestors — it was not the Muslim way — but he believed Allah would approve of his reasons for doing so. They weren't supposed to die! Grieving was his way of focusing his hate for the West, and it made him stronger to think they looked down upon him — his father deprived of the seventy-two virgins Allah promised all believers in paradise — as he planned his Great Assault, his personal *jihad* against the West.

He let his chest swell at the thought. The Great Assault would begin soon, and the entire world would see it as it played out. The Nation of Islam would rise as one and would applaud Jafar and those alongside him for their deeds, their own acts of defiance against the unholy West. It would be his legacy for Islam, something of which Islamic historians would praise him. The historians of the West would vilify him — if he left any of the bastards alive to recall it. This sole act of terrorism would earn him his seventy-two virgins, and even more than that: Jafar believed Allah would double or even triple that total if he succeeded in his task.

This plan of his had been in the works for some two years, and he knew that it would rival anything that his hero, bin Laden, Islam's Hide and Seek world champion for the near-two decades since the 1993 World Trade Center bombings, could come up with. He wanted to go for more than just shock and awe, to use the infidel American phrase. He wanted to do more than just terrorize a country, or the West as a whole.

He wanted to terrorize the world.

"*Bismillahir Rahmanir Rahim.*" In the name of Allah, the Most Beneficent, the Most Merciful.

I will be merciful, Jafar had thought — *merciful to those who begged Allah for forgiveness, forgiveness from their blasphemy, their wretched infidelity. It was no matter. Allah would be merciful and give them the death they so desperately deserved.*

Jafar had allowed himself another smile, but it did not last long. It turned into a grimace as his knees started to hurt, as if the memory foam cushion he knelt upon gave way to the hardwood floor beneath it. He had been at the window for how long? Five minutes? Ten? Could it have been twenty? He did not know. The arthritic pain that shot through him did not matter right now. He was not finished with his prayers. He constantly embraced the pain for Allah, and gladly did so. It was Allah's command, and he would follow it. *Allahu Akbar!*

Once he completed his prayers, though, he would meet with those loyal to him — he despised video conferencing over the Internet, but it had its uses — and finish planning his Great Assault, Allah's Grand Scheme.

He had promised it all to Allah, and Allah would guide him.

His face was slick with sweat — it was a warm day, and Jafar did not have the window open — as he rose from his kneeling position. His knees had cracked as the weight lifted. He had winced, but pushed the pain aside. He staggered across the room to his desk, which sat in front of a panel of large monitors. Each was already on, and staring back at him were the faces of five men who were ready to assist him in his plan to bring about the domination of Islam.

He had encrypted the patch; he wanted no one listening in. He had cleared his throat and turned his microphone on.

"I apologize, my brothers in Allah. Excuse my tardiness. I was merely saying my afternoon prayers, asking our gracious god to bless our mission," he said.

"No apology is necessary, brother Jafar," said one of the men, his voice coming through the speakers clear as a bell. "Allah is worthy of our praise and prayers."

Jafar had nodded curtly, then continued: "That He is. He has so graciously awarded us this mission to cleanse the Earth of infidels. It is nearly time for us to do his noble work, and it begins in a few days' time.

"Brother Adham, has the truck been rented?"

"It has, brother Jafar."

"Good. Make sure the explosives are set inside. I have already taken the liberty of making sure none of the security teams are on that side so you can do your work without interruption. When you complete the job, make sure you destroy the truck. Our hands must be clean of this.

"Now, how about the second target? Are things ready to go?"

"Yes, *musahib*. The water shall flow like rain, and glorious Allah shall wash the stench of the infidels away."

Jafar allowed himself a grin.

"Very good. You all have ways out of the country?"

They nodded. Jafar had been pleased. He, however, would stay in the country to oversee the entire operation. He knew his people were loyal to him, and they would not reveal his location to anyone. But just to be sure…

"Do you have your cyanide tablets in case of capture?"

Once again, they nodded. Jafar had noticed, even through the computer monitor, that they firmed their upper lips before nodding.

They are willing to go to the deaths for Allah, to protect the mission and the identities of their brothers, he thought. *They are good soldiers of Islam. Cyanide may be a crude method of suicide, but when in a tight pinch, with the mission on the line, it would be an easy way to avoid the authorities.*

"Good. Make sure you are not captured," he had stressed, looking directly into the web cam. "Allah would hate to lose any of you in this *jihad*, even though he will be with us until the end. Go now and pray. Clean up any loose ends and make sure our contacts know what they are supposed to do. *Allahu Akbar!*"

"*Allahu Akbar!*" they repeated. One by one, the connections severed.

Jafar had then picked up his mobile and dialed the twelve digits. It rang twice before the person answered.

"Good morning, *musahib*," the voice said.

"Good *afternoon*," Jafar replied. "It is much too late in the day in our homeland for morning."

"Yes, I know. It is morning here in Jamaica though, Jafar."

"Has everything gone as planned?" Jafar had cut him off.

"Yes it has. The old man charged the account." The voice at the other end spoke low, as if the person speaking did not want his conversation overheard by others. "I will be watching in my office, and as soon as I get the signal, everything will be taken care of."

"And the money will be back in the account?"

"Yes, *musahib*. The chargeback will take place at that time, as well. It will be as you command."

"It will be as *Allah* commands," Jafar had corrected. "I am but a man, brother Naqil. Allah is our leader, and he commands this mission. He wants the money back in our account. He does not want the West to sully our funds, brought to us by the sale of our own heroin and the Saudi's precious oil, bastardized by OPEC. Is that understood?"

Jafar could almost feel Naqil trembling through the connection.

"It is, brother Jafar. Forgive my ignorance."

"You are forgiven as long as Allah deems you forgiven. He may ask for your blood in exchange for repentance. Are you willing to give it in his glorious name, Naqil?"

The silence on the other end had been deafening. It had lingered far too long for Jafar's liking.

"Are you there, Naqil? Allah does not like to wait for his followers' answers. He demands immediacy and unwavering loyalty."

"I am here," the underling said. "Someone came to my desk."

"Right," Jafar had replied. "What is your answer, Naqil? Are you willing to give your blood for Allah?"

"Of course I am. You know this, *musahib*."

Jafar had smiled.

"Of course I do. I will call you before it occurs. *Allahu Akbar*."

"*Allahu Akbar*."

Jafar had hit the end key, tossed the mobile on his desk and leaned back in his chair, sighing contentedly. He had then looked toward the window and his prayer cushion. The sun streamed through the glass, the dust showing through its rays. He held off the urge to go to the window, throw it open and yell to the masses that their deaths were coming.

No, he had thought. *Allah does not want them warned. He wants them off-guard so that when the end comes, they are praying to him to save them from what approaches.*

There will be no saving this time. London shall fall first, and then Washington, D.C. The Western world will finally capitulate and bend its collective knee to Allah. Those who refuse Allah will die. The only way to salvation and paradise is through Allah alone.

Jafar believed that.

Soon, everyone would believe that.

***

Seeing the sun rise caused Jafar to breathe in the musty, sweat-filled air of his flat. He let it caress his lungs as if it were made of the finest silk a Sheik gave to his harem. Even if he had opened a window, the warm, London air would not be much better than the air he breathed right now.

The air Londoners and everyone else who had come for the Olympics would be breathing would not be suitable for anyone, if Jafar had anything to say about it.

The air may not be breathable after tonight, he thought. A grin began to form.

Seeing the sun rise also angered the Afghani. As it was the holy month of Ramadan, it meant that he would not be able to eat for well over 15 hours, and he did not have anything since before he remotely set off the explosives the night before. It would be nearly a full day since he had last taken sustenance in by the time he sat down and ate *Iftar*.

I wanted to wake up earlier and take part in Suhoor, Jafar thought, *but Allah must not have wanted me to do so. He wants me to be sharp, to let my anger fuel my rage. He wants to see if my desire to eat will attempt to drown out my desire to do his will. I will not allow it to be so! I will show Allah that I am worthy to be his subject, and that I shall sacrifice my body's needs during Ramadan. I will show Allah that I am stronger than the others, and that* Suhoor *makes a Muslim weak!*

Jafar lowered himself to his knees and clasped his hands in front of him. He bowed his head and began to pray:

"Allahu Akbar. Subhan Allah, Al-hamdu Lillah, La ilaha illa-llah. A'uzu billahi minashaitanir rajim. Bismillahir Rahmanir Rahim. Allahu Akbar."

He kept his head bowed as he repeated his prayers, lifting his hands to Allah and asking for his blessing. Jafar smiled as he felt dawn's light caress his face through the windowpane, as if he could feel Allah's presence warming him. He lowered himself and praised Allah's name, rising after one rotation of his prayers. He felt his back tighten and spasm.

Jafar bit off the pain and resisted the urge to grab his back, even though it would have been the prudent thing to do. Instead, he continued his prayers, not sacrificing his devotion to Allah for his body's own weaknesses. He feared Allah's retribution for such a betrayal.

His morning prayers lasted for another half an hour. He rose, felt his knees crack, and walked gingerly to his couch. He grabbed the remote and turned the television on.

The BBC led with last night's attacks on Wembley — Jafar smiled again — but the ticker on the bottom drew his attention.

The scrolling black text read: "UK authorities to shut down commercial flights out of Heathrow, outbound Eurostar service to Paris and Brussels, roads leading to Wales and Scotland; authorities suspect terrorists on Monday's attack upon Wembley Stadium still in country."

37

A shiver of fear ran up Jafar's spine. Doubt began to gnaw at him. He began to gnaw his fingernails as he painfully paced the floor.

Do the Britons know I'm involved? he wondered. *No, it's impossible. There are no traces of me whatsoever. Everything has been erased — the account, the rented truck, both are gone. My operatives have vanished, as if they never existed; they emailed me after they destroyed the truck and let me know they did it. The authorities have no leads, and if they ever manage to find one, they will be chasing ghosts. I am as good as in the clear.*

What if they manage to find something tangible on you? a little voice whispered into his consciousness. *They could ask the Americans to send in one of their wire-tapping spies and email-slicing sleuths to find you, and you have nowhere to go. You can't get out of the country, unless you slither into Scotland on foot. And what if they were to find you, a Muslim in the highlands of England, all alone with your backpack? Those zealots would use you for target practice, Jafar. You know this. It's why you stay in this cramped flat with its broken air conditioning all day, planning world domination and breaking the codes of Mohammed.*

"No, no! Stop! Stop!" Jafar yelled, slapping his hands over his ears. "Allah commands you to stop!"

Allah has no power over me, Jafar, the voice whispered. *You believe you are the second coming of Mohammed. You are wrong. You are going to go to hell, Jafar, and the West will laugh at you. Your Muslim brothers will laugh at you. You are but a fly on a camel's hump, and unlike how you think you are this strong, militant Muslim who can handle a strict Ramadan regimen, a camel can go longer than you without water.*

Jafar felt his mouth ache with thirst, his tongue fat and dry. It felt like home. He yearned for a glass of water.

You are weakening, the voice taunted.

"No, I'm not weak," Jafar said. "You will be quiet in my mind, or I will stop you. I will kill you!"

The voice simply laughed at him.

She is coming, Jafar. Your doom is coming, and there is nothing you can do about it, it said. Beware your next move. She will find you, and she will kill you.

Jafar heard the voice trail off. He did not know what it meant by *she.*

The voice must be confused. No woman can stop me, Jafar thought. He began to breathe easier as he comforted himself.

Chapter 4
Heathrow International Airport, London, England
31 July, 2012 — 06.00 GMT/1 a.m. ET

Somewhere over Greenland, Jaclyn fell asleep. She spent several hours during the flight reviewing the information Dupuis sent to her iPad, including the video the terrorist made bin Laden style, as well as the video of the explosions. Just from this, she had a good bead on what happened before she hastily boarded the plane in Flushing.

She changed in the car en route through Midtown Manhattan, the tinting in the limousine adequate enough for her to have plenty of privacy as she shucked off the thing Charlie made her wear during the shoot. In exchange, she replaced it with a white blouse she left untucked as well as a gray skirt that would reach her knees. It was not exactly her style now, but when in open service to the CIA, she did not dress provocatively. It was in these clothes that people would think of her as just another unimportant pencil pusher.

Her other outfit, safely tucked away on the plane with the other "necessities" Dupuis had her bring — *I love these necessities*, Jaclyn thought with a smile as she inspected the contents when she arrived at LaGuardia — was the one that the government knew would give terrorists and other enemies of the United States pause.

The Gulfstream's descent shook Jaclyn out of her slumber over eastern Ireland.

Unlike on a commercial flight where she had to stay in her seat during the plane's descent and approach, Jaclyn, on a government plane and the only passenger, was under no such restrictions. She unfastened her seat belt without a second thought, stretched her arms above her head and went to the bathroom to freshen up.

And unlike most women, freshening up did not take her forever.

She returned to her seat and looked out the window. St. George's Channel was calm, and dawn had already shed the darkness that had bathed Britain. They barely encroached Wales, passing over Swansea and sliding ever so silently into England. The Gulfstream leveled out and made a direct line for Heathrow. They would touch down within the hour.

Jaclyn was slightly nervous. This was her first assignment out of the country. She wanted to prove Dupuis was right in sending her overseas to represent the United States, and she wanted to show President Forrister that he could call on her in times of unrest.

She took a deep breath and slowly exhaled. Her heartbeat quickened as they flew closer and closer to western London.

The hour passed just as quickly.

They landed at Terminal 5, where MI5 was to pick Jaclyn up on the tarmac. A quick pass through customs — Jaclyn would show her diplomatic identification, allowing her and her necessities to pass through unscathed — and they would be on the M4 moments later.

Squeaking wheels hit the runway at speed, and within half a minute, the Gulfstream began to slow down and taxied toward the SIS hangar. The plane turned left, and Jaclyn saw an older man standing next to a black car. The car reeked of diplomacy.

That must be Messingham, she thought.

She stood up and donned her jacket, which she thought she wouldn't need in the stifling heat but would wear it anyway. She did not wear her Walther P99 under it and would not until she cleared customs. Taking the jacket off until after would be the prudent move: She did not want anyone to know she was carrying.

The Gulfstream stopped, and the attendant lowered the door. Bright sunshine flooded the cabin, along with the heat and humidity of London in very late July.

For a moment, Jaclyn wished she were home in comfortable Seattle.

She walked down the small set of stairs holding a rather hefty bag. The MI5 agent walked forward.

"Welcome to England, Ms. Johnson. I am Nigel Messingham, MI5. Let me take that for you," he said, grasping the handle at the same time. "We have a busy schedule, so if you'll please follow me to the car."

"But my other things?" Jaclyn asked. Nigel paused and turned to face her. "I still have another bag on board."

"Well go on, then. Don't dilly-dally about it," Nigel replied.

Jaclyn turned and walked up the stairs and grabbed the second bag, which was just as heavy as the first. This one, Jaclyn recalled from a few hours ago, had her necessities, items she hoped she would not need until, at the very least, later that night, when she could begin her own investigation.

Nigel took this one from her — Jaclyn dragged it — and he immediately felt his upper body give way.

Jaclyn hoped he did not break anything important. She was relieved though, because even if he did, the swirling fumes of ether would affect neither of them, since her bags were made of thick leather.

Nigel strained as he picked the bag up again and heaved it toward the car. He was practically duck walking the bag between his legs.

Jaclyn was slightly amused.

"You can bloody well help me, James!" he yelled at the driver. "I'm not as young as you are."

James the Driver hurried over, grabbed one end of Jaclyn's bag and easily lifted it. He backed the bag toward the car's trunk. They gently put it in, and James closed the lid.

"I am not taking that thing out of the boot," Nigel said, sweat pouring into his eyes from the strain. "How the devil did the CIA get them onto the plane in the first place?"

Jaclyn walked toward the open door that James held.

"They used professional wrestlers," Jaclyn said. "The Rock, Hacksaw Jim Duggan. They are on CIA retainer for heavy lifting."

"Hacksaw Jim Duggan?" Nigel said. "That creepy fellow who stuck out his tongue all the time?"

Snapshot nodded.

"Surprised he never bit his tongue off. A disgusting man, sticking his tongue out. I'll never understand Americans and their fascination with the tongue. Although I must say the missus does fancy that Gene Simmons from KISS."

Jaclyn giggled as she slid into the car, followed by Nigel. James shut the door, opened his own — Jaclyn realized that the steering wheel was on the right-hand side of the car, and that he would be driving on the left-hand side of the road — and pulled away from the Gulfstream.

A few minutes later, James drove north on Stanwell Moor Road for several hundred meters before he bared off to the left toward the A4 onramp. Once on the highway, Nigel raised the barrier between the driver's cabin and the rear space.

Jaclyn tensed.

"My Director Willows and your Director Dupuis have spoken at length over this issue, Agent Snapshot."

"Yes."

"I am to take it that you understand what is at stake here."

"Of course you can. I am to assist you and MI5 in whatever is necessary during the mission. Director Dupuis told me that, yes, but she did not tell me your code name."

"She probably does not know it."

"Then how do you know mine?"

"The SIS makes it a point to know all operatives who come openly into our country. We have to know who we are dealing with. You may not know it, Jaclyn, but the CIA is the same way. Of course, if you snuck in, we would not know anything about you."

41

"And you'd probably have orders to kill me."

Nigel chuckled.

"Probably. Probably not. Who am I to say? But SIS requested your file — it's not that thick now — and Director Willows had it in his hands within five minutes."

Jaclyn felt slightly unnerved by that fact, but she did realize that the United States and United Kingdom were allies. They shared information freely.

"Of course, if I were to work a mission in the United States, Director Dupuis would know my code name was Midwicket and that my son is also in the clandestine service. He's about your age, too."

"Midwicket?" Jaclyn asked, ignoring the part about his son. "I'm not familiar with the term."

"Of course you wouldn't. You Americans don't know anything sport-related unless it has to do with baseball or basketball or your utterly boring version of football. Midwicket is a defensive position in cricket. It also has to do with when the batsman pulls the ball behind him. Cricket has 360-degree hitting, unlike your baseball. And instead of between one and four runs scoring when the ball is hit over the wall, cricketers get six runs. Our cricket is far superior to your baseball because of this."

"So I take it you enjoy cricket, then."

"Enjoy it? Cricket is an absolute joy to watch. It's a gentleman's game, unlike the barbaric football you Americans play or the football the rest of the world plays. I played a little cricket while at Oxford, but I was more of a bowler than a batsman, but when I wasn't bowling my overs, they stuck me at midwicket. I guess the name carried on with me longer than I thought. Would you like some tea? Freshly brewed and all."

Nigel indicated the hardwired Keurig machine that was nestled into the middle of their row.

"Sure, thank you. I'd love a cup."

"We try not to use it while in transit, but I'm sure you're absolutely famished from your flight, so we can make an exception. Is Earl Grey fine with you?"

Jaclyn nodded.

Nigel prepared a cup for her and a cup for himself, taking all of two minutes to do so.

With their escort, James practically flew down the A4, passing the airport proper on the right and Cranford Park on the left. As she sipped her tea, she passed many different residential areas.

It let her to wonder…

"Nigel, why didn't we take the M4? That would have taken us right into London, right?"

Nigel took a deep sip before he said, "Quite right, it would have — as soon as it merged with the A4. But we're not going directly into London proper. Director Willows wants you to see Wembley and the carnage for yourself so you can make a full report to Director Dupuis and the president when you are back in the hotel."

Jaclyn accepted that with a nod. She sipped her tea, wishing she could have flown down the M4 — *surprising that Dupuis mentioned the M4 and not the A4,* she thought — the greenery of Heston Park and Osterley Park unfolding in front of her, wondering how nice it would be to live in such serenity.

Soon the A4 ran alongside the M4, and a few miles later, James found the traffic circle for the A406, which wound its way from Gunnersbury through Ealing Common. They bared to the northeast at the Hanger Lane Tube station, travelling on North Circular Road until they approached Stonebridge Park on the left.

Another left-hand turn onto Harrow Road this time, and the glass bulk of Wembley came into view. They approached the Wembley Stadium Rail station.

Jaclyn finished her tea and turned to Nigel.

"Has there been any update on the death toll? When I got on the plane in New York, I believe the toll was up to two thousand. Surely it has gone up?"

Nigel looked grim.

"Yes, it has. It's up to twenty-seven hundred. They are finding bodies under seats, collapsed concrete, everything. They are finding bits and pieces on the pitch. If you'll excuse the term, it's been bloody devastating. And I hate to say it, but you could say that this is our September 11."

Jaclyn's face fell.

"I hope England never has to deal with something like that. I lost my parents that day."

Nigel's expression matched his American counterpart's.

"Oh, I'm dreadfully sorry, Jaclyn. I feel like a cad now. Please, I apologize."

Jaclyn saw Nigel was truly sorry.

"It's okay, Nigel. I know you didn't mean to say it the way it came out and how it sounded. You can make it up to me later with another cup of tea."

Nigel smiled. He looked out the window. His eyes brightened at the sight of Wembley.

"There she is. The National Stadium. The Home of Football, the Venue of Legends. James," he said, lowering the barrier, "be a good lad and don't pull onto South Way. There's plenty of rescue vehicles there. It will probably be best if we don't disturb their access. Diplomatic plates will probably send the locals all into a thither."

He turned to Jaclyn.

"Are you carrying, by any chance?"

Jaclyn blinked.

"Not at the moment. Should I be? We're only looking at the crime scene, right?"

Nigel shook his head.

"Rookies. You should always be armed, Agent Snapshot, especially at the scene of a crime. You never know what is going to happen."

"Then James is going to have to pop the hood of the trunk —"

"The boot," Nigel interrupted.

"The boot?"

"The boot."

"Okay, James is going to have to pop the boot," Jaclyn said, shaking her head, "so I can get one of my Walthers and a holster."

Nigel blanched.

"One of your Walthers? Dear me, Jaclyn. How many of the little things do you need?"

"The Walther P99AS isn't a little gun for a woman, Nigel," Jaclyn shot back. "Besides, Sean Connery's James Bond preferred a Walther PPK, and those things are tiny compared to the P99. And I carry at least six of them at a time. You should have been able to glean that from the file SIS conned out of Alex last night."

Jaclyn looked knowingly at her British counterpart. She could see he was adding two and two — and two — together, realizing that the clandestine American packed a heavy punch in the way of firepower.

James pulled up at the intersection of Harrow Road and Wembley Hill Road, a stone's throw away from the White Horse Bridge. He popped the trunk, and Jaclyn, once out of the car, removed her jacket. She opened the bag on the right side and grabbed an undercoat holster, then pulled out one of her Walthers. She checked the magazine, snapped it back into place, slid it into the holster and secured it. She put her jacket back on, then followed Nigel over the footbridge.

"Everything looks fine on this end," Jaclyn said as they walked over the bridge. They were still some one thousand feet from the stadium.

"Quite right, but the damage is on the north side, and inside the stadium. We'll just tuck in to the old girl and see what the devil is going on."

Jaclyn gave a semi-tight smile and just sighed, slowly getting used to Nigel's British banter. She adjusted her sunglasses so that the sun's rays didn't find her sensitive eyes. She pressed a small, undetectable button on the side of the frame. Within seconds, her heads-up display came into view.

She filtered through the display and found the temperature reading — it was a balmy 92 degrees Fahrenheit, which converted to 33 degrees Celsius according to the small, red digits in the upper left-hand corner — as well as a quick scan of the area conducted by the micro-sensors in her sunglasses' frame. She wanted to make sure that she was ready for anything, especially if anyone wanted to get the drop on her: The CIA taught her to exercise caution, and her whole "unarmed" bit she said to Nigel was a simple, professional tease. The fantastic piece of technology she wore on her face played a huge part in helping her accomplish her tasks. If it detected anything remotely dangerous about the scene surrounding Wembley, Jaclyn would be the first to know.

There was nothing to be concerned with at the moment, she saw. Her HUD had nothing out of the ordinary to report.

She and Nigel walked along South Way to the stadium's southern entrance. Both showed their identification. The concourse was full of corpses, pulled from the rubble on the north side.

Jaclyn gasped. Her HUD was able to give her an idea of what she would have seen had she been able to see without visual enhancement. What happened in Boston a year ago also came to her mind. She made a mental note not to lift the shrouds. Another memory triggered of New York, post September 11, and a photo of covered bodies in a makeshift morgue near Ground Zero.

Wembley Stadium was normally a place where a country's World Cup hopes faded in the floodlights.

Now it was a morgue of a different kind.

"And that's not all of them," Nigel said. "Keep walking, I'll show you."

Jaclyn braced herself for the worst as she walked.

The two agents slid through a curtained partition and up the ramp to the loge level. And where there should have been the green pitch unfolding before their eyes — "Holy shit," Jaclyn exclaimed — instead bodies covered in white sheets, much like the concourse, filled their vision. Jaclyn kept her sunglasses attuned to the pitch. It wasn't until a minute or so later that she was finally able to see the wound the terrorists dealt to the five-year-old building.

When she finally saw the gaping hole cut into the inner area of the stadium, she strengthened her resolve.

Someone is truly going to pay for this, she thought. *And I hope I'm the one who catches up to them.*

IOC Conference Room, London, England
31 July, 2012 — 07.15 GMT/2:15 a.m. ET

Delegates swarmed into the IOC offices the morning following the attack on Wembley. Every single one of them, speaking in their various languages and dialects, had the same message for the IOC president.

Send the Americans home, or we will go home.

The Belgian president of the IOC was sympathetic to the delegates — he understood exactly where they were coming from — but he expected this. With the terrorists' message broadcast on every news channel around the world, the delegates believed the Americans were the cause of it. His conversation with Forrister last night only strengthened his resolve, though.

The Olympics would go on.

"Get rid of the Americans!" the delegate from Australia yelled.

It was matched by the delegate from Spain. And France. And Iran.

Practically every country, save the Great Britain and Canadian representatives, were against the United States' inclusion in this Olympic Games.

"My friends, please settle down," the Belgian said.

"No!" came the joint reply. "Send the Yanks home! We're in danger because of them! They were wrong to spread war after they were attacked, and now it's going to cost our athletes their lives!"

"It will not," the president said. "Please, calm yourselves."

He waited until everyone settled themselves. He saw scowls and crossed arms as he looked out at the crowded room.

This is not how I want my tenure to end, he thought. *I have brought the delegates together to stand on an issue before, and I shall do it now.*

The Belgian took a deep breath before he continued:

"It is indeed a great tragedy that has occurred during this Olympiad. Without a doubt, it has rocked the foundation of sport to its knees. It has torn the fabric of our Olympic fellowship. These terrorists are out for one thing: To scare us, to make us fear them. I will tell you now and forevermore that we will not tolerate terrorism at the Olympic Games.

46

The Olympics promote peace and harmony in our world through sport. The mindless aims of these monsters, these talentless beings, must not be allowed to tear down our will, or our collective strength as a body of nations. We must stand together, especially with the United States and our host nation. Right now, they both need our support. We should not shun them at this difficult time."

He took another breath as his lungs began to burn from his speech. He looked out among the sea of delegates and saw their scowls replaced with deep, thoughtful looks. The president could see they were shedding their anger, their hearts re-opening to the true Olympic spirit.

And then there were some, those from Middle East and those whose countries generally disliked the United States and Great Britain, who were still of the opinion the American delegation should be chucked out of London entirely.

Overreacting meatheads, he thought.

He continued.

"I have spoken with President Forrister, as well as the British Prime Minister. I have even spoken with Her Majesty, the Queen. I have received every assurance those nations will not rest until the culprits are caught and are brought to justice. I have also given them my guarantees that our security forces will be on the lookout for any additional terror plots against this Games."

The delegates became noticeably angrier than they had when they walked in. More terror plots? None of our athletes are safe.

I never should have said that, the president thought.

"Please, calm down," he said. "In the interest of safety for all athletes, their trainers and coaches, every inch of the venues will be swept. Until the venues are thoroughly checked, we will not allow any athletes into the venues. What happened at Wembley yesterday must not happen again."

Another breath.

"The Olympics have been targeted before. In 1996, our Centennial Olympic Park in Atlanta saw an attack. In 1972 in Munich, our Olympic Village was the scene of bloodshed. And now, a football match was the scene of our greatest tragedy, the greatest loss of life in any terror attack against us as a whole.

"This was not just an attack against the United States, it was not just an attack against the United Kingdom. It was an attack against every single nation in this room: In other words, ladies and gentlemen, this is an attack against all of us." The president spoke with such clarity and incredible pacing that he made it sound like he turned into a lecturing professor.

He looked down at his notes.

"During the Munich Games, our esteemed IOC president Avery Brundage, an American, said that 'every civilized person recoils in horror at the barbarous criminal intrusion of terrorists into peaceful Olympic precincts.' He continued by mourning the dead Israelis and ordered the flags put at half-mast. He finished his speech by saying, 'I am sure the public will agree that we cannot allow a handful of terrorists to destroy this nucleus of international cooperation and goodwill we have in the Olympic movement. The Games must go on.'

"I believe in every word of that speech. Therefore, I am ordering every flag in our Olympic Village lowered to half-mast, and that we shall mourn the American and British fans that came to watch a football match, only to be killed by the heinous acts of terrorism. I also say to you all now, and I am fully expecting the support of you and your national federations — the Americans will stay, and these Games must, and will, go on."

Chapter 5
Wembley Stadium, north side
31 July, 2012 — 07.25 GMT/2:25 a.m. ET

Jaclyn had nothing important to do.

She already saw the result of the attacks and tapped out a message to Dupuis on her 3G BlackBerry Curve. Her message to the Director of the CIA was simple: "Carnage, Chief. Absolute carnage."

She did not have to go into specifics, since Dupuis had already seen video of the blast. But to see the devastation and the hole in Wembley's interior was something television cameras could not adequately project. One had to see it with their eyes to believe it.

In Jaclyn's case, her HUD was her eyes.

What she saw through the HUD nearly brought her to tears.

At that moment, she sat outside of Wembley Stadium's north side, her back resting against the legs of Sir Bobby Moore. She was in the process of reviewing the files on her iPad, mainly looking at the file Dupuis sent her of the terrorist's message. She saw evil welling deep inside the oasis of his dark eyes, and his skin, brown like the desert, perspired heavily. The terrorist made no move to wipe the sweat away. He just stared at the webcam, spouting his message of hate.

It was all about sports, too, Jaclyn thought, shaking her head. *It's not only about the United States' involvement in the Middle East, or our foreign policy. There's a focus, an evil focus, behind the man's words. And it's about sports.*

That's what makes this son of a bitch mine, she thought. *He killed some twenty-seven hundred people over sports.*

Jaclyn looked up and saw Wembley Way beginning to fill up with curious early-morning gawkers who wanted to get a glimpse of the stadium. Some paid out four quid in order to take the Tube to northwest London, then pay the same amount headed back into the city proper, just to see if anything else happened since last night. She wondered if someone from the stadium's security team would notice them and keep them at bay.

She shrugged and returned to her iPad.

That is until Nigel called to her. She turned her head, and her HUD indicated that he was waving to her. She walked over to the entrance doors.

"What's up?" she asked.

"The head of security has found something out," her MI5 counterpart said. Nigel nodded to the burly man, who wore a rather bulky sidearm on his right hip.

"Our head overnight watchman never showed up for his shift last night," the guard said. "After everything settled down, we paid calls to everyone on the shift and told them to come in as scheduled," — Jaclyn noticed the guard, like Nigel, had pronounced it "shed-yuled" — "but this bloody wanker never showed up."

"So why would that be important to tell MI5 and the CIA?"

The guard looked to Nigel, who nodded. Jaclyn took that as an indication that he had already heard what was about to be said and was playing his part in this drama well.

The guard leaned in.

"He's Arabic."

Jaclyn wanted her body to tense up — she commanded it to tense up — but it didn't. She just saw a man on her iPad that was possibly of Arabic descent; she really could not tell because of the balaclava, and the clothes he wore in that video could have been of African make for all she knew. This whole Arabic business was hearsay until she heard otherwise.

"So?"

The guard looked stunned, but Nigel looked cool, calm and collected, even in the early-morning humidity.

"Go ahead Peter, drop the bombshell," Nigel said with a slight smile. Jaclyn looked between the two and wondered what the pair played at.

"The man's name is Kafil Abdul Mohammed."

That caused Jaclyn's body to stiffen. She had heard it several times in the past six hours or so, and she immediately added one and one together. The evidence was now officially convincing, but still, she had her doubts. It's how she was trained: While gathering facts, disregard each in turn until a fact that makes perfect sense is brought to the table. So far, she had a name, a nationality — *somewhat*, she thought — and the fact that this man was a security guard at Wembley and didn't show up for work last night. It made her dismiss all of them; after all, many people of many different nationalities didn't show up for work last night.

Still, her brain processed that an Arabic man with the same name as the terrorist claiming responsibility for this attack works here and didn't show up last night.

If that isn't a coincidence Lord, I'll break my HUD and wander through London blind, she thought.

"Okay, he has a name which could be any one of a million people in the world. How many Kafil Abdul Mohammeds are running around?"

Jaclyn replied, somewhat sarcastically. She was poking holes in his theory, trying to parry around his defenses.

Then he dropped his riposte.

"This Kafil Abdul Mohammed happened to re-arrange the overnight security schedule the other night," he said, sliding a piece of paper her way. Jaclyn took it and increased her HUD's visual amplification. As she read the words, the guard said, "Everyone scheduled for duty on the north side of the building was either given a two-hour break or was shifted to the south side, and then those on the south side were given a two-hour break or shifted to the north afterward."

Now that is more like it, Jaclyn thought, smiling internally, finally getting hard evidence in front of her. *This is not a coincidence. This is something tangible, especially with the north side of the building practically blown apart.*

"Alright, let's play with that theory. When did this occur again?"

"Two nights ago. The night before the attack. Says so on that sheet I handed you."

Jaclyn began to pace in front of the two men.

"So we have to presume that our Mr. Mohammed shifted the security schedule," — she pronounced it like the Aussie did — "to keep prying eyes away from this side while his people worked; he couldn't have done it all on his own, the stadium is too big. Have any of your men found any explosives or detonation devices in your travels?"

"No, ma'am," the guard said. "We really haven't been able to do any searching because the authorities have roped off the entire area. I'm surprised they let you lot walk through this area."

Jaclyn ignored it.

"Are there any surveillance cameras that would have been able to show this side of Wembley Park? You guys do use CCTV, I understand."

"For security cameras, no, not for the outside of the stadium, but for the interior concourses, yes, we have them inside up on the third floor. But there is a CCTV camera right over there on top of the arena." The guard pointed to the left. "And there's another one on another building, too."

Jaclyn looked to where the guard pointed.

Wembley Arena loomed nearby, even though its neighbor cousin dwarfed it by a considerable margin. And at the very top…

"HUD, magnify image," she said.

"What the bloody hell did she just say?" the guard asked Nigel.

"Pay her no mind," the MI5 man replied. "She's doing her job."

Jaclyn's HUD complied with her request, and soon the roof of the arena came into clear focus for her eyes to process. The CCTV camera pointed right at her.

The HUD then began to blare at her; a small red light flashed on the right-hand side of the device. It meant only one thing.

Jaclyn dropped the paper and drew her Walther P99 from underneath her jacket, holding it up in a defensive position. She looked around, awaiting the next attack. One of the curiosity seekers said, "She's got a gun!"

"Snapshot, what in the devil —?" Nigel began, but Jaclyn's voice drowned his out.

"Draw that gun, Midwicket. There's danger about. You may want to draw your gun, too," she said, indicating the security officer.

They did as they were told, and within seconds they echoed Jaclyn's posture. They looked like Charlie's Angels.

The seconds ticked by. Jaclyn's HUD continued to flash the warning, but nothing had happened. She hoped the HUD was not malfunctioning. *That would not be good*, she thought. *I didn't bring a spare unit.*

The HUD's beeping began to scream in her inner ear. Sweat stung her eyes. Her breath rattled her teeth. Her heart pounded up against her breastbone.

She turned her head back to the left.

A rocket emerged from the CCTV placement above the arena, venting fuel, its steady hiss displacing air.

Her eyes widened.

It came right at them.

Chapter 6
The West End, London, England
31 July, 2012 — 07.25 GMT/2:25 a.m. ET

Jafar exited the bathroom — his urine was a deep yellow in color, a sure sign of dehydration — and walked to his laptop, tuned to the CCTV feed overlooking the north side of Wembley. He saw the rescue personnel mingling together. He figured some of them had just awoken and were drinking coffee.

They are all slaves, he thought. *Slaves to caffeine and other pain-numbing stimulants. Allah would spit on them. They are not worth saving if they cannot save themselves from the crutches of humanity.*

He did not see any of the gawkers in Wembley Park — he could have turned the CCTV view, but he chose not to — but the woman seated at the base of Sir Bobby Moore's statue drew his attention.

Jafar's eyebrows rose a sliver. The skin around his eyes scrunched up as he observed this woman. He sat down, felt his knees crack, and ignored the pain. He studied the woman on the screen.

Who is she? he wondered. *Why isn't she scurrying around like the other infidels, trying to help the dead? She's not acting like one of the predictable infidels.*

Wait. He paused. *There's something different about her. She's not dressed like one of the others.*

Jafar tapped the keys of his laptop and commanded the CCTV to zoom in upon the statue's feet. It took a brief moment to zoom and focus. Once it did, he had a clear look at her. She had her face down, looking at one of those dratted iPads. She could have been reading, but it was a strange place to sit down and catch up on the latest steamy romance novel.

He focused on her clothes. Black skirt, white blouse, black jacket, dark sunglasses. No burqa.

She's definitely not a rescue worker, Jafar thought.

He rubbed his chin, letting his fingers dangle through the several inches of goatee hair. Small flecks of dandruff floated from it. He pulled at the hair thoughtfully, as is he was trying to straighten it.

Then he saw the woman's head come up, looking north. His eyes widened.

"She looks incredibly familiar," Jafar said. "Where have I seen her face before?"

He searched his memory. His lips twisted as he thought about this woman. He let his posture relax and leaned toward the screen. He studied her closely.

She turned her head toward the stadium, then saw her slide the device into a pouch. She stood and walked toward a pair of people standing in the entranceway.

He tapped the keys again and zoomed in ever closer. The pair were males.

Infidels if I ever saw them, he thought. *Now what do those two — wait. I know* that *one, the one wearing the uniform of a Wembley security officer. The same uniform hanging in my closet. That's my bloody* boss. *But this other one…*

Jafar focused his attention on the taller man. Older, wearing nearly the same type of outfit as the woman. *He isn't helping with the search and rescue, either*, Jafar thought. *Maybe if I run him through the facial recognition system, I can find out who he is.*

He thought about it for a brief moment.

"Yes, let's do that. I'll find out who this infidel is. He does not belong there, which means he is in a position of importance."

He squared the cursor over the man's face, then typed in his commands. He returned his attention to the other man, and watched intently as the security chief handed the blonde-haired woman a piece of paper. The top of the sheet bent downward as he handed it across to her. The CCTV visual imagery was so clear he could see the logo at the top of the page.

It was the logo that gave Jafar pause. His dark eyes widened with fear.

"That's security log stationary," he breathed. "I would be a camel's hump if it isn't. I recognize it!"

A beep from the search distracted him. He opened that window and saw the facial recognition spat out its search results.

No such person exists, it said.

Strange, Jafar thought. He leaned back briefly, then had another thought. Let's check to see if Peter shows up in the system.

He clicked the security chief's face and then ran it through the system. The woman just began pacing, getting a somewhat clear look at her face. He quickly ran her face through the system in another window. Wasting time was not something Allah would approve.

Seconds later, the facial recognition beeped, and Jafar saw Peter's information — his name, his date of birth, his address; he had several unpaid parking tickets outstanding — spring off the screen. Jafar knew now that the first man was off the grid, since Peter came up so quickly.

The laptop beeped again, this time with the woman's results. Jafar opened it and read:

No such person exists.

Jafar leaned back and lifted his arms above his head. The woman turned toward Wembley Arena and looked like she was staring it down.

So, he thought, *there are two people who are completely off the grid at the site of my first attack. What are they doing there if they supposedly don't exist? There has to be a reason, but that is not my concern.*

If they don't exist in the system, then I will make them not exist in reality.

He grinned, then opened the CCTV controls — for the false placement above Wembley Arena. He had it installed weeks ago, even before the explosives were set inside the stadium two nights ago. He had prayed about it, and Allah instructed him to make sure the infidels found out nothing. If they found any evidence, he must take care of it. Allah wished it so.

If it came down to it, he must get rid of the evidence.

All of the evidence.

Are you sure it's the evidence you left, Jafar? his inner voice taunted. *You could be mistaken. You could be destroying nothing. You could be overreacting. You know, the mind is the first thing to go.*

Jafar ignored the insults, ignored his inner voice's laughter. He was deep in concentration on the task at hand.

The rocket launcher would do it, he thought. He was sure of it. It was easy to fool the infidels. They had so many of these CCTV placements throughout London proper that they would not notice a false placement.

It was time to put Allah's next step in the Grand Scheme into motion.

Jafar quickly tapped away, keeping an eye on the CCTV monitor as his fingers danced across the keys. The launch sequence initiated as he pressed a series of keys. The words *missile armed* flashed on the screen.

Almost immediately, the woman reached into her jacket and yanked out a gun, holding it up as if she was waiting for something. She said something to the other two, and they, too, pulled out sidearms.

Funny, Jafar thought, *that they look like that old television show right now.*

He bit off a curse. He hated the West so much for their culture and their blind allegiance to television that he could not help the draw to it during his time in New York City. The fasting he had to do in penance stayed with him.

He looked to the three gunslingers through the laptop.

"I want them dead," he said. "And if the rocket doesn't kill them," — he didn't see how they could avoid it, though; the arena was practically on top of the stadium — "then this will."

Jafar quickly entered another set of commands, then set it for a delay. Then set up another set of commands, then delayed those. He slapped his hands together and rubbed them.

It will be a cloudy day in northwest London, he thought with a smile. He pressed the button.

The rocket released.

"Get away and down!" Jaclyn yelled, finding her voice. Without a second thought, she ran two steps, curled herself into a ball and somersaulted forward, while Nigel and the security guard, a split second later, ran in an attempt to keep up with her.

The rocket dove in behind them, colliding with the glass façade and shooting through. The glass shattered, but the rocket's ensuing explosion did more than just cause the glass to break.

A rolling fireball emerged from the north side of Wembley, melting the steel frame. It sent waves of flame and energy outward. Shards of glass flew like a discus. The people who had come to gawk at the stadium were certainly getting an eyeful. Some of them screamed in terror.

Jaclyn felt the heat on her back as she rolled, the glass pelting her and the ground surrounding her like hail stones. The force of the blast caused her to roll farther than she intended to, her momentum carrying her down the right side of the pedestrian walkway ramp.

She finally stopped, but she stayed down until she was sure the glass had stopped falling. She waited until the clinking sounds ceased. When that ended, she finally looked up.

She felt Nigel's hand on her shoulder as she moved her head.

"Are you alright, Snapshot? Your back is cut up a bit."

"I'm fine. How deep are the cuts?"

Nigel looked.

"They don't look that bad; just a few abrasions. Up you get. Now," he said, "where's Peter?"

He only got the first syllable of the security guard's name out before he saw him, laying face down by the statue of Sir Bobby Moore. The second syllable came out as a resigned sigh. Nigel's face fell.

The security guard had a very large shard of glass embedded in his back.

Jaclyn ran and kneeled next to him when she got there. Nigel came up behind her. Jaclyn checked the guard's pulse.

"It's very weak, Nigel," she said without looking at him, before she yelled, "We need a medic here!"

"I don't know if he can be saved, Jaclyn. That glass looked like it's in there well and good."

"It's about to come right out well and good." Jaclyn quickly stowed her Walther in its holster, then whipped her jacket off and covered her hands with it. She grasped the glass.

"Get down here and get ready to stop the blood flow," she ordered. Nigel quickly walked over to the other side of Peter and went to his knees. "I'm going to pull it out and give him a fighting chance, at least."

"Whatever you say Jaclyn, but it will probably only be a 50-50 chance."

"Where I come from, 50-50 is better than 0-100."

Nigel couldn't argue with that logic. He put his hands on Peter's back and pressed down. Blood began to cover his fingers.

Jaclyn began pulling at the shard. It gave way somewhat, but the flesh inside held onto it like a vice.

"It's not budging any more than that; if I pull any more, I could rip his heart out."

"Don't try it, Jaclyn; he didn't have a chance."

"Where the hell is that damn medic?!" Jaclyn yelled. She turned to Nigel and gave him a piercing stare through her HUD. "He's a witness, Nigel."

"He gave you the evidence; it'll show Willows plain and simple what happened. We'll give it to him."

Jaclyn checked her pockets. It wasn't there.

"What did I do with it?"

Then she remembered. She smacked her forehead. Blood smeared her blonde hair.

She looked back toward the stadium entrance, which looked wider than she remembered it. Burning lattice framed the statue of Sir Bobby Moore. She looked beyond the former England captain and, through her HUD, saw the sheet of paper lying on the ground, a lake of flame and debris protecting it.

"I see it!"

"I thought you were blind?"

"Partially blind." She tapped her sunglasses. "I'll be right back. Keep your hands on that wound." She rose from her crouch and ran toward the entrance.

The heat from the conflagration tried to warn her away, but she steeled herself and gave the blaze a mental flip-off. She tiptoed around the burning steel and luckily still had her shoes on, for there was plenty of glass lying about. She reached down for the paper and had her fingers on it.

Her HUD whined in warning.

"What the —?" Her fingers were on the paper, but the distraction made her delay her task.

The next sounds made her forget it altogether.

A light rumbling from deep inside the stadium made Jaclyn look up. The sound became a rolling thunder, and then she noticed what that sound was in all actuality.

Explosives.

That son of a bitch set more, she thought. *That's why he moved everyone to the north side, so he could have them set on the south side.* Thought quickly caught up to her while the explosions made their way around the stadium just as quick.

Her eyes widened with dawning comprehension.

"Oh, shit," she whispered.

The incriminating paper now long forgotten, Jaclyn made a mad dash away from the northern entrance, her feet barely touching the concrete. She waved toward Nigel in an imitation of Han Solo running away from the Imperial bunker.

"Nigel! Get moving! She's going to come down!" she warned.

"What the bloody hell are you talking about?"

She grabbed his arm and, with strength unbeknown to her before, yanked the Briton to his feet, pulling him away from the downed security guard.

"The terrorist set more explosives. Wembley's going to be a Ground Zero-like crater in about five seconds."

"But what about Peter? What about the people inside?" Nigel asked.

They were now 10 yards away from where Peter lay.

Jaclyn looked back at Wembley, her face worried, its fate already sealed by the detonation. She realized the detonation also sealed the fate of the rescue workers inside. If they weren't already dead, they soon would be.

Peter, though, was another story.

"Help me get him," she said.

The duo moved forward a step, a step that led them back to danger. A much louder rumbling met their ears. The sound made them freeze in place. It was the sound of collapsing steel, breaking glass and crumbling concrete. Another three explosions, this time outside of the building, went off with the power of a howitzer.

Jaclyn's internal hypothesis was right.

Wembley, iconic arch and all, was on its way down.

They looked up at the looming hulk of the northern façade and stared in horror as a larger plume of smoke and dust rose from the southern end.

The cloud began to swarm around and pushed the clean air away. It penetrated the openings of the parking garage next door. Particles of Wembley's remnants covered abandoned cars. Visibility quickly became nil.

The cloud headed this way.

"There's no time. Move!" Jaclyn said, pulling her MI5 counterpart away from Peter, abandoning him to his fate. They ran down the ramp and pounded Wembley Way as the northern entrance began to collapse behind them. The arch swayed, then began to fall toward Bobby Moore.

"Move, damn it!" she waved to the people still gathered on Wembley Way. Most of the people scattered when the rocket struck the building. Those who stayed were rooted to the spot.

The cloud came ever so quickly.

Jaclyn, in her heels, tried to beat it. She grabbed the nearest person, a balding man wearing a black suit, and tried to pull him to safety.

"Take your bloody hands off me, woman!" he protested. "You're going to rip me suit!"

"You're going to wear that suit to your fucking funeral if you don't move right this minute!"

Jaclyn didn't see the shock in his face, but she felt his body begin to finally move. Nigel was moving people, too. The others moved as the cloud encroached their personal space. It turned into a stampede. Narrow Wembley Way turned into Estafeta in old Pamplona.

"Keep going," Jaclyn said. "Don't stop until you get to the Tube."

They kept running.

IOC Conference Room
31 July, 2012 — 07.45 GMT/2:45 a.m. ET

The door flew open on the delegates. The IOC president, who was speaking with the delegates from Canada and Portugal — and trying to decipher their accents — looked toward the disturbance. One of his aides stood in the doorway.

"Wembley's gone!" the woman said.

A ripple of shock flew around the room. Eyes were wide. Mouths hung open.

The president, though, stood there as if the words weren't registering.

"What did you say, Bernadette?" the Belgian asked.

"Wembley Stadium imploded," she said. Her face was completely white. "It happened about five minutes ago."

"Are you sure?" said the delegate from Germany.

"I'm positive. British television was showing it live. We were watching it as it happened. The stadium is gone, I tell you. Gone!" She broke down sobbing, hitting her knees. Several of the female delegates rushed to her side.

The other delegates looked to the president.

His reaction was not what they expected.

They saw a defeated man standing there, one who looked like he was about to crumble under the weight of their combined stares. His posture was slumped, as if Bernadette and her purple size six pumps just leveled him with a drop kick to the solar plexis. He couldn't breathe. The president was in shock, and these people were looking to him to lead them through this second attack. He suddenly realized he was not Avery Brundage, not Juan Antonio Samaranch, not Jacques Rogge.

Right now, he wished he was not in charge.

"Mr. President, what are we going to do?" the delegate from New Zealand asked.

The Belgian heard the question, but it took him a moment to move. He gulped and turned to the questioner.

"Pray," he replied.

Chapter 8
The West End, London, England
31 July, 2012 — 08.05 GMT/3:05 a.m. ET

Jafar saw everything happen on the BBC broadcast, along with millions of others watching throughout the United Kingdom. It would lead the news broadcasts in the United States in a few hours.

As he watched, he smiled wide throughout the entire ordeal.

Wembley Stadium, including the arch, was gone. He destroyed it.

His false CCTV camera placement atop Wembley Arena was gone. A nice five-foot hole graced the roof now.

Wembley's security chief, as Jafar saw through the real CCTV camera, suffered a fatal wound in the initial blast. He was certainly dead. He believed the two faces he could not get to register on the recognition system were dead.

They are certainly off the grid now, he thought.

Jafar walked to his prayer window and opened it. He didn't do it so fresh air would enter his dry flat. No, that was not it at all. He wanted to hear the screams when the British found out their national stadium, their iconic Wembley, was now rubble.

He took a deep breath and hit his knees.

Allah has blessed this mission, and it will come to fruition, he thought. *The West will fall. The Middle East will rise. Allah has ordained it. It will happen.*

The destruction of Wembley is far from the end of my attacks.

***

Jafar was born in 1969, ten years before the PDPA called the Soviets in to help with the *muhajideen* problem that had been growing in the country. The Soviets already aided Afghanistan with billions of dollar in economic and military aid. It was only a matter of time before the *muhajideen* saw the writing on the wall and revolted against the Communist government.

Being a youth, Jafar did not know what was happening, and his parents, Allah-fearing parents, kept him sheltered from the world of Afghani politics. It was easy for him to be brainwashed by the *muhajideen* after they were gone, not understanding why his parents were killed in the Soviet invasion.

"The godless Communists are at fault! They do not belong here! Go back to where you came from, you dogs!" the *muhajideen* screamed from their pulpits and their caves, brandishing the weapons American senator Charlie Wilson convinced President Carter to provide to them: The Americans did not want the Soviets in Afghanistan, near their precious oil supply, and arming the *muhajideen*, part of Operation Cyclone, made sense at the time.

Little did the Americans know those weapons would be trained on them.

Orphaned by the Soviet invasion, Jafar took part in raids against the Communists. It was not unusual for youths to do so; they saw it as their part in the war effort. It was either kill or be killed. The number of Soviet soldiers taken out by Jafar and his friends, whether with incendiary devices or with American machine guns, were staggering.

Soon, Jafar was the only one of his friends who remained. He became a loner by nature, answerable only to Allah. He had shown prodigious skill in warfare and an uncanny knack of avoiding capture. Eventually, he rose to the rank of commander, and for his efforts against the godless Soviets, he was educated in many things.

Yet when the Geneva Accords were signed, the Soviets and the Americans pulled out of Afghanistan, leaving behind a wasteland. It was not to be so, the *muhajideen* believed. Jafar even wept, because he knew the Americans gave their word that they would help Afghanistan rebuild.

Then Osama bin Laden came.

The Yemen-born bin Laden had been fighting with the *muhajideen* for some time, when he suddenly became the face of Islam to the West. He began to point the blame to America, pretending they had not helped against the Communists. It stirred Jafar and the populace into such a fervor that they began to hate the West. Jafar could feel his heart racing as bin Laden spoke. Bin Laden made sense to him.

But when his superiors asked Jafar to go abroad and learn about the West, to ignite his hatred of the West, he did so with relish.

His handlers told him, "Do not arouse suspicion. Lie to them. Do not tell them you are from Afghanistan. You are Saudi now, and you are there to learn business. We are sending you to England, to attend Oxford University. There are possible exchange programs with American schools. Take in everything you can. Be mindful. Assimilate. Learn about their culture and why we hate it. They thumb their noses at Allah, and praise their own God. And then, when you have learned everything, you will return so that we can launch great attacks against the West, attacks that will benefit Allah and show them why they are wrong not to worship Him!"

And so, with tuition paid for by the sale of Afghani heroin, Jafar Abdullah Mohammed went to England under the assumed name of Kafil Abdul Mohammed. There he learned the ways of the West, learning everything from the ways the West governed its people to the ways the West relaxed. He grew fascinated — on the outside, that is; on the inside, he could have spat upon them and not thought twice about it — with the games of football and cricket, if just to fit in with his English classmates. He saw women dressed in shorts and t-shirts, and tried not to vomit at the sight.

As he learned about Western culture and the influence the United Kingdom and the United States had on the rest of the world, he now knew why bin Laden was right to denounce them. He went to New York City and Columbia University, where he saw the United States aid Kuwait when mighty Saddam invaded that tiny country. Recalling what happened in Afghanistan, he quietly wondered what the Americans promised the Kuwaitis in exchange for their assistance.

Of course, he knew exactly why the Americans in their jets and their aircraft carriers went to the Persian Gulf. It was because of oil, something the Afghanis wished they could have offered the Americans.

It was too late, though. The Americans had worn out their welcome, the Afghanis believed. The Americans were on the other side now, collaborating with the Soviets. They were the enemy, and they had to take them out.

Time went on. Jafar's hatred for the West grew. When September 11 occurred, he knew it would happen beforehand. Like a good Muslim, he kept his mouth shut. He was in New York, watching from afar. He kept his elation down as the planes slammed into the towers, the field in Pennsylvania, and the Pentagon. He then watched on television as the towers came down.

It was then and only then, in the safety of his apartment, that he could hit his knees and properly praise Allah. With a smile on his face he spoke his prayers proudly, uncaring if his American neighbors heard him shouting Allah's name in joyous praise.

Jafar then found his way out of America before Bush's imminent witch hunt began. While in Toronto, he watched on television as Bush proclaimed that the coming attacks were not against the people of Afghanistan, that Americans had a great respect for the people of Afghanistan.

Jafar had to laugh at the Texan. It came out as vitriol.

"That is a lie!" Jafar yelled. "If you cared or respected us, then you would have helped us recover from the Communists! You lying infidels! *Allahu Akbar!* Allah, bless Osama, our hero!"

When the Americans invaded Iraq to find weapons of mass destruction, Jafar, now safely in England once again, had to laugh at Bush's desperation.

When the Americans took Hussein out of office, it sent ripples through the Islamic community.

Jafar could not believe it. He believed Saddam, mighty Saddam, would be in control until he passed the torch of Allah on to Usay or Quday. He could not believe the dirty Americans won the battle.

And then, with what the Americans called Operation Neptune Spear, Jafar's heart dropped. The West had killed bin Laden. The pictures of infidels celebrating in front of the White House made his eyes leak with sadness. His hero was gone.

He decided that the West, especially the Americans and the Britons, needed to be stopped. With Moscow, Paris, Madrid, a recovering New York City and London in the running for the 2012 Summer Olympics, he followed Hussein's death by planning a stunning attack that would shock the world and bring the winning city to a standstill. He had operatives in each city, waiting to carry out his plans. When IOC voters eliminated Moscow first, Jafar bit his lip: It would have been sweet justice to carry out an attack against the Russians. He hoped to get his revenge upon the Soviets.

New York was the next city eliminated. That took him off guard. He felt for sure that New York, with its planned state of the art stadium in the West End, would have been one of the two finalists to get the Games. So sure he was that he had double the operatives in Manhattan than he did in any of the other cities.

Madrid was next to go. Not surprisingly, Jafar felt nothing for the Spanish city. At that point, Spain was not a fan of America, and had not chosen to get involved in Bush's War on Terror. He only had one operative there, one who had not been involved in the train bombings in 2004. It would have went unnoticed if Madrid came under attack, Jafar had to admit.

That left Paris and London as the potential hosts. Jafar's heart raced with anticipation as the vote neared. Beads of sweat ran from his temples, down his cheeks, and beaded on his brow. He wondered how it all would play out: Would his operatives make trouble on the Place de la Concorde or at Trafalgar Square, or would they wait a day, as they had been ordered, and attack the London Underground or the Metro? It was this alone that caused Jafar the most of his anxiety.

Then it happened. The vote came, and even through his closed windows, he heard the celebrations erupting from two kilometers away. London's fifty-four votes won the Games of the XXX Olympiad, and Jafar let loose a grin. He had nothing to worry about: His operatives would take care of everything tomorrow, and all he had to do was sit back, enjoy the spectacle of everyone running around, trying to keep the populace of Greater London calm. He could not wait to watch the BBC the next morning. He sent an email to his Afghani handlers back home, saying everything would proceed as planned.

It happened the next morning, July 7: The Underground came to a halt as three bombs exploded within fifty seconds of each other. A fourth exploded an hour later. Fifty-six people, including Jafar's bombers, died as a result. Seven hundred others were injured.

It was chaos personified, contagious and necessary.

While the terror lingered, Jafar reveled in it.

He would do the same seven years later.

Chapter 9
Wembley Park Underground Station, London, England
31 July 2012 — 08.45 GMT/3:45 a.m. ET

Jaclyn did not think an email tapped out to Dupuis would explain this. No, letting her fingers dance over the keypad of her BlackBerry would not do this justice one bit. She knew Dupuis needed to hear her voice and tell her what just happened. To hell and back with the time difference. To hell and back with security. Dupuis had to know now.

Dust covered her as she stood in an alcove of the Wembley Park Underground station. Nigel was nearby, talking on his cell phone, presumably to his superiors. Jaclyn, overstepping her bounds a bit, told him she wanted to get a good look at the CCTV tapes from two nights previous.

Wembley had been gone for an hour. Smoke rose steadily from its remains.

They had already lost precious time.

Jaclyn dialed Dupuis' home number, one she knew to be secure. It rang three times and almost went to Dupuis' voice mail before the Director of the CIA, half asleep, picked it up.

Please don't let her be pissed off, please don't let her be pissed off, please don't let her be pissed off, Jaclyn prayed.

"This had better be damned good, Jaclyn," Dupuis' groggy voice demanded. "Is London still on the map? It's quarter to 4 in the morning. If London is still on the map, I hope to God you have a much better reason for calling me when it could have waited for two more hours."

Damn it, Jaclyn thought, biting her lip. *She's really pissed off.*

She ducked further into the alcove. The sun pierced the dust cloud. She had on her sunglasses, but the dust was thick. It was stinging her wounds; London EMS hadn't checked her out yet.

"Yes Chief, London is still on the map," Jaclyn replied calmly, "but this couldn't wait. Wembley, though, isn't on the map any longer."

She heard silence on the other end for several beats of her heart.

"What do you mean? Did aliens lift the entire section of Wembley?"

Jaclyn smiled for the first time in nearly 90 minutes. She was thankful Dupuis had a sense of humor this early in the morning with no coffee running through her bloodstream.

"I mean the stadium, Chief. It's gone. The terrorist destroyed it an hour ago. Wembley Stadium is Ground Zero."

Another four beats of her heart went by without Dupuis speaking.

"Wow. And the dead Americans?"

Jaclyn grimaced.

"Buried under dust and steel," she replied. She told Dupuis of how the British turned the southern concourse of the stadium into a makeshift morgue, as well as the pitch. Her narrative continued, informing her of what the now-dead security chief — there was no way he could have survived the dust cloud, not to mention the arch falling — told her and Nigel about Kafil Abdul Mohammed before the rocket surged toward them.

"Do you have the evidence?" Dupuis asked.

This time, Jaclyn cringed.

"That, too, is buried under steel, dust, and glass. I went to get it when the explosions started and the stadium came tumbling down like a house of cards."

"Nice imagery."

"I'm sorry, Chief."

Dupuis sighed.

"Don't worry about that. You did what any person would have done. People will probably vilify you and want you strung up," — Jaclyn cringed again — "but that information will never get out, at least not from us. By the way, are you secure right now?"

Secure in what way, Alex? Jaclyn thought, biting her lip. *Secure in my bed? Secure in someone's arms? Secure in the knowledge that we have a terrorist on the loose…*

"No, the cube is in my bag, and that's in the car, which we haven't seen in about two hours. Hopefully James and the car and my stuff are okay."

"Don't worry about the car right now; worry more about being overheard. You couldn't send this in an encrypted email? That's why you have a BlackBerry. That's why you have an iPad."

"I would have sent one but I didn't know when you would get it. This was the best possible way, secure or not. I thought it would be best to let you know this way so you could inform the president before he found out about it on CNN in 75 minutes. He would have come down hard on both of us if I didn't take the initiative and call you. Fuck secure, Alex: The whole breadth of England knows what happened. This really isn't an international secret."

She said it before she could close her mouth. Thought overrode better sense. She had just told off the Director of the CIA. Her boss. The one person who took care of her and showed confidence in her abilities after her parents died.

She was more ashamed of herself now than she ever had been before. She tried to speak, but the words wouldn't come.

But Dupuis shocked her by speaking first.

"You're right, of course," she said. "I'm sure you gave it plenty of thought before you acted. I'm sorry for accusing you of not knowing your job. The best trained you. And you're right: It would be best if Forrister found out from me instead of some Larry King wannabe."

Jaclyn grinned.

"Thanks for the vote of confidence, and I'm sorry for yelling at you. You know me; sometimes I let my mouth do my thinking for me."

"Don't worry about it; I haven't had coffee yet. What's your next move, Snapshot?"

Back to the terminology of the clandestine, Jaclyn thought.

"Midwicket is on the phone right now with SDW," she said, using the initials of the MI5 Director, Sir David Willows, to confuse anyone who may be eavesdropping. "I have the feeling we're going to go to Millbank for a debriefing and to view footage."

"You haven't been to bed yet, have you?"

"That's a big 10-10, Chief," Jaclyn said, replying in the negative. "We came straight here via the A4 and some back roads."

"Scenic route, eh?" Dupuis paused as she yawned. "Get some rest when you can. Send a message through your BlackBerry when you learn anything else. I should be at the White House in about two hours, so you can reach me on my cell if you find anything."

The pair hung up, and Jaclyn turned to see Nigel finishing his call to Willows.

"What's up?" she asked.

"Sir David is not happy one bit."

"Neither is Alex. I had to wake her up. At least Sir David has had his tea and crumpets this morning."

Nigel shot her a scowl.

"He's not happy because he had tickets to the football final."

"Oh, what a bummer," Jaclyn replied sarcastically. "What does he want us to do? What's our next move?"

Nigel took a deep breath, then coughed. The air was incredibly heavy with the after effects of Wembley's very premature demise.

"As soon as James brings the car around, we're going to get sorted by my superiors. You may be able to get a spot of breakfast, since you haven't had anything to eat since last night, I suppose. Neither have I, for that matter."

"I think I may have lost my appetite when we walked into Wembley, but I may be able to choke down an English muffin or two."

"And once that's done," Nigel continued as if Jaclyn had not interrupted him, "we're going to check out the CCTV feed from two nights ago. Sir David is already leaning hard on Scotland Yard for that footage. We should have it by the time we arrive on Millbank."

"We may want to stop at EMS first," Jaclyn said. "I still haven't been checked out, I don't know if there's any glass lodged in me, and you don't look so hot yourself, champ."

"At least I'm still wearing my jacket, Snapshot. Yours is buried under dust and who knows what else was inside the bloody stadium."

That was my favorite jacket, too, Jaclyn thought, turning her HUD back toward the crater that had once been Wembley Stadium. It would smoke for another few days. Fire rescue companies were on the scene, pouring many cubic liters of water on the site to dampen flames.

It just made it worse, if it wasn't already.

Jaclyn thought about the initial rescue efforts. Those had now gone to waste. They would need more hands on deck as soon as the fires and hot spots were put out to not only move debris, but to re-dig all the bodies — those who were killed in the explosion yesterday, and those who were inside the stadium when she came down.

The sounds of people speaking off to the side interrupted her reverie. Her enhanced hearing, sharpened by the affliction to her eyes, could easily make out what they said:

"You know something, maybe the terrorist is from Wales, in all actuality," the man said. His friend looked aghast at what he was suggesting. "Think about it. This bloke is probably a member of the Welsh FA, I'd wager. Now The FA has to move the League Cup and FA Cup semis and final back to the Millennium Stadium. The sound of Wembley falling is like the sound of a cash register opening for Cardiff."

Jaclyn was stunned. Blinking, she turned to Nigel.

"Did you hear what that creep just said?"

A blank look passed over Nigel's face.

"No, I didn't. What did they say?"

"He said that the terrorist was probably with the Welsh FA, whatever that is, and that the FA — he didn't say Welsh before it that time — would have to move the League Cup and FA Cup matches to Cardiff."

Nigel ran his hand over his face to hide his scowl.

"That is just bloody sickening."

"That is what I thought, too: Thinking about sports in a time of crisis. People died an hour ago, and these people only care about their fucking sports."

The car pulled up onto Bridge Road.

"We'll get sorted by EMS at Box 500. I don't think you should be around this place much longer, at least for today," Nigel said, opening the back door of the dust-covered car and allowing Jaclyn to slide in first. "Besides, I may go deck the bastard myself if we don't leave now."

Chapter 10
Thames House, Millbank, London, England
31 July 2012 — 10.00 GMT/5:00 a.m. ET

Rush hour traffic on the Westway took a little more than an hour to get the intelligence officers from Wembley to Millbank. Nigel was quick to point out to Jaclyn that the Olympic Stadium used for the 1908 Summer Games would be approaching on the right once they passed Shepherd's Bush.

Jaclyn wasn't paying any attention to him, though. She was deep in thought about the whole situation: Wembley's use as a prop in this terror strike, the fact that the terrorist worked at Wembley, how the FA would have to move their season-ending match to Wales...

Then the thought struck her right between the forehead.

"Nigel," she said, turning to her counterpart. She winced as a slight pain attacked her. "Tell me about this FA nonsense."

"There's not much to tell, really," he replied. "Why do you ask?"

"Professional curiosity. I don't want to leave any stones unturned."

Nigel sniffed.

"Very well. When the old Wembley was torn down, the FA — the Football Association — needed a place to hold events for the national football team, the League Cup and the FA Cup."

"Cups?"

This time, Nigel smiled a kind, fatherly smile.

"Trophies, to you American lot. We call them cups, silverware, you name it."

"There are two? My older cousin followed English soccer a long time ago, but I never cared for it. What's the difference?"

Nigel now felt like a teacher in school.

"Well, there are actually more than two cups, Snapshot. There's the Premier League Cup, the League Cup, the FA Cup, the European Cup — honestly, there are so many to keep track of that I bloody well don't know what all their names are now. But the League Cup is a half-season competition that takes place during the autumn and winter months between the 92 teams in the Football League."

"That's a big league."

"Yes, and no. You see, the Football League is divided into four divisions: The Premier League, which is generally the best clubs in England, followed by the Championship, League One and League Two. The FA Cup is open to clubs all throughout England and starts in July with many qualifying rounds. The teams in the Football League don't enter the tournament until November at the earliest, while the Premier League doesn't have to worry about the FA Cup until after the Christmas holiday.

"At any rate, the FA had to move everything in their offices over to Soho Square while the new Wembley was constructed, but the matches went to Cardiff; at the time, there were no stadiums in Greater London that could hold more than 60,000 fans. The Arsenal was in the process of building the Emirates. The Tottenham and Chelsea's stadiums were too small. The Millennium Stadium in Wales had just opened and served as a proper replacement until Wembley was ready in 2007 for the FA Cup Final.

"Now with Wembley out of commission again, the FA will have to find a new replacement site for those matches along with a stadium for the national team. They could go back to Cardiff, but I would bet the loo on the Arsenal getting those. Tottenham wouldn't be happy, I can wager."

"Why is that?" Jaclyn asked. They passed Notting Hill.

"The Arsenal and Spurs have an intense rivalry, to say the least, much like your Yankees-Red Sox rivalry in the States. This one is worse, though: Instead of some 200 miles separating the two sides, only a few kilometers separate the Emirates and the Lane." Jaclyn looked confused. "Basically, put a stadium in Georgetown and a stadium at the Pentagon, and you've got Arsenal-Spurs. That in mind, I would not even fathom a guess as to how bad the rivalry would get if one of those two got both the FA Cup and the League Cup finals, as well as a little piece of the gate to boot."

"Okay," Jaclyn said, "I think I've got it. So what happens with The FA as a body now?"

Nigel leaned back. He ignored the pain that shot through him.

"I really don't know. They were at Wembley for the past few years, but I think they moved out temporarily while the Olympics were in town. Gave everyone a holiday, moved their stuff to some place in London; probably went back to Soho Square. I'm pretty sure they will stay put for the time being now."

I won't take that bet, Jaclyn thought. She looked out the window and saw they were coming up on Marylebone Road.

"We're going to make a quick detour to get back on the right track. We won't be long. We'll be at Millbank shortly, so don't let the eyelids droop."

The suggestion caused Jaclyn to feel the fatigue. She had been running on pure adrenaline for a couple of hours now, and the mere mention of sleep made her feel like she was running on fumes. She took a deep breath and tried willing herself awake.

The car turned onto Edgware Road, following it south to Oxford Street.

The terrorist's lair was 16 blocks to the east.

James pulled the car onto Park Lane, edging to the east of Hyde Park. Nigel looked out toward Hyde Park, while Jaclyn's head looked toward another patch of greenery straight ahead. Buckingham Palace Gardens, located behind the British Monarch's residence, approached.

As they made the turn around Grosvenor Place, Jaclyn had her left hand in her skirt pocket, where she kept her BlackBerry. She didn't need to see the keys. She knew them simply by touch, and she only took messages from one person. She simply typed a message out to Dupuis:

Investigate English FA, new location desired? Personnel files needed. Have an idea. Earliest convenience, or delegated to Salt. JJ

Jaclyn double-clicked her BlackBerry's mouse as James turned left onto Buckingham Gate, then felt her BlackBerry vibrate as the message went through at Birdcage Walk. St. James's Park was on the left.

She smiled as the phone purred. She hoped Salt — the CIA code name for their high-tech computer cracker named Daly — would be able to give her more insight into the identity of Kafil Abdul Mohammed.

Minutes later, the car made the right-hand turn onto Whitehall, making its way south. They passed the Houses of Parliament. Jaclyn wondered if the talk inside was of issues of crown and country, or if the murmurs in the House of Lords and House of Commons chambers were focused on this morning's incident at Wembley.

If she had to bet, she would say the talk was of the latter.

James turned the car into Thames House, pulling into a waterproof garage underneath the building.

***

Thames House was an 82-year-old office development on the Victoria Embankment side of the River Thames. Built on land cleared following the river's 1928 flood, located just south of Lambeth Road and down the road from various government offices on Whitehall, the building had many uses until Her Majesty's Government purchased it in 1994. After an intense renovation, it became the home of MI5, while MI6 took possession of the newly constructed Vauxhall Cross, located a stones' throw away on the other side of the Thames.

And as MI5 was in charge of not only internal security in the United Kingdom but also site of the UK's counterterrorism division, there was quite a bit of pressure upon this agency to find out what happened not only last night and this morning, but also for them to bring those responsible for these reprehensible acts to justice.

After being checked out by EMS the moment they arrived at Box 500 — EMS workers had dressed their wounds, and even gave Jaclyn a place to change her blouse so she did not have to meet the General Director wearing a glass-torn rag — both Jaclyn and Nigel headed upstairs to meet with Sir David Willows.

To Jaclyn's HUD-enhanced sight, Willows was everything she figured an older British gentleman to be. A gentleman, no doubt, but he was also slightly pompous and arrogant, sounding more like the late Bernard Lee than the late Robert Brown, whose voices Jaclyn heard whenever Willows spoke. He wore heavy suits and was slightly heavy-set, but through the HUD Jaclyn could tell the man carried his weight — literally and figuratively — rather well. A pipe stuck in his mouth, sending soft tendrils of gray smoke toward the ceiling of his office. Jaclyn tried not to cough. His gray hair was in such an impeccably-combed state, as if he saw a barber first thing in the morning, but Jaclyn noticed the barber forgot to trim back his eyebrows, which were rather stuck out and pronounced.

She tried not to stare; with her HUD though, Willows would be none the wiser, thankfully.

"Agent Midwicket, Agent Snapshot, I am most relieved you are both alright," Willows said, his pipe still clamped between his teeth.

"Thank you, David. A little dust in the lungs and a couple of scrapes and knocks, but other than that, we're in the pink," Nigel said. "Has the threat level been elevated?"

Willows nodded.

"The highest it can go," he said. "We've been at critical since last night. All flights in are being allowed as long as they go through security," — Jaclyn fidgeted ever so slightly — "but no flights, trains, or boats are leaving. We've also closed roads into Wales and Scotland. Heaven forbid a Welsh citizen in Swansea had to go to work in Bristol this morning. He may never bloody get home."

Willows turned to Jaclyn.

"Agent Snapshot, I am told you'd like to have a look at the security footage recorded around Wembley two nights ago. I've put in a call to Scotland Yard, and the boys at CTC will wire them to us shortly; I expect you have a hypothesis, my dear?"

Jaclyn nodded, but said nothing. She simply looked at Willows through her sunglasses. She wasn't giving Willows, though an ally to the United States, anything more than he needed to know. It was a little game occasionally played among clandestine agencies. She shouldn't play it now, and she knew it. If Dupuis were here, she would probably reprimand her and apologize to Willows. Jaclyn was the rookie, Willows the veteran, so to say. This was Willows' playground, and he was in control. When the CIA needed something from MI5, they usually showed a certain amount of respect. It was the same in reciprocity, quid pro quo of the highest order.

Willows could have thrown her out on her ass without even a glimmer of those files. But when he grinned at her, it seemed as though he knew he was dealing with a rookie. He would let her slide this one time.

"I have the feeling our Mr. Mohammed was on the inside when all of this occurred," she said. "As I'm sure Nigel has told you, the Wembley security chief accused one Kafil Abdul Mohammed, who happens to share the same name as our terrorist, of failing to show up for work after he was instructed to come in for his shift last night. He also alleges that Mr. Mohammed re-arranged the security schedule two nights ago. If my hypothesis is correct, then we have our terrorist pretty much dead to rights."

Willows leaned back, puffing on his curved pipe.

"Where is the security chief now?" he asked.

"Dead, sir," Nigel replied. "At least we believe he's dead."

"What the devil do you mean, Midwicket?"

"The security chief was more than likely killed when the rocket embedded in a false CCTV placement on top of Wembley Arena exploded outside the stadium," Jaclyn said. She inhaled. "We were running from it."

Oh my, I said that rather quickly, she thought.

"The what embedded in the what?" Willows said incredulously. If his eyebrows could shoot out any further, they would have tickled Jaclyn's forehead. "Midwicket, what is this rubbish?"

Nigel proceeded to tell Willows of the false CCTV emplacement, the rocket stored inside of it, the glass shard sticking into the security chief's back. He told him of how he and Jaclyn tried to save him, but once the stadium began to come down...

Nigel had to pause for a moment.

It took Nigel several minutes to relay the events in full. Then they analyzed it from every angle possible.

79

Someone knocked on the door. Willows told the person to enter.

"Sir, the files from CTC are here. Shall I route them to your computer?"

"Midwicket? Snapshot? What will you both require?" the General Director asked.

"This is Jaclyn's baby, so to speak, sir," Nigel said, looking to his American counterpart.

Jaclyn gulped. She never thought MI5 would give her the point in this mission, especially given her orders: In MI5's presence, she was to be an observer. Outside of MI5, though, was another story.

She had to think quickly.

"Possibly someone to run the computer, I would say. The ability to freeze images and such is beyond my comprehension of computers."

"Consider it done," said Willows. "Have you two eaten yet?"

Both shook their heads.

"I'll arrange for something to be sent up, and I'll have James bring your bags and things to the hotel we've picked out for you. It's a very nice place over by the University of Westminster and Regent's Park. Very comfortable, too, I'm sure you'll find. I stayed there myself when I was a lad."

Jaclyn did not have the heart — nor the curiosity — to ask the General Director of British Intelligence what he meant by that.

Both she and Nigel rose to their feet — Nigel saluted Willows — while Jaclyn saw in her HUD that a text message was coming in. The vibration in her skirt pocket confirmed it.

"Excuse me, General Director, is there a ladies room on this floor?"

"Of course there is. William, will you show Agent Snapshot to the ladies loo, please?"

As soon as she was in the bathroom, she pulled the phone out and read the message Dupuis sent:

Salt has your information; the data packet is on your iPad right now. Be glad Salt was up at the crack of dawn and in the office by 5. AD

That boy moves fast, Jaclyn thought as she sat on the toilet lid. She didn't say anything about what was said in the message out loud; she didn't know if MI5 bugged their bathrooms for this very reason. *Hopefully he came up with something good for me to sink my teeth into when I get to the hotel, whenever that will be.*

She typed out a quick thank you to Dupuis, waited several moments, flushed the toilet, then left the bathroom.

Time to see exactly how our scumbag pulled the stadium down, she thought.

***

The top floor of Thames House housed MI5's secondary communications facility. Inside, a wall of panel monitors were stacked one on top of the other, then wired together to give the appearance of a movie theater-type screen.

Upon that screen was a darkened Wembley Park.

It was clearly night. They could only see the silhouette of Wembley Stadium's north side. The time stamp on the lower right-hand corner of the screen — it was so large that it took up the breadth of one 32-inch television — showed that it was the earliest part of the morning — 00.10 GMT — when the attacks occurred.

Jaclyn sipped coffee, her second cup, while Nigel stared intently at the screen, his mouth savoring a cup of tea and Eggs Benedict. Jaclyn paced. The tech at the computer looked behind him and scowled at the American.

A light came on screen, illuminating the pedestrian walkway at 00.11 GMT.

"We've got something, sir," the tech said, causing Nigel and Jaclyn to stop eating and pacing, respectively, and turned their attention to the screen. "Light just came on."

Several minutes passed. Nothing had happened yet. Not even a bird had swooped down onto the pedestrian walkway. Sir Bobby Moore's statue looked clean, the bronze reflecting the light to make the bust dazzle.

Then...

"Door is opening, sir. Can't tell who it is exactly just yet."

"Can you close in on the man?" Jaclyn asked. "That may be the only way to figure it out."

"I'm five steps ahead of you."

The tech commanded the screen to freeze with a simple keystroke. Another two keystrokes zoomed in toward the man. The image looked grainy.

"Let me clear this up a bit. Will only take a second."

"Half a second would be better," Jaclyn said.

"Hold onto your knickers, love," the tech replied. "You can't rush art."

"Art," Nigel said, causing the tech to look at him. "Just be quiet and do your job."

"It would be easier to do me job if SuperChick here would stop giving me flak about it."

Jaclyn looked like she would go through the roof, but she closed her eyes and breathed in through her nose. She calmed herself and paid no further heed to Art's barbs. She opened her eyes and saw Art's fingers playfully pounding the keyboard.

Her HUD saw the screen shimmer and de-res, and within seconds, a clearer picture of the man showing up.

"Alright, who is this son of a bitch," she asked.

"Running him through the facial recognition system," Art said. He clicked the man's face, causing a square to appear. Art's fingers depressed open apple and the letter J, and that made the square shimmer. "System accessed."

Seconds passed slowly. They turned into an agonizing minute. Nigel continued to sip his tea. Jaclyn looked on, anxious to see the results.

The screen darkened. Jaclyn wanted to shout "What happened?" but saw the room-sized bust of Kafil Abdul Mohammed staring into the room.

Jaclyn felt the eyes upon her. Even though it was a still image, the dark eyes made her skin crawl. Her HUD processed the information. She placed an imaginary balaclava over the photo's mouth.

She wasn't sure, but it appeared to match.

Her skin crawled even more.

"What do we have?" Nigel asked.

"Kafil Abdul Mohammed, Guv. Born in Saudi Arabia in 1969, according to the file. Attended Oxford and did an exchange with Columbia in New York in the early 90s. At Oxford, he graduated from the Said Business School, then the Graduate School of Business at Columbia. He minored in chemistry at both."

"My kind of guy," Jaclyn said sarcastically.

"That would totally make sense," Nigel said. "He would have used his knowledge of chemistry to create his own explosives. Pretty smart, if you ask me."

"We didn't ask," Art said, issuing his retort without peeling his eyes away from the screen. "He applied to be a security guard at Wembley in 2005, shortly after London won the Olympics."

"That also makes sense," Jaclyn said, but Art interrupted her.

"No, it doesn't. What would he have had to be a guard of in 2005? Wembley was in the process of being built at the time; it didn't open until 2007, a year later than it should."

Jaclyn detected a hint of anger coming out of Art. She looked to Nigel.

"Don't mind him. Art's a Spurs supporter; he missed out on going to Wembley when Spurs won the League Cup that year. Wembley was finished late, and Spurs haven't been to a final since," Nigel said, grinning. The MI5 man noticed Art's hand clench. Nigel leaned in to Jaclyn and said, "If you want to stay on his good side, don't mention anything about Cesc Fabregas and the North London Derby 2009 at the Emirates. He may punch a hole in the monitor."

Jaclyn rolled her eyes.

Men and their sports, she thought.

"Mohammed's file ends there," Art the Tech said. "No known address, no next of kin."

"Good," Jaclyn said. "Then there will be no one to notify when I crack his skull."

Art couldn't help but grin at that. Neither could Nigel.

"Alright, it seems as though that is a dead end for now," Nigel said. "Let's go back to the main screen and see if we can learn anything else about what happened the other night. The tape obviously doesn't end there. He opened those doors for a reason. It's not like he was going out for a breath of fresh air."

Art tapped the keys and Mohammed's likeness minimized, returning them to the enlarged view. He clicked another series of keys, the shot zoomed back out, and within seconds, the trio saw Mohammed motioning with his hand, indicating he wanted a vehicle to back up.

The truck came into the shot. It slowly backed toward the pedestrian walkway.

Jaclyn could hear the truck's beeping in her mind.

Once the truck stopped, doors on both sides opened, and two men exited. Several more men walked up the ramp, presumably from another vehicle parked on Wembley Way.

"I want facial recognition on all of them," Nigel ordered.

"One thing at a time, Midwicket. Truck first, people second. We'll be able to find out who owns that truck before we can find out who those people are."

"As you wish, Your Majesty."

"And if you want, I can even tell you how many liters of petrol that thing drinks by the time Parliament bangs the gavel."

Jaclyn noticed the sarcasm playing out between the agent and the tech. She figured this was SOP for this pairing.

"No thank you, but by lunch would be adequate, Arthur."

"Do we have a clear look at the plate?" Jaclyn asked, leaning over Art's left shoulder.

"No, but that doesn't surprise me. But this does," Art replied. "Look at this. The company name is right on the side of the bloomin' truck."

"Magnify that for me," Jaclyn asked.

"With pleasure."

Art froze the image and moved his mouse over the truck, clicking and dragging the cursor to form a tight rectangle. He clicked the rectangle, and it seemed as if the truck exploded into the room. It filled the screen.

If Jaclyn weren't already partially blind, she would have been fully blind by the brightness of Wembley's lights reflecting off the enlarged image.

"Holy U-Haul, Batman," she exclaimed. She staggered back a bit until her sunglasses dampened the light to a tolerable degree.

"Maybe it would be best if we magnified the image to a lesser degree, Arthur," Nigel said. "Our guest is a little susceptible to brightness."

"Sorry about that. I got a little carried away with me mouse, there. Guess I didn't feed it the right cheese and it rebelled on me. Tricky little blighter, it is." Art gave a slight laugh.

Jaclyn didn't.

Art's cheek twitched with embarrassment.

"Enough of that, Arthur. Just give us the information we require and hop to it."

"Yes, Guv."

Art lowered the resolution and the image shrunk. The wording on the side of the truck became clear as the day is long.

"Fenton's Rent-A-Truck," Jaclyn read. "Do we have a location for it?"

"Give me a tick," Art replied. His fingers were madly dancing away, as if he knew every locale in Greater London was open to him. The seconds passed quickly, the waiting excruciating.

"Come on, computer. Spit it out," Jaclyn pleaded.

"You can't rush a computer, even with a T1 line," said the tech. "Patience, young grasshopper."

"Yes, sensei."

"Aha!" Art exclaimed. "Ask and ye shall receive." He looked a little closer at the screen. "Blimey, their home office is in Yorkshire. I don't think we'll get the information we need that quickly."

"Why not?" Jaclyn asked.

"Yorkshire is a few hours away, Snapshot," Nigel answered. "I'm sure you want to get a little sleep."

Jaclyn swooned.

"I need more coffee."

"Arthur, do they have an office closer to London, by any chance?"

"Looking that up now, Guv."

Ten seconds later, Arthur's eyes scrolled down.

"They do. They're in Shepherd's Bush. Just a stones' throw away from White City."

"Right. Jaclyn?"

"That's me."

Jaclyn stirred a cup of coffee as she walked back to the pair.

"We have a lead. We're going to Shepherd's Bush to check out this rental company."

"No, you're not."

Willows entered the room. An aide stood with the General Director.

Nigel fixed his boss with a quizzical stare.

"Why not, sir?"

"Because Metropolitan Police have something they want us to check out. They've stumbled upon something very interesting in Osterley Park. Take Snapshot with you."

"Did they say what it was?" Nigel asked as he grabbed his jacket and swung it around him.

"Why yes," Willows said. "Apparently a truck was burning. Metropolitan smelled petrol. But that's not why they called us."

Both Jaclyn and Nigel waited for Willows to speak.

"Why, then?" Jaclyn asked.

Willows turned to her.

"Because they found the blueprints to Wembley a few meters away."

Jaclyn shivered.

This is definitely a lead, she thought. She felt her BlackBerry in her pocket. It yearned to be pulled out and tapped upon. Dupuis needed to know what was going on.

Nigel turned to Arthur.

"Run that plate through DVLA and see what the VIN of that truck comes back as. Send me a message as soon as you find out anything." He began to move toward the door. Jaclyn followed.

"You got it, Midwicket."

"Midwicket?" Willows said.

Nigel stopped and turned to face his boss.

"Yes, sir?"

"Be careful out there. We're not sure exactly what we're dealing with," he said, before turning to Jaclyn. "Are you armed, Snapshot?"

"Yes, sir. I'll know about any danger before anyone else does."

"Good. I'll see you both when you get back. James is waiting downstairs, a little lighter in the boot, but the car is a little cleaner than when you last saw it."

The pair nodded to the General Director, before they headed out into the hallway.

Jaclyn pulled out her BlackBerry and typed out a quick message to Dupuis:

Following lead on truck. Will advise. JJ

With any luck, Jaclyn thought, the lead would open many more doors into this mystery.

Chapter 11
Osterley Park, London, England
31 July 2012 — 12.15 GMT/7:15 a.m. ET

James' lead foot got Jaclyn and Nigel back up to the A4 quick. The diplomatic car, heavy with flashing blue and red lights, caused cars on Vauxhall Bridge Road to move to the side. They did the same on Grosvenor Place.

As soon as they got to the A4, Jaclyn began wondering when she could begin her own investigation. She had been in London for six hours, had not yet gone to sleep — she yawned heavily — and she had yet to break away from MI5.

Sooner or later, she thought, *I'll need some time to do what I was trained for. And I have an idea of what I'm going to check in to first.*

The trip, even with James doing his best to break the land speed record, took nearly half an hour to get out to Osterley Park. They crossed underneath the M4 and continued until they came to Syon Lane. They followed Syon for several hundred yards before coming to Jersey Road. A side street off Jersey would take them to the burning truck.

They could see black smoke pouring into the sky off in the distance.

Jaclyn adjusted her sunglasses.

"Has Arthur sent you the VIN yet?" she asked Nigel.

The MI5 man checked his iPhone.

"Yes he did. Such a good lad for a football supporter."

Jaclyn chuckled, but as the truck came into view, she became serious about the investigation. James turned the car around a small lake in the middle of the park. Trees were on either side of the road leading up to the bend. A green lawn flowed away from the road.

Smoke poured off the truck, burned to a crisp, as the saying went. Firefighters had already suppressed the flames with foam.

As Jaclyn and Nigel stepped out of the car, the scent of gasoline was on the air.

"I guess Arthur will have his answer on how much gasoline this girl drinks," Jaclyn said across the roof to her British counterpart. She indicated the truck. "Considering the stench in the air, I would say she drinks a lot."

"Bloody petroloholics."

The pair showed their identification to the Metropolitan Police officers on scene. They walked up to another officer, one holding a roll of papers in his hand.

"You bloody well took forever to get here," the officer said when Nigel and Jaclyn identified themselves to him. "Traffic that bad on the A4?"

"Not really," Jaclyn replied. "I wanted to see the sights."

The officer growled.

"Bloody Americans, thinking they are comedians," he said under his breath.

"What do you have for us, officer?" Nigel interrupted.

"Truck was fully engulfed when we got here," he said, not looking at Jaclyn at all. "Crews put her out. I'd say she's a total loss, though."

"Looks it. Those are the plans for Wembley?"

The officer looked at Jaclyn as if he wanted to draw his revolver and put a few slugs in her.

"Yes they are. You won't be bloody touching them, though. You Americans should never have even scored against us."

"That'll be enough, officer," Nigel said impatiently. "This is officially a matter of crown and country now. Hand them over."

The officer did so, albeit reluctantly.

"Now, has anyone checked the VIN on that truck?" Nigel asked.

"No sir, there were no plates on it, either. There were no witnesses to it, except those people right over there," he indicated toward the building off to the left. "They heard the truck pull up, but they didn't notice anything out of the ordinary until they heard the wind whipping about. Turns out they heard the truck on fire."

"Naturally," Jaclyn said. "Nigel, I'm going to check that VIN." She turned to the officer. "I'll need a pair of gloves."

Once again, the officer looked like he wanted to punch Jaclyn in the face.

"What do I look like, bloody Harrod's? Get a pair from one of the firemen over there," he said, before he walked toward the truck and waved everyone away.

"That guy has an attitude problem, doesn't he?"

"He must have lost a few quid on the match," Nigel replied. "Serves him right for gambling."

"Too bad the match ended at halftime," Jaclyn said. "Maybe we would have scored a few more times."

"He would have been worse than he is today."

Jaclyn shook her head, smiling at the same time. She walked up to the truck and borrowed a firefighter's gloves. Another firefighter opened the door for her.

"Such gentlemen," she cooed before she grasped the hot metal frame. She didn't feel a thing.

She wiped the area where the VIN was and peered down at it. Using the magnification in her HUD, she was able to read off the number to Nigel, who stood behind her. He confirmed it as soon as the American agent finished.

"Well, we know this is the truck that Mohammed used," Jaclyn said, hopping off the cab and onto the ground. "Finally, some hard evidence."

"I think we knew it was when Sir David told us the Wembley plans were here," Nigel replied, brandishing the plans almost like a sword. "This was almost like a terrorist's calling card."

Jaclyn conceded the point.

"So our next move is to pay Fenton's a visit, I guess," Jaclyn said, before her HUD began to beep again. "Oh, shit."

"What is it, Snapshot?" Nigel asked.

Jaclyn ignored the question. She let her HUD roam about, looking for the threat.

It viewed the truck's storage area, and the beeping went insane.

"Get away from the truck!" she yelled. "It's going to blow!"

Nigel backpedaled away from the truck while Jaclyn walked with hurried steps.

"Hey, where the bloody hell do you two think you're going?" the officer with the attitude said. He was still standing near the truck.

"Getting as bloody far away from that truck as we can!" Jaclyn mimicked, turning her head. The cop looked flabbergasted. "I advise you to get your fat British ass away from it before it —"

The truck exploded. The ensuing fireball caught the cop and a few other officers, not to mention a firefighter, in its wake.

"Explodes."

Several people began to yell at each other. Firefighters grabbed extinguishers and covered the cops with foam. The storage area of the truck had blown apart, flames tickling the metal.

"Excellent timing," Nigel said dryly. "You did warn them, though."

"Yeah, well, the HUD doesn't have a time ticker on it. Maybe the next software update will have one."

Nigel immediately called Thames House and told Willows they were on to something. Sirens blaring in the background caused Nigel to put a finger in his ear so he could hear what the General Director said.

"Yes sir," he said. "I will make sure we do that when we question him, sir. I'll check back in with you after we have information."

Nigel hung up.

"And how is Sir David?" Jaclyn asked.

"He's smashing, as always. Sends his best, as always. Wants us to find this bastard quickly, as always."

"He doesn't ask much now, does he?"

"No my dear, he does not. We have to go to Shepherd's Bush and question this rental truck owner, maybe rough him up a bit."

"Good, I haven't roughed up anyone in a while."

"I was joking, Jaclyn."

"Who said I was?"

She wanted to wink at the British agent, but the Foster Grants impeded her.

"I believe we're all set here," Nigel said, changing the subject. "The emergency medical teams are on their way, and they'll get these people sorted right quick. Our chariot awaits us."

The pair walked to the car as ambulances sped up the side road.

Instead of getting off the A4 at North Circular Road like they had done when en route to Wembley, James drove some 65 meters further and took Chiswick High Road. It became King Street, and after a while James took a left onto Goldshawk Road, the A402.

It took them right into Shepherd's Bush, their next destination.

Shepherd's Bush lay directly south of White City. It was mainly a residential area — Jaclyn was quick to point this out to James, who eased off the accelerator — but what made Shepherd's Bush what it is today was the Westfield Shopping Centre, the largest urban shopping center in all of Europe. The Westway was only a mile away to the north.

James pulled into Fenton's drive, located just off Shepherd's Bush Road. The Royal Guest House was right across the street.

"The proprietor must be in now, seeing that it's just after lunch," Nigel said as he sipped his tea down to the dregs. "Let's go see what we can dig up on this mysterious truck."

"I'm only along for the ride, Midwicket. I'll hold the shovel, you tell me where to stick it in."

They got out of the car and walked right inside.

The owner stood behind the counter, swallowing some Pepto Bismol. He was a small, older fellow, with not a follicle showing on his bald head. He wore overalls that said OshKosh B'Gosh on them.

Jaclyn saw that on the HUD and wondered how the man fit into them.

"Rough lunch, I take it, sir?" Nigel asked.

"You would be right about that. I tried one of those new places up at the Westfield; I bloody won't do that again. Now," the owner said, "what can I do for you good folks?"

"You can tell us about the account for this truck." Nigel gave him the plate number of the truck that became a carbeque.

"I'm sorry, lad," the owner said; Nigel bristled at being called lad. "I can't give you that. It's me company policy not to give out information about me customers. It's bad for business, you see."

Nigel gave a soft chuckle.

"And it would be bad for you, sir, if you do not cooperate. I'm from Box 500."

The proprietor blanched.

"Well," he said, taking another swig of Pepto Bismol. "That's a horse of a different color, then. Let me see." The owner began to check his computer records. "Oh bollocks! This bloody system is too slow."

"Windows 7?" Jaclyn asked.

"No, it's a blooming IBM."

"Maybe it's time for an upgrade."

"What the devil are the sunglasses for, love? It ain't that bright in here."

Smirking, Jaclyn removed her sunglasses. The whites of her eyeballs knocked the old man backward a foot. The man's face went pale.

"Mother Mary Gertrude!" the man exclaimed, a slight Irish brogue coming through. "Alright, now I see why."

She put her sunglasses back on, sliding them behind her ears.

"I would suggest speeding up. This is a matter of international security."

"Right, I'll do that," the man said breathlessly.

He typed away until he found the entry he sought out. It took several minutes. Jaclyn rapped her fingertips on the glass countertop. Nigel twiddled his fingers and whistled.

"Well here we are," he said. Jaclyn and Nigel waited anxiously. "Kafil A. Mohammed, and he is listed as doing business as Allah's Cleansing Service. He wanted the truck for a couple of big jobs, as I recall."

"A couple?!" Jaclyn said. Her voice raised in timbre.

"What do you mean a couple?" Nigel asked. He was just as shocked as Jaclyn.

"I don't really know, sir. It's not me business to ask questions about what me customers are going to do with me trucks when they use them."

"I suggest you change your policy," Jaclyn said, leaning on the counter. "This truck was used to haul explosives to blow up Wembley Stadium."

If the man was shocked when Jaclyn lowered her sunglasses, he was even more shocked this time.

"Is that right?" he said after a moment. "I'm downright dumbfounded. If I knew that, I would have never given him the trucks."

"And if you did that, he would have probably killed you," Jaclyn said. "This guy is a religious fanatic."

The rental truck owner clutched his heart. He grimaced.

"You know something," he said, "I had a funny feeling about this guy. It sounded like he was up to no good. Bloke said '*Allahu Akbar*' like it meant something to me."

He paused.

"Wait, hang on a tick. How do you know it was one of me trucks involved in the thing at Wembley? I saw it on the news last night; I must admit, I just turned into a Premier League guy with QPR up the street, but I do follow the national team like every good Englishman does. Was here late, though, and missed the kick off."

"We found the truck in Osterley Park," Nigel replied. "You won't get the truck back unless you're bringing marshmallows."

The owner looked at him as if he had three heads.

"The truck is destroyed," Jaclyn said, looking at Nigel as if the British agent was a little out of his mind. "The terrorists burned her a couple of hours ago, then detonated a bomb inside the storage area. A couple of people were hurt during the explosion."

The owner quickly made the sign of the cross.

"Well," he said, recovering from that shock, "it looks as though this bloke won't be getting his deposit back, and he'll be paying for a new truck, to boot." He quickly tapped away at the keys for a few moments. Jaclyn saw the man's forehead crinkle before he shouted "Bollocks!"

"Something wrong?" she asked.

"You're damn right something's wrong. The account is blocked; I'm getting error messages. It won't let me charge back on it through his bank. And the bloke's deposit is gone, too! Bloody hell!"

"Does the account have an address, by any chance?" Jaclyn asked.

"Yes it does, but —"

"You can't give it to me?"

The proprietor nodded.

"Look, friend," Nigel said, walking up to the counter, putting his hands on it. "This wanker has screwed you over enough, don't you think?"

The proprietor nodded again.

"How about doing us a favor and help us screw him back?" Jaclyn added. "Give us the bank name and the address of this 'cleansing service,'" — she cringed, knowing the meaning behind the name — "and no one will ever know you gave it to us."

She cringed once again, knowing her words to be partially false. Knowing that the terrorist has been three steps ahead of them for the past 16 hours meant that she wasn't completely sure the man would be alive tomorrow.

If that happens, she thought, *I'll never forgive myself.*

Jaclyn's HUD confirmed the man's heat signature shooting off the charts. His breathing was also slightly erratic. Jaclyn was worried that the man would have a heart attack right then and there.

He stumbled forward and grabbed a pen. His hand shook. Jaclyn grabbed his hand. The man looked like he wanted to scream.

"It's okay," she said with a smile. "Tell me what the address is, and I'll write it down. And if you have all the information for the bank, too, that'll be a big help."

The owner took a breath, smiled at Jaclyn, then did so. Jaclyn's penmanship was flawless. She was able to scan it through the HUD and filed it to the tiny memory chip. She put the paper into her pocket.

She and Nigel left the rental store.

James had the engine running.

"Alright, I want to go to the hotel now. I'm beat and I want to get some shut eye, maybe a shower. How far away is it?"

"Oh, it's not that far. We'll just hop on the Westway, and that'll bring us right to Regent's Park. It's not that far from the hotel, actually."

Weary from the day's events, Jaclyn nodded and slid into the car, pulling her BlackBerry out and sending Dupuis an update, as well as the address for the Jamaican bank. Nigel slid in opposite her. Once the doors closed, James hit the accelerator and took them away from the rental shop, dust trailing.

***

As soon as they left Fenton's, though, a curtain in one of the Royal Guest House's second floor suites moved to the side. The window opened only a few inches. The assassin's gun barrel inched its way outside, stuck between two well-placed flowerpots, a perfect camouflage. Not even an infidel passerby would know what he was looking at if he looked up and saw it.

The assassin, under Jafar's strict orders, pointed it right at Fenton's entrance.

It was only a matter of time before the owner would leave his store again.

The assassin waited patiently.

The West End, London, England
31 July 2012 — 13.25 GMT/8:25 a.m. ET

Jafar's cell phone rang. He stretched for it and felt winded as a result.

"Hello," he said. His voice was tired, but he had barely used it all day. His mouth was parched. He needed water.

Surely Allah, you will allow me this one transgression? he prayed. *I must have some water.*

"Brother Jafar, the government has visited the rental truck dealer. They have just left. My weapon is on the front door. He will die the moment he leaves."

"Was it the pair I described to you?"

"Yes *musahib*. A man and a woman. Both looked like they've had a long day."

They still live, Jafar thought.

"It's going to get even longer. When you finish with your task there, I want you to go to the next destination we spoke of in e-mail. You know what to do. Allah will bless you and your family for this."

Jafar could almost hear the assassin's smile through the phone.

"Thank you, my brother in Allah. I shall not let you or him down."

"I know you won't," Jafar said before pressing the end key.

He threw the phone down.

"I love causing chaos," he said. "It is the reason Allah put me on this earth. The pitiful Americans and the Britons are running around in an attempt to stop me. They can't stop me, because Allah is not behind them. He is on my side, and I shall be blessed the most among them all!"

Are you sure you will be blessed, Jafar? the voice called out. *That seems a little presumptuous, even by you.*

"Oh be quiet. You know that Allah has reserved many virgins for me. It shall be as Allah wants it to be."

But have you given any thought to these two beating you? They've already escaped once.

Jafar cursed. *Yes, they are a resourceful pair, getting away from not only the rocket, but the stadium imploding. They avoid the death that awaits them. It is like...*

He shook off the thought before he had the chance to speak such blasphemy.

Oh come now, Jafar, the voice added. *Your thoughts betray you and Allah. Am I right in thinking that you believe them to be somewhat blessed by Allah?*

"I did not say that."

You were thinking it.

"I was not!" he bellowed, the sound of his voice ricocheting off the walls. He had shut the window an hour ago. His flat became stifled once again. He wasn't even sweating. There was barely any moisture left in him to sweat out.

He needed water.

He swooned and fell onto the couch face first.

You are weakening, Jafar. You must have something to drink or else you are going to perish before you can see Allah's works through to the end.

"It would be a sin to do so," Jafar choked. "It is Ramadan. I am fasting from sins of the flesh. I must not be weak."

You will die if you don't. You won't be honored by Allah if you die, and you won't get your virgins, either.

"Shut up, you know nothing of what Allah has promised me."

But I do, Jafar. I do know. I have heard Allah converse with you. I know of his designs, his plans. If you're going to triumph over the Americans and Britons, you must drink. You are dehydrated. You are slowly becoming delusional. You will see spots before your eyes, and your body will stop functioning altogether. If you had not stayed up last night to watch the devastation unfold, you would have woken up in time for Suhoor. *Allah is punishing you, Jafar.*

The terrorist suddenly found new strength. He became enraged. He propelled himself up onto his knees.

"No! Allah is blessing me! I will not fail him!"

His inner voice wasn't having it.

Take in water, Jafar. It is the only way for you to survive, the only way for you to make it to tonight. You may win your battles tonight, with or without you, but you know that nothing will go right after today if you are no longer on this earth to monitor the buffoons you call associates. Your efforts will fail. Take in water, Jafar. Do it. You must drink.

Jafar's mouth suddenly felt drier than Kabul in July. He lurched forward and got to his feet.

He couldn't take it any longer. The voice got to him.

He needed a drink.

Jafar stumbled into the flat's modest kitchen. He opened the refrigerator door and pulled out his filtered pitcher. He didn't even bother with a glass.

"Allah, forgive me," he whispered.

His mouth was so ravenous to find relief that he over-compensated the lift under the pitcher. Liquid flowed into his mouth, but also into his nose. Liquid spilled to the floor.

He drank deeply. He drained the pitcher.

Before he could refill it, though, he swooned, lightheaded. His vision instantly clouded and became fuzzy. The pitcher dropped from his hand.

He hit the kitchen floor with a thud.

Jafar heard taunting laughter in the back of his mind.

You are indeed weak, Jafar, the voice said. *You are like any other Muslim. You proclaim that you are greater than other Muslims, but you are not. You have just proven it to me. You goaded yourself into breaking sacred Muslim law by thinking you would not make it until tonight. You needed a drink. You would have drunk anything that you saw. You would have drunk sand if I convinced you it was water. You didn't need much convincing, though. You are so weak you did not even check to see what was in the pitcher. Your dehydration was your worst enemy.*

Jafar's eyes widened in horror.

It was beer. Alcohol. Allah changed your water into beer, and you drank it without stopping. Enjoy the floor, Jafar.

The voice continued laughing, the sound bouncing around in Jafar's mind.

The inner laughter made him groan. Seconds later, he felt the bile rising. He vomited. His insides spilled onto the linoleum, last night's *Iftar* on display.

As soon as the nausea passed, he put his head down and passed out, vomit coating the side of his face.

***

An hour passed. Jafar still lay on the kitchen floor.

His front door creaked open. A slight breeze from outside filtered into the room.

The hooded man slid into Jafar's flat, looking around for his boss. Shutting the door quietly, he moved further inside. He hoped he would not find Jafar lurking about.

When he saw Jafar sprawled on the kitchen floor with a pool of vomit surrounding him, he smiled.

He now knew he would have plenty of time to pull off his treachery.

He walked back into the parlor without worrying about the sound of his heavy footfalls disturbing sleeping beauty. He sat down at Jafar's laptop and opened a browser. He typed in the URL for Yahoo.com and immediately logged in.

Once in, he checked Jafar's files and looked for the target for later in the day. His eyes widened when he saw the plan sketched out.

His heart skipped a beat not once, but twice.

This is incredible, the man thought. *No wonder Jafar is very secretive and doesn't let those not involved in certain elements of the "Grand Scheme" know what else is going on. He doesn't trust anyone.*

I'm going to make him pay for not trusting me. Time to make him a little more paranoid than he already is.

The man copied the information and pasted it into the e-mail. He typed in the destinations and subject before flagging it as urgent. He clicked send without a second thought.

As soon as it was on its way, he closed the browser, closed Jafar's files and made for the door. He left nothing amiss, just in case Jafar noticed a difference when he woke from his impromptu slumber.

Chapter 13
Situation Room, White House, Washington, D.C.
31 July 2012 — 18.45 GMT/1:45 p.m. ET

Alex Dupuis hurried into the basement of the West Wing as quickly as she could. The Secret Service waved her through, before one of President Forrister's aides escorted her down to the Situation Room.

This is too hot to even discuss over secure lines, the Director of the CIA thought as she passed staffers rushing through the corridors, the business of the country at stake in their travels. *This is way more important than the business of the country.*

Peoples' lives are at stake.

She walked into the Situation Room, where Forrister and Bennett — *that slime ball*, Dupuis thought — were deep in discussion over a trivial issue.

"Has she even called in? Sarah made her report in every six hours during the Boston mission. She's a young agent and she shouldn't be trusted with a mission of this much importance," Bennett told the president. "She should be recalled and a more experienced agent put in her place."

"There's a problem with your logic, though, Dick," Dupuis said, causing heads to turn her way. "There are no 'more experienced agents' available for this type of work. Agent Snapshot has performed admirably so far."

Bennett's eyes widened in shock.

"So you have been in contact with her? That's good. Glad you let us know, Madame Director."

"I did let the president know," Dupuis countered. "If he chose not to disclose that information to you, then you must not be as important as you think."

"Alex —" Forrister interrupted.

Bennett's face grew red.

"I'm sorry, sir, but I will not let your chief of staff deride the workings of the CIA to gain your ear."

"The CIA has done nothing but fuck up our relationships with other countries due to your warmongering and undercover work."

Dupuis fired right back.

"Mr. Bennett, since when did the CIA change its acronym?" She looked to Forrister. "Did you change it to BUSH while I slept last night?"

Forrister couldn't help but smile. Bennett slammed the table in frustration. Forrister ignored it.

"What's up, Alex? What do you have?"

Dupuis slipped several sheets of paper out of her attaché case and slid a copy over to the president. She hesitated; she wanted to make Bennett think he was not getting a copy of this highly sensitive information, but she relented and gave him his copy anyway.

"An anonymous tip was sent to us through a Yahoo account from England. Our terrorist is looking to strike again quickly. The Aquatics Center will be hit tonight in some shape or form."

"Tonight our time, or tonight England time?" Bennett asked.

"England time. We don't have a gauge as to when the terrorist will strike, but we can be reasonably certain it will be take place around the time our swimming champion races. The terrorist attacked during the soccer match last night, and since there is an American champion racing tonight, well, I think even you can add one and one together, Mr. Bennett."

If Bennett's face wasn't red before, then the color in his face was darker than maroon.

"Mr. President, I must object to the way the Director of the CIA is treating me!"

"Can't take it but you can dish it out, eh Dick?"

"That's enough out of both of you," Forrister said. "There will be no more petty squabbling in this room, the Oval Office and on Air Force One. We are supposed to be on the same side. Do I make myself clear?"

Dupuis smiled. She knew the rebuke was more for Bennett's benefit than hers. She knew the president had her back.

"Yes sir," she said as Bennett hung his head by an inch.

"Alex, what is the move?" Forrister asked.

"As soon as I hear from Jaclyn again —"

"You mean you haven't heard —"

"Dick, enough already."

"Mr. President, this agent has not checked in with her superior in how long? How do we know she hasn't gone off and gotten killed?"

"If she had, MI5 would have contacted me. She has been working very close with the British since she touched down at Heathrow while you were in your paisley PJs, Dick. I happen to trust Snapshot more than I trust certain people. She is probably catching a couple of winks right now; you do know we sent her to England on very little sleep."

"Sleep is unimportant when it comes to the security of a nation," Bennett said pompously.

Dupuis rolled her eyes and took a deep breath. She looked to the president.

Forrister leaned back.

"Alex, when you next hear from Snapshot, tell her that she is to go into the Aquatics Center and make sure that nothing happens to the athletes or the spectators. We've already lost plenty of lives; we cannot afford to lose more. Let her know that the full support of the White House is behind her, and that I will call anyone to clear her path."

Dupuis nodded.

"I will try to call her right now," she said, pulling out her cell phone and dialing Jaclyn's BlackBerry. "If she's sleeping, hopefully she won't scream at me like I screamed at her this morning."

"I'm sure she will forgive you, Alex."

Dupuis brought the phone to her ear and waited for Jaclyn to pick up.

The Regency Hotel, Nottingham Place, London, England
31 July 2012 — 19.15 GMT/2:15 p.m. ET

Jaclyn was unable to sleep long. Her internal clock already out of sync due to the transatlantic flight, she caught a brief nap before her eyes sprang open. She looked at the clock.

It was nearly 7 p.m.

She wondered what was going on back home, but she refrained from calling Dupuis just yet. She needed to shower.

Jaclyn dug into her bag of necessities and found several one inch by two-inch devices to help her surveillance while she washed. These black boxes contained miniature cameras built in, along with a transmitter to connect with Jaclyn's HUD. She mounted another black box in her shower, one with an audible tone, to alert her to the presence of intruders.

With what had happened to her so far today, she was not taking any chances.

She strategically moved about her hotel room placing the black boxes in areas where her HUD could keep tabs on a particular section. She monitored the doorway as well as the windows. She even covered the path to the bathroom with a black box. After checking the HUD, she grabbed her Walther P99 from the bedside table.

Jaclyn disrobed in the bathroom before turning the water on full blast. Her HUD and Walther were next to each other on the sink. She felt the towels, and they were soft enough. She lifted one to her nose and inhaled the freshly laundered towel's scent.

Someone's been using Downy, she thought with a smile. She stepped into the shower and drew the curtain closed.

Jaclyn felt the water pelt her skin, the spray thrumming against her upper body. She tilted her chin upward, allowing the water to caress her neck. She spun and felt the water assault her upper back like rice thrown on one's wedding day. Once again she tilted her head back, this time letting her clover honey-colored hair turn the color of caramel. She felt the trickles of water cascade down her back and drip off her buttocks, while other trickles rumbled down her chest and clung to her breasts and abdomen. Some of it flowed around the sleek curvature of her hips to the backs of her legs. Water droplets exhausted themselves, especially if they started running down her 5-foot-9 frame from the top of her head. She lathered her hair with the hotel-issued shampoo, scrubbing the excess Wembley dust from every follicle and from her scalp. If any of the security guard's blood remained in her bangs before she bathed, it was gone now. She rinsed her hair out well and good; as a model, she didn't need dry skin showing up in her photos.

Then again, she thought, *that's what Photoshop is for.*

Several minutes later, her shower ended: She did not like long showers — long soaks in a luxurious bath tub full of bubbles, now that was a different story — and with terrorists on the loose, she had to be ready for anything. Brevity in the shower was of the utmost importance.

The short, audible tones of the HUD echoed softly once she turned off the water. Her eyes moved directly to the unit and thumbed it off, then stepped out of the shower and grabbed the HUD. Sliding the Foster Grants on next to her slicked-back, dripping hair, she saw the intruder's back through the magnification. The room was, for the most part, dark. The fading sunlight on that side of the hotel did not help. Identification was not feasible.

Damn it, I thought I left the lights on. All I can see is the intruder's heat signature.

Jaclyn grabbed a towel and wrapped it around her waist, then grabbed her Walther. She inched her way to the door. Water dripped onto the floor. Her wet feet made puddles on the linoleum. She heard the intruder come near the door.

Maybe I should have left the water running, she thought. *They know I'm out of the shower now.*

Jaclyn breathed hard, her pulse racing. She took a calming breath, then gritted her teeth as she reached for the doorknob. She grasped it and yanked the door open, pointing her gun right into the intruder's face. The barrel rested just inches from the person's nose.

It was Nigel.

"Did I come at a bad time?" the Briton said, not letting the awkward moment detract from his sense of humor.

Jaclyn lowered her weapon, then realized she was naked from the waist up. She ducked back into the bathroom and grabbed a towel, unfurling it and draping it across her shoulders, covering her breasts. The fluffy fabric felt comforting to her.

"You could have knocked, you know," Jaclyn said, a touch of anger on her lips.

"Oh, of course I could have, and I did, actually," Nigel replied. "When there was no answer, I used the key the desk gave me to open the door. I couldn't be too sure with a terrorist loose in London. I wasn't sure if they got to you or not."

"Have they gotten to you or your family?"

"No. Well, not that I know of. One of the girls would have called me if something was wrong, but they haven't done so."

"That's a relief," Jaclyn said, before thought caught up to her. "What are you doing here, anyway?"

Nigel walked back into the main room. Jaclyn followed him.

"Interesting reason, actually. Sir David got off the phone with your Director Dupuis not too long ago. She told him she has been trying to get a hold of you for quite some time, with no answer on your end. Sir David sent me to check on you, since there are no other American agents in England to do so."

"I was sleeping and, as you know, I was just in the shower. I leave my BlackBerry on silent when I'm asleep so I'm not disturbed."

"Even when the emergency call is a matter of international security? Was it not you who told the owner of the rental truck shop — oh, let me correct that, the now deceased owner of the rental truck shop," — Jaclyn stiffened — "that a matter of international security meant 'hurry your blasted arse up?'"

"What do you mean he's dead?"

"Dead. He was killed an hour or so ago, bullet right to the head as he left his store. Witnesses told Metropolitan Police that he exited the building and turned to lock the door when someone shot him in the back of the head. He has no head any longer, and his next of kin is going to have to replace the glass in the door."

Jaclyn's head dropped, her chin coming to rest between the towel ends.

I knew something like this was going to happen, she thought.

She took a deep breath and composed herself. She stood up and held onto the towel around her waist so it wouldn't slip off. She walked to the bedside table.

Several missed calls were on her BlackBerry.

Jaclyn quickly dialed Dupuis' number and waited as the pesky system took forever to process it.

"Come on, ring!"

"There's no use shouting at the bloody device, it'll take its sweet time, regardless if we are in a hurry or not."

Jaclyn shot Nigel a look of pure spite. Nigel simply chuckled to himself.

Dupuis answer half a second later.

"Jaclyn, you need to keep that phone on at all times," Dupuis said. "Dick Bennett is screaming from here to eternity that you haven't checked in lately."

"I'm sorry, Chief. I was just catching a nap to recharge the batteries a little. I wanted to tell you some stuff, but I have a little company right now." She looked to Nigel. He waved.

"Nigel's there, I take it." Dupuis sighed. "Whatever it is will have to wait, unless it's something he already knows."

"Well," Jaclyn said, sitting on her bed. Her towel around her shoulders moved away from her body. The inner curve of her right breast became visible. Nigel paid it no mind. "We did find out the terrorist used a rental truck to haul the explosives to Wembley, but the truck is destroyed, the account canceled, the owner to the rental truck service dead…"

"This guy is rather meticulous, then."

"I would say so."

"Then you wouldn't be shocked when I tell you we've received an anonymous tip that there's an attack planned for tonight," Dupuis said.

The words made Jaclyn flop backward onto her bed. The towel moved again. This time, her entire right breast was exposed. The warm air tickled her flesh. She covered it up after a moment's hesitation.

So much for having a little nighttime skullduggery, she thought.

"Where are they looking to hit this time?"

"The Aquatics Center in Stratford."

Dupuis and Nigel said it at the same time, as if in stereo. Jaclyn looked at her British counterpart and moved the mouthpiece over to her cheek.

"You've known about that all this time and you are just now saying it?" she said.

"Jaclyn, are you talking to Nigel?"

"Yes, Chief, I am. He knows about it, too."

"Of course, because I told Willows when I spoke with him earlier."

"I love being the last one to know."

"The last one to know is usually the one taking a shower at 7 p.m. London time," Dupuis taunted.

Jaclyn sighed.

"Alright, so what's our scenario?"

"You're going to have some time," Dupuis said, "but not a lot of it. I've checked with NBC, and they said that the swimming event won't air until 10:30 p.m. our time. It's taking place at 9 p.m. in London."

Jaclyn looked at the clock.

It said 19.34.

"Less than an hour and a half," she said, more to herself than to Dupuis or Nigel.

"That means you don't really have much time, Jaclyn."

"Yeah, I know."

"You need a plan."

"I know that, too."

Jaclyn began to pace. She tightened the towel around her waist.

"I'll let you know when I come up with something, Chief. I need to think."

"Don't think too long. There are going to be several thousand people inside that arena. You need to get to Stratford now." Dupuis hung up.

"What's the poop?" Nigel asked.

Jaclyn stopped pacing and looked at him.

"What's the poop? I wouldn't have thought that is a very British thing to say, Nigel."

Nigel smirked.

"We do let American sayings infiltrate our vernacular every so often."

Jaclyn chuckled.

"What's the plan, then?"

"I don't know. Apparently they are going to attack the Aquatics Center around 9 p.m. We have to get all of those people out of there."

Nigel stood and began to pace slowly, his right hand rubbing his chin as he walked. He made several passes until he stopped quickly and slapped his hands together.

"The BBC is broadcasting it live," he said.

"I suppose so?" Jaclyn said.

"No, it is. They are broadcasting every event live in the UK, while your NBC is broadcasting on tape delay."

"That doesn't surprise me," Jaclyn said. "They do that for every Olympics not in the United States or Canada."

"Right, but I don't think you're listening, Jaclyn: The BBC is broadcasting the event live."

Jaclyn tried to follow where Nigel was taking this. The look on her face, though, showed that she clearly had no idea if Nigel was on the same map as she was.

Nigel sighed.

"Her Majesty's Government has closed off outgoing flights from Heathrow, outgoing Eurostar, and highways leading to Scotland and Wales. It means that whoever our Mr. Mohammed is, he is still in the country. He's ordering hits on rental truck owners, he's remotely triggering rockets to fly at us. He is a slippery little snake, yes, but he is still on British soil."

Comprehension began to dawn upon the American.

"So if he's in the country," she said, "and he's attacking the Olympic sites, he's going to be watching on television to see the devastation first hand. He won't be on scene."

"Now you're catching on."

Jaclyn swore.

"That means he is going to watch the swimming event while it's taking place. I'd bet every last pound me and the missus has in the bank that this bastard is going to wait until the American takes the lead — that's what happened yesterday before the bombs went off at Wembley — before the world collapses under them."

The mere thought of this left Jaclyn shivering from head to toe. It was then that she realized she was still only wearing a towel around her waist and over her shoulders.

"I need to get dressed. Is James downstairs with the car?"

Nigel nodded.

"I'll be down in a few minutes," Jaclyn said as she walked to the bathroom. "I can call Alex from the car, you can call Sir David, or we can conference call somehow. I have a little idea; I want to run it by the president." She removed the towel from her shoulders and began to dry her hair vigorously. "Luckily for us, James has a lead foot and a half, so we can get to Stratford rather quickly."

"Right," Nigel said, walking for the door. "I'll see you downstairs."

He left.

Jaclyn checked her HUD and saw that he was gone. She dropped the towel from around her waist and walked into the bedroom nude. She bent over her necessities bag and pulled out a maroon colored clothing bag with a clear window, showing a black top. Jaclyn unzipped the bag and pulled out her one-piece jumpsuit.

Made of the finest Lycra polymer ever constructed by government-paid scientists, the form-fitting jumpsuit was the major necessity of her work in the clandestine service. It had six custom-made holsters with which to store her weaponry: Jaclyn placed her Walthers there, and they did not add any weight to the jumpsuit. She had holsters strategically placed with one on either side of her latissimus muscles, just underneath her armpits, one on each hip, as well as one on each quadriceps muscle. She was able to carry multiple magazines on the backside of her utility belt, which had several pouches in front that she used to carry small incendiary devices of her own creation, as well as other little hidden tricks provided to her by the CIA's quartermasters. Slapping a button on her utility belt would give her protection on 96 percent of her body in a firefight.

In short, if she wanted to take over a small country, she could do so with the impressive arsenal she carried on her person.

Jaclyn slid into the small-looking jumpsuit, feeling the Lycra expand over her legs. She pulled it up to her waist and felt the protective covering over her groin and her buttocks; the covering would look smooth against the skin and would prevent any personal embarrassment.

Of course, if anyone said anything about that, she would have simply shot them to shut them up.

She moved her arms into the garment, pulling the back up onto her neck and the front to cover her breasts. She zipped the top up, then covered the zipper with a Lycra flap. The jumpsuit molded her body like a second skin. It would have made Sue Storm blush. Catwoman was not even in the same ballpark of sexy. In the jumpsuit, she was no longer Jaclyn Johnson. She became Snapshot, a deadly weapon of the United States clandestine services.

It was a name terrorists would soon fear.

Jaclyn quickly filled the utility pouches with her incendiary devices and other goodies, then covered herself in a long, black trench coat. She pulled on long, spiked boots, making her look several inches taller than normal: standing straight, she would now be 6-foot-1.

She checked out the rest of her necessities bag — it was still half full with spare magazines and more of her "chemistry projects," as she called them — before checking herself out in the mirror.

She gave a little grin as her HUD showed her reflection.

"Jaclyn, Jaclyn, Jaclyn," she said with a slight laugh, rubbing the Lycra smooth, "if Charlie could see you now, he would probably bust in his pants."

Jaclyn hooked her iPad inside the trench coat, then grabbed her BlackBerry, her key card and headed out of her hotel room, walking as quickly as she could to the lift.

It was 7:55 p.m.

***

Jaclyn slid into the backseat of the diplomatic car and pulled out her BlackBerry.

Nigel's eyes bolted when he saw what she wore, then quipped, "Going out for a night on the town afterward, Jaclyn? James knows of a good S and M club in Soho, don't you, James?"

Jaclyn did not react; she was used to these types of taunts from men that she simply began to dial Dupuis' number.

"No Guv'nah, I do not. I wouldn't believe all the rumors around the coffee pot. But I think Miss Snapshot may make a few rumors herself with that get-up," James said as he took a look into the rearview mirror. Jaclyn sat behind and opposite the driver. He adjusted it to grab a look at the sexy American.

Jaclyn grinned to herself.

"Just drive, James. We need to make tracks and get to Olympic Park in the next 63 minutes."

"Yes ma'am."

Nigel raised the barricade between the compartments as Jaclyn engaged the speakerphone. She pulled the wave-dampening cube and pressed the button.

"That was quick," Dupuis said as she picked up her phone. "Let's hear what you're thinking about."

"Are you still in the Sit Room? Is Forrister right there?"

"Yes to both."

"Put it on speaker; it would be good for everyone to hear this plan."

Jaclyn and Nigel heard a muffled, "Mr. President, Jaclyn wishes you to hear this," before Dupuis pressed the speakerphone button. A rush of ambient sound filtered through, but Jaclyn tuned the sound to detect voices, not excessive noise.

"Hello, Jaclyn," Forrister said, his basso voice coming in clearly. "I believe one of Britain's finest is with you."

"Nigel Messingham, MI5, Mr. President, an honor to speak with you."

"The pleasure is mine. Jaclyn, what have you come up with?"

Jaclyn looked to Nigel, who nodded. She took a deep breath.

"Mr. President, Nigel tells me that the BBC is broadcasting every event live to the Home Nations. And with the BBC in the Aquatics Center, that means they are going to broadcast us evacuating the building. We have a hunch, sir, that the terrorist is still somewhere on British soil, which means —"

"Which means he could watch what you're doing as you're doing it," Forrister finished. "Instead of pulling the rug out from under his plans, he's going to get the drop on you. Damn it, we cannot allow that fucking piece of trash to do that."

"Right, which means we need to somehow cut the BBC off the air."

"Mr. President, I must be frank: it's going to be very tough to get the BBC to stop broadcasting," Nigel said, leaning over the phone. "It is the bastion of British journalism, the watchdog of the people. If Jaclyn or I were to go in there and flash a badge, a gun or some leg, the BBC would come down hard on Her Majesty's Government. And if Jaclyn were identified, it would touch off a firestorm in the American media, too, and I'm sure the Republicans in Congress would, respectfully speaking, sir, have a bloody field day."

"Some of the conservative and moderate Democrats would have one, too," Forrister said.

"I'm sure you can understand the severity of the situation that our respective governments are drawing toward, Mr. President."

There was silence on the other end.

"Sir?" Jaclyn asked.

"What will you need, you two? Government intervention?"

"That would be a start, sir," Nigel said. "The head of programming is who you'd have to call."

"Oh, I won't be the one paying the call to the BBC," Forrister said.

"Sir!" Jaclyn screeched.

"Mr. President! I must implore on you to reconsider this; this will be the easiest way to do it safely. We can't do this alone, and we can't put steel to the on-site producer's forehead. That will not look good for any of us."

"You both misunderstand me. I will be making a call to England as soon as I hang up with you two."

"Downing Street?" Nigel asked. "I'm sure the PM would be happy to help, sir."

"I was thinking of going a little higher, Nigel."

"The House of Lords? I don't think the BBC would listen to them, sir."

"Higher."

Nigel blanched.

Jaclyn's jaw dropped, but soon turned into a sly grin.

"You don't mean — *her*, sir?"

"It took you both long enough. I have no question she'll be able to handle the BBC and put them in their place. I'll ask her to tell the BBC to take orders from you both on site until the situation resolves itself."

"Hopefully the bloody broadcasters don't decide to be arseholes and blow the whole bloody operation before we get everyone out of the arena," Nigel said.

"Be positive, Midwicket," Jaclyn said. "I trust the president, and you trust the queen."

"And if she can't convince them to do it?"

Jaclyn took a deep breath.

"Then we better hope this bastard is away from the television when we go in there."

Nigel firmed his face and nodded.

"Alright you two, I'm going to call Buckingham Palace and get this underway. Jaclyn, call in after this task is over. We'll monitor the BBC from here."

"Thank you, sir," Jaclyn replied.

"Jaclyn, you know what to do. We have every faith in you," said Dupuis.

"Thanks, Chief."

The connection cut. Jaclyn pressed the button on the cube, cutting out the eavesdrop-proof waves.

"Turn that back on, Jaclyn," Nigel asked. "I'm calling Sir David."

"What for? Forrister's calling the Queen; what do you need Willows to do?"

Nigel gave her a roguish grin.

"He's going to scramble the heavy artillery for us."

Chapter 14
The West End, London, England
31 July 2012 — 20.05 GMT/3:05 p.m. ET

Jafar stirred.

He groaned as he became fully conscious. He felt hammers pounding his skull, the hangover beginning. He grabbed at his head and tried squeezing it like a grape. He knew that no amount of Tylenol would kill the pain.

The pain continued nonetheless.

He groaned again when the smell of his own insides finally hit him. The smell of bile, released a quarter of a day ago, lingered in his nose. It squished as he rolled his head.

"Must find incense candle," he said, his voice weak. He pushed himself up and felt his arms jiggle under the weight of his own body.

The room spun as he lifted his head. He moaned.

"Steady Jafar," he said.

The Afghani raised himself to his knees before finally lifting his upper body. He was still rather weak.

"Thanks be to Allah," he said softly.

He began wondering what happened to him. It didn't take long for him to recall succumbing to his mortal desires and drinking liquid during the day. He would have to perform a harsh penance for his sin.

Maybe I will kill another infidel in lieu of penance, he thought. He raised his left eyebrow as he considered it. A tired grin came to his lips. *Yes, that is what I shall do. Another infidel killed in exchange for Allah's blessing and forgiveness. It sounds like the right thing to do.*

He forced himself to crawl through his own vomit on his knees. He made it to the counter after 10 knee movements. He raised himself up. It was a struggle, but he managed to do it without collapsing. His head swooned as soon as he got to his feet.

If he hadn't been dehydrated before listening to the voices inside his head and committing a dreadful sin, he was certainly dehydrated now. His mouth felt like he had stuffed his socks inside, with the same taste. His muscles ached after six hours of non-use.

I will punish the one who changed my cool, clear water into alcohol, he thought, his eyes narrowing and becoming darker. *It is their fault that I am like this!*

Jafar staggered slightly as he moved his body a little to the right, bringing himself even with his kitchen sink. He looked outside and saw bumpy red clouds surging into view. Within half an hour, London would be totally in the dark.

A storm is coming, Jafar thought.

He grabbed a glass and immediately loosened the tap. Fresh water flowed into the glass. He brought it to his lips and drank without a moment's hesitation. He tried to keep the water in his mouth, but he drank so fast that a trickle spilled out and caught in his goatee. There was no doubt in his mind the liquid he now drank was indeed water, surging out of the tap from the city's vast Brent Reservoir. There was no subterfuge here. There was no way that anyone could introduce poison: The British Government, he knew, would not poison the entire city of London's water supply just to kill one terrorist. He drank safe in that knowledge.

He let the water continue running as he drank the water down, then refilled his glass three more times until he felt adequately hydrated. He popped two aspirin into his mouth and drank another half glass. He shut off the tap. He turned and stepped around his vomit — he would clean it later — reaching the fridge and taking out *Iftar*, his evening meal. It was nearing *Maghrib*.

Jafar returned to his dark living room with his food. He sat down and saw his laptop went to his screen saver. He rolled his finger over the mouse pad and noticed the time.

He panicked.

I have not prayed to Allah since this morning! he thought. He suddenly became anxious as his eyes strayed from his meal to his prayer window in the corner. Doubt gnawed in his gut.

He sighed.

A few more minutes won't hurt me, Jafar thought. *I need to eat, though. It has been a day since I have tasted anything as wonderful as Iftar, and I have communed with Allah several times since then. Allah will understand. My level of devotion has not changed. My body needs nutrition. Allah can wait.*

He checked his emails and noticed his assassin had completed his task; he was onto the next assignment and would be ready for the infidel to arrive.

Jafar nearly jumped out of his seat and praised Allah then and there if his body would allow it. His smile, though, was unmistakable through his black goatee.

That link is dead and can no longer tell lies, Jafar thought. *Soon, the next link will be dead. That will mean the trail dies.*

He inhaled deeply. The stench from his kitchen hung about his flat. He crinkled his nose at the smell of his own insides. It nearly put him off his meal. He walked to his prayer window and opened it, allowing the disgusting fumes of his own body to filter out.

He checked the clock again when he got back to his laptop and noticed it neared 8:15 p.m. He pursed his lips, going through his calculations of this event one more time.

The attack shall begin in approximately 45 minutes, he thought. *I must be done with Iftar and my prayers before then. I cannot miss the American diving into the pool.*

He began eating like he had never eaten before.

Aquatics Center, Stratford Olympic Park, London, England
31 July 2012 — 20.25 GMT/3:25 p.m. ET

Without a direct link to Stratford from downtown London other than the Tube, it took James a few extra minutes, even with the lights of the diplomatic car flashing away, to get to the Olympic Park.

During that time, Jaclyn watched as cars dashed out of the way to avoid the speeding limousine. Time was of the essence. She wondered how long it would take Sir David to scramble the "heavy artillery" that Nigel requested, and how long it would take to get from Box 500 to Stratford.

Hopefully not long after the Queen pulls some royal strings, she thought. *The quicker we can get the entire operation finished, the quicker I can begin my own special investigation. I don't want this to be rushed, though. The safety of hundreds of people is at stake.*

To go through that building and deem it safe after what she had been through at Wembley earlier in the day would not be a prudent exercise.

"How much farther until we get to Stratford, Nigel?" she asked her partner.

Nigel peered out the window.

"We just passed under the A12. We should be there in moments, my dear."

"Good," Jaclyn said, fiddling with one of the buttons on her trench coat. "We're going to have to hope Her Majesty has applied the right amount of pressure or else this trip is going to be for nothing."

"Relax, Snapshot. You are far too tense for such a young woman. It's all that coffee you drink. You should drink more decaffeinated tea. Puts a little zing in your step and keeps you calm."

"Coffee puts zing in my step."

"True, until you're having a bloody heart attack at 35. You'll change your ways then."

"We'll see when I get to 35."

If I get to 35, she thought. *With someone out looking to get me, I'll be lucky if I make it 26.*

James breezed down White Post Lane and crossed the River Lee Navigation, the western border of the Olympic Park. He pulled the car to a stop some distance away from the Aquatics Center.

A security agent walked up to them as soon as they got out of the car. He took a double take at Jaclyn's outfit, especially when he saw she bristled with weaponry.

"You two must be whom the bells tolls for the BBC," he said with a roguish grin.

"That would be us," Jaclyn replied. Neither she nor Nigel returned the grin. "Would you lead us to the truck, please?"

The guard nodded and turned, leading them away from the car to the BBC truck, situated some 50 meters away.

Jaclyn turned her head toward the Aquatics Center, its wave-like roof drawing her attention. People filed into the building, unknowing the terror about to unfold inside. She noticed the people weren't boisterous or talkative, though, the two attacks upon Wembley still on their minds.

Once they got to the truck, located away from the Main Press Center, Nigel opened the door and entered, identifying himself. Jaclyn slid in behind him and closed the door.

"What the bloody hell are you supposed to be?" the producer said to Jaclyn.

Jaclyn simply pulled her trench coat back, revealing her form — and her six Walthers, ready for her to snap them up.

The producer saw the guns and nearly wet himself.

"I'm Her Majesty's Enforcer," she said in a fake British accent. "Do you have a problem with that, mate?"

"No, no, no problem with that, love," he replied, his voice shaking with fear. "So you're the ones the Queen has sent to yank us off the air. Terrorist threat, is it? The people have a right to know what's going on."

"Not immediately, they don't," Nigel said. His face filled with blood rushing to his cheeks. "This is a matter of crown, country, and your mates' lives at stake. Do you know what's going to happen if there is a bomb or two or fifty inside there? They're going to be dead, and you and your little broadcasting company are going to have to explain to their wives and families why you decided to be chicken shit pinheads and let the cameras roll on us evacuating that place when you could have bloody done them a favor and broadcast something else like the Queen requested." Nigel took a deep breath. "If that wanker is still on our soil, he's going to be watching. If he sees us evacuating, there's going to be a 300-meter crater right in the middle of Olympic Park a second later. And I can bloody right tell you that if I didn't have my security clearance, I would run directly to Sky — you remember Sky, right? — and tell them exactly what happened. I would bet my mum's britches that Sky's Olympic ratings would be well higher than the BBC's."

"So would I," Jaclyn proudly said. She leaned toward Nigel. "What's Sky?" she whispered.

"Not now, my dear."

They looked directly at the producer. Jaclyn edged past Nigel and looked directly in his eyes, fixing him with a long stare.

The producer wondered what was behind the Foster Grants.

"Do you seriously want to have the blood of nearly twenty thousand people on not only your hands, but the hands of everyone in this truck?" she said, rattling off the near capacity of the watersports arena. "Don't think about it too long, friend; you have about 30 minutes before the end of the world. And if you thought Wembley coming down was a picnic, the death of the Aquatics Center and everyone inside would be beyond the magnitude of You Know What."

"Alright," he said, "you guys win. You convinced me better than me boss did a little while ago."

Jaclyn's face showed her surprise.

"What did he say?"

"He said the Queen called him up personally, dialed the number up herself, no aides or anything. He didn't believe her when she said who she was, obviously; the Queen doesn't make her own phone calls now, does she?"

Jaclyn crossed her arms. Her hands came treacherously close to the handles of the twin Walthers on her sides. She fixed the producer with a stern look that only showed in her mouth.

The producer blanched.

"Well, Her Majesty had him call the Buckingham Palace switchboard and ask to speak with her. They put him right through and she said that if we don't help you, she would have us all mysteriously shepherded away and taken to Siberia sometime in the next fortnight."

Jaclyn's hands were faster than a light switch turning on. She had two of her Walthers out in a heartbeat, both barrels pointed right at the producer's forehead.

The smell of urine rose to the roof of the trailer.

"I could have been a real bitch and done the job for her," Jaclyn whispered. "After all, I am Her Majesty's Enforcer."

Nigel stepped past his opposite number, lowered her guns with his right hand and grabbed the producer's headset.

"Holster them, Snapshot," he said. Jaclyn reluctantly complied with the order. "You, sir, can take a powder. And I would change your pants, too, if I were you. You're in a right state."

He put the headset on just as James opened the trailer door.

"Sir, the heavy artillery has arrived with the cuddly ones."

"Very good, James. Tell them that Agent Snapshot will lead them into the building as soon as we get the place evacuated," Nigel said. He turned to Jaclyn. "You're ready to lead the team in?"

"As ready as I'll ever be."

"Good." Nigel donned the headset. "Alright, who the bloody hell do I have on this thing?"

A chorus of voices answered. Nigel jumped.

"Alright, one at a time. Here is what we will be doing from this site until further notice: Viewers who have swimming on will be shifted to Newcastle for," he paused briefly while he looked at the broadcasting itinerary, "the Germany-Brazil football match. We will not show cameras of the Aquatics Center interior until I give the go-ahead to do so. No shots of Olympic Park will be shown either, for that matter." Nigel put his hand on the boom mic and turned to one of the technicians. "How long do we have until the next event inside the Aquatics Center starts?"

"Ten minutes, sir. Please don't let her shoot me."

Nigel grinned.

"No, she won't shoot you unless you betray us. Get to work, you folks."

Nigel took the headset off and followed Jaclyn out of the trailer.

"Follow me, I want to introduce you to the team; they are Box 500's gold-medal winners when it comes to the biathlon."

"Nigel?" Jaclyn said.

"Hmm?" He kept walking.

"The biathlon is during the Winter Olympics."

Midwicket paused in step for about five seconds.

"Of course it is!" he said, turning to face the American. "I bloody know that. They train up in the hills of Scotland during the winter. Right quick on skis, they are."

Jaclyn smiled and shook her head as she followed Nigel away from the broadcast truck.

116

Chapter 15
Olympic Aquatics Center, Stratford, London, England
31 July 2012 — 20.58 GMT/3:58 p.m. ET

"Ladies and Gentlemen, *madams et monsieurs*, may I have your attention please, *mai je avoir votre attention s'il vous plait*," the public address announcer said. "We are asking everyone inside the Aquatics Center to please evacuate the building in an orderly fashion. Please hold onto your ticket stubs, as you'll need them for re-entry to the Aquatics Center. We will allow people to return as soon as it is possible to do so. Thank you very much. *Nous demandons à tout le monde à l'intérieur du Centre de natation s'il vous plaît à évacuer l'immeuble de manière ordonnée. S'il vous plaît garder vos talons de billets, car ils seront nécessaires pour la rentrée au Centre de natation. Nous allons permettre aux gens de retourner dès qu'il est possible de le faire. Merci beau coup.*"

Jaclyn seemed surprised when there was little panic in the crowd's voices. They did as the announcer requested, calmly filing out of the building. Some were startled as they passed the black Escalades filled with barking dogs. The building was empty save for security personnel.

For now.

Jaclyn watched as the so-called "heavy artillery" — better known as SO-15, a Specialist Operations branch within Metropolitan Police — armed themselves and geared up to sweep the building. She inserted a small earpiece into her right ear.

"This is Agent Snapshot, do you copy?"

"This is Agent Midwicket. I copy, Snapshot."

"I think we're ready to go in. Stand by."

Nigel clicked his mic in acknowledgment.

"Are we ready?"

The agents all nodded. They tightly held onto the leashes of their bomb-sniffing dogs.

"Let's go then." She clicked her mic. "Midwicket, this is Snapshot. Agents are bringing the cuddly ones into the target. Operation is a go to proceed."

"All interior cameras are off, Snapshot. I'm monitoring operational activities from the lead agent's head-mounted camera."

"Jolly roger that."

With one of her Walthers drawn, Jaclyn led the crews into the Aquatics Center. The onlookers watched them enter the building, a wave of black and fur flowing up the stairs.

"We're inside now, Midwicket," Jaclyn said. "The puppies are straining against their master's leashes."

"I bloody hope they don't have to use the bathroom. The IOC will never forgive us."

Jaclyn smiled as she wandered through the halls of the Aquatics Center.

"Check under the bleacher area," she said to the team. "That was how the terrorist got the drop on the fans last night."

The crews scoured every inch of the building's interior. They had yet to find anything after being inside for 10 minutes, for 15 minutes, for 20 minutes.

At 9:30 p.m., they struck the mother lode.

"Blimey!" the lead agent said. "Are you getting this, Midwicket?"

"That's a 10-4, Agent Five. Snapshot?"

"That's me."

"Ping Agent Five, he's found something interesting."

"Roger that, on my way."

Jaclyn picked up Agent Five's signal. She hurried down the hall and down the steps into the basement of the facility. She found a wide-open door leading off to the open-air wings of the building. She saw the agents looked at the steel columns holding up the wings, and she noticed someone covered the columns with —

"Holy shit," Jaclyn said, holstering her Walther. "There's enough C4 here to turn Stratford into a gateway to China!"

Several of the agents snickered.

"Cut that," Nigel said. "Jaclyn, how long do you think it will take to get rid of it all?"

Jaclyn's face belied her surprise. She had no idea she would have to remove it all; she figured that's what the SO-15 guys were for.

"I'm hoping you don't expect me to carry this stuff out."

"No Jaclyn," Nigel said. "Ask the team."

"Oh, right."

She turned her mic off.

"How long do you think it'll take to dispose of this stuff?"

"Fifteen minutes, give or take a few. And we need to check the other wing for more explosives, so tell Midwicket that it will be half an hour."

"Snapshot to Midwicket, Agent Five requests half an hour to forty-five minutes more before the world is safe again. Will that be enough time for you?"

Nigel gave a soft chuckle in her ear.

"Oh yes, quite enough. I'm just getting used to this producing gig. It looks like we're going to show gymnastics for the time being."

Jaclyn smiled.

"Surprised our terrorist hasn't hit that yet."

"It was men's gymnastics tonight."

"That explains it. Midwicket, I'll be headed off for a bit. These guys can handle the rest."

"Roger that, Snapshot. I'll catch up with you later on."

There were a few seconds of awkward silence before Jaclyn turned to the team.

"Half of you go into the other wing and check and see, then report to Midwicket. You also want to check the building for secondary explosives: That's what knocked Wembley down. I'm headed off."

They all gave her a two-fingered salute.

Jaclyn ran out from underneath the wing.

I hope they thwart that bastard, she thought. *I would love to see his face when he finds out he didn't get to play in the pool.*

She took out her BlackBerry and began typing a message to Dupuis:

AC crisis averted. Beginning personal personnel investigation. Will be dark for some time. Will check in when task is done. JJ

She pressed send. It gave the short vibration when it acknowledged it went through.

Jaclyn walked toward the Stratford Tube station, oblivious to anyone who saw her depart.

Chapter 16
The West End, London, England
31 July 2012 — 21.41 GMT/4:41 p.m. ET

Jafar rose from his kneeling position. He felt his knees crack. He stifled a wince.

He returned to his couch, where his laptop lay in wait, his remote control for his television next to it. He checked the time.

Damn it, he thought. *I'm late. I must have engrossed myself in my worship of Allah that I lost all track of time.*

He immediately turned on the television. The blue jerseys of Brazil and the black jerseys of Germany shined under the floodlights. St. James' Park's Sir John Hall Stand practically swayed under the 1-1 score line.

Football? Swimming is supposed to be on, he thought. *Oh, there's that ticker at the bottom.*

Due to a power outage in Olympic Park, the BBC will show full coverage of the men's 200-meter freestyle when power is restored.

"At least I will not miss anything," Jafar said to the screen. "They are only delaying their deaths. They should thank Allah for the delay, but they should welcome death to come quickly."

Jafar reached over and grabbed another glass of water — he intended to stay incredibly hydrated this evening, no matter if his kidneys shut down — and drank deeply. The sound of pebbles against his prayer window distracted him. Those pebbles became a cacophony of sound.

He grinned.

Yes, Allah. Wash the stain of these infidels away. Let them know your patience with them is at an end, and that this is only the beginning of the storm. Let them know their miserable lives will be at an end soon, and that they should make arrangements with you. Only through you, Allah, and your messenger, Mohammed, may they be saved from what is to come!

Are you so sure they are without power, Jafar? the voice taunted. *They have been known to lie in the past. They are infidels, as you say. A power outage would be a nice way to throw you off.*

"They are not that smart," Jafar replied to himself. "They would never come up with something like that."

But Jafar had to stop himself. Could the infidels be leading him astray?

The dulcet tones of his cell phone began to ring.

Jafar accepted the call.

"What is it?"

The voice on the other end sounded panicky.

"Brother Jafar, there is a problem."

Jafar's eyes narrowed, his brow furrowing as he waited for his agent to tell him what was going on.

"Yes, I had a feeling there was one. The BBC has switched programming. What is going on there? Is there a power outage in Olympic Park?"

There was a pause on the other end. Jafar could hear people talking in the background. He couldn't make out what they were saying, but there was no panic in their tones.

"No *musahib*. The lights are all on, but the people are all outside the building. There are government types milling about; they've sent dogs inside. They've been in there quite a while, too."

"How long?"

"Half an hour, at least."

Jafar's eyes sprung open in anger.

"And you are now just reporting in? What is wrong with you? Allah will not forgive you for such a breach!"

"A thousand pardons, *musahib*. I have no excuse. I waited for the explosion and saw nothing. I waited too long. I throw myself on your mercy."

"You better hope that the infidels do not escape this," Jafar warned. He took a deep breath. He felt the sweat pour off him in buckets. He looked to the window. It was very dark in the West End, and rain continued to pelt the glass. The humidity continued rising, the air saturated. "Has it begun raining in Stratford yet?"

"Not yet, *musahib*. There are clouds rolling in, though."

"Be prepared to find cover for the time being, as close to the diplomatic cars as you can. As soon as I destroy that building, I have a task for you to do. I will encrypt a message to your device."

"I await the message, brother Jafar. I shall do it as Allah wishes and as you command. *Allahu Akbar*."

Jafar did not bother with the closing salutation. He ended the call and threw the cell phone onto the table. It landed with a clunk. His mind raced with possibilities.

The infidels are smarter than I give them credit for, he thought. *They have thrown me off, but briefly. It is no matter. Allah shall win the day, no matter what they do to try to stop me.*

He decided he would simply wait for the BBC to return programming to its planned schedule; he now knew there were delaying tactics at play. He would let them have their little fun. He wanted the infidels to think they had won the day, to think they had foiled the terrorists.

As he smiled his feral grin and ran his fingers through his slightly graying goatee, he knew it was the furthest thing from the truth.

It just so happens I have a back-up plan, Jafar thought as he leaned back into the coziness of the sofa. *I have been anything but sloppy in my planning; I have been as meticulous as can be. There will be another crater in London that will rival those on the moon before I am done. A matching set. But first, I must take care of another problem.*

He grinned as he found the images from earlier today and emailed one to his assassin's BlackBerry.

He emailed the other to another operative.

Chapter 17
Temporary Headquarters of the FA, Soho Square, London, England
31 July 2012 — 22.00 GMT/5:00 p.m. ET

With the Olympics in town, Salt discovered that The Football Association moved its offices from Wembley Stadium back to its prior home in Soho Square. Many considered it a classy move: the IOC, in turn, moved into Wembley to keep a closer eye on the football tournament. Number 25 Soho Square had been the home of the FA while Wembley underwent its reconstruction, and the FA kept payments up on it and kept it vacant. The FA moved everything — their computers, their files, and the third version of the prestigious FA Cup – back to Soho, so it could prepare for the upcoming season, which would begin in just a smidge over eighteen days from now.

Now with Wembley on the ground, the FA would run the sport from the same place it did while Wembley went back up during the last decade.

Jaclyn made the eight-stop Central Line trip from Stratford to Tottenham Court Road in 19 minutes. The train was not entirely full, as only a few of the people who went to Olympic Park for one of the events there — including the swimming events — decided to leave at the exact same time Jaclyn slipped away from the Aquatics Center. Several boys in their late teens gawked at her, for they didn't see gorgeous blonde women wearing body-length trench coats and black one-piece jumpsuits walking through London every day. She was quite the sight to their hormone-laden eyes.

Jaclyn ignored them.

Her HUD timer said it neared 10 p.m. She hoped she could return to Olympic Park before midnight, that way she could confer with both Nigel and their respective clandestine heads so they could disseminate whatever information Jaclyn covertly swiped. She figured it would take several minutes to find a way inside the building, plus a few more minutes to find the personnel office. She trusted her sleuthing skills to the point where she could make herself undetectable by security camera; the little gadgets in her utility belt were also helpful. She felt that she would be in and out within 10-15 minutes, and she would be back on the Tube headed to Stratford again by 10:30 p.m. at the very latest. Midnight was her deadline, just in case she ran into trouble while performing her skullduggery. She didn't anticipate it, but she felt it wise to have a back-up plan.

The train rumbled into Tottenham Court Road station, and she quickly got off the train. The boys stayed on, sorry to see her go.

Jaclyn made her way to the escalators, allowing the other departing passengers to walk ahead of her. She followed the sea of people as they all walked on evenly placed, eggshell-colored bricks until they came to the motorized stairway. Jaclyn kept her HUD trained on every single person near her. She feared nothing from the couple with the sleepy kids, but she focused her attention on the bald, burly man who looked like her male double: he wore leather, but the fang dangling from his ear looked big enough to stab someone. If he made a move, though, she could detect a rise in his pheromones before he even acted.

Once at street level, Jaclyn heard the pulse of London as she came to the Oxford Street portico. She could hear the dim sounds of rain pounding against the glass windows of the station, as well as car engines purring along. Her footsteps echoed softly off the concrete floor. She paused at the entrance, checking back and forth. Her HUD showed no threats; the indicator light stayed green. She exited onto Oxford Street, turning left, heading west.

The rain drenched her immediately, her hair plastered to her scalp. She activated a sensor in her HUD that bounced droplets of rain off her Foster Grants, keeping her already-limited vision intact. She knew there were no natural lakes along Oxford Street, but with the rain coming down at near-Biblical proportions, it wouldn't have surprised her if lakes started forming in the westward-running gutters. Sheets of rain fell with such force that car alarms went off. She hoped for minimal lightning sightings, but with it being London in late July, she didn't want to place wagers on that.

She walked several minutes until she came to Soho Street, the northern entrance to the square. Even before she made the left-hand turn, she looked like a drowned rat. Luckily for her, the trench coat was just as waterproof as her sunglasses, as was the jumpsuit. She made a mental note to have the quartermaster construct a small umbrella that she could easily store in one of the trench coats' inner pockets, just for these types of emergencies.

Despite the heavy rain, gay partygoers still got their dance on at The Edge, the tall building looming over Soho Square. Several stood outside smoking, the rain not deterring them from their hourly nicotine doses. They paid her no mind, though. She surreptitiously glanced at the email Salt had sent her with the address of the FA's temporary headquarters and plugged it into the BlackBerry's GPS application.

She saw that she was only steps away from her intended destination.

Once inside the square, she saw very few cars; only a few puttered about slowly, looking for a parking space. She stepped into the street and felt water run over her boots. She sloshed through and hurried to the middle of the square, where the trees gave little protection from the rain. Jaclyn walked to the Tudor-style hut in the middle of the park.

Her destination stood tall in the southeastern corner. White concrete blocks formed the lower half of the building while brown bricks sent Jaclyn's HUD looking toward the heavens. A flag of England stuck out from the building on a pole. Brisk winds bent the pole to near-snapping.

Time was not on her side, but at that moment, that corner of the square was devoid of human life. A tight smile emerged as she hurried across the street to the building. She tried her best not to splash as she ran; she didn't want to draw unnecessary attention. She ducked into a doorway next to the entrance ramp to her right. Large paving stones formed the sidewalk. Jaclyn could see not a puddle upon it.

She took a deep breath. She pulled out a comb and slicked her wet hair back before she looked up, calculating the building's height with her HUD.

The building was six stories high. She checked the building's schematics on her iPad — *now would be a great time to have that umbrella*, she thought — and found the personnel office was on the sixth floor in a corner office to her right. A rooftop entrance looked inviting.

She smiled even as a fat raindrop landed on her lips. She ran her tongue along the bottom lip in anticipation of her scheme. A bolt of lightning pierced the sky.

With a quick two-handed movement, Jaclyn ripped the front of her trench coat open. Her right hand dove in to her utility belt, opening a pouch on her left hip. She pulled out a folded, cylindrical object and snapped it open. One press of a button later, she had a small crossbow in her hands. She aimed it for the roof and triggered the mechanism. She heard a *thwoof!* before a cable shot out and hooked atop the lip of the roof. She gave it a tug and found it secure.

Jaclyn pressed another button. She immediately began to rise against the raindrops until the edge of the crossbow reached the top some 20 seconds later. She hefted herself up and onto the roof. She unhooked the crossbow, stored it, took two steps and, as soon as she saw the security device attached to the doorknob, dug her iPad out from inside her trench coat. She placed the edge of it against the device and held her breath.

Her fingers danced along the touch-screen surface as she tried cracking the FA's security code, but not only that, she wanted to make sure she did not alert security to her presence. It took less than a minute. Jaclyn also got a look at the security log.

Security last made a pass of the sixth floor 10 minutes ago, and had done so every half an hour on the half an hour.

"I can easily get out before security even realizes I've been here," she said to the door. She used the *Keys, Keys Everywhere!* icon on her iPad to unlock the door. She pressed it and heard the lock click.

She tentatively opened the door and did not hear any alarms go off. Her HUD did not detect any inaudible alarms, either. She entered the building and closed the door, free of the rain for now.

Jaclyn drew one of her Walthers as she stalked the darkened corridors until she came to the personnel office, located in the rear of the building. She tried the doorknob; it opened freely. She bit back a smile as she slid into the room.

The sensors in her glasses told her that there were several desks nearby. The HUD's scanner showed her exactly where those placements were. She scanned the room and found the filing cabinets.

Jaclyn walked over to the three-drawer cabinets and used her HUD's fine micro-flashlights to illuminate the front panels. She looked for the drawer with 'M' on it. It was on the second cabinet, top drawer. She tugged at it. It easily sprang open.

So much for security in London, she thought.

She rifled through the files until she came to the one she craved to know more about. The tab had a white sticker on it that read "Mohammed, Kafil A." It looked like the sticker was the third or fourth used on this particular file. She heard rain tapping at the windows and at a metal fire escape on the other side of the wall.

Jaclyn pulled the file out and laid it flat on top of the others. Opening it, she found a single page, as well as a photo. No write-ups from superiors were inside. Mohammed appeared a model employee who crossed every t and dotted every i. In Jaclyn-speak, it meant that he was too good to be true, which also meant…

"I think we've got our terrorist," she said.

She checked his address against what the address Fenton's gave her and Nigel; the words EXACT MATCH flashed inside her Foster Grants, telling her the addresses were one in the same. She decided she would delay her return to Stratford.

I need to check out this address, she thought. She yawned.

"I need some sleep, too."

Jaclyn reached into her utility belt and grabbed a small digital camera, taking a good shot of the suspect's file picture. She saw his dark eyes and triggered a memory from earlier in the day. She wanted to go through her iPad at that moment and check out the broadcast the terrorist made last night, just to see if they matched. She tried to visualize Mohammed with a black balaclava.

Her HUD pinged its warning tones. Jaclyn froze. She looked toward the door. Security was on its way, and it was close.

Jaclyn bit back a curse.

Damn it! They weren't supposed to show up for quite some time, she thought.

Not needing anything else in the file, she folded it back up and stuffed it into the drawer in its proper place. She slid the drawer closed without a sound. She turned and looked to the door.

She saw a flashlight's beam under the doorway. Security was right outside. Keys jangled.

She heard the key slide into the lock. Her pulse began to race. She couldn't make it to the fire escape door in time. Jaclyn lunged for the nearest desk, pushing the rolling office chair out of the way and ducking underneath the desktop. Her trench coat rustled as she moved. She slid the chair back toward her as far as she could without causing herself discomfort. She waited. Seconds seemed like hours.

She heard the door creak open. Her breath echoed the sound. She tried not to move; even if she could maneuver better in this cramped space, she wouldn't dare do it. A simple quiver from her muscles would betray her hiding spot. She couldn't even reach for the button on her utility belt that would protect her from gunshots without making a sound. She had to stay silently still, or else compromise the mission.

A beam of light bounced around the room. Jaclyn heard the guard open his mic connection.

"A1 checking Personnel. Motion sensors went off at my cube."

"Nothing reported here, A1. All clear?"

The guard delayed his answer. The beam continued to bounce around the dark room. The rain continued tapping against the fire escape outside.

"All clear," he finally said. He extinguished his flashlight and closed the door.

Jaclyn let out a slow breath and waited a moment. Her HUD still reported a threat nearby, and it wasn't going further away.

That's strange, she thought. *I don't hear footsteps, either. That can only mean –*

She bit off another curse.

Damn it, he's still in here.

Without caring that her trench coat made a noise now, she reached into her utility belt's right hip pouch and grasped two small marble-sized balls. She kicked the chair away. It rolled to the back wall. She leaned out of her hiding place and tossed one of the balls toward the wall nearest the fire escape door, then reached around and smashed the other against the desk.

Two large clouds of gray smoke emerged from the balls. The balls themselves disintegrated upon impact. Jaclyn heard the security guard unsnap his holster.

She slapped the button on her utility belt, positioned right under her navel. A millisecond later, she felt her jumpsuit form up as its Kevlar lining expanded against her body. She grabbed the Walther nestled on her right thigh. She leapt away from the desk, pulling the gun out of the holster as she went into motion. She brought the gun around and fired off a round as she ducked behind the cloud of camouflaging smoke. She did not intend to kill or injure with her shot. She only wished to distract.

The guard fired two shots, but neither of them hit. The guard could not see his target, his shots going where he thought this intruder would be.

Jaclyn opened the fire escape door and stepped into the storm, closing the door behind her. She pulled her crossbow out and pulled the trigger. It wrapped around the railing. She didn't have much time; in seconds the security guard would be on top of her.

She leapt over the bar with a gymnast's grace, her weight allowing her to repel the 25 feet with ease. Five seconds had passed when her feet touched the ground. She pressed a button on the crossbow, sending an electrical charge up to the hook on the railing. The gadget retracted the hook, allowing it to coil right back into the crossbow. Jaclyn folded it as she ran for a small wall, leaping and throwing her weight up, around and over. She landed on the other side just as the security guard stepped out onto the fire escape.

She scampered away from the wall, putting the folded crossbow back into her utility belt as she walked east on Goslett Yard, passing another gay nightclub. Luckily for her, Goslett Yard was a darkened alley, save for several lights from the nightclub's marquee. She walked toward Charing Cross Road, but she knew she only had a few moments until the FA's security called Metropolitan Police to the scene.

Jaclyn hurried. She needed to catch a taxi.

The West End, London, England
31 July 2012 — 22.20 GMT/5:20 p.m. ET

London's news is so boring, Jafar thought as he watched the BBC. *Other than when I'm causing the chaos, of course.*

Jafar wanted to grin, but he easily stifled it. He still had no idea what was going on; the BBC hadn't shown anything from Olympic Park yet. He had his assassin's report, that was true. But he wasn't banking on his information. He wanted the official report.

The television flashed a "Breaking News" bulletin with the BBC logo on the bottom right-hand corner. Jafar turned his attention to it.

Once the bulletin faded, a view of the Aquatics Center pool came into focus. No one was in the stands. The waters were calm. Only a few security guards were standing poolside.

Jafar intently watched the screen.

The anchor began:

"You're looking at the Olympic Aquatics Center in Stratford where UK authorities have averted a major disaster, according to the Ministry of Defense."

That's what you think, Jafar thought.

"Within the past 75 minutes, agents from Metropolitan Police's SO-15 Division as well as from Her Majesty's Secret Service evacuated the arena after an anonymous tip was sent to the United States' CIA. The tip was that the Aquatics Center was the next Olympic venue attacked during the 200-meter men's freestyle event this evening. This follows last night's attack on Wembley Stadium, and it we should note that like at Wembley, an American athlete was to take part in the swimming event.

"Agents arrived shortly before 9 p.m. and had the arena evacuated within minutes before bomb-sniffing dogs entered the building. What they found was incredible, and officials on site allowed the BBC to take these exclusive pictures of C4 nestled into every single one of the Aquatics Center's stanchion beams on the removable wings. Experts from SO-15 told the BBC that if this amount of C4 went off, it would have wiped Olympic Park off the map, and in excess of 20,000 people would have lost their lives."

The camera switched to outside the Aquatics Center, where people were filing back inside the arena. The line to go back inside the building stretched quarter of a mile away.

I'll wait for the line to shrink before I set off the next set, Jafar thought.

The BBC then showed a familiar face on the screen. Jafar recognized him instantly. The Afghani's eyes were nearly sticking out on their stalks. It took him a few seconds to realize that they were still live, and the camera had panned to the Aquatics Center.

On second thought, I'll do it now, he thought. Jafar quickly typed in the remote detonation command. He looked to the television.

It took a second to register, but the chaos began as soon as the first explosion caused the earth to shake. Thunder roared as the explosion rocked the building. Glass from the Aquatics Center shattered and fell like crystal rain as the gigantic fireball rolled outward and upward. Thousands of people, still in line, screamed in panic, and those at the front of the line stared up in horror, unable to move away as the glass fell, cutting arteries and embedding shards deep into their faces and bodies. The sail at the entrance crumbled and fell in on the building, while the wings toppled inward. Falling stone crushed the people inside, unable to escape. The metal framework of the building became twisted, pretzel-like. Smoke and dust, much like at Wembley this morning, rose into the Stratford night.

Screams of terror filled Olympic Park as panic ensued. People ran as far away from the Aquatics Center as they could, as quickly as they could. They rightly suspected that another bomb could go off at any time. Ripe and rank, the pheromones of fear rose from their pores. Rescue crews, on scene just in case the building exploded during SO-15's initial sweep, tried fighting their way through the escaping mob. The rush of people became too much for rescue workers that some of them found themselves knocked to the ground and trampled. Several of them died in the harshest way possible: they were only trying to help those who were injured or near death. The insanity of the situation, coupled with the sheer amount of people fleeing Olympic Park, prevented help from coming.

A short distance away, fans trying to get away from the destruction inundated the Stratford Rail and Tube platforms. Security authorities on the platforms were concerned that they would have another situation like Hillsborough on their hands: they hoped people would show courtesy to those in front of them, not crush them or send them falling off the platform onto the tracks below. Trains were entering with such regularity that it would be difficult to save anyone who fell. Stewards stationed themselves at the edges of the platforms, their arms outstretched to keep people as safe as possible. Others were located at the ticket booths, trying their best to keep order on London Underground property. They tried their best to keep people calm.

They failed.

Families were huddled together on the platforms, and those who could not find their families or their friends became hysterical. The sound of a train rumbling into the station caused small children to wail, and some people wondered if the sound was of the platforms crumbling under the sheer weight of the travelers. The apprehension that the terrorists would go to any lengths to commit mass murder had everyone fearing for their lives. Flesh trembled under extreme exhaustion. Anxiety lingered everywhere.

Jafar smiled, pleased with what he had caused. He didn't have to see everything to know that he had done his utmost to keep the West on edge.

He heard the screams. He saw the rush of bodies. He felt their panic, even through the television.

Allah, Jafar knew, was pleased with what he accomplished tonight.

Jafar immediately went to his prayer window and hit his knees one more time. He still needed to know of two more events before he made his way to bed.

He prayed for them to happen soon.

Chapter 18
White Hart Lane, Tottenham, London, England
31 July 2012 — 22.51 GMT/5:51 p.m. ET

Jaclyn caught the taxi just as it drove through Soho Square and told the driver, a Pakistani, to bring her to an address in North London. The driver complied, just before he adjusted his mirror to get a better look at his newest fare.

He hit a button behind the mirror. He pulled away from the curb right seconds before Metropolitan Police cruisers made the turn onto Charing Cross Road.

Jaclyn didn't need to glance out the window to know she just avoided capture.

Like getting out to Stratford, there was no real easy way to go to this section of London. The driver, though, seemed to find a path that took him eastbound along Oxford Street until he bared left onto Bloomsbury Way. The taxi wound its way through Islington on the A1 until the driver turned onto Essex Road. The A104 soon turned into the A105. Finsbury Park, on the left-hand side, was all aglow, even at this late hour.

Jaclyn yawned. She wanted to pass out.

Why do I have the feeling I'm making a mistake? she thought. *I should have gone right back to the hotel. Too late now, though. I might as well make the best of it.*

This road took them all the way into Tottenham and White Hart Lane. A few turns later, the driver slowed down to a stop. A school stood on the right-hand side of the road. A community center lay on the opposite side. There were no other houses.

The address in Mohammed's file, not to mention the billing for Fenton's, was phony. She knew it had to be.

She paid the driver to wait for her so he could take her to Olympic Park afterward. She slid out of the car and walked over to the school. Its blue fencing looked black to Jaclyn's HUD. She began to scan the area for possible threats, even at this late hour.

Nothing was there. She and the driver were the only beings awake on this section of the Lane. There were several cars in the parking lot of the school, but a scan of the building indicated they belonged to the janitors who were busily working in the boiler room.

She turned away from the school and made her way behind the taxi, strolling across the street. Her heels slapped the pavement. Crickets chirping in the grass of the nearby rugby pitch were harmonizing together. It was an eerie symphony of insect and footwear. All she needed were a few firecrackers, and it would have been July 4 all over again.

Jaclyn stepped up and stopped on the sidewalk. She exhaled heavily out of her nose. She moved her hands inside her trench coat and firmly fixed them on her hips. Pursing her lips, she knew she had reached a proverbial dead end on this case.

Three beeps in her ear told her to move quickly. She somersaulted to the right just as the taxi driver pulled a gun on her. She tucked and rolled several feet. Her trench coat billowed out behind her.

The blast blistered the night. The shell lodged in a tree in front of where Jaclyn once stood.

When Jaclyn came up again, she had two Walthers in her hand, both pointed right at the taxi, her hip holsters empty. She lowered one and pulled the trigger, causing the left front tire to deflate. The second one shattered the windshield. The shots caused the driver, leaning out the passenger side window, to lose his grip on his weapon.

Jaclyn sprang at the taxi driver in that one instant. Before the driver knew it, Jaclyn had the barrel of one Walther pointed in his throat, the other at his forehead.

"Where the fuck is Mohammed, bitch?" she asked. "You're a dead man if you don't tell me."

The driver didn't seem to hear her. He simply smiled tight, his teeth coming together in the back of his mouth.

A slight crunch came from driver's mouth. Seconds later, a trail of bubbly ooze came out. His body went limp.

Jaclyn removed the guns and holstered them.

"Cyanide," she spat. "A crude but painless death. Someone's been reading up on the Nazis and their methods, it looks."

She pulled out her BlackBerry and called Washington. She leaned against the taxi while the phone went through the rigorous task of international dialing. She crossed her ankles, right over left, just as the phone began to ring. It neared 6 p.m. on the east coast. She knew Dupuis would still be in the office. It was only Tuesday.

The phone rang three times, unusual for Dupuis. She normally picked up on the second. It went to a fourth ring.

Finally, after six rings, Dupuis picked up.

"Everything okay, Snapshot?" Dupuis said. "It's late there."

"You ain't kidding, Chief. It's so late I can see the sun coming up."

"Cut the sarcasm, Jaclyn. What's going on?"

"Well, we averted the crisis at the Aquatics Center. I snuck off and began my own investigation, Chief, but it looks like it's a dead end: the address our Mr. Mohammed gave the truck rental agency and the FA seems to be a fake. I'm standing on White Hart Lane in Tottenham with a dead taxi driver who just tried to take me out. Bastard committed suicide before I could get anything out of him. He had a late cyanide soft drink before he went to bed."

"That sounds gruesome to the stomach and the teeth. But I have to correct you on one part: the crisis wasn't averted."

Jaclyn uncrossed her ankles and pushed herself away from the cab. She didn't think she heard Dupuis clear enough.

Surely, the wireless reception in Tottenham sucks, right? she thought.

"You want to say that again, Alex? I thought I heard you say the crisis wasn't averted."

"You heard correctly."

All of the wind left Jaclyn as if she wasn't wearing a Kevlar-lined jumpsuit. She leaned back against the taxi.

"How? The team said they were going to clear the beams of C4 before I... oh shit. Don't tell me they cut the wrong wires."

"The terrorist had a secondary set of explosives in the building, just like at Wembley. They have no idea how many people are dead, but Olympic Park was a mob scene about half an hour ago. They've finally restored some semblance of order and the last train left Stratford a few minutes ago. Hopefully no one other than yourself and the other law enforcement agencies go there the rest of the night."

Jaclyn knew exactly what Dupuis wanted her to do.

"Chief, I'm exhausted. I've gotten all of four hours sleep in the past 40. I need some rest or I'm not going to be any use to the service for the rest of this mission. And I told them to check for secondary explosives."

"Snapshot, the president wants you on scene. We really don't know how many are dead, and there are reports that our swim team is among the missing. The president is on the phone with the IOC president right now, and there is talk of possibly delaying the Olympics a day so authorities can check the other venues, or possibly canceling the Games entirely. Forrister said he would convince every delegate he had to in order to have the Games delayed to ensure everyone's safety, not just American athletes' safety."

"Is it a direct order?" she finally asked.

"It is. Now, what happened after you snuck off?"

Jaclyn relayed her adventure to FA Headquarters as well as her escape — "You better hope to God that security guard didn't get a good look at you, Jaclyn; there will be absolute hell to pay if you're identified, even with diplomatic immunity. What do you think would happen if Nigel broke into Major League Baseball's offices? Americans would want to throw another tea party with Nigel as the bag!" chastised Dupuis — and her clues to Mohammed's "address" as well as his identity.

"Chief, I think this is the guy," Jaclyn said. "I haven't had the opportunity to go over the photo and compare it to the video, since I really haven't been alone in the past half an hour. And I don't know if this taxi has been rigged with listening devices. The driver was clearly working for Mohammed, but I'm at a loss at how he knew that I was at Soho Square."

"We'll probably never know that reason, Jaclyn. Don't worry about it now. All you need to worry about is getting back to Stratford and be the president's voice there. Sir David is already on the scene; I've asked him not to tear into you for going off on your own. He's rather upset at me, since it wasn't exactly in our purview to start our own investigation."

Great, Jaclyn thought. *Now the old man is going to get all blustery.*

"Call me again when you get back there and tell us all what you've found out, and maybe by the time you get there Willows' anger will have died down a bit."

"I will do that, but Chief?"

"Yes, Jaclyn?"

"I'm stuck in Tottenham."

"You didn't shoot anything out on the cab, did you?"

Jaclyn bit her lip.

"Yeah, I did. I shot out the windshield and the left front tire."

"Is that area secure?"

Jaclyn looked around.

"For the most part, yes. There are no lights on in the houses down the street, and I don't see any flashing red and blues coming. Hopefully the residents didn't hear anything out of the ordinary out here."

"Call Nigel and have him send your car. I would bet someone did. Jaclyn, you need to get out of there, and I'm talking about get your ass out of there five minutes ago. I suspect you're wearing the necessities?"

"Your suspicions would be correct as usual."

"Great. Get the fuck out of there. Get as far away as you can. There's a soccer stadium a few blocks away from there. It's on High Road, but ironically, it's called White Hart Lane, the home of —"

"Tottenham Hotspur."

"Wow, you did your homework on the flight over."

Jaclyn began to walk east on White Hart Lane.

"No, I just have a friend who likes them, and since I'm currently stuck in Tottenham, I find it ironic the bastard isn't here to pick me up."

"Call Nigel then and have his driver —"

"That's who I'm talking about!"

"Jaclyn, shut up for a minute. Walk to the stadium and call Nigel. The faster you walk and talk to him at the same time means the faster your ass is out of trouble. If you can't get a hold of him, you need to steal a car. I expect your call by 7:30 east coast time."

"A.M. or P.M.?"

"Take a guess, Snapshot."

"I'll call ASAP. Is there anything new with our banking friend?"

"Not yet, but we'll have him. I dispatched the team immediately, so it'll take some time."

Dupuis hung up as Jaclyn passed the turn off for Rivulet Road. She dialed Nigel's number and crossed the street and into a park, keeping her body low to the ground.

She found herself in a mainly residential area by the time Nigel picked up the phone.

"Where the bloody hell are you, Snapshot?" Nigel said angrily. "We've had a blasted couple of hours since you left, and blasted really isn't the word I should use right now."

"I'm in Tottenham," Jaclyn whispered. "Long story short, my ride decided to kill himself."

There was silence on the other end for a few minutes. Jaclyn presumed Nigel was listening to someone else speak.

"Maybe I shouldn't introduce you to my son," he said, his first syllable drawn out slightly.

"Nigel, quit trying to play matchmaker for me and send James to White Hart Lane to get me. I'm under orders to come back to Stratford."

"I don't see why, there's nothing to see here but smoke."

"Nigel," Jaclyn said as she crossed the A10. She just noticed it wasn't raining here, and that the roads were not wet.

"Oh alright," Nigel replied. "I'll send James around to fetch you. Hold tight, will you? It will take a bit to get up there. Probably about 20 minutes or so at the latest."

Jaclyn looked at her HUD and noticed that it was about 11:15 now. That meant she would get back to Stratford around midnight, and who knew how long she would be there before she finally got to sleep.

"Alright, I'll be there with bells on," she said. "See you in about 45 minutes."

Jaclyn disconnected the phone. She headed east.

Chapter 19
Olympic Park, Stratford, London, England
31 July 2012 — 23.51 GMT/6:51 p.m. ET

James fetched her at the West Stand entrance of White Hart Lane — it was difficult to see her, as Jaclyn blended in well with the shadows — and brought her back to Stratford so quickly that Jaclyn arrived before her target time. Nigel met her at the BBC truck where they had seen each other last nearly three hours ago.

Once she stepped out of the car, Jaclyn looked toward the smoking pile of rubble that had been the Aquatics Center. She saw the devastation through her HUD and could not find words adequate enough to describe it.

Olympic Park was calm now, as Nigel said on the phone earlier. White shrouds covered the bodies of the trampled rescue workers. Grass leading away from the rubble looked worn to the dirt. Jaclyn looked over to the site and saw fire crews pouring water on the wreckage, trying to cut down on hot spots before rescuers dug bodies and any survivors out.

At that moment, she did not hear anyone yelling for help, nor could she hear the suppressed moans of anyone trapped. She feared that the only ones who survived this ordeal were either at a pub taking the edge off, or at home, trying to make sense of what happened tonight. She wondered if those who went to Wembley last night did the same thing after they left the stadium.

I wonder how I'm going to handle this when I get back to Washington, she thought. *And here I'm thinking I was about to do some heavy duty complaining about my gear.*

Nigel escorted her to a command post, where Sir David waited for her. Jaclyn entered and looked at the head of MI5 with a bit of apprehension. He didn't seem to want to look at her.

"Welcome back, Agent Snapshot. Glad to see you remembered where your duty was."

Bite your tongue, Jaclyn, she thought.

"I'm sorry, sir. I had other duties assigned to me."

"You are a guest of Her Majesty's Secret Service, and you would be quite right to remember that," Willows said. He stuck his pipe back into his mouth. "What did you find out?"

"Let me call Alex first," Jaclyn replied, pulling her BlackBerry out and quickly dialing Dupuis' number. It rang twice this time.

"Hi Jaclyn, long time, no hear," Dupuis said jovially.

Jaclyn suppressed a grin for sake of not blowing her orders.

"Chief, I'm here with Midwicket and Sir David."

They quickly exchanged pleasantries.

"It turns out that my mission failed. The information given to Midwicket and I earlier today was not entirely accurate. It looks as though the terrorist threw a dart at a map of London and used that address as the front for his operations. The same address was in his file at the FA."

"And how the devil did you find that out?" Willows growled.

Jaclyn took a deep breath and explained everything once again to her British counterpart and the Director General. By the time she was finished, Sir David's face was the color of strawberry ice cream.

"Looks like I have to smooth things over with Scotland Yard and the FA about that now," he said. "Alex, your agents always get into so much trouble over here, I can't remember the last one who played by the book!"

"I can't remember either, David, but you have to admit my agents do have a certain *je ne sais quoi* about them that gets the job done."

Jaclyn grinned internally at her boss's praise, while Willows grumbled something unintelligible to her ears.

"I trust your judgment, Liberty. We're not used to these types of attacks over here, I'm surprised we can handle these things."

"We would prefer that no one has to deal with these types of attacks, Parliament. Jaclyn is the best available agent."

Willows breathed out through his nose. He finally looked at Jaclyn.

"What would you suggest we do next, Snapshot? You don't mind playing second fiddle to a woman, do you Midwicket?"

Nigel shook his head.

"If Jaclyn doesn't mind taking the lead; she seems to have a knack for this sort of stuff, what with her sunglasses giving her warnings every five minutes." Nigel gave her a little wink. "I would follow her into the heart of Argentina and announce that Maradona cheated in 1986 — as long as she had an escape plan, that is."

Willows chuckled.

"Right now," Jaclyn began, not understanding a word of what Nigel just said, "I think we need to concentrate on getting whoever is under the rubble here and at Wembley so we can give them proper burials. Who knows what we're going to find under there." She jerked her head toward the Aquatics Center. "Our leads on Mohammed seem to have dried up for now, but I'm sure that we will be able to get new ones as soon as there is another attack."

She quickly remembered.

"Oh, and I was able to get this." She reached into her utility belt and grabbed her digital camera. She also grabbed her iPad from inside her trench coat and uploaded the picture she grabbed of Mohammed.

That seemed so long ago, she thought as she showed Nigel and Willows the photo compared to the broadcast video from a night ago.

"It seems that it is a match, Snapshot," Willows said. "Alex, your agent is impressive."

"Only an hour ago you wanted her deported for dereliction of duty, David," Dupuis countered.

Willows' face turned white.

"Never mind that now," he said, brushing it aside. "Times have changed. We need her in on this one hundred percent, and she will have carte blanche on this operation." Willows coughed.

"Will we be able to share intel as normal, David?" Dupuis asked.

"Of course," Willows replied immediately. "As long as it's not sensitive material that will compromise Her Majesty's Government or President Forrister's administration, we will be glad to do so, as usual."

Jaclyn heard Dupuis breathe as if relieved.

"Good. I will let the president know everything. Jaclyn, call in if anything breaks. Get some sleep."

"Will do, Chief. You too, after you watch the Nationals game, of course."

Dupuis cut the connection. Jaclyn stashed her BlackBerry back into her utility belt.

"Nigel, have James bring Agent Snapshot to her hotel room, and you call Jane and let her know you will be home soon. Jaclyn, if you could e-mail that photo to my people, we will have them get in touch with Oxford in the morning and have a dossier on him by the time you have your tea and crumpets at Thames House," Willows said.

Jaclyn pulled the iPad back out and shipped the photo to Box 500's techs.

"Good, now go get some rest. You've both done well today."

"Other than the fact that more people died, sir?" Nigel said.

Willows coughed again.

"I'll see you both in the morning." Willows stomped out of the command center and headed to his car.

Jaclyn and Nigel looked at each other and wondered what tomorrow would bring, before they both left the command center, walking into a swirling dust cloud. The wind had picked up a bit in the last half an hour and had brought it from the Aquatics Center site to their position. The Olympic flag was at half-mast, but it stood stiff in the breeze.

The dust got under Jaclyn's sunglasses. She removed them and began to wipe her eyes as they walked toward the limousine.

The gunshot cracked as Jaclyn's thumb and forefinger were digging near her eyelids. The sound caused her heart to shoot into her throat. Jaclyn dropped to her knees when she heard a squelch nearby. She put her sunglasses back on and before she drew her Walthers, she slapped the button to make herself bulletproof. Security guards yelled for their partners to draw their weapons.

Jaclyn searched for the gunman. Willows had his own gun out and tried to keep as low as possible as he sauntered back to give Jaclyn backup.

Her HUD picked the assassin up almost immediately, and he wasn't that far away. She saw the assassin positioned on top of the Tube station, and before she could fire, he let loose another two shots, both aimed for her torso.

The American agent deftly dodged the bullets. She fired three times with each gun, each bullet coming close to hitting her target. The bullets compressed against the façade of the station and fell harmlessly into a flowerbed at the base of the wall. One of the assassin's shots hit her in the chest. She staggered briefly but didn't go down.

The assassin, high above the station, stared in disbelief.

Jaclyn ran toward him and fired away, exhausting both guns as she approached. If she did not have the Kevlar-lined jumpsuit offering her cover, she would have ducked behind something solid for protection. Then, she would have either re-loaded or re-holstered her spent weapons, and then would have drawn another two guns. In the open like this, she had no choice but to drop them and draw two more.

Stupidly, the assassin chose to stand up and offer more of himself to Jaclyn's aim as he fired off a couple more shots in her direction.

Jaclyn dropped and rolled to the left before she righted herself to one knee. She squeezed the triggers twice and hit him in the pectorals. He spun and hit the deck, dropping his weapon in the process.

"Target is down!" she yelled as she got to her feet. "We need him alive!"

She raced to the platform and beat other security personnel there. She found a few Underground security guards rushing up a flight of stairs, and she was quick to run up behind them. They all had their guns drawn as they reached the roof.

Jaclyn saw the wounded assassin reaching for a sidearm pistol. The security officers told him not to move, but she wasn't sure if the bastard spoke English. She didn't wait for the assassin to pull the weapon, nor to heed the security guards' order. She fired.

A blood-curdling scream erupted from the assassin's mouth. His right wrist bled where Jaclyn shot him.

Jaclyn stalked in with her gun raised.

"If he makes another move, put another bullet in him. His screams are music to my ears," she advised the security officers. They all nodded as they acknowledged her order.

She knelt in front of him.

"Did Mohammed send you? It's okay, we know Mohammed is responsible for all of this," Jaclyn said. "You can admit it to us."

"I will never admit anything to a woman," the assassin said just before he spat in her face. "Allah does not recognize your authority over me." He moved his left hand up to his mouth quickly, using the distraction to toss a cyanide tablet into his mouth. He bit down before the security guards could even raise their weapons.

The sound of the plastic crunching under his molars was one of defeat in Jaclyn's ears.

The cyanide flowed out of his mouth, his eyes becoming glassy. He died immediately, his link to Mohammed severed.

"Fuck!" Jaclyn screamed. Enraged, she emptied half the magazine into the dead man's brain. Half of his head was gone by the time she finished.

The security guards stepped away from her just as Willows stepped onto the roof of the station.

"Snapshot, what the devil? What happened?" he asked.

Jaclyn was still on her knees. She dropped the Walther on the tar.

"The bastard killed himself, just like the taxi driver did. Cyanide caplets; the security guards can confirm it. I only blew his head off afterward. This son of a bitch Mohammed is so fucking meticulous it makes me sick. This holy war, these terrorist acts, makes me sick."

Jaclyn looked at the dead man and saw she had shot half of his head away. She tried not to vomit.

Willows walked the remaining few feet to her. He couldn't find the words to agree with her.

Jaclyn turned her head to the MI5 boss and saw Willows looking into her sunglasses, trying to find her eyes.

"Nigel's dead, Jaclyn."

Jaclyn knelt there, stunned, unmoving. Like earlier when she spoke with Dupuis while partially stranded in Tottenham, she did not think she heard Willows correctly. She could not breathe. She rocked back onto her haunches and fell on her Lycra-covered behind.

"No," she mouthed, but no sound came out. "No, he can't be. He was just walking with me."

"He is. This bastard," Willows said, pointing at the dead terrorist, "shot him right in the temple, in the same fashion that Fenton was killed earlier today."

Jaclyn couldn't believe it. She vaulted toward the wall, stepping over the dead assassin. She nearly stepped on his chest. She looked out toward Olympic Park.

She saw him, lying in a pool of his own blood. The pool grew by the millimeter. His eyes, Jaclyn could see through the magnified image, were open, unaware that he had just been shot.

Jaclyn's mouth opened in disbelief. Her heart dropped from her throat to her spiked boots. She finally closed her mouth. Her eyes, hidden behind her Foster Grants, narrowed in anger.

Chapter 20
The West End, London, England
1 August 2012 — 00.15 GMT/31 July 2012, 7:15 p.m. ET

I just love closed circuit feeds, Jafar thought as he watched the scene play out in Stratford once again. He played the DVR again and again, savoring each moment of his assassin putting a bullet in the Briton. It was clearly his favorite part: He smiled every time the bullet hit. He rewound and played the man staggering so much it appeared like the dead man danced toward his grave.

He knew the British would either capture or kill his agent during this operation. The agent was expendable, of course. He was not sad about that. His assassin gave his life for Allah, of that Jafar had no doubt.

As it should be, Jafar thought. *The Imams had foreseen that there would be so many Muslim men lining up to die for what they believe in: an Islamic world, a Muslim world. A world that is pure. It would be a world where the Jews and the Christians finally recognized Allah's greatness and power, where they ultimately bend their knees to Him. Until they did, however, Allah would exterminate them until they capitulated.*

I will be victorious, which means Allah would be victorious.

You are wrong, Jafar.

There it is again, Jafar thought. *That blasted voice in my mind. The voice that made me sin, the voice that just will not listen to reason, the voice that blasphemies Allah to no end.*

"Go away with you," Jafar said aloud. "You are selling crazy, and we are not buying here."

Of course not, Jafar. You have plenty of that stocked up for a long, winter's hibernation.

The voice laughed madly in Jafar's mind.

The Afghani clamped his hands over his ears, but the laughter increased in volume just the same.

"Stop it, Allah commands you!" he pleaded.

The voice was having none of it. The laughter died down, but the voice's power made Jafar tremble under its deep, basso pitch.

We've had this conversation before, Jafar. You are not Allah, despite your complex. You only think you are Allah. You may share the name of Allah's Messenger, but you are not nearly as great or respected as he was. You are less than Him. You always have been. You always will be.

Jafar tried to stay strong under the voice's powerful, mind-reducing assault, but he whimpered and choked back tears. The voice's words were relentless, never-ending. The voice was like a father who was never pleased with what his son did, even if it was the greatest thing on earth.

The tears finally rumbled down his face. They fell uncontrollably.

Jafar had had it with the voice. It was time to do something so that he could never hear the voice again.

He rushed into his bedroom.

He hurried around his bed, pulling open the drawer of the bedside table. He cringed when he saw the pornographic magazines he had purchased while in New York City, and he hoped that Allah did not see them. He reached in and tossed aside the box of unused condoms. He reverently pulled out his pocket copy of the Koran and placed it on the bed, before he found what he was looking for.

His gun.

He stared at it for the longest time. The voice needed to die. The voice in his brain must be stopped.

He brought the barrel to his right temple. His breath caught in his throat as the cool metal touched warm skin.

Do it, Jafar. Put me out of my misery, the voice taunted in his ear. He felt an invisible tongue graze his inner ear, and it caused him to shiver.

"Go away," Jafar sobbed, "or I will do it."

No, you won't. You don't have the balls to do it, Jafar. You're a pathetic piece of shit that can't do anything right.

"I killed thousands of people today!" he nearly screamed in protest, but he remembered his neighbors. The walls were somewhat thin. "I killed thousands yesterday. I did it for Allah."

You did it for your own twisted belief that you are Allah, the voice said, as if he was circling his prey, ridiculing him with every revolution. You are a disgrace to Muslims everywhere, a disgrace to the peaceful Muslim faith.

Jafar cried.

Poor little jihadist baby you are, Jafar.

Jafar closed his eyes and pushed the gun deeper into his temple. He pulled the hammer down.

Come on, Jafar. Pull the trigger. End my life, and end yours, too. Do what your agents do willingly, in Allah's name, not yours. Give yourself to Allah. Go on, do it. You know it's what you crave to do.

Jafar's eyes flew open. Rage filled them. He pulled the gun away and manually brought the hammer back into a fixed position.

"I will give my life to Allah when I am good and ready to do so," Jafar said. "You are nothing, and your taunts are not what Allah wants me to do. He still has work for me to do. My agents know exactly what they were put on earth for, and that was to follow me to victory, to whatever end."

Suit yourself, Jafar. You could have ended it yourself just now. But the woman who killed your agent —

"That bitch did not kill him! He gave himself to Allah!"

Keep telling yourself that. She shot him after he killed her partner. He only did it to save himself the pain of having his brains splattered all over the roof of that station. Go watch the footage again. She would have killed him, and he would not have received his virgins.

Jafar's lip curled. He tossed the gun onto his bed, then stalked out of his bedroom and rushed to the television. He had frozen the image of the British agent being shot.

He pressed play.

He saw the woman crouched. Then like a blur, the woman pulled out her weapons and danced away from his assassin's shots. She exhausted the weapons and pulled out two more, as if from nowhere. It didn't seem possible that a woman could do this. It was unheard of.

It was a blasphemy of Allah's teachings, Jafar thought, plain and simple. War was the domain of men. This was not a place for a woman.

He saw her shoot his agent, just as the voice said. He dropped his weapon. He fell. The angle of the camera showed it perfectly. The audio captured every gunshot and his agent's crash to the station roof. A commotion followed.

Then, for the first time, he heard the woman speak.

"If he makes another move, put another bullet in him. His screams are music to my ears."

Jafar saw the woman kneel.

"Good, kneel in front of a man," Jafar whispered. "Know your place."

"Did Mohammed send you? It's okay, we know Mohammed is responsible for all of this. You can admit it to us."

Jafar's eyes went wide.

"I will never admit anything to a woman," he heard the assassin rasp. The sound of expectoration hit the woman's face. "Allah does not recognize your authority over me."

Several seconds followed.

"Fuck!" the woman said. Bullets flew.

Jafar saw his agent had killed himself. He heard another Brit coming up the stairs, before the man said, "Snapshot? What the devil happened?"

He paused the DVR.

"See! He killed himself! He gave himself to Allah!" he yelled to the voice.

The voice simply chuckled in response.

Perhaps you're right. For once. But this woman, she may be the death of you. You can choose the manner that you meet Allah: You can give yourself freely, or you can be killed by the woman. It is your choice. Allah would be most displeased, though, should a hearty man of Islam like yourself let a woman kill you.

Jafar's eyes shifted back and forth. He bit his fingernails. He began to pace the floor.

I cannot allow that to happen, Jafar thought. *If she is to be the death of me, I must make my escape plans.*

Your other agent failed to kill her.

Jafar grinned.

"She must die, of course. She must not get near me. I have sent another agent to take care of her in the morning."

The Afghani noted the time and saw that it was nearly 12:30 a.m. He needed to sleep, and he knew he could only get about four hours before he woke to partake in *Suhoor*; he would not allow himself to do what happened earlier in the day. He said a quick prayer to Allah, then laid down on the couch.

He would awake four hours later, like clockwork.

It was to be his day.

Midwicket KIA in OP. My fault! Headed to hotel, must sleep. JJ

Jaclyn sent that text to Dupuis as soon as Willows herded the American toward the limousine. She tried not to cry any longer while en route to the hotel. She succeeded, for the most part. She was incredibly ashamed of herself for letting her guard down.

I never should have taken off my sunglasses at that moment, she thought as James headed west. *Nigel would still be alive if I kept them on. I have no doubt of that. My sunglasses are the key.*

Her BlackBerry vibrated as soon as James pulled up to the hotel. Jaclyn held her breath as the message downloaded.

Flying to Heathrow immediately. Will be at your hotel in the morning. Will discuss further action then. Islamic banker dead. Sleep well. AD

Jaclyn let the breath escape. She let her head fall backward to the rest. She looked to the limo's ceiling.

"Alex is coming," she whispered. She closed her eyes tight and felt the trickle of tears escape. She quickly took two deep breaths, though, to calm herself. She wiped the tears away before James had her door open.

She thanked the MI5 driver. She could tell he hurt, too, but he wasn't letting that show. He hopped back into the car and headed back to Thames House.

Jaclyn watched the car disappear before finally entering the hotel.

Inside the relative safety of her suite, she shed the trench coat and stored her weaponry — she retrieved her exhausted Walthers and replaced their magazines almost immediately after leaving the roof — and other devices before sliding the sweat-slicked jumpsuit off her body. She showered quickly, ridding herself of her rain-drenched hair and her clammy skin, dried off and slipped into bed.

In the safety of her dreams, she wasn't safe. Not one bit.

As soon as her subconscious relaxed, scenes from not only Nigel's death, but of the near death experience they shared at Wembley plagued her mind. Her dreams became nightmares. She lost her HUD in each scene, each replay. In some, her HUD failed to work as intended . She didn't hear the hissing of the rocket until it was much too late to do anything. The gunshot in Olympic Park was one of a vicious thunderclap, the shot much like a too-close lightning strike.

The sight of Nigel sprawled on the ground, blood pouring out of him, soon followed. It flowed like the River Thames, meandering this way and that. It encroached her private space, even upon the roof of Stratford Station. It flooded her. Plasma swallowed her. She drowned in Nigel's life.

Jaclyn shot straight up. Her eyes were wide open. Sweat poured down her face, coating not only her skin but her HUD. Her sheets were soaked. She felt her pulse. Her heart tried to break her breastbone.

She swung her legs out of bed and found they ached. She had run on so much adrenaline since she arrived at Heathrow a day ago that she didn't notice her own exhaustion. She was more concerned with the well-being of others than her own condition.

Poor Nigel, she thought. It wasn't the first time she had thought that.

She couldn't have cried even if she wanted to. She had cried enough. Crying only made her more dehydrated than she already was.

She stood and walked to the bathroom, drawing several glasses of water.

Jaclyn looked at the time. It was nearly 9 a.m.

"It didn't feel like it was eight hours of sleep, that's for sure."

She showered once again, then put on some loose-fitting clothing and awaited Dupuis' arrival.

It came too quickly. The knock on the door startled her. She was putting on her sneakers to go for a run; she already had on a blue Seattle Mariners t-shirt as well as black Victoria's Secret shorts with "Pink" written in bold, pink letters on the behind.

"Who is it?" she asked.

"It's Liberty."

Jaclyn breathed a heavy sigh of relief. She opened the door.

Dupuis stood there, holding her briefcase.

She was not alone, though.

Standing next to her was Alexei Zhirkov, the CIA's top clandestine services' psychiatrist. Tall and bald, the former KGB man loomed over Jaclyn like a high, steel curtain.

Jaclyn knew why he was here. She looked at him through the HUD and saw him smiling down at her.

She nearly slammed the door in both of their faces.

"Hi Jaclyn," Dupuis said. "I'm sure you know Dr. Zhirkov."

Jaclyn nodded.

"May we come in?"

"Of course." Jaclyn stepped aside and let them in. She tried not to show her agitation.

"Were you about to go somewhere?" Dupuis asked.

"Actually, I was about to go for a run. You know me, Chief. A run usually helps me see things clearer. Pounding the pavement helps clear the head."

Dupuis nodded.

"But you were going unarmed?"

Jaclyn raised her t-shirt to show a holstered Walther P99. She grinned.

Dupuis matched it.

"See Alexei, I told you she was a smart girl. Maybe a little too smart."

Both Dupuis and the doctor sat down, while Jaclyn remained standing. She wanted to remain somewhat on guard here, especially after her boss ambushed her like this. Bringing a psychiatrist halfway around the world didn't seem like something Dupuis would normally do. If anything, they would recall Jaclyn.

Thought caught up to her.

Of course, she thought. *No flights are leaving Heathrow, not even diplomatic flights. If you can't bring the patient to the shrink, bring the shrink to the patient.*

It also didn't make sense, since it would mean the shrink would have to stay in London.

Unless he's to follow me around like a fucking bloodhound. He's going to stick out like a sore thumb here, she thought.

She decided to smile and play coy. She could do that. The CIA had trained her to play dumb on occasion. But Dupuis knew that, too: She trained her.

"So," Jaclyn said, finally sitting down. "I know why Alex is here. Why are you here, doctor?"

The doctor spoke with a rich Russian accent. Jaclyn couldn't quite place it, though. Her first guess was St. Petersburg.

"It's the Olympics, of course. I was going to go to the gymnastics to see my cousin, Svetlana, perform. It has been years since I have seen her, and I know she has the ability to medal," he said with a smile.

Jaclyn mimicked it.

"Cut the bull shit, doc," she said, cutting her smile short. "You have no intention of seeing any cousin. I've read your file; your family was wiped out by the KGB in order to get your cooperation, and you defected to the West in 1985. Cousin Svetlana must be incredibly distant for you to even know about her."

Jaclyn crossed her arms over her chest. She looked at the doctor with defiance written all over her face.

"So as I asked before, why are you here?"

Her HUD detected a twitch in the doctor's cheek. Dupuis shifted in her seat.

Jaclyn didn't take pleasure in knowing she had thwarted their efforts to pull a fast one over her. She should have, though. She should have been pissed that Dupuis would pull this sort of stunt, and she was surely pissed that the shrink had the audacity to sit in her hotel room and lie to her face.

She didn't really give a shit about the doctor's lies, but there was a part of her, a very small part, that appreciated Dupuis' concern for her sanity.

"Dr. Zhirkov is here at the request of the president, Jaclyn," Dupuis finally explained. "It is only as a precaution for your well-being. The president holds you in very high esteem. If he didn't, he would have ordered you home without a second thought to the mission priority. The United States nor the United Kingdom can afford to lose you. Not right now. Not the way things are unfolding."

"I wouldn't have been able to come home, and you know this. You know the British have closed off Heathrow to outgoing flights. I'm stuck here until the embargo is lifted, and now so are you."

"Very true, but you could have swum across the English Channel and found your way to Paris. I have my bathing suit. Where's yours?"

Jaclyn pursed her lips. She never gave that any consideration, as ludicrous as the idea was.

Dupuis smiled. It took the edge off her agent, if only a little bit.

Jaclyn's posture slumped. She knew she had to go through with this, despite her misgivings on the matter. If they pulled her from this case, any new agent Dupuis decided to send over to London would have been behind the proverbial 8-ball right from jump street.

No, Jaclyn thought. *This mission is my baby right now. Nigel, God rest his soul, would want me to go through with it. He would want me to find the son of a bitch who ordered those killed at Wembley and those killed at Olympic Park found and brought to justice — if I didn't kill him first, that is.*

"Alright, if Forrister wants me to have my head shrunk by this guy, I'll do it. Besides, it's on the taxpayers' bill. How can I refuse?"

Dupuis grinned.

"Quite right, because if you refused, I would have yanked your little ass from the case so fast you'd think the English Channel was the

Hudson River compared to swimming across the Atlantic all the way home."

Chapter 22
The Regency Hotel, London, England
1 August 2012 — 10.00 GMT/5:00 a.m. ET

"Agent Snapshot is fine, Director Dupuis. She has come to terms and accepted Agent Messingham's death as being her responsibility. She exhibits the same mental capacity as any other agents, who have been at this game longer than she has."

Dr. Zhirkov and Dupuis stood in the hallway, right outside Jaclyn's room. Jaclyn did not want to eavesdrop. She and the doctor spoke at length, and she admitted she had a little bit of survivor's guilt regarding Nigel's death. She explained she respected Nigel and felt bad for the British people, for they unknowingly lost an incredible agent, one who protected them without ever receiving a thank you.

"Alright," Dupuis said. "Thank you for helping her out, doctor. We don't need Jaclyn stationed at a desk job at Langley. That would not be in our nation's or our allies' best interest. She is much too good of an agent to not let her do what she does best."

"Very true," Zhirkov said, nodding. "And think of the outcry from the taxpayers if they discovered all of their tax money went to programs that just didn't work out the way they intended to."

Zhirkov winked.

Dupuis smiled at the irony.

"I'll be sure to let my Congressman know that. I'll see you in the car; I just want to talk to Jaclyn for a minute."

Zhirkov bowed to Dupuis before he walked toward the lift. Dupuis watched him go before she re-entered Jaclyn's hotel room.

She found Jaclyn pacing slowly, deep in thought.

"You're going to wear a path in the floor if you keep doing that. The taxpayers won't like that if they have to replace a hotel room floor in London. They'll wonder which president or member of Congress threw a party here," Dupuis said, grinning at her operative.

Jaclyn stopped and turned to face Dupuis.

"So what's the verdict, Chief? Am I nuts? Am I being pulled? Because I will tell you right now I'll be damned if I give up this mission."

"Jaclyn —"

"I've come too far in the 24 hours I've been here."

"Jaclyn —"

"Sure, we had a set back with the whole wrong address thing."

"Jaclyn —"

"And then there was the whole Aquatics Center coming down, but that wasn't my fault. I told them to check for secondary explosives."

"Jaclyn!"

Jaclyn froze.

"Yeah?"

"You're not being pulled from the operation."

Jaclyn looked stunned.

"I'm not?"

"No, of course not," Dupuis said, walking to Jaclyn and grabbing her upper arms. "There was no way I would pull you after what you've been through. I would not have listened to Forrister even if he said it would have cost me my job. You are way too valuable. I wasn't lying to Willows last night when I told him you are a selfless agent. As I said, Dr. Zhirkov was only here to make sure you were okay to continue. He says you are."

Emotions flooded Jaclyn, but she stopped herself before she started to cry. She took several calming breaths.

She looked Dupuis in the eyes.

"Thanks, Chief."

"No thanks are necessary. Just get this fucker before he causes any more damage in Lon—"

Jaclyn had heard her HUD tones, causing her to interrupt Dupuis as she slid her hand up her t-shirt to grab her holstered Walther.

"What's going —"

Dupuis never got the word out, but she had been around Jaclyn far too long to know that if she reached for her sidearm, something was about to go down. A heavy hiss of rapidly shifting air and an explosion drowned it out. It was close by. Anyone standing outside the hotel would be dead or suffer from severe hearing loss.

The two women rushed to the window and looked out at London. They saw the smoke rising from the diplomatic car — the same car Jaclyn rode in yesterday — parked in front of the hotel.

The flames encompassed the vehicle. No one tried to escape.

Jaclyn knew immediately that anyone inside of it was already dead.

"Let's go!" she said, rushing for the door. "Are you armed?"

"Are the Nationals going to finish last in the NL East this year?" Dupuis retorted.

"Sorry I asked."

The pair rushed into the hallway. They were the curious pair: two women, both armed, one in running gear, the other in business casual attire. Anyone looking at them would have immediately looked for the movie cameras.

They didn't wait for the lift to return to the second floor, instead running down the two flights of twisting stairs, skipping steps after every five. Jaclyn increased her already-lengthy stride as she ran out through the lobby, mere seconds ahead of Dupuis. Jaclyn was a blur of Mariners blue and Victoria's Secret black while the concierge spoke with Metropolitan Police.

She had her gun up the second she emerged onto Nottingham Place. Her HUD immediately scanned the surrounding area. The crackling fire sent large amounts of heat at her, causing the fine hairs on her arms to rise under the warmth. She heard the sounds of burning upholstery and metal merging with the sounds of fire engines wailing in the background. It sent waves of anxious excitement coursing through her.

Dupuis came running out a second later. She tried to see who was inside the car. She made out the charred forms of James and Dr. Zhirkov, sitting there as if waiting for her to come down. She lowered her gun, if only for a second.

Jaclyn slowly spun with her Walther ready to fire. Nothing showed on her HUD. The surrounding rooftops appeared clear.

A man exited from a nearby building on the other side of the street. His hat was pulled down low, and carried a long green bag that resembled a US Army duffel, but it was thinner than the one Jaclyn carried during her initial CIA training 11 years ago. Jaclyn turned her head just as the man, a man with tanned, Middle Eastern features, turned his head to look at her.

Jaclyn's breath stuck in her throat as the man nearly paused in his stride. She took two cautious steps forward.

He ran.

Not waiting for Dupuis to give her the order to follow, Jaclyn took off after the man. Dupuis' voice echoed in her mind, but the blood pounded in her ears, drowning it out. She sprinted the length of Nottingham Place toward the busy Marylebone Road. She saw the man toss the bag behind him in an effort to distract her, but she easily avoided it when she crossed its path.

He had a 50-foot lead on her.

She watched as the man ran right across Marylebone, making westbound cars peel to a halt, the sound of tires screeching, the smell of rubber hanging in the air. Eastbound cars did the same as he crossed to the far side.

Jaclyn raised her gun at drivers, causing them to stop as she ran across. One driver didn't see her coming. He slammed the brakes and came several feet away from hitting her.

Jaclyn's HUD beeped at just the last second. Jaclyn swerved her hips to avoid the inevitable collision, her feet churning the pavement in the same movement.

She, too, crossed to the other side, picking up the pace.

Jaclyn was right: she loved to run, and her troubles of the past 24 hours vanished as the sidewalk groaned under her vicious, bipedal assault. This chase was more than just a mind-clearing exercise, though. This was a chase that would save hundreds if not thousands of lives. If Jaclyn couldn't catch this guy, more people were certain to die from Mohammed's acts of terrorism.

The man turned left onto York Gate, the entrance to vast Regent's Park.

Jaclyn had no choice but follow him.

She had him in her sights as he crossed the York Bridge. She turned up her cadence as she ran, trying to catch up with Zhirkov's murderer. She crossed the bridge seconds later, before the path meandered to the left. The chase took them beyond the tennis courts to the right of the path.

They were between 300 and 325 feet to the north of the Outer Circle.

The man looked over his shoulder as he ran. Jaclyn could see the man's fear etched on his face now. She knew the man had cyanide capsules on him. He wouldn't take them until absolutely necessary, not until she caught up to him.

I need to prevent the fucker from taking them, she thought.

They quickly crossed the Inner Circle, and the man's kick continued down the path. Jaclyn's kick was just as strong. They approached a fountain, but the man purposely avoided it, instead skirting off to the left. A copse of trees was the perfect place for him to lose his shadow.

He made a beeline for them.

Jaclyn followed. She was within 15 feet of him now, and definitely within yelling distance. She saw him look over his shoulder again. He started showing signs of panic. He was also slowing down a bit.

She almost had him.

Across the green lawns they ran, crossing another line of trees. They approached the multiple football fields inside the park, where kids and adults alike played the national sport. Jerseys of all different colors — red, white, blue, and the unusual combination of claret and blue — were visible, but Jaclyn only had eyes for the green shirt of the terrorist. His hat flew off his head.

Ahead, he breathed heavy, but he went on until he started to stagger.

Jaclyn took the opportunity. She took two more steps and launched herself at him in dropkick-like fashion. She swiped his legs out from under him, her right foot connecting with his right leg, bringing it over to trip his left leg up. The terrorist hit the ground hard. People who watched the ending stages of the chase "oohed" as Jaclyn brought him down hard. Some men ran to Jaclyn's aid as soon as the man's torso crashed to the earth.

But when they saw her turn the man over onto his back and pistol-whip him in the face, knocking him out cold, most of them froze; they turned to their buddies.

"I think the bird has it all under control, don't you, mate?"

Others didn't stop.

One man wearing a blue shirt bearing Samsung on the front along with a Chelsea badge over the left breast came running up to her just as Jaclyn began searching the terrorist for cyanide capsules.

"Blimey! That was the most impressive sliding tackle I've ever seen!" he said, his eyes wide with fascination. "Do you play football?"

Jaclyn took a seat right on the downed man's chest. Despite a light bead of sweat on her forehead and a racing pulse, she didn't appear to be laboring after her strenuous exertion.

"You don't happen to have a cell phone, would you? I need to make a call."

The man shook his head.

"My mate does, though." He turned his head. "Oy, Roger! Bring your mobile over here, mate!"

Roger hurried as quickly as he could, handing his cell to Jaclyn. She dialed emergency.

"This is Jaclyn Johnson, CIA. Connect me to Sir David Willows at Box 500, PDQ. It's a matter of international security," she said when the connection was made. She waited a few more seconds.

"I didn't know the CIA were experts at football!" The man in the Chelsea jersey continued to babble freely. Roger, who turned back toward the field they were on, wore a Fulham jersey with Dempsey 8 written on the back.

"I don't play football," Jaclyn said. "Women aren't allowed to play football in the United States. It's too rough of a game for the fairer sex, I'm afraid."

The man's eyes widened.

"On the contrary, the Yank women are great at football! They won the World Cup back in '99, remember? The Chastain bird ripped her shirt off after they won."

Jaclyn shook her confusion away.

"Oh, you mean soccer. I thought you meant 'football' football. No, I don't play."

The man's face immediately soured. He turned and walked away, and Jaclyn thought she heard him say, "Bloody Americans demeaning football by calling it soccer. Blasted throwball lovers should all be shot."

Jaclyn shook her head.

"Men and their sports," she said, just as the phone began to ring again.

The pompous voice of the Director General answered. He sounded like he had his pipe lodged between his teeth.

"This is Willows."

"Sir, this is Snapshot. I have a terrorist under arrest. I'm sitting on him in Regent's Park. We're over by the soccer fields."

"You mean the football fields."

"Whatever."

Jaclyn shook her head again.

"Please contact Alex; I don't have my BlackBerry. And I need someone to carry his ass back to Thames House for questioning. *Aggressive* questioning."

Willows knew exactly what she meant; aggressive questioning was a euphemism for torture.

He coughed.

"I'll call James and have him come get you; he's not too far away from Regent's Park."

"Sir?"

"Yes, Snapshot, what is it?"

Jaclyn gulped. Roger the Footballer waved toward a passing constable, who then came running toward them.

"James is dead. This bastard killed him and the CIA shrink."

Willows, Jaclyn could tell, didn't hear her correctly. His "What did you say?" only confirmed it.

She repeated herself.

"Good gracious," said Willows. "We have to stop these blasted terrorists before they take out all of London."

"Yes, sir, I couldn't agree more."

"How the devil did it happen?"

Jaclyn told him that she didn't know exactly what had happened, except that the diplomatic limousine now doubled as a stretched barbecue.

"Remind me to skewer this bastard when he gets here so I can rake him over the coals."

"I will definitely do that, sir. You can count on me."

"I'll round up a squad and send one over."

"Sir, there is a police officer coming this way."

"I'll handle him; hand him the phone the moment he gets there. Meanwhile, you hang tight and make sure the bastard doesn't take his cyanide pills."

Jaclyn hefted her Walther and smiled into the cell phone. The constable had started huffing and puffing by the time he got there.

"No sir, I don't think he will be doing that any time soon. I'll see you in a few minutes. Here's the nice officer."

Jaclyn handed the phone to the constable, who quickly — and unexpectedly — received an earful from Sir David. The constable handed his cuffs to the American, who easily restrained the prisoner for transport.

Chapter 23
Thames House, Millbank, London, England
1 August 2012 — 13.33 GMT/8:33 a.m. ET

London in early August was much like Washington, D.C.: humid, hot, and hazy. Jaclyn was used to it, even though she would have preferred her native Seattle.

Thames House, though, was just the opposite of the outdoor temperatures. It was perfectly air-conditioned, and it wasn't a stretch to see agents wearing short-sleeved Oxford shirts as they headed to and fro on Her Majesty's business.

Jaclyn, though, was still dressed for her run. She would have gone upstairs to her hotel room to change when they drove past, but she told the driver to keep going. The SIS would send a car for Dupuis as soon as she finished giving her statement to Metropolitan Police.

She quickly became chilly as she stood outside the interrogation room. The terrorist had not spoken much to MI5 other than his name, Maqil Gnosh. He was shivering more than Jaclyn was, and he was wearing more clothes than Jaclyn was at the time being.

"You look cold."

Jaclyn turned. She gasped.

Her HUD showed a young agent wearing an Oxford shirt and a black tie. The face was very familiar to her. It was if —

"I'm Tom Messingham," he said, cutting off her thought. "I am – was – Nigel's son."

Jaclyn froze. She thought she had been seeing a ghost of her British counterpart, only 20 years younger.

"I'm Jaclyn Johnson." She extended her hand.

Tom shook it. Jaclyn noticed he had a firm grip.

"Yeah, I know. Loads of people are talking about you this morning, about how you took out this bloke out with a sliding tackle Paul Scholes would have been proud of." He jerked his thumb toward the glass.

She looked quizzically at him.

"I'm sorry, Paul who?"

Tom grimaced.

"Paul Scholes, bloke played for Manchester United. Belongs in a nursing home, he played for the Red Devils for so long. He's probably one of the best defensive midfielders ever to play in the Premier League. But since you're an American, I'm sure you know nothing of what I'm talking about."

The young man, according to Jaclyn's HUD, was blushing a bit. He sounded much like the man in Regent's Park, but he had a boyish charm to him that Jaclyn could not deny was appealing to her.

She felt her heart skip a solitary beat.

"No, not really, but I've been learning a bit about British sports since I've been here."

"Would you like something a little warmer to wear?" he asked. "I've got a spare shirt and a pair of running trousers that may fit you. If they don't, I'm sure one of the female agents has something that would be comfortable."

Jaclyn felt goose bumps rising on her arms. She didn't know if it was from the air conditioning, though.

"Why yes, that would be very nice, thank you," Jaclyn replied.

Why yes? That would be very nice? Who are you and what have you done with Jaclyn Johnson? her inner voice echoed in her mind.

She paid it no mind as she followed Nigel's son toward the dressing rooms, but an all-too familiar voice stopped her advance.

"Jaclyn!" Dupuis said.

Jaclyn and Tom stopped and turned toward Dupuis' voice.

"I have to congratulate you on bringing this one in alive," the Director of the CIA said as she walked toward her operative with Willows in tow. "I don't think Congress would approve of you pistol whipping him, but I must admit, your methods bring results."

"Thanks, Chief."

"Agent Scouser, may I present Alexandra Dupuis, the Director of the Central Intelligence Agency," Willows said to Tom. Dupuis and Tom shook hands.

Jaclyn leaned toward Tom.

"Scouser? What does that mean?" she whispered.

"It means that I'm a Liverpool supporter."

"Liverpool?"

"Eighteen-time league champion, five-time European Cup champion."

Jaclyn sighed.

"Men and their sports," she said.

"Alright you two, no flirting on the job," Dupuis said with a knowing smile.

This time, it was Jaclyn's turn to blush. Tom simply bit his lip.

"I'll go get those things for you, Jaclyn," Tom said before he hurried away, eager to put some distance between himself and Dupuis. Willows simply chuckled and walked to the interrogation room, where he stood outside and watched the prisoner shiver.

Jaclyn looked at Dupuis and wanted to strangle her.

"Don't look at me like that," Dupuis warned with a smile as they walked slowly to the interrogation room. "We can talk about that later."

"Talk about what later?"

"Don't be coy with me. You know exactly what I mean, Snapshot. Young Agent Scouser may have just met you, but I can tell when there are budding sparks. He most definitely finds my top female agent attractive."

If Jaclyn's heart didn't skip a beat earlier, it certainly did now. She tried to hide it.

"How do you know?"

Dupuis looked incredulous.

"Jaclyn, I'm 45 years old. I was married twice. I had two kids by the time I was 21. I know when a young man fancies a young woman, and I could see it in his eyes. And don't for one second think you didn't see it either. Trust me, I can tell that you are excited.

"However," Dupuis lowered her voice, "as your boss, I must warn you about sharing the bed of a foreign intelligence officer."

Jaclyn's jaw dropped.

"Alex! I just met him not five minutes ago!"

"I'm serious, Jaclyn. There are consequences here beyond your oath to serve and Tom's oath to crown and country. I can tell there are sparks between you two, and I'm telling you right now that you must tread carefully. I'm not putting the kibosh on it, I'm telling you to go slow. We may have coddled you for the past 11 years, training you in every form of combat known to man. We may have denied your adolescence by not letting you meet teenage boys for a fling or having your heart broken, but Jaclyn Ann Johnson, you are a very beautiful young woman with a lot to give to a man. I made a promise on your parents' graves that I would look out for you, and yes, that includes this. I know we haven't been close, but I'm telling you that as a friend, don't let your emotions shift your focus."

Dupuis turned and walked toward where Willows was keeping an eye on the two American women, while Jaclyn wrestled with what she had just heard.

She slowly walked to where the intelligence heads stood.

"How do you like our young Agent Scouser, Snapshot?" Willows said through the pipe smoke.

Jaclyn bristled.

"That's classified, sir."

Dupuis stifled a chuckle. Willows gave a "Hmph" before returning his attention to the prisoner.

"So how would you like to proceed, Snapshot?" he said.

"Excuse me, sir?" She seemed baffled by the question.

"As I said last night before, well, you know," he said, causing Jaclyn to stiffen slightly, "you are the lead in this case. You've shown you can handle it. How would you like to proceed with this? My agents are getting nowhere here. Maybe a little American ingenuity and know-how will work wonders."

"David," Dupuis interrupted. "Jaclyn has never done a full-scale interrogation before."

"I'm not going to let that stop me from getting what we need."

"You can't torture him. Congress would frown on it and demand the British turn him loose."

Jaclyn looked aghast at the mere thought of letting this bastard go. She could taste the revulsion rising. She didn't want bureaucracy standing in the way of her investigation. This was a solid lead!

"I'm afraid the Houses of Parliament would agree with Congress," Willows added, "although not about letting him go. They would probably find the nearest gibbet and hang his sand-slinking arse, but only at night and only after giving him a brandy first."

Jaclyn had to grin.

"Whoever said courtesy was lost on the British needs a reality check," she said.

"Courtesy? We bloody well invented it! And speaking of courteous —"

Tom returned with a long-sleeved Oxford from his locker as well as a spare pair of MI5 jogging pants a female agent gave to him for Jaclyn's use.

"I'm sorry it took me so long," he apologized. "I wasn't sure of your size, and I know how bloody picky women are about their clothes —"

"Tom?"

"Yes sir?"

Willows smacked him off the back of the head.

"That was from your father. Stop making a bloody fool of yourself over the girl. Just give her the clothes and be done with it."

Jaclyn couldn't help but bite her lip as Tom sheepishly handed her the garments. She murmured her thanks before she pulled the shirt on. She left it unbuttoned and it hung to mid-thigh, covering her shorts. She slipped the jogging pants on over her shorts.

"I like the fashion statement, Snapshot," Dupuis said. "The new business casual. I'll mention it to Forrister and see if he'll approve of it."

Jaclyn flashed a scathing look at her boss.

"Is there a translator for this guy?" Jaclyn asked.

"He speaks our language pretty well, it seems," Willows said. "But we have an agent who speaks Farsi rather well, so if we need him, we can send him in to assist you."

"And who would that be?"

Tom stepped forward as Willows waved his arm toward him.

Jaclyn suddenly felt warm. Tom smiled.

"You better come in just case he decides to clam up on me," Jaclyn said, opening the door and stepping inside the room. Tom followed.

The room was like an ice box, even colder than the main corridor, Jaclyn thought.

"Enjoying your stay in Camp Antarctica?" Jaclyn taunted. She threw the file on Mohammed onto the tabletop.

The terrorist shooter didn't even glance at the file. Instead, he looked at her with a glare of revulsion. He wanted to spit at her, but it seemed his salivary glands had frozen. He had his arms wrapped around him in a self bear hug.

Jaclyn could tell he was freezing.

"I will not talk," he chattered. "The British men have tried to get me to talk; I certainly will not talk to an American woman. Send in a Muslim Imam, turn up the heat, and I may talk to him. I refuse to say another word to you. This is torture, and you know it, bitch."

Jaclyn kept her enhanced stare upon the terrorist.

"Oh no," she said, taking a few steps toward him. "This isn't torture. This is far from torture. If you want real torture, we could take you outside and submerge you in the Thames, not letting you breathe until we were good and ready to let you. I know that would be real torture for you."

The terrorists' nostrils flared at Jaclyn's remark.

Jaclyn's sneer matched his. She grabbed the chair, spun it around and sat down. Tom kept an eye on the proceedings from the wall.

"We know you killed the people in the car. We have your rocket launcher and your itty bitty prints are all over it."

"You can't prove anything. I was just walking."

"Right, walking through London with a rocket launcher," Tom said. The way he said "launcher" made Jaclyn's insides dance. "I'm sure you were taking it out for coffee."

"Of course you were, Maqil. That's what you want us to think. Of course, rocket launchers aren't like guns: We can't do a paraffin test on your hands to prove it. But we know you did it. Just admit it and we'll raise the temperature on you a little."

The double entendre didn't work. Maqil clammed up.

Jaclyn grabbed the file and opened it. She showed him the picture of Mohammed.

He looked at it as if he never saw him before.

"Get a good look at your boy Kafil. We know he put you up to this," Jaclyn said. She wanted to add, "We know he put you up to targeting me," but she didn't think Dupuis would go for that.

Because that's exactly what Kafil is doing now, Jaclyn thought. *He's made me his newest target. He has somehow found out about me, and now he wants to have me taken out of the equation. He tried to have the taxi driver kill me. Now he wanted to shake me by killing my driver. I'm not going to let him get to me.*

She suddenly felt vulnerable not having the jumpsuit on. She didn't let it show.

"That's not his name," Maqil said.

She didn't let her shock at this revelation show, either.

The terrorist became quiet once again, not looking at either Jaclyn or Tom.

Tom turned the monitor on.

"Let's lower the temperature in Interrogation 1 a few more degrees and see if that loosens his tongue a little bit."

"It won't," Maqil said. "I will not give you any more information. The West will lose, and you infidels will both die. Prepare to meet Allah."

"We'll be sure to send our regards, since you're going to hell," Tom replied, before opening the door. He let Jaclyn leave first before he threw the terrorist a look that would kill.

"Well that was certainly interesting," Dupuis said. "He gave us more information than before."

"So we've found out that our terrorist is not Kafil Abdul Mohammed," Jaclyn said as she paced in front of the three of them. "Just another in a web of lies."

"That doesn't shock me, Snapshot," Willows said, pulling his pipe from his mouth. A curtain of pale gray smoke lingered around his head like a crown. "That's the way terrorists work: They feed misinformation and pull complete 180's and do the opposite."

"I think that before we do anything else," Dupuis interrupted, "is what we're going to do about sleeping arrangements. It's obvious that whoever this terrorist is knows where Jaclyn is staying. We need to arrange for her to move immediately."

"There are plenty of hotels near here," Willows said. "Exquisite rooms, beautiful views of the city."

"I was thinking more along the lines of a safe house, David: A place that is under MI5 surveillance 24-7, with agents checking in with Thames House every half an hour or so."

"There is the new safe house in Islington, sir," Tom said. "Over on Essex Road."

Willows raised his eyebrows a sliver as the young agent spoke his idea.

"How new are we talking about here?" Jaclyn asked.

"Within the past few years, actually," Tom replied. "The building was bought by Her Majesty's Government under a front company. It was supposed to be turned into a church, but that's what the public was told." He gave Jaclyn and Dupuis a wink and a nod.

Jaclyn desperately wanted him to wink at her again. Her temperature rose. She grabbed the hem of the Oxford and surreptitiously fanned herself.

"What's the name of the place?" Dupuis asked.

"The old Carlton Cinema. It became the Mecca Bingo Hall."

Jaclyn grinned.

"That's ingenious," she said.

"We seem to think so," Tom said, his grin matching hers. "We picked that building because we know those militant jihadists would never attack a building with the name 'Mecca' on it, nor would they ever think that we would exploit that fact."

"They are anything but predictable."

"They seem to think that way about us," Dupuis countered.

"How would we get her things out of the Regency and over to Islington," Willows said, "without attracting the terrorists' attention? Surely they are monitoring the location, surely they must know we have the shooter."

"Could we take the Tube to Highbury?" Tom asked. "It's a straight shot right up the Victoria."

"That would get her there," Willows said.

"What about her things?" said Dupuis.

"Oh, don't worry about me," Jaclyn said. She tapped her HUD. "I do have this handy little gadget. I will be able to get my things after the sun goes down."

"Yes, but —" Dupuis began.

"But nothing, Alex. It's what, 2 o'clock right now? I can hang out here for a while."

"That's not what we mean, Snapshot," her boss said. "We need to get your things out of the room without the hotel people knowing we've done it. If the terrorists find out that you've left the hotel, they could torture the concierge and anyone on duty into giving them information on where you went and what car you drove."

Jaclyn grimaced. She hadn't thought of that little issue.

"Oh," she said soberly. "Right."

She sat down, but immediately jumped up as an idea hit her.

"I need a car," she announced. "I need one, like, yesterday."

"What's going on, Jaclyn?"

Jaclyn looked at all three of them.

"I know how I'm going to get my stuff. I'm going to need an assistant, though. I'm not going to drive on the wrong side of the road."

She looked at Tom.

"Care to help a lady?"

Tom grinned before he looked to Willows.

"Would that be okay, sir?"

Willows nodded.

"By all means, Scouser. But make sure you're back here to finish your duties."

"Yes sir."

Tom blushed as he escorted Jaclyn down to the carport; several of Tom's co-workers exclaimed, "Would you like a little something for the weekend there, lad?" Jaclyn didn't follow him immediately. Dupuis handed her a manila envelope as well as her BlackBerry. Jaclyn waved her good byes, then headed off for the carport with Tom.

"What's your plan?" he asked as soon as they were driving on Whitehall a few minutes later.

"Just a hunch I have," Jaclyn replied. "Remember what Alex said a couple of minutes ago: If I were to leave the hotel, there would be some sort of register notice about my checking out. The terrorists can't torture the hotel staff for information on me if the hotel doesn't know I've left, right?"

Tom's eyes lit up as he realized what the blonde-haired American had in mind.

"A little bait and switch, I believe."

"Right. The concierge will see me re-enter, but he won't see me leave."

"Which means he'll think you're still there, at least until the shift changes. How will you pull it off?"

Jaclyn grinned at him.

"With a little American ingenuity and know-how."

Tom smiled as he made his way through Trafalgar Square.

The Regency Hotel, London, England
1 August 2012 — 14.25 GMT/9:25 a.m. ET

Jaclyn explained her plan to Tom as he drove. He, like James, had a lead foot, and it was only luck that they avoided two accidents.

Jaclyn suddenly had the urge to have him pull over so she could drive. She dampened it, though. This whole other side of the road business was not for her.

Once they arrived at the hotel, Jaclyn nodded to Tom. She got out and walked into the hotel. Tom kept his eyes forward, despite every urge to turn his head to the left. He pulled away toward Marylebone. He turned left and made it appear like he was headed back to Thames House.

He ducked down Bingham Place, the road just to the west of Nottingham Place, and pulled up just short of the Regency's other entrance. Jaclyn did not want him seen.

Within 20 minutes, Jaclyn gathered everything she needed. She used her iPad to discover which rooms on the Bingham Place side were empty. It didn't take her long to crack the lock of one on her floor, shove her things inside and bring them to the window. She opened the window and stepped out onto the balcony.

She dug out her crossbow just as Tom stepped out of the car. She tied the handles of her necessities bag and hooked the grappler to the railing. She hit the repel button, and the bag was lowered down to Tom. He was careful not to jostle it too much.

Jaclyn looked back and forth.

No one was coming.

She checked her HUD and detected no one on the rooftops.

Tom unhooked the bag and hit the scale button. The crossbow lifted to Jaclyn's grip.

Much like she did in Soho Square last night, she dropped over the railing to the sidewalk. She released the cable and walked to the passenger side of Tom's diplomatic car. Once settled inside, they left the hotel and made their way to Islington, taking a roundabout way to throw off anyone who could spy on them via CCTV emplacements.

No one would be the wiser.

At least that was what Jaclyn hoped.

As they drove away, Jaclyn turned to what looked like her new partner.

"I take it your mother is handling the funeral arrangements today."

Tom kept his gaze forward, the A503 continuing to stretch out ahead of them.

"Actually, dad took care of it years ago. Smart, actually, if you think about it. He didn't want mum to worry about anything, so everything was taken care of around the time me and my sister were born."

"How many siblings do you have?"

"Three, and all of them are bloody females," he grinned as he said it. Jaclyn smirked. "Chloe, Lien and Maria. Lien is my twin. Chloe is two years older than us, and Maria is two years younger. All three of them went blubbery this morning when mum told them."

Jaclyn noticed his voice went up slightly when he mentioned his sisters' grief.

"How about you?" Jaclyn asked.

"What do you mean?"

"How did you react when you heard your father was killed in action?"

Tom slowly pulled the car over to the curb and put it in park. He turned off the engine.

Jaclyn knew there was a reason why he did this. She was ready for it. Deep inside, she was scared for what he had to say.

"I knew something like this could have happened," Tom said after a few minutes. He had a rapt audience right from the off. "I mean, it can happen on any given day. Being in the service to Her Majesty, it could happen at any given minute. Dad served in the Middle East, and he didn't die then, so I got the feeling he was practically invincible. I joined the service as soon as I could, right out of college three years ago. We lost a couple of agents, but not dad. He was always there.

"Now he isn't."

Jaclyn reached out and rubbed his shoulder.

He was about to break.

"It's okay to cry, Tom. It's okay to grieve." She spoke to him in a loving, caring voice. It sounded incredibly peculiar to her. It was not the voice she had grown to know. It was soothing, like that of a nurse to a patient. It wasn't the voice of a cold-blooded killer. "He died protecting his country. He was about to go home to your mum."

She watched through the HUD as he began to shake. His left hand rose to his face, covering his eyes. Tears fell like rain.

Jaclyn reached for him, her arms wide open. He felt her pull and fell into her warm embrace, separated only by the stick shift. His wet eyes hit her right shoulder. Her hands slowly ran up and down his back, comforting him.

She held him for the longest time.

Chapter 24
The West End, London, England
1 August 2012 — 15.00 GMT/10:00 a.m. ET

Jafar adjusted the memory foam pillows, trying to get comfortable on the couch. He tried to put one under his knees to relieve the pain, but he had no such luck. His upper back was sore, and he was afraid to pinch a nerve in his neck if he somehow twisted his frame the wrong way.

His face turned into an eternal grimace.

How could he get captured like that? he wondered. *Even worse, that woman ran him down, in front of a bunch of infidels! Allah will not look upon him with favor; a woman bested him.*

And not just any woman: it was an American. Another thing for the arrogant Americans to taunt us with.

Jafar breathed heavily through his nose. He felt the air move the hair inside. He lifted his head and scratched his nose, the cartilage moving back and forth. His head dropped back onto the circular pillow, his eyes drifting to the stucco-laced ceiling.

One agent dead, killed by his own hand; Allah will bless him, Jafar thought. *Most of my other agents are out of the country. Allah will bless them, as well.*

But this one captured agent, he will not — unless he keeps his mouth shut.

Jafar managed a smile. He brought his hands together behind his head. He knew that neither the British nor the Americans would use torture methods in order to extract information from the prisoner: Both governments have frowned upon its use. The one thing the jihadists always counted on was the American liberals wanting to protect everyone's rights, especially those captured in a war zone. They didn't allow them to be tortured.

Of course, if we were to capture a dirty American, we wouldn't hesitate to turn the screws to them. That is where the West will lose this war, he thought, turning his head in toward the back of the couch. *They do not have the stomach to vigorously interrogate our operatives, like we do to them. The American government and their soft, human rights activists don't understand what it takes. Winning a war takes treachery and using methods not necessarily approved by civilized people. If it was they facing the prospect of us torturing their citizens, though, I wonder what they would say. I bet they would cry for their government to allow torture.*

Besides, they won't get anything out of my agent. I trained him myself. He is impervious to interrogation. He is above every method of torture, since I put him through every type of torture known to man. The hills of Afghanistan continue to shudder under his screams.

Jafar cursed. He still could not believe his agent was unable to sacrifice himself before the American caught up with him.

That is why I gave them the cyanide! There were reasons why I did that! They were to go to Allah of their own volition!

You are worrying too much, Jafar.

"Oh great, not you. I don't need you right now," Jafar said to the ceiling.

The voice chuckled deeply. It seemed to rattle the walls, the table, the laptop upon it.

That is what you think. You are alone in the world right now, Jafar. You need someone to help you maintain order in the world you wish to create. I will help you.

Jafar looked to the ceiling as if it had two heads. He immediately shot up from the couch and pointed his finger upward.

"You?! You wish to help me? Don't make me laugh. You mock Allah. You mock me. You do not believe the way I do. You do not believe my plans will work. Go away."

That is where you are wrong. The voice sounded as if it were circling the couch, reverberating off the walls, tiptoeing across the floor. It was incredibly deep when it became angry, but this time, it sounded like it was wind blowing across the desert after a storm.

Jafar felt his pulse slow. He lay back down. He felt as if he were lighter than air.

I want to see you achieve victory over the infidels. They are the ones who mock Allah, not I.

"You said that I think I am Allah."

Who? Me? I never said anything of the sort. If I said anything of the sort, then I apologize for making it seem like I did. Forgive me. *Allahu Akbar.* And all that.

Jafar narrowed his eyes. I am not convinced.

"You sound like one of them, you know."

One of whom?

Jafar's lip curled into a sneer. His anger rose. Electricity zipped through his body.

"One of those ugly Americans! One of those bastards who we torture, those blasphemies of Allah who run around believing they are better than Muslims. They say 'and all that' and 'just saying.'"

But unlike the Americans, I'm going to tell you what to do.

Jafar was slightly intrigued. He had thought out every little thing, and every little thing had gone correctly — until now. What happened today was an unforeseen development.

"I don't need you to tell me what to do. I know what to do. I need to grind the West down under my heel. These Britons and Americans think they are going to get something out of my man. They are severely mistaken."

And what if they somehow do get something out of him?

"Impossible."

This woman may do it, Jafar. Like I said — this woman may kill you. She has escaped death several times. She may prove more cunning than you have given her credit. And you have said that you've seen her somewhere before. Maybe you should do some more research before you jump the gun about this.

Jafar bit his lip. *The voice is right*, he thought, trying his best to keep the thought hidden from the despicable voice. *I have seen her before, but I can't remember where.*

The terrorist stood, inched around the table and began to pace, his hands set behind his back.

Think, Jafar, think! he told himself. *Allah help me. She is familiar. Where have you seen her before?*

The frustration showed in Jafar's face. Without a second thought, he walked to the bathroom and began to whack his forehead against the molding until he saw stars.

Instead of stars, though, he couldn't see. His vision became fuzzy, as if he had a migraine developing.

And then it hit him.

He looked toward the empty magazine rack just opposite the toilet; it belonged to the flat's last occupants, but they failed to take it with them. In it had been various magazines, all with high gloss covers, many depicting gorgeous women — even a devout Muslim like Jafar could not deny they were beautiful in the face, but they wore too much make-up, and many needed a burqa — on them. Fashion models from the West, all of them. There was one, though, who stuck out because of her sunglasses. He looked at the wording of that one, and it said the model was blind. At first, he thought it was a publicity stunt, but as he flipped through and found the story, he recalled reading she wanted to enter public service.

Jafar's eyes, though blurry, were wide. His smile matched it.

Tracking down terrorists was a public service to the infidels, he thought. It was, however, a pain in the arse to terrorists.

179

Jafar sprang toward his laptop, feeling no pain in his head and knees. The blood rushed in his ears. He had a lead. He was on to something.

The voice didn't bother him. For once today, things were going the way Allah wanted them to go.

He quickly executed a Google search for blind fashion models, and his search came back rather quickly. The first entry, cosmopolitan.com, had the name Jaclyn Johnson next to blind model in bold print. He opened the link and as soon as the page loaded, he saw the cover model's flawless face staring at him.

Jafar quickly opened the file from yesterday. He scanned his eyes over the image of the woman sitting at Bobby Moore's statue, then ran the woman's Cosmopolitan cover photo through the facial recognition system.

Within five seconds, a dialogue box with "Central Intelligence Agency: Classified Information. Access Denied" popped up on the screen.

Oil strike, he thought. His grin was malicious. Every single one of his teeth showed.

"I knew I've seen her before!" he shouted.

He immediately closed the window, not letting the Americans detect even the slightest breach of security.

"A major fashion model is an undercover government agent. How ingenious. But, alas, I know their secret now," Jafar said, still grinning. He leaned back

You may know their secret, Jafar, the voice said, but do not forget that this woman, as I've said before, has eluded death and tracked down one of your operatives.

"She is blind," Jafar reasoned. "Take away her sight, and she will be vulnerable."

Keep telling yourself that.

"Be quiet. I must now use this information to my advantage. I must make another broadcast to the world and expose the Americans for their folly."

Besides, he thought, *no woman would ever take me down. I can remove her from the equation simply by mentioning her. The weak-willed Americans would never want to see a woman hurt in the crossfire. They would want to protect her and remove her from the situation. They'll send in a man to try to take care of me.*

Jafar clapped his hands together and got up to fetch his balaclava. He had a message to record, and he was still not ready to reveal his true identity to anyone outside of his circle.

Chapter 25
MI5 Safe House, Islington, London, England
1 August 2012 — 20.51 GMT/3:51 p.m. ET

Jaclyn made herself at home in the Carlton Cinema. She had been in Islington for about five hours — she did not want Tom to leave, but he kept his word to Sir David — and was thoroughly bored. She caught a little nap, though, supplementing last night's nightmarish sleep.

Her dreams were not of Nigel's death this time: They were of her future. Tom's face was prominent in her dreams.

Recalling them, Jaclyn blushed furiously. She wiped a slight bead of sweat that caked her forehead. She felt sweat drip down her spine. It was a steamy night in London, that was true, but in her dreams, London's dusk was bitter cold in comparison.

She walked barefoot to the back window, looking to the northwest. Through her HUD, she could see the floodlights of Emirates Stadium glowing off in the distance. The Olympic Committee had awarded some of the football matches to the Emirates after another stadium pulled out of the competition a few years ago.

The HUD filtered the light, but at the same time, it detected an incoming call on her cell phone. She did not recognize the number. She debated, very briefly, sending the call to voice mail.

She took a slight breath.

She pressed receive.

"This is Jaclyn."

"It's Tom."

Jaclyn's heart skipped a beat.

"Hey," she said, smiling.

"You may want to turn the telly on. We've received intelligence that BBC One has something coming on which concerns you."

She froze. He sounded pensive. She had only known Agent Scouser for a few hours, but she had a bead on him rather quickly. Other than that brief spell in the car — she could still feel his tears — he seemed to be a very strong person, and one that was not scared easily.

"Why? What did they get?"

"Only your bloody identity, Snapshot."

Jaclyn gasped, then briskly walked to the television. She flipped it on and saw a commercial playing.

"How did they get it?"

"Apparently the terrorists sent a digital recording to the BBC a few hours ago," Tom said. "They didn't look at it until about half an hour ago and after they disseminated it, they paid a call to us. Sir David told them to censor it. He's on the phone with Dupuis, and I'm sure she will be on the phone with the president the second she hangs up."

"That wouldn't surprise me. Damn it, how did the terrorists find out?"

"Your guess is as good as mine, Jaclyn. It's not like anyone can break through the CIA's encryption, nor can anyone break through MI5's. We'd be on their arses quicker than they could blink."

Jaclyn allowed herself a grin, despite the situation.

He is so cute, she thought.

There was silence as the BBC broke in:

"We will get you back to the Emirates for the second half of Spain and Portugal in a few moments, but first breaking news to our desks: The terrorists reportedly behind the Olympic attacks say they have only just begun, but the balaclava-wearing man has called out the American agent assisting Her Majesty's Secret Service."

The screen flicked to a shot of the terrorist, Mohammed, sitting in his darkened flat, a balaclava covering the bottom of his face. He spoke perfect English with a British accent, just like the last time. Jaclyn did not let that fact escape her.

"I know who you are —" A censor tone covered her name. "I know you are an American secret agent, and you are everything wrong with America: A woman in a position of power. I sneer at you —. You will not have a chance to find me, because I know how the American mind works. They will pull you, a weak woman, before you get the chance to strike. Your American handlers will do this. I know they will. They are predictable."

I will not allow them to pull me, Jaclyn thought. *This is my case. Alex better not pull me.*

"Jaclyn, are you listening to this?"

She nodded, forgetting Tom could not see her.

She heard every word, every accented syllable as if the terrorist screamed it at her from a foot away. If she had been deaf, she could have heard every word and then wished for her ears to shrivel off. Mohammed's inflammatory words left her speechless.

"This American bitch thinks she can get away with this utmost of treacheries," Mohammed said. "Allah will not let her get away with it, because no woman should be in a position of power. A woman's place is a step behind her man. The West has become too lenient in this, and Allah will remember your reluctance to follow Him! He will make you all bow to me as I will level London, starting with," the transmission's audio cut out as his mouth moved, disguising his next target, "and I will kill —. I killed her British partner last night. I will kill her before I move on to destroy Washington, D.C. You have been warned, America. I suggest you make things right with Allah before you all burn."

The video cut out abruptly, leaving Jaclyn staring at the television, the BlackBerry at her ear. Tom's voice was dim compared to what she just heard the terrorist say: He had killed Nigel, and she was next on his list.

He was calling her out.

She exhaled through her nose, her face frozen not in fear, but in intense concentration. If she could spout flames from her nose, she would have incinerated the safe house. If her eyes had pigment in the pupils, there would have been murder seen inside them.

If he wants a battle, she thought, *then he's got one.*

I just have to be in the country to give him one.

"Jaclyn, are you there?"

Tom's voice shook her from her vengeful reverie. She breathed as she turned away from the television. She hit the power button on the remote.

"Yeah, I'm here, Scouser."

"This bastard is as mad as a hatter, Jaclyn. Blimey, this situation is kicking off now, especially if he's coming for you."

"I'm not worried, Tom. If he wants me, he's going to have a fight on his hands. I'm not easy to kill."

Jaclyn paced. She took several feet at a stride.

"I mean that Sir David and Dupuis are probably going to pull you," Tom said softly. "They aren't going to want to lose you over this useless tosser."

"Tom," Jaclyn said forcefully, "I did not get into the clandestine service to be coddled by my superiors, or by men stronger than me. I got into the service to bring terrorists to justice, either capturing or killing them outright. I don't run from threats. If this fucker wants to try to kill me, he's going to have to find me first."

"And you're holed up in the middle of bloody Islington."

"But no one knows where I am except you, Sir David and Dupuis, right?"

"Of course not. No one will ever find out where you are, love. Not from me, not from anyone here."

Jaclyn closed her eyes and smiled.

"I know, Tom. I need to get out of here and find this bastard. Have we made any progress with our captive?"

Tom laughed.

"Not at all; this guy is shut up tighter than a nun's arse. He's not saying a word about Mohammed."

Jaclyn grimaced.

"We need to drag it out of him, and fast."

"We can't torture him, Jaclyn. That's against the rules."

"Fuck the rules, Tom. This guy has information that we can use to bring not only him but his boss to justice."

"Jaclyn —"

"No, Tom," Jaclyn sharply cut him off, "I know what you're going to say. Our governments agreed not to torture prisoners of war. 'It's the humane way to be,' they say. Fuck that, Scouser. They are sitting up on Capitol Hill or on Whitehall, so fucking far away from the bombs going off and from the bloodshed, sitting on the fat campaign donations that protect them from all that. And here we are, risking our asses for those pompous jackasses, and now the terrorists are making it personal. To tell you the truth, Tom, I'm a little tired of playing nice and by the rules when someone targets me."

"They always make it personal, though," Tom replied. "It's what we're trained to be prepared for. And I know how you feel: I don't like it when my family is targeted, either. Look what happened to my old man last night."

That sobered her. She stopped her pacing and tried to say something. Her lips moved, but nothing came out. Not that she had anything to say that would have been appropriate at this particular moment.

"I know," she said softly.

"I'm not looking for revenge."

"You should be."

"But that would be against my oath," Tom replied. "We're not in the revenge business. We seek out and take out terrorists, yes, but we don't get revenge on them."

We let the presidents take care of that, Jaclyn thought.

Her HUD flashed an incoming call. She checked the number, and immediately her chest tightened.

It was Dupuis.

She tried to breathe normally as she brought the phone to her ear.

"Tom, let me call you back; Alex is calling."

"I'll be here. Call me if you need anything."

"I will."

Jaclyn pressed end, then heard the phone ringing. She pressed send and brought the phone back to her right ear.

"Hey, Chief."

"Did you see the broadcast, Jaclyn?"

"Yeah, I did. Tom called and let me know it was coming on."

"What do you think about it?"

"He's fucking with the wrong agent, Alex. No one makes me a target, especially not a sexist camel jockey like him."

"Completely understandable. That's why we're pulling you from this assignment, Jaclyn."

Jaclyn stiffened. She was ready for this; she knew there was the possibility of this happening. But now that it was reality, she didn't understand it. Nor did she really want to. She just wanted to shoot this terrorist and end the mission.

"Why?" she asked.

"The president feels it to be best," Dupuis replied. "You're too good of an agent to lose to a threat like this."

Jaclyn strenuously objected and read Dupuis the riot act, much in the same tone she used when she issued the same argument to Tom only a few minutes ago.

"And that is reason number two, Snapshot. You are taking this threat on your life too personally."

"Like you wouldn't do the same thing, Alex? What if you were the one the terrorist targeted? What if it was one of your kids, Alex?"

"I would step back and let the professionals handle it."

"Bull shit, Alex. You're a mother, that is your profession. And I am a professional: I'm a professional terrorist killer. Not letting me go after this coward and show him just exactly what it takes to kill someone when you're looking right in their eyes would be a waste of my training."

"Jaclyn, I know you want to do this, and I don't want to recall you, but this is coming higher than me. I have no choice but to follow Forrister's orders."

"Forrister can shove his fucking orders," Jaclyn shouted.

"Jaclyn," Dupuis said a little more forcefully, "I'm sending MI5 agents to retrieve you. You're on a plane in two hours."

Jaclyn's head swam. *This can't be happening*, she thought. *I need to stay here. I need to get this fucker. I know too much about this case; another agent will need days to catch up. If I'm not here, it will give Mohammed carte blanche to attack this city. I can't let him attack London any more. And if my own government won't help me find this asshole, I'm going to have to do it by myself.*

She steeled herself for what she was about to do next. She couldn't believe she was going to do it, let alone say it.

"I won't be here, Alex. Don't bother sending them."

"What do you mean, Snapshot?"

"I mean what I say I mean. I won't be here, so don't bother trying to find me."

The silence on the other end roared in her ears. Jaclyn couldn't make heads or tails of it, but she was afraid she had knocked Dupuis for a loop.

"You can't be serious, Jaclyn."

"I am dead serious, Alex."

"What you're talking about is treason. Treason, Jaclyn! Think good and hard about your next course of action. It could mean your freedom."

Jaclyn knew it was a stalling tactic, giving MI5 enough time to get to Islington.

"I know what it means, Alex, but I feel that it's the right thing to do. I'm sorry. I quit."

She didn't even wait for Dupuis to reply. She hung up the phone.

It shouldn't have come down to this, she thought as the tears ran down her cheeks. *My government, the group that trained me and supported me through the most awful period in my life, should have my back.*

She quickly took a deep breath and calmed herself. She looked at the digital time read-out on her HUD. She figured she had a good 20 minutes before MI5 started crawling through Islington looking for her, especially if she was going to make good on her promise.

She decided she had to make a quick getaway, but with no car and too much to carry, she would abandon her old life here and now. She would only carry a couple of magazines. She took no more than two of her Walthers to protect herself. She couldn't wear the jumpsuit 24/7, mainly because she would stick out and because the sight of it would be a major tip off to authorities. Hanging up on Dupuis like that, and especially her last words to her, meant she was now a traitor to the United States, an enemy of the state. She wouldn't have doubted that Dupuis would call Scotland Yard and give them every detail on her that she could remember. The mere thought of it made Jaclyn want to cry again, but she did her best to hold the tears off until she could leave Carlton Cinema and Islington as a whole. She knew that every police officer would be on the lookout for her; she wouldn't have been surprised if they put the meter maids on her case. She couldn't wear anything recognizable. She decided to leave the iPad and the BlackBerry; they could be traced and lead authorities right to her location. She also replaced her HUD with a pair of contact lenses, and she took a pair of

Ray Bans. She would literally fight blind if she had to; she didn't know if there was a tracking device inside the Foster Grants.

Jaclyn stuffed everything she could carry into a duffel, then accessed the iPad. She called up the schematics of the building and found a drop shaft that would allow her to escape the building undetected. It led to a series of tunnels from World War II which led into Highbury, not that far from where she now stood. If anyone knew about the tunnels, they would capture her. She hoped the youth of Britain — Tom included — had no idea about them.

She erased the browsing history on the iPad and grabbed the duffel while walking to the drop shaft. She hooked the grappler of her crossbow onto a circular piece of metal, then pressed a button as she stepped into the dark nothingness.

Jaclyn became a rogue agent.

***

Without lights or sirens, agents from Her Majesty's Secret Service pulled up in front of Carlton Cinema. The black car was out of place on Essex Road.

The agents sauntered onto the sidewalk and up the steps as if they belonged there. They slipped inside the building and looked all around for the American. They found her BlackBerry and her iPad, as well as the tools of the trade that she used the other night.

They couldn't find her, though. That concerned and baffled them.

They had missed her by 10 minutes.

The lead agent called in to Thames House.

"Sir, the American isn't here. We've checked the loo and under the bed. The bird isn't here."

"Check the Tube and the Essex Road station," Willows said. "I'll let the CIA know that she is missing."

While Willows called Dupuis — "I already spoke with her, David; she's gone," Dupuis said, "and now I have to call President Forrister and tell him his best agent has committed treason." — the agents on scene scoured Islington, looking for the rogue agent. They checked the Overground station as well as every yard on Essex Road. They received assurances from the priests at St. Paul's that she wasn't there, even though they didn't exactly have to tell them if she had requested sanctuary.

They even checked the Highbury & Islington Underground station, hoping to catch her impersonating a drunken hobo.

187

And while Dupuis was on the phone with Forrister, the IOC president met with the media, imploring the terrorists to leave the Games alone. There was no mention in his speech about Jaclyn. The fact the Americans had a rogue agent in England didn't even register to him.

She wasn't even news to him.

But in America, she would be known in every household by the time early risers were slurping coffee.

They would brand her as a traitor.

Eric Forrister didn't have time for coffee this morning. He hadn't slept the night before, and he was certainly irritable. Dupuis' message disturbed him. Hearing that his best agent had gone rogue did not sit well with the president.

He felt grateful to the BBC. The "Bastion of British Journalism" came through and did not allow Jaclyn's name to venture upon their airwaves. He doubted any of the others — Al-Jazeera, for one — would do that. He made a mental note to send a letter to London thanking them for their cooperation when everything settled down.

But as he opened *The New York Times*, his heart sank. The headline, "American agent turns back on USA" ran under the masthead.

He quickly thought things through: If the BBC censored Jaclyn's name, and the American networks didn't say anything about it — he made sure someone watched all the networks last night — then who did?

Forrister came to a quick conclusion.

There was a leak in the White House. There had to be. No one other than a select few knew about Jaclyn's sudden disappearance. Now everyone knew, thanks to a blabbermouth in his administration.

This concerned him.

"Have you heard from her, Alex?" Forrister said when he called Dupuis back. Bennett sat off to the side.

"No sir, I haven't," Dupuis replied. "She's been missing for a little more than half a day. She hasn't been seen, which means she's laying low. It's what any agent would do in such a situation."

"She's a traitor, Alex," Bennett said. "She probably has ties to al-Zawahiri that we haven't even thought of." He was pacing in front of the president's desk. Unlike Forrister, who looked at his chief of staff like he had two heads, he drank coffee and looked as though he had slept soundly the night before. He had no concerns for the missing CIA agent.

In fact, he looked simply jovial at the prospects of Jaclyn's treachery. He was going into spin control for the president.

"Now you're just talking nonsense," Dupuis said. "I know Jaclyn, and I've known her since she was a teenager. Jaclyn Johnson is an All-American girl. Besides, her parents were killed on September 11. I began training her a week later. Think about what you're saying: How could she have ties to al-Qaeda?"

"Exactly," Forrister said. "Dick, Alex is right. You're talking nonsense. Shut up."

"Mr. President, I must object. I'm the only one thinking clearly. I'm the only one in this room and in this conversation who does not have a personal tie to this traitor. I think both of you are a little too close to her to make a rational decision."

Forrister looked at his chief of staff and wanted to punch him dead in the face.

"Dick, I would sit down and shut up right now if I were in your shoes. I haven't had coffee yet, and you're really close to pissing me off."

"Mr. President," Dupuis said as Bennett finally sat down opposite the president, "Dick is right about one thing: I've known Jaclyn since she was a young girl. This is her first mission outside of the country. I can tell you that she has to be scared to death. In fact, I know she is: I could hear it in her voice last night. She's afraid the country has turned its back on her by recalling her. I told you that it was the wrong decision ordering her home."

Bennett tutted. Forrister waited for the Director of the CIA to finish.

"Any agent that we send in now would be so far behind that we'd finish dead last, and all of London would be wiped all off the map. That would not look good for any of us. Jaclyn should have been allowed to stay on the job."

"And have her killed by this lunatic?" Bennett said.

"Why Dick, are you showing compassion for the CIA?" Dupuis said. "I never would have expected it from you."

"We already have many Americans dead in London, Alex," Bennett said, his face flush with anger at Dupuis' thrust to the gut. "I don't want to see any more Americans dead, not even from the CIA, as corrupt as you folks are."

"Dick," Forrister warned.

"Eric, the CIA has no regard for laws. This rogue agent is going to violate every treaty and law we have on the books, and she's going to make this country look incredibly bad in the international community."

"Worse than it was before Eric took over the White House, Dick? You're sounding like a Republican now," Dupuis said, hiding her smile with the phone.

"Worse," Bennett replied, obviously not catching Dupuis' sarcasm. "Eric, we need to reel this organization in and make sure they play by the rules."

"We?" Forrister asked. "I didn't know 'we' was a euphemism for us. My administration will handle this, Dick."

190

"I hope so. I wouldn't want to leak it to the press that you're not handling this properly."

The Oval Office became deadly silent. In London, Dupuis' eyes widened slightly.

The look on Bennett's face was that of a pompous know-it-all, one without a care for anyone else but himself. At that moment, Forrister knew Dupuis was correct: Bennett was looking like a Republican in Democrat's clothing.

It took Forrister long enough to realize it. He didn't know why he hadn't noticed it before.

"You leaked it to the press corps," he said. He was sobered with the realization.

Bennett's shit-eating grin betrayed him.

"Of course I did, Eric. The public has a right to know when it is betrayed by one of its own."

"The public had no idea what Jaclyn was doing on their behalf," the president said, raising his voice. "They had no idea what she did in Boston. Her missions are classified; they had no idea Jaclyn existed until this morning. If anyone wasn't playing by the rules, Dick, it was you."

"Fuck you, Eric. You are too close to the situation. I told it to Sarah, and I told it to you: you need to reel the CIA in before they fuck this up. I reeled them in last night. I leaked it. You should thank me by kissing the ground I walk on."

Forrister was on his feet in half a second. His hands were on his desk.

Murderous intent was in his eyes.

"You're lucky I don't have you executed for treason, Dick."

Bennett stood and put his hands on Forrister's desk, too.

"I did it to save your presidency and Sarah's legacy. That's not treason. The Republicans are screaming for your removal, and with the election coming up, we need to get those undecided voters on our side."

"It isn't your side any longer, Dick. You're fired."

"Fired?" Bennett was incredulous.

"That's right, you're fired. Pack your shit and get out of here. Your security clearance is revoked. The Secret Service will see your ass out of here."

"You can't fire me, Eric. I quit!"

"Good, that will make it a lot easier on the unemployment line," the president shot back.

Bennett walked out of the Oval Office, slamming the door in his vicious wake.

"Are you still there, Alex?" Forrister said as he recovered.

"Yes sir, I heard every word. I've had a bad feeling about Bennett for a long time. He has not been a fan of the CIA, nor have I been a fan of his. He's lucky I didn't have Jaclyn fly back to D.C. and shoot him that day."

Forrister grinned.

"Let's not throw that idea away yet. This is at a crisis stage, Alex. We need to fix this, and we need to fix this yesterday."

"I couldn't agree more. Eric, we have been betrayed — no, you have been betrayed — by someone close to you, someone you trusted. The country is going to look to you for leadership. We can spin this your way and keep Bennett's camp off the air and out of the papers, but first, we need to help Jaclyn."

"She's gone rogue, Alex. She's completely off the grid now. The British said she left her BlackBerry and her iPad behind in the safe house. There's no way to get in contact with her. I wouldn't even know how to get in contact with her."

"There is always a way. I'm about to head to Thames House to talk to Sir David. We can't let Jaclyn operate without some semblance of support."

Forrister sighed. He leaned over his desk.

"No, we can't. The only question is 'How do we do it?' The terrorist must know that Jaclyn has gone rogue by now; hell, half of the free world knows by now. Only the west coast and Hawaii don't know. Maybe Australia doesn't know, either."

"We don't have to announce it to everyone that we're going to help her. But Eric, you have to agree with me on this: We owe it to her to give our support. She thinks we're against her. We need to clear her mind of doubt. We need to give her the green light to go after this guy."

Forrister turned and looked out at the South Lawn, leaning against the wall. He stared out at the greenery, the sunlight reflecting off the grass. He didn't shield his eyes.

"Mr. President, are you there?"

Forrister didn't answer. He was deep in thought. He had to make a decision that he knew both sides of the aisle would criticize.

At that moment, he didn't care what Congress thought.

It was the moment of truth.

Chapter 27
Islington, London, England
2 August 2012 — 17.20 GMT/12:20 p.m. ET

Jaclyn spent the night in the subterranean tunnels underneath Highbury, sleeping soundlessly as soon as she finally dozed off. She spent a good portion of the night crying and wondering how everything happened, finally allowing herself to fall asleep, content in knowing that no one – not even Tom, not even Alex – could find her here. She slept as peacefully as she had since before she left New York.

But without her BlackBerry or anything to tell her the time, she was lost as to how much time had elapsed since she had left the Islington safe house, and more importantly – since she had last eaten.

Just thinking about it made her stomach rumble with hunger.

"I need to find a way out of here," she said, her voice echoing off the wet, gray concrete. She wasn't panicking, but her stomach certainly was.

She quickly changed her clothes, slipping out of the shorts she wore all day yesterday and put on the MI5 running pants Tom had given her at Thames House; it was all she had that was somewhat comfortable and didn't smell. She slid a Walther into the waist holster she had worn and slipped it around her body. She left her other belongings in the tunnel, confident no one, human or animal, would disturb them. She put a pair of Ray Bans on; they would be adequate to protect her eyes.

"Now would be a great time to have my iPad," she said. "I have absolutely no idea where in London I am, and I don't know where I can eat without drawing attention to myself."

She emerged from below the ground near the tennis courts on Highbury Grove. Trees and bushes kept the entrance well hidden, so she had no doubts she would be able to find it again. She pushed herself up and came up feeling fresh air on her face.

She headed south on Highbury Grove, careful not to attract any unnecessary attention. She chose to jog slowly.

A cruiser passed by just as slow. Jaclyn's heart sped up, and not because she was running. It made a turn. Jaclyn was able to breathe again. She checked to make sure the cops were not spying on her. She turned her head and looked over her shoulder every so often, making sure no one followed her.

For a split second, she felt like the terrorist she had caught yesterday morning.

How had everything gone south so quickly? she thought.

She turned left onto St. Paul's Road and found a pizza place not too far from the Highbury & Islington Underground and National Rail station. She ordered a turkey sandwich — she called it a turkey grinder much like Seattle residents call them, only to get a blank stare in return from the proprietor — with a little bit of lettuce, tomatoes, pickles and black olives and a water on the side, before she sat down facing the door. She began to dig in when the door opened.

Her entire body froze.

Tom stood there, looking at her with a smile on his face. Jaclyn, disarmed by it, couldn't help but match it. Her eyes, hidden by her Ray Bans, began to water.

The MI5 agent walked up to the counter and ordered a cold meatball sub with shredded mozzarella and a Coke before he slid into the booth, sitting opposite from her.

"We've been looking for you all bloody night and day," he said. "Where have you been?"

His tone put Jaclyn immediately on the defensive.

"If you're going to talk down to me like I'm a little girl, then you might as well leave me alone, Tom," she replied.

Tom took it like a slap to the face.

"There are a lot of people concerned about you, me included. Sir David is barking, Director Dupuis has been at Thames House for the past two hours trying to get your credentials reinstated. Scotland Yard has been on the lookout for you, but not to arrest you."

"Alex has been trying to get my credentials reinstated?" Jaclyn said, disbelieving.

"Yes ma'am, and she's making sure it's kept quiet, too. No idea what that's about; you'd think the president would want to back you after all the shit that's been said about you since the sun rose over Manchester."

Jaclyn didn't hear a word. She was stunned and she wanted to cry. She sat silently for a few moments while Tom fetched his own meal.

When he returned, Jaclyn asked, "So what does that mean?"

"What it means, little lady, is that you're in the clear," he said before bringing half of the sandwich to his mouth. He chewed and swallowed a minute later. Jaclyn nibbled at her own meal. "Director Dupuis has cleared up the misunderstanding."

He reached into his pocket and pulled out Jaclyn's BlackBerry. He slid it over to her.

"You'll find that she has sent you a text message." He continued to scarf his food down while Jaclyn anxiously opened the text. Her meal lay forgotten. Tom reached over and grabbed the long pickle spear resting near the potato chips.

She scrolled through the message:

JJ, Meet me in St J's Park behind Number 10. On the Island. Have things to discuss with you regarding situation at hand. Will be there at 0100. Respond promptly. AD

Jaclyn looked up and nearly dropped her BlackBerry on her sandwich.

"So are you going to respond to her, or should I tell her you're going to be a stubborn little witch and not show?" Tom said as he finished the first half of his sandwich and immediately began the second.

Jaclyn threw a potato chip at him.

She quickly tapped out a reply in the affirmative.

"Now," Tom said as she put the BlackBerry down, "where were you staying last night? There aren't that many places to sleep that we don't have our eyes upon. We couldn't find you at all."

"That's because I didn't want to be found. I'm sure you could understand the predicament I was in."

Tom nodded.

"But now that you are fully in the graces of the good guys and gals, you can stay at the safe house once again."

Jaclyn's mouth dropped.

"Are you serious?"

"I am very serious. Sir David wants to keep you as safe as possible. I can take you there as soon you're done eating." Tom brought the sandwich back to his mouth.

"I would have to get my things from my hiding spot."

"I can drive you over to wherever you were hiding and help you. How much do you have?"

"Just a few things."

"I can see you're wearing the pants I gave you."

Jaclyn nodded.

"You wear them well."

The flirtatious tension was palpable.

Jaclyn shook her blonde hair back over her shoulders.

"I can't wait to get back to the safe house," she said just as Tom took another bite. "I feel so disgustingly dirty that I think I am going to shower for at least an hour."

Tom choked.

"Are you alright?"

"Yeah, I'll be fine. Just swallowed wrong," he said as soon as he recovered.

Jaclyn grinned inwardly. She could see that he was sweating a bit, and she knew it wasn't from the stifling air wafting into the restaurant.

Chapter 28
The West End, London, England
2 August 2012 — 17.35 GMT/12:35 p.m. ET

Sweat poured down Jafar's face. *Iftar* was nearing. The Afghani was starving.

The only thing that kept his mind off food were his prayers to Allah. He knelt on the memory foam cushions, giving his knees some semblance of comfort. He faced the southeast as he always did. His mouth moved silently, his soundless words touching the ears of his god.

A shrill ringing interrupted his meditation. His head popped up several inches, but his eyes did not open.

My landline phone has the most annoying ring, he thought.

The phone rang twice more before it went to voice mail. He completely forgot that he had a landline phone. Whenever some called him, it was on his cell phone.

Who has my landline number? he thought.

But thought caught up with him very quickly.

He stifled a wince.

Allah, I did not mean for the distraction to keep me from you, he prayed. *Forgive me, merciful Allah.*

He repeated this prayer rapidly until he heard his voice mail's speaker blare throughout the house:

"Brother Jafar, it is me, Yusuf," the voice mail said.

Jafar's eyes widened. He recognized the voice. He didn't need to hear who it belonged to.

"I am still in the country."

"What?!" Jafar screamed, completely breaking his meditation.

Using more speed than he usually mustered coming off the prayer cushions, Jafar sprang for the phone. He picked it up and turned off the voice mail as soon as the feedback squeal met his ears.

"What in the devil are you still doing here?" Jafar demanded. "You were supposed to be out of the country three days ago!"

"I am sorry for disobeying you, brother Jafar, but I felt my place was by your side, to carry out the will of Allah."

Jafar grinned. *He is honest and grovels well*, he thought. *Allah shall reward him for both.*

He wiped the grin from his face and let his ire take over.

"You have broken Allah's commandments, and you have broken my sacred communion with Allah!" Jafar roared. "You must pay for these breaches of etiquette!"

"I will, brother Jafar; I will do as Allah commands me to do," Yusuf pleaded.

"Double your prayers! Allah wishes it to be so!"

"Yes, brother Jafar!"

Jafar breathed into the phone. He tried to walk away from the wall phone. He needed a longer cord. He bit back a curse.

"Where are you now, Yusuf?" he asked.

"I am not far from you. I am at King's Cross."

"Take the next train and come to me. We will eat *Iftar* together, and we will speak of what is next to come in Allah's Grand Scheme."

"I will leave right now."

"Yes, do hurry," Jafar said. "You should be honored that I have invited you to join me as I break my fast."

"Oh yes, I am, brother Jafar. Most honored to be looked upon by Allah's most faithful and unerring servant."

Without saying good bye, Jafar hung up the phone. Only then, with the adrenaline of annoyance leaving him, did he feel the pain in his knees surge through him. His eyes widened in pain.

Luckily, his couch was there to break his fall. He clattered to the cushions.

"I'll just wait here for Yusuf to come and help me up," he said, feeling the pain slowly ebb. "Yusuf can fetch my meal. It is his fault that I am in pain. All his fault. If he had left the country as he was supposed to —"

Then he would not have been able to help you with the next stage of the plan.

Jafar's mouth opened.

You thought of it earlier, Jafar. Don't pretend you didn't see his usefulness as you conversed with him just now. You are only complaining because you are in pain. And I told you long ago that knee replacement surgery works wonders. But did you listen? No, you did not.

"Oh, be quiet. Allah commands you," Jafar said, but it lacked the punch he used with Yusuf.

As you wish, musahib.

Jafar did not hear the bodiless voice properly. He groaned as he tried to get up. The joints popped as he finally was able to stand up. He was surprised his tendinitis had yet to flare up.

"You are saying he should be in on the plan, then."

Of course I am. Allah brought him back to you. You would be most unwise not to see his arrival as a blessing from Allah. You should utilize him in any way you see fit. Or you could continue the prayers that were interrupted and ask Allah what role He sees you using Yusuf in. Just a suggestion.

Jafar's interest was now piqued. His right eyebrow rose as he considered the voice's proposition.

"I shall do that," he said, walking to the window and easing himself down onto his prayer cushions.

He clasped his hands and began to mumble once again, calling upon his god to bless him with the wisdom to continue His noble work.

"Allah, inspire me. Let me know your purpose. Let me know what it is you want me to do with my operative."

He remained kneeling for several minutes until he recalled what he read in the Telegraph earlier today. His eyes flew open as dawning comprehension came upon his mind.

"Yes," he thought. "That would be perfect. I just need to get Yusuf to agree to it — or I could command him to do it. Yes. I could command him. Allah would be most displeased if he did not perform this task."

He laughed hard.

Are you sure that is what you want him to do, Jafar? Or is it what Allah wants him to do?

"What do you mean?" Jafar asked, not turning his head.

It's quite simple, Jafar. Is this Allah's will, or your own will?

Jafar barely gave the answer any thought.

"It is Allah's and mine. Allah wants what I want, and I want what Allah wants. They are interchangeable."

I knew it, the voice said, laughing at the same time. *You think you are Allah!*

"Shut up! You know nothing! Allah spits on you, you infidel voice!"

I have said it once before, Jafar. Allah means nothing to me, and you mean nothing to Him. You bastardize His teachings in the same manner your wicked Imams do. You should read your Koran more closely, and think about what you read before you react. Perhaps then you will learn that the West is not your enemy: only those who say they know what Allah and Mohammed preach and turn it around to fit their grandiose schemes are the enemies of Muslims.

"You are wrong!" Jafar screamed. "The West is our enemy! They abandoned us in the 1980's, and they bombed us a decade ago! They continue to bomb us! They will not rest until they destroy all of Islam! The criminal Bush lied! *Allahu Akbar!*"

Make your peace with Allah, Jafar, the voice taunted. *Your fate is in His hands alone.*

The voice disappeared.

That did not stop Jafar from grabbing his silenced weapon and putting several bullets into the ceiling. The weapon smoked as he dropped it on the table.

"I must not let anyone stand between myself and Allah. Allah is the only one who matters, and no one will shatter my faith in Him.

"Now," Jafar continued, "I must prepare for my loyal operatives' arrival."

He didn't have much time. His operative would be there within minutes.

Chapter 29
St. James's Park, London, England
3 August 2012 — 01.00 GMT/2 August 2012, 8:00 p.m. ET

If it had been any other time than just after midnight, Jaclyn would have had a much easier journey to get to the Victoria Embankment side of the River Thames. She would have been able to take the Tube's Victoria Line from Highbury & Islington Station and make the journey to Victoria Station, then transfer onto either the Circle or District lines — the District line would have been a smidge quicker — to Westminster Station for her secret meeting with Alexandra Dupuis.

Seeing as it was just after midnight, she had two options: walk from North London, or take a bus to Trafalgar Square.

Saving her feet from a lifetime of fallen arches, she chose the latter.

Jaclyn made the walk from the Essex Road safe house to the station in 15 minutes. Canonbury Road and its houses on either side were peacefully slumbering, unaware of the woman in black making her way past them. She didn't even look to see if any lights were on; she was sure no one looking out the window would be able to see her anyway, save her blonde hair. She didn't even turn her head to see if she was being followed; her HUD gave her a 360-degree view of the area. She walked with confidence.

She turned onto Upper Street and passed The Famous Cock on the other side, careful not to draw attention to herself from the patrons spilling out. One thing was for sure, she thought: despite the terror warnings Mohammed issued, there was still plenty of carousing from the younger set, those who still felt invincible, believing themselves to be fearless, immortal.

She came to the bus stop and waited. Only a few minutes passed, but they seemed like a lifetime. In a few minutes, she would be seeing Dupuis again.

Jaclyn was, of course, slightly wary of this meeting, despite the confidence she showed. As the hours between her impromptu meeting with Tom in the pizza place to now elapsed, she began to have slight misgivings: hours of uninterrupted thought usually did that. She did not know if this was a trap, but then thought caught up with her: Tom could have arrested her right then and there after he spilled marinara on his trousers. But it still could be a set-up. If anything, Dupuis had taught her operative to be cautious in the field. This was as much the field as anything.

Jaclyn decided to go to St. James' Park armed as heavily as she could. She would not be easily taken, if that was Dupuis' plan.

The N41 bus rolled to a stop in front of her. It was empty. Thinking nothing of it, Jaclyn paid the driver and took a seat in the middle of the bus before it pulled away and drove south on Upper Street.

In the 40 minutes it took to ride from Islington to Trafalgar Square, Jaclyn noticed the bus did not slow down to pick up passengers at any of the stops along the way. She immediately sensed that the driver was, quite possibly, MI5. She tried to stay as calm as possible. She didn't want to alert the driver that she knew anything was out of sorts.

"Sir, could you stop at Trafalgar Square, please?" she asked.

"That's the last stop, love. We'll be there shortly," the driver replied.

You mean it's the only stop, Jaclyn thought. She leaned back into the seat and began to think about her upcoming meeting with Dupuis.

In what seemed like five minutes, the bus pulled up onto Charing Cross Road. Jaclyn hadn't even noticed skirting the edges of Soho until the bus passed Leicester Square. She prepared herself to disembark.

Once they pulled into Trafalgar Square, the driver said, "There you go, love. Trafalgar Square." Just as Jaclyn came toward him, he reached for her arm. Jaclyn bristled. "The Mall will be deserted. No one will disturb you and the director. Go through the Arch and turn left onto the Horse Guards Road."

Jaclyn nodded and stepped off the bus, her suspicions confirmed.

Trafalgar Square, like every other night of the year, was busy on this warm night. Remaining inconspicuous would be a difficult task, especially in her jumpsuit and trench coat.

Not only that, she wanted to avoid the pigeons. Even this late at night, they toddled here and there in the square, occasionally hopping onto the LED-lit fountains while others pecked away at the ground. They cooed lovingly to each other, completely oblivious of a stranger in their midst. Many feet had trod upon the square that day, and it seemed a new visitor would not distract them from their late-night feeding frenzy. Jaclyn recalled a story a few years ago of a woman committing suicide here, burning herself in a religious statement. The birds carried on long after they carried her corpse out. If that couldn't disturb the pigeons, then a woman walking innocently across the square certainly would be less of a nuisance.

Jaclyn headed for the Admiralty Arch that separated Trafalgar from The Mall. Her HUD was ever searching for threats.

As she reached the Arch, she looked across the breadth of The Mall. It was as the bus driver had said. She could only see a few people walking up and down the sides, picking up trash from the day's activities. White traffic horses blocked off the road from Trafalgar Square heading to toward Buckingham Palace as well as Whitehall and Millbank to the south of Trafalgar, preventing any cars from travelling along the Victoria Embankment.

She walked under the Arch. A sheet of black fabric fell behind her. This did not startle her, nor did she even notice it happening. If she was to turn her head, all she would have seen was a black curtain. On the other side was a perfect rendition of The Mall, seen as if no one walked along the road.

Jaclyn, though, walked along The Mall. She passed by several of the street cleaners, who paid her absolutely no mind. She heard them speak softly into their broomstick handles.

Clearly, MI5 is keeping this area secure, she thought. *Alex must have leaned hard on Willows to prevent any eavesdropping.*

She found the Horse Guards Road some 500 steps after passing under the Arch. She turned left and started skirting St. James's Park. As she walked, she could only hear her footsteps; not even a cricket chirped, nor frogs croaked. She came to the back side of Downing Street. A bell rang out. She turned and, from above the Prime Minister's residence at No. 10, she saw the clock of Big Ben illuminated.

It was 1 a.m.

She took several more steps before she saw two cars parked on the right-hand side of Horse Guards Road. Both were black: one was an armored limousine, the other a Citroën C6.

Jaclyn whistled when she caught sight of the latter. She walked slowly and inspected the rear end of it. She brushed her hand along the Citroën's spoiler.

An alarm rang out throughout St. James's Park. Jaclyn stepped back from the car, her hands up.

Seconds later, the alarm cut out with a double beep.

"Don't touch the merchandise until it is given to you, Snapshot."

Her heart thundering away, Jaclyn turned to see Alex standing on the path leading onto the island, holding the keys and alarm deactivator for the Citroën. The Director of the CIA, Jaclyn could tell, was pleased to see her, but the look on her face said plainly that she was annoyed because her operative just alerted half of London to their supposedly secretive presence.

Jaclyn didn't grimace or swallow awkwardly, though. Instead, she looked at Dupuis as if she hadn't seen her in a long time.

"Alex," she said, running toward her. She embraced her boss in the tightest hug imaginable.

Dupuis held her motherly, patting her back.

"Come on now, Jaclyn. We have a lot to discuss."

She led Jaclyn deeper onto the tree-covered island.

Jaclyn saw a small fortress, one hastily constructed for their meeting. Large rivets sprang from the corners of the steel, which dug deep into the earth, as if it had been here for years. She saw that there were no spotlights aimed down upon her, lights that would have rendered her weakened.

Her HUD let her know that all was okay. She was among friends.

"You're late, Snapshot," Dupuis said, steering Jaclyn into the building.

"Sorry about that. I asked the driver to let me off in Trafalgar Square; I didn't know exactly how far away we were meeting."

Dupuis waved Jaclyn's explanation off.

"This island gives us complete secrecy and security. The British have taken care of everything. They are very concerned for your safety, as am I."

"You should know that I can take care of myself, Chief." Jaclyn didn't want to sound too defensive or argumentative, but she couldn't hide her disappointment in her boss's reluctance to disobey President Forrister. "After all, you trained me yourself, and you gave me this nifty little outfit to wear. I am better protected than Forrister is when he is abroad."

"Well relax," Dupuis said. "You don't have to worry about being recalled. The president wishes me to convey to you his apologies. He wanted to tell you himself, but I'm afraid he had a party fundraiser to attend and wouldn't be available until 3 a.m. London time."

"I probably would have woken up for a call from the president, Chief."

"I know, but you are going to need your rest."

"What's the assignment, Alex?"

"The assignment is the same, Snapshot," Dupuis said, now pacing in front of her protégé. "You are to find this bastard and kill him. You are to use any means necessary to accomplish your mission.

"But," she continued, "there are some restrictions."

This confused Jaclyn. She was able to use any means necessary, but there are restrictions? It sounded somewhat hypocritical to her.

"And they are?"

Dupuis took a deep breath and continued to pace.

"The restrictions are that you are working as a rogue agent; the press back home has all but vilified you as a traitor."

Jaclyn's heart sank at the news. Her posture noticeably slumped.

I can't go home...

"This is to keep up appearances, Snapshot," Dupuis continued. "We have to assume the terrorist knows you to have gone rogue. It would not look good if the United States came to a rogue agent's beck and call. We are helping you achieve your mission parameters with the tools given to you tonight in addition to the tools currently on your person.

"There is another restriction: President Forrister is invoking deniability, Snapshot."

That knocked Jaclyn back a step.

"Why?" she asked.

"It is quite simple. You are off the books from this moment until we deem it reasonable to put you back on. There is unrest back home; the president's now former chief of staff, Bennett, is raising hell about the CIA and our corrupt methods and tactics. He is raising the voter's ire, and now Bennett is firmly against the president. I feel he's been against us and the president from the start, only acting covertly."

"That doesn't surprise me, Chief. Bennett is slime; I wouldn't be surprised if he turned out to be a Republican, either."

"You are also to stay away from MI5 and the Secret Intelligence Service as a whole."

Now that was a slap to the face. She couldn't see Tom. She wanted to resign — again — right then and now. She didn't say anything, but her face began turning red.

"MI5 may be our allies, but in your position, they are not yours. They are allowing you the leeway to operate your mission on their soil, though, and that should be good enough for you. If they have any intel for you, they will send it to me for dissemination before it is passed along to your BlackBerry."

Dupuis walked to a shelf and grabbed a box, then brought it over to Jaclyn.

"Here, it's a box of spare magazines. I know you don't like to carry more than six at a time, but I have the feeling that you're going to need every single one you can get your hands on."

Jaclyn grinned.

"And before I forget, the British will allow you to stay at the safe house —"

"I know, Tom told me earlier," Jaclyn interrupted.

"— provided you don't blow it up."

Jaclyn shifted her body weight from her right foot to her left. She grinned at Dupuis.

"Now Chief, when have I been known to intentionally blow something up?"

"What usually happens when you're around something, Jaclyn?"

"Right off the top of my head? Let's see, anarchy, chaos, life insurance pay-offs, destruction, fire, death —"

"That reminds me," Dupuis said, cutting her off. "Nigel's funeral is this morning."

Jaclyn reeled.

"Tom didn't tell me that."

"I wouldn't have thought so. I'm sure Agent Scouser is trying to put on a brave face and is trying to forget all about it. Of course, I'm sure you want to pay your respects to your counterpart, but you're not allowed near MI5 personnel."

Jaclyn slumped again.

"I have taken the liberty of getting you this," Dupuis said, brandishing a black veil from her pocket. "I won't tell Willows that you're there. It's at St. Paul's, not too far from where you're staying. Sit in the back, wear this, and no one will notice you."

"Thanks, Alex."

"I know Nigel would have wanted you there. Now," Dupuis said, escorting her out of the makeshift meeting place and back into the warm, London air, "Parkerhurst will give you a rundown of your car."

Jaclyn looked giddy at the prospect.

A young man, Parkerhurst, stepped out from the back of the limousine as the two women approached. He was clean shaven with no gray in his hair. Jaclyn had worked with him during the situation in Boston as well as during their respective government training periods. Jaclyn enjoyed teasing him. He was relatively handsome, but deep inside, she knew the man in front of her could never compete with Tom Messingham in the looks department.

Just thinking about him made her pulse race. She calmed herself down and pulled at the collar of her jumpsuit.

"Hello again, Agent Snapshot," Parkerhurst said. He spoke with a deep Boston accent; Jaclyn immediately tossed the letter R out the window. "The British have been kind enough to outfit you with a Citroën C6. It comes standard with a V6 engine, six speed automatic transmission, 0 to 60 in just a bit under nine seconds and a max speed of 149 miles per hour, 18 inch Atlantic alloy wheels, about 28 miles to the liter in the city, 49 miles to the liter on the highway —"

"Thank you for the television commercial, but I highly doubt Agent Snapshot is going to do much driving outside of London, Parkerhurst," Dupuis said, her tone suggesting to the CIA quartermaster to get a move on. "Just tell her the options."

"Sunroof, heated leather seats, heat-resistant windshield, wide-angle mirrors —"

"Parkerhurst!"

The young quartermaster became startled.

"Yes, Director Dupuis?"

"Give her the non-standard options, if you would."

"Well," he continued, grimacing all the while, "it has the standard triple-plated armor on the windshield and chassis, as well as three adjustable license plates, valid in any country. The trunk is loaded with 14 miniature surface-to-air missiles; the switch is in your center console. Front-loaded quarter panel machine guns, oil slicker on the rear bumper. It has hover capability to 50 feet — I advise you to use that only at night, just to keep the citizens of England in the dark — but if you need to make a fast getaway, you'll find we installed a rocket-propelled exhaust. The manufacturer tinted the mirrors to hide your identity, and it comes completely with the most highly updated anti-theft device: No one can get into this car but you once you set your personal code.

"Now look at this, Snapshot." Parkerhurst slid his hand into his pocket. He pulled out a flat box that resembled the surveillance devices she used in the shower three days ago. "This device will disrupt surveillance video signals for up to two hours. It will force the video to replay the same image of the last five minutes up until the 10 seconds that you enter any room, so you'll have to be quick about it. It is far more advanced that what we gave you before."

Parkerhurst slipped back into the limousine while Dupuis walked up and handed Jaclyn the keys to the Citroën C6.

"It's all yours for now, Snapshot. Do take good care of her, will you?"

Dupuis walked to the open limousine door.

"Chief?"

"Yes, Jaclyn?" Dupuis said.

"How do you know the car is female?"

Dupuis smiled wide. She slid into the limousine.

"Because it's going to last quite a while longer than the last car we gave you to use, or else."

"Or else what?" Jaclyn said, but Dupuis closed the door hard before Jaclyn could even get the words out. The limousine pulled away from the curb, leaving her alone.

August's heat surrounded her as she watched the limo's tail lights turn right onto Birdcage Walk. Jaclyn stood there holding the new provisions Dupuis and Parkerhurst provided for her.

She checked the digital readout on her HUD and noticed it was 1:20 a.m. If she were going to get some rest and be awake in time for Nigel's funeral, she would have to get back to Essex Road very quickly. Six or seven hours of sleep would be plenty.

It was then she noticed what side of the car the steering wheel was on. She slapped her forehead as she came to a brutal — yet truthful — realization.

"Oh, shit," she said. "I have to drive on the wrong side of the road!"

Chapter 30
St. Paul's Church, Islington, London, England
3 August 2012 — 10.00 GMT/5:00 a.m. ET

Sleep came easy for Jaclyn that night. She had the first good night's sleep since she arrived. She woke up refreshed, showered without worry, then got dressed for a very somber occasion.

The church was not that far from Carlton Cinema, so Jaclyn was sure to have plenty of time to make it to the service. She drove the Citroën C6 north on Essex Road and found a place to park on one of the side streets.

The funeral procession had yet to begin. She entered the church to find it packed.

Jaclyn slid into one of the pews in the rear of the church. She lowered the veil so no one could recognize her.

Five minutes later, the doors entering the sanctuary opened, and Jaclyn saw Tom clutching his mother's hand as the family walked in. Nigel's daughters walked in behind their brother and mother. Jaclyn also saw Sir David walking among the mourners.

She tensed. She hoped no one would see her; remembering her conversation with Dupuis earlier this morning, she was not to be around MI5.

Surely they would let her show her respects, she thought. True, she and Nigel had only worked together for a day, but still, that was no reason to keep her away from his funeral.

Jaclyn breathed as Sir David and the rest of the mourning party took their seats. No one noticed her. Her HUD did not detect anyone coming toward her. She was safe.

Then they brought in the casket. Nigel's remains were inside, ready for preservation, a red and white flag of England draped upon it.

Jaclyn's HUD followed it as it rolled down the aisle.

The service began moments later. The celebrant came to the pulpit and spoke of Nigel's life, of his education at Oxford, his long marriage to Jane. The priest spoke of how he baptized all four of their children, and the way Nigel had accepted Christ for each of them.

By the end of the priest's sermon, tears flowed to the carpet. Nigel was an upstanding citizen, a great father to four wonderful children, and Jane's soul mate.

Jaclyn couldn't argue with any of that. She had known him a very short time, but she felt Nigel was an exemplary person.

"Now, with an assassin's bullet," the priest said, causing Jane to wail louder, "the head of this family has been taken from them. May God have mercy on the soul of the dead assassin, killed by Nigel's partner, and may God bless Nigel's family. May God give them comfort in their time of need, and let God bless those who aid them. May God bring an end to the terrorism that has struck this country in recent days, and let those who stand against terrorism stand as one unit in Christ's love and grace."

The service was soon over, and before they could wheel Nigel's casket out of the church, Jaclyn chose this time to depart. She slipped out of the sanctuary and down the stairs, walking swiftly to her car. She drove to the corner, waiting for them to bring the casket out immediately across from her.

She held her breath.

A minute later, the church doors flew open, and the blue casket, without the flag of England, came out first, held by six pallbearers, followed by the family. Tom had sunglasses on, much like the pair Jaclyn wore without the HUD yesterday afternoon.

They brought Nigel's casket around the rear of the hearse, which sat pointed north toward St. Paul's Road. The pallbearers loaded the casket into the car.

They didn't see the missile coming at them.

The weapon shifted air with a hearty hiss as it sped directly toward them from the northeast, just to the right of where Jaclyn sat. The missile caused her to jump and gasp, as her HUD did not even acknowledge being in the line of fire, or warn her with its steady beeping. A trail of flame seared the air before it hit its target.

The hearse, with Nigel's casket half way inside, exploded not once, but twice in five seconds. A fireball enveloped the car, as orange flame mixed with black smoke rising into the North London morning. Screams rented the air. The blast startled those at the foot of the casket. They lost their grip on it, and the now-burning sarcophagus fell to the pavement. Those close to the hearse were lost in the fireball. Bodies lay in the street, flames surrounding them. Those who were in the missile's path died without knowing what had happened.

The second explosion took everyone by surprise, since it came from inside the casket. It forced the lid off, sending shrapnel in many directions. Those on the stairs leading into the church — mainly Nigel's family — took the brunt of the explosion. MI5 agents surrounded the family, guns drawn, searching the skies for the attack. Smoke and flame rose from the inside of the funerary box.

Jaclyn's heart leapt into her throat. The desecration of Nigel's body angered her. She wanted to jump out of her car and see if Tom and his family was okay, but that would have been a direct violation of her agreement with Dupuis. That and she wasn't armed —

Wait a second, she thought. *I have a whole arsenal at my disposal right here!*

Jaclyn gunned the engine of the Citroën C6 and sped around the corner onto Essex Road, parking the car right in the middle of the street by the rear end of the hearse. Voices rose, wondering what she was doing. She quickly searched the rooftops to the northeast, looking for a smoking fissure trail.

There was a faint hint of smoke in the sky across the way. The building looked to be vacant for some time. The heat signature of the building's roof, though, gave it away as being the source of the missile.

The assailant isn't going to try to blow anything else up again, Jaclyn quickly surmised. *He may try to escape, though. Hopefully there isn't a back door to that place.*

Jaclyn flipped open the center console and hit two switches. The quarter panel machine guns opened, the circular barrels revolving and protruding from both sides of the Citroën's hood like a shark's dorsal fin. A mechanism in the trunk drew open, before the surface-to-air rack rose above the roof.

The sight of the Citroën's armament caused several people to scream and rush away from the church, heading to the safety of their cars. Those still inside the church scrambled away, too, for fear of someone bringing the building down on top of them. MI5 agents tried to keep order. None ran toward the car wondering what the driver was doing.

Jaclyn figured MI5 already knew what she was driving and what it was capable of doing.

She breathed easy. Jaclyn calmly looked through the armored windshield and patiently waited for someone to emerge. She wanted to look to see where Tom was, but she figured he had already led his family, his sisters weeping heavily, away from their father's charred body.

Just add that to the list of things this terrorist is going to answer for, she thought.

A split second later, a door to the building opened. A man stepped out, but when he got a good look at the commotion and the Citroën in front of the burning hearse, he paused. He backpedaled quickly and shut the door behind him.

"That's my little bitch," Jaclyn said.

She revved the engine and pulled forward one hundred feet to the intersection.

Stopping right in the middle — cars gave her a wide berth, since the vehicle was armed with who knew how many tons of explosives rigged to it — Jaclyn waited until she saw the bastard again. She knew he would look out the window. He had to make sure he was safe.

He was dead the moment he stepped outside the door.

She pulled her iPad out and quickly ran a diagnostic on the building. There was no one on the second floor, but one of the heat signatures on the first floor — there were two — went to the window and looked out.

"Get a good look at this," she whispered.

She acquired the target and quickly punched in a command.

A guided rocket on the right side of the magazine ignited immediately, venting steam as it surged away from the Citroën. Jaclyn watched as the air shifted around the weapon in a fiery mix of oxygen and hydrogen.

The rocket collided with the vacant building, causing it to explode, sending brick and mortar flying toward the south and into St. John's Road. The southeast end of the building collapsed in on itself seconds later.

If the target wasn't dead when the rocket exploded, he was certainly dead now, Jaclyn thought.

Her only question now was simple: Where did the other bastard go?

She consulted the iPad and saw the heat signature of the building go off the charts. There was only one casualty inside, it said. That meant —

"Shit!"

She backed the car to the side of the road, flipping switches as she pulled to the curb. The machine guns revolved back into position, while the missile magazine lowered itself, the trunk panel sliding shut.

Jaclyn got out of the car, set the security system and ran toward the church.

I'm breaking the rules, but I don't care, she thought. *I can't let this son of a bitch get away. I'm the only one who knows where he is.*

She had tossed the veil away. Tom came running toward her, trying to speak. Flames crackled in the hearse nearby.

Jaclyn cut him off before he even had the chance to speak.

"I need a gun; a Walther, if you've got one," she said.

"What the hell is going on, Jaclyn?"

"A gun, give me a gun. I can't let that bastard get away." Tom unholstered his weapon, a Walther SP22-M2, and handed it over to her. It was slightly larger than her preferred Walther, but she felt its balance and deemed it satisfactory.

"Thanks," she said, before she ran off back toward St. Paul's Road without another word.

"Hey, wait!" Tom shouted, but she didn't acknowledge him. She was already out of earshot. Several other MI5 agents ran up to him.

"She's not supposed to be anywhere near us."

"What the devil is she doing?"

Tom stared after the quickly departing figure of Jaclyn running quicker than any person he had seen run before. She had just made the left-hand turn onto St. Paul's, his shiny Walther reflecting the sunlight.

"I have no idea, and right now, I don't care," he said, his voice cracking. "I just hope she finds that son of a bitch and puts him out of his misery."

Chapter 31
The West End, London, England
3 August 2012 — 11.08 GMT/6:08 a.m. ET

Jafar praised Allah as the missile launch succeeded. His agents, planted perfectly in a building adjacent to the church, were able to cause a great deal of chaos as the funeral for that infidel Briton finished. They executed his plan as well as he expected, and he had to give his operatives credit for suggesting they plant a bomb inside the casket itself only a few hours ago. It was brilliant. It was audacious. It was something all of them would be heaped glory upon by Allah.

The Britons thought we would rest while they grieved, Jafar thought. Theirs was a thought of folly. Allah will not allow us to rest until we eradicate their blasphemy from civilization!

He watched the entire episode transpire on the CCTV emplacement down Essex Road. He zoomed in and waited for the funeral to end, and when it did, the fireworks began.

"*Allahu Akbar!*" he shouted as the missile made impact. Flame wreathed the bodies. The hearse became useless metal in seconds. Pandemonium rang out on the steps when the casket exploded a few heartbeats later. More people fell victim to his attacks, their bodies cut up by flying debris.

It was so exciting, he cursed himself when he forgot to make popcorn beforehand.

Then *she* came.

"What in the name of Mohammed?!" he screamed. He watched as the black Citroën C6 sped around the corner and moored itself to the end of the flaming hearse. The trunk's roof began to peel backward, revealing — "Allah bless me!" Jafar shouted in disbelief. "That thing is nuclear!" — its surface-to-air missile launcher.

He did not see the machine guns. If he had, he would have fainted.

Moments later — it could have been an hour, but Jafar would not have noticed any difference since his eyes were riveted to the screen — the Citroën drove forward, coming up to the intersection. The magazine began to move slightly.

The missile blasting away made his heart skip a beat.

The missile colliding with the building made him choke.

"Oh my," he said. At that moment, he showed compassion for his operatives. This was completely unforeseen.

The Citroën went into reverse and pulled up to the curbing just as his cell phone began to ring. Jafar picked it up and immediately praised Allah when he saw who was calling.

It was Yusuf, his agent in the building.

"Yusuf, thank Allah you are alive," Jafar said as he pressed receive, relieved.

"It is not Yusuf, it is Achmed, his loyal lieutenant. *Allahu Akbar*. That was close. Brother Yusuf, though, has perished."

Jafar nearly choked. *Yusuf was a loyal agent. Allah will bless him*, Jafar thought.

"That was completely out of the desert. We had no counter for —"

Jafar's voice became caught somewhere between his larynx and his mouth. He was looking at the screen. The door of the Citroën had opened and —

"Oh my Allah! It is her! The rogue woman! And she is running toward MI5! They are going to arrest her —"

"What is happening? I cannot see a thing; I am in the subterranean tunnels. I am making my way to the Tube station near the stadium. I will sneak aboard and make my way to you, *musahib*."

"No! No, this can't be happening!" Jafar yelled.

"What is happening?" Achmed asked.

"The Britons are not arresting her; that mourning infidel bastard gave her a gun. And now she's running away." Jafar sounded amazed and frightened at the same time. "She didn't take the car. Brother Achmed, if I were you, I would stay where you are. Allah commands it. He does not trust that woman."

"Yes," Achmed said, disbelieving. "Do you want me to take her out? I am armed."

Jafar gave it only a few seconds' worth of thought. With Achmed taking the woman out, it would foil Jafar's internal voice's plans. The voice said this woman — *Why isn't she in custody?! I thought they would take her in!* — had the ability to kill him.

She was free.

Jafar was sweating.

Achmed needed to do this.

"Yes, brother Achmed. Take the woman out. Take pictures of her remains and send them to me. We can use them in our next broadcast to the world. It is as Allah commands. *Allahu Akbar*."

"*Allahu Akbar*."

The connection ended quickly. Jafar could not see the woman any longer. He could have checked the CCTV emplacement at the Highbury & Islington Underground station, but he wasn't thinking properly.

He shouldn't have been worried; it was only one mistake.

The voice, though, had him very worried. The voice was *right*. The voice called it.

This woman was a very crafty individual.

"I hope Achmed can do the job," Jafar said, mostly to himself as he sipped water.

The voice, to his surprise, stayed silent.

Chapter 32
Islington Tunnels, London, England
3 August 2012 — 11.15 GMT/6:15 a.m. ET

Despite her heels, Jaclyn used a decent amount of speed. She had been a relatively good sprinter in her junior high track meets back home in Seattle, but the strides she took down St. Paul's Road left the cinder track behind.

She churned the pavement, hardly breaking a sweat as she ran west along the sweeping road. She made a slight turn and, without looking, was able to cross to the other side of the road, the bracers giving her enough speed to cross between the passing cars.

The Walther, of course, gave her a wide enough berth to make the cars hit the brakes.

She came to the Highbury Grove Bridge. She ran slightly to the left, giving her enough room to skim the corner. She ran north, her arms pumping.

Six hundred feet passed in less than 15 seconds. Jaclyn ducked through the trees when she came to Baalbec Road, maneuvering around the low-lying branches, the downed leaves dumped here last autumn crunching under her feet.

She opened the cement hatch and kicked her heels off. She descended the rusty ladder as she grabbed the handle to close the hatch, leaving her in darkness. She activated the small flashlights on the HUD, making the darkness shriek under the light. She hefted Tom's Walther as soon as her feet touched the bottom.

She walked toward the southeast.

Her HUD scanned the area for possible threats. Jaclyn knew that anyone targeting her because of the flashlights would trigger the warning tones. She breathed as slowly as possible as she walked forward, her right foot leading her left. Her bare footfalls didn't make a sound on the cement.

Water dripping from the ceiling nearly distracted her, but she detected the sound of running feet coming toward her from the south. She quickly extinguished the flashlights with a mental command and waited patiently, leaning against the wall. Her prey would come right into the maw of the Walther.

She was ready to spring.

Seconds passed. The sounds of hurried footsteps became louder. The target drew near.

The warning tones went off that time, audible only to Jaclyn. She turned her head and let her HUD scan heat signatures. A bright orange spot emerged from around a bend some fifty feet away and came toward her at a rapid pace.

The bright spot grew. It would be on top of her within seconds.

Jaclyn took a deep breath and lunged away from the wall, raising the Walther and leveling it upon her prey. She turned the flashlights back on as soon as he was within twenty feet.

"Freeze! Don't move a muscle! Don't even quiver!" she shouted.

Her prey took two steps before he froze in place. The flashlights shone in his eyes, causing him to squint painfully. He had been down here for 10 minutes and his eyes had adjusted to the dark.

"Get on your knees slowly," Jaclyn ordered, moving in cautiously.

"I am unarmed," the man said as he dropped to his knees.

The voice gave Jaclyn pause. It was certainly Middle Eastern, but it didn't have that scared-for-his-life, panicky tone she would have expected from a just-captured terrorist.

She moved in and began to pat him down, moving from his latissimus dorsi muscles to his waist, checking the pockets of his pants and down to his ankles. She found no weapons, hidden or exposed, and she didn't find any cyanide capsules in his pockets.

"Why did you do it?" Jaclyn breathed into his ear. Her breath caused him to shiver.

"You are mistaken, Agent Snapshot. What you saw happen and what actually went on inside that building are two distinctly different things."

Hearing her code name shot back at her gave her a sickening feeling in her stomach. Had the terrorists infiltrated CIA security and looked at her file? That had to have been close to impossible. She felt dirty.

"What are you talking about?"

The man, Jaclyn saw, oozed a confidence she had never before seen in a terrorist. The ones she ran across had arrogant attitudes that made her skin crawl. They were all about praising Allah and going on about infidels. This one was different, but until he proved otherwise, she would treat him just like any other dirty Islamic jihadists.

"It wasn't me who pulled the trigger on that missile," he said. "I saw the man who did. He is dead now. You killed him."

"But you were still in the building," Jaclyn said through gnashed teeth. She jabbed the barrel of the Walther into his left temple. "I could shoot you now and leave you for dead. Barely anyone knows about these tunnels. No one but the rats would find your stinking carcass."

"Except for my superiors," the man countered. "They will know something occurred if I do not report in after this meeting with you. They know I'm down here. They'll send in a search party and send me back to my homeland."

"Yeah, and I'm sure they'll give you a glorious send-off during *al-Dafin*," Jaclyn spat.

He took a deep breath and tried to turn his head to look at Jaclyn. She dug the barrel harder into his skin. He winced. "You don't understand. If you kill me, you may feel something of a personal victory over the terrorists, Jaclyn, but it would be the furthest thing from the truth.

"Do you want to know the truth?"

Jaclyn was confused. The man, this terrorist, had an implacable calm about him. He had not mentioned Allah or going to see his god, or about the 72 virgins he would receive in heaven. There was definitely something different about him, but Jaclyn couldn't pinpoint it just yet.

Jaclyn saw the man's eyes through the HUD. There was no sign of betrayal in them.

She eased the Walther off his temple, but she kept it in contact with his skin, just to let him know that any lie would lead to his death.

"Go ahead," Jaclyn said. She noticed her heart raced. "You have five minutes until the end of the world as you know it."

The man smirked.

"I am not what you think I am, Jaclyn Johnson. I am not a terrorist. I never have been one, nor will I ever be one."

"Then who are you?"

The man took a deep breath.

"My name is Lavi Witz."

Jaclyn's breath lodged in her throat. Her chest heaved.

That's not an Islamic name, Jaclyn thought.

He dropped his bombshell.

"I'm with Mossad."

***

"You want to try that one more time?" Jaclyn said, disbelieving what she just heard. The barrel of the Walther slipped a couple of inches. It now rested on his upper jaw.

"I am with Israeli Intelligence. I have been working undercover in Afghanistan for nearly seven years."

If hearing the man did not have an Islamic name, hearing that Witz worked for Israel's version of the CIA knocked Jaclyn back a few steps.

221

He was an ally.

And Jaclyn could have killed him without knowing the truth.

She didn't let that fact dissuade her from interrogating him.

"How did you get involved with Mohammed?"

"That's classified, as I'm sure you can understand."

"I'm sure you can understand me not believing you and putting a bullet in your brain."

Witz, for the first time, showed fear. He gulped hard. He expelled a great deal of bad air into the tunnel. Jaclyn could hear his teeth tremble.

"I can tell you that I came under the tutelage, you may say, of one Yusuf Mohammed Diop during my years in Afghanistan. Through subterfuge and murder, I became one of his trusted lieutenants. With the Olympics coming, he told me that plans were underway, plans made by an associate of his here in England —"

"Mohammed?"

"Yes," Witz said. "Yusuf was going to be involved in several of the attacks and wanted me to help carry them out."

"And of course, you had to follow his orders."

He nodded.

"How many of the attacks were you involved in?"

"I was involved in the Wembley attack," Witz said. "No one outside of Mohammed and his immediate lieutenants were to know of this. The ones outside of Mohammed's special circle did not know of what was to happen until the night before. They removed all communication devices to the outside world from us: Mohammed is extremely paranoid about leaks. His immediate lieutenants are all loyal to him, but he does not trust anyone else.

"We were told by Mohammed to leave the country before the stadium blew up. I, of course, had orders to stay as close to Mohammed as possible. I did not get a phone again until the next day. I reported in to Tel Aviv as soon as I could get away from Yusuf — he kept us all on pretty tight leashes — and let them know of my involvement."

"Tell me about your involvement today."

Witz took another deep breath.

"I found out about today late last night. Yusuf told me to be ready for his call. He told me to stay close. He called Mohammed and went to his flat. I got the call last night. Yusuf wanted me to scope out locations for an attack the British would take great offense to."

"I think they did. I took offense to it, too. I'm sure if we attacked one of their funerals, the Muslim world would be up in arms, demanding the blood of disrespectful infidels."

Witz conceded this time.

"He wanted me to find a vacant building near the church, but I couldn't find one. Yusuf chose that building. He went in and shot the people there. He had me stash the bodies in the tunnel underneath. He set up the missile launcher as the hearse pulled up to the church and decided to wait. He called Mohammed and told him what was going on. He wanted me to pull the trigger, but I refused.

"He backhanded me and called me a traitor to Allah. He told me to wait downstairs while he attacked the funeral procession out of the church. By the time he came back downstairs, we heard the rumble on the street. He tried to go through the front door to see what it was, but the sight of the heavily-armed Citroën made him head back into the building."

Jaclyn grinned as she remembered the look of fright on the terrorist's face.

"He told me to arm myself and prepare to shoot our way out of there. I refused again, I grabbed his cell phone and hopped into a shaft leading into the tunnels. Luckily he picked a building that had an escape into the fallout shelter tunnels. I made it in just before you blew the building up.

"I called Mohammed and let him know that Yusef was dead. He explained to me that he saw everything on CCTV and that he wanted me to kill you."

Jaclyn bristled.

"I told him I was armed, but as you have already realized, I am not. After I spoke with him, I contacted Tel Aviv. They said you had gone rogue and that I should avoid you at all costs. They trust my judgment, and I said I would put my life in your hands.

"Yusuf didn't tell me if there were any additional attacks planned, but without him in the fold, it will be difficult for me to get information. In fact, I do not believe I will be lucky to get close to Mohammed, and if I do, there is no guarantee he would keep me in his cadre of associates. He is a very dangerous man. If he detected a lie, my life would be forfeit."

"What do you suggest?"

Witz took another deep breath.

"Let me complete my mission. It seems as though our missions are closely linked."

"I'm a rogue agent, though. I'm not anyone's ally right now. I'm getting my intel through my own two eyes." Witz didn't have to know the US government was helping her on the sly; she was sure he was holding out on her. "My mission is my mission."

"You have to bring Mohammed down."

Jaclyn breathed. Then she nodded.

"I can help you as much as I can. I can't promise much, but I'm going to try to get closer inside Mohammed's circle."

"You still have your phone?"

"Am I allowed to move for it?"

"Yes, but do it slowly." Jaclyn still had the Walther trained on him. She believed his story. It didn't mean she trusted him.

Witz took his cell phone out of his right pocket. Jaclyn cursed herself for not searching him better.

"Call up the number. I can memorize it to my HUD."

Witz held up the phone so Jaclyn could see the screen. The HUD recorded it – as well as the name for the phone number, too.

It said Jafar.

I hope this guy isn't lying to me, Jaclyn said.

"Alright, done. I won't call him yet. I want you to get close. When you get close, call me." Jaclyn gave him the number for her BlackBerry. "It's scrambled, so no one can get a trace on my location."

"I will do that."

"I will only call him after he gets a sense of security. Then he'll panic. I want him to panic."

"Of course. It would be the perfect way to end this heinous terrorism against the world."

"No, the perfect way to end this heinous terrorism would be to kill the son of a bitch."

"Very true."

Jaclyn stuffed the Walther in her suit coat pocket. Her fingers hooked onto something else inside.

"You're ready to head to Mohammed's?"

He nodded.

"Good. Enjoy his company."

"I don't think I will, but I will do my best to represent the institution. I'll tell him you never found me."

"Good. And I'll do my part," Jaclyn said with a grin, "but you won't see me doing it."

She removed her hand from her pocket and threw down a silver ball right in front of Witz. It cracked and sent heavy plumes of camouflaging smoke rising in front and around him. He immediately grew disoriented.

Jaclyn took off the way she came, her bare feet making no sound on the concrete.

The scene around St. Paul's had been chaotic, for the most part. Two Mercedes-made ladder pump companies came from the Islington Fire Brigade station on Upper Street, screaming down St. Paul's Road seconds after Jaclyn sprinted to Highbury Grove. Several curious passersby tried to get a good look at the souped-up Citroën C6, but MI5 agents, despite still being in shock at what happened to their fallen brother, were able to keep people away from what some were calling a nuclear holocaust on four wheels.

Jaclyn did not go straight back to St. Paul's to pick up the Citroën. Instead, she returned to Carlton Cinema, where she waited for the flashing lights up the street to vanish from view.

It was nearly dark before the authorities cleared the scene.

After counting to one hundred once the last lights flickered out, Jaclyn grabbed the keys and her iPad. She hurried as quickly as she could down Essex Road, inputting the security system's deactivation codes as she walked in front of the church. Black scorch marks covered the pavement where Nigel's hearse burned. Her HUD also picked up shards of shrapnel from the casket lid strewn across the church lawn. Yellow police tape surrounded the church steps as well as the place where the hearse sat through the service.

Even though she heard Witz's reasoning for what happened, she couldn't have been more disgusted with what happened this morning. She didn't have time to make sense of it all, though. The past few hours flew by in a blur, and her stomach began to rumble again. She hadn't eaten since the night before; she wouldn't have been shocked if her Lycra jumpsuit hung off her body the next time she put it on.

She had the sneaking suspicion she would put it on tonight.

Jaclyn slipped into the car and made a quick three-point turn before driving south on Essex. She came to the Essex Road Rail Station and turned right onto River Place, then hooked a left as soon as the rear end of Carlton Cinema opened. She got out of the car and reset the security code.

She let her HUD do a quick scan of the surrounding area just in case. She entered the building through the rear door.

Being back in what was slowly turning into home allowed Jaclyn to breathe easier.

The knock at the door forty minutes later gave her reason not to. No one was supposed to know she was here — or visit her here.

Jaclyn put down the Chinese take-out and grabbed her personal Walther. She stalked toward the door, apprehensive and cautious. Her HUD, unfortunately, could not see through doors. She would have to open it and hope it wasn't a bunch of Mohammed's cronies.

She inched her hand out, grasped the doorknob and turned it. There was no need to use stealth; the person on the other side could see it turning.

She flung the door open and brought her Walther up to fire.

The barrel was sticking right in Tom's face.

The corner of Jaclyn's mouth flinched as she saw who it was. Tom, on the other hand, smiled.

"At least you're wearing bloody clothes this time," he said. "Although I wouldn't mind if you —"

"Oh shut up," Jaclyn said, nixing Tom's cross thought. She walked back into the confines of the safe house. "You could have called before you barged in here."

"I didn't barge in here; I knocked. And I did call. You didn't answer. Did you check your voice mail? I left at least one message for you." Tom stayed in the doorway.

"Going to turn into one of those obsessed boyfriends now, Tom?" Jaclyn slapped her mouth closed before she could stop herself from saying it.

Tom smiled, but let it go.

"I can't believe I just said that."

"Don't worry about it."

"So why are you here?" Jaclyn said, breaking an awkward silence. "I was under the impression that I was not to have contact with MI5 any longer."

"I think that agreement was broken when you ran up to me this morning and demanded the use of my sidearm."

"Oh," Jaclyn said, slightly blushing at the fact. "Yeah. I didn't think I would need a gun at a funeral."

"No, you just ended up bringing a car with more firepower than the bleeding RAF." Tom's mouth curled into another grin. "I'm here for two things, actually. First, I want my gun back."

Jaclyn looked around and found it next to the bag of Chinese. She grabbed it and handed it to him, handle side out.

"You're lucky I had a spare in the boot. It would not have looked good if I didn't have a gun when I was trying to keep people away from the scene. Right blooming difficult, I'll tell you," Tom said as he grabbed his gun and slid it into his holster. "So, where did you have to run off to so quickly? Did you end up catching the guy?"

"Is that the second thing you came for?" Jaclyn said playfully.

"Consider that part of the retrieval of my gun."

Jaclyn knew she could trust Tom; he trusted her with his secret two days ago. And since it had to do with the devastation this morning…

"Yes, and no," she replied.

"I don't understand, Jaclyn. What happened?"

Jaclyn took a deep breath, then looked into his eyes.

"You need to hear the whole story before you react, okay?"

"Should I sit down?" Tom asked quickly, noticing her pause.

Jaclyn shook it off.

She told him of the sprint down St. Paul's Road and into the tunnels on Highbury Grove. She explained how she apprehended the suspect.

Then she told him who the suspect claimed to be.

Tom's head nearly hit the roof.

"Mossad interrupted my father's funeral? I don't get it. Why would they —"

"I'm not done yet."

"Oh, by all means, proceed."

She continued to tell him about Witz's mission for the past seven years, infiltrating al-Qaeda's regimes until he found the one preparing to strike at the heart of London.

"You see, he refused the assignment," she said, putting her hands on his chest. She felt his heart beating rapidly. She feared for his blood pressure. "He abandoned the bastard —"

"Right before you brought the roof down on the fucking muppet."

Jaclyn breathed a soft laugh.

"He's on our side, Tom. He's trying to get close to Mohammed now. He probably already has. He hasn't called me yet."

Tom's eyes widened.

"You gave him your blooming number?! For Christ's sake Jaclyn, you have no bleeding idea if he's truly with Mossad. He could have said that to throw you off the trail that he's really one of Mohammed's goons, and only said that to keep you from killing him."

Tom yanked out his cell phone and began to dial feverishly.

"What did you say his name was?" he asked.

"Lavi Witz. Who are you calling?"

Tom held his hand up as he walked around in a small circle. His pace clearly told Jaclyn he was slightly furious.

227

"Hello, this is Agent Scouser. I need to cross-reference a name with Mossad and see if he's on the active roster. The name is Lavi Witz. He was in on the attack today. I'll hold as long as I need to."

He turned to Jaclyn.

"I'm just double-checking his story."

"He's probably off the books like I am. The Prime Minister probably has deniability, just like the president."

"You never know."

Jaclyn sat back down, not worrying about what Tom came up with in his search. She dug into the roast pork lo mein and twirled the noodles on her fork before bringing them to her mouth. She savored the MSG assaulting her taste buds.

Within five minutes, Tom had his information.

"Alright, thank you." He shut his cell phone. "He's clear and definitely on the books, too. Mossad didn't want to give that information up, but when we told them he was in on the attack today —"

"He wasn't really in on it."

"He didn't stop it."

"He couldn't; who isn't thinking clearly now. He couldn't blow his cover, Tom."

Tom's eyes hardened, his lips pursed. Jaclyn could have sworn that her HUD's heat signature recorded vapor pouring out of his ears.

After a few deep breaths, he finally calmed down. He grasped her upper arms softly.

"You're right, I'm sorry. I'm not excited about you giving your number to this guy, though, even if he's Mossad."

"Why?" Jaclyn said, a teasing smile coming to her lips. "Think I'm going to run away with him?"

Tom smirked.

"No, I didn't think —"

Jaclyn put her fingers on his lips and shushed him. She leaned up on tiptoes and whispered into his left ear, "What was the second reason you came here?"

"I —" he said, his mind failing him at that very moment. Jaclyn's sweet voice, sure of itself even at a caressing whisper, had rendered Tom's mind incapable of thought. She had disarmed him mentally and emotionally, and if she wanted to flip through the files inside his heart, learning his secrets and his desires, he would have been unable to stop her from doing so.

Not that he wanted to try stopping her. His mind was not his at that moment. It would have taken quite a bit of resistance on his part to defend himself, and as a 25-year-old man who had not been given the attentions of the feminine gender growing up, his resistance to her was disabled the moment he laid eyes on her at Thames House.

"Tom?" Jaclyn said, her voice returned to its original tone and timbre.

His eyes were glassy, as if they were not on this planet.

"Tom? Thomas? Hey, Tom? CIA to MI5, come in. Do you read?"

Tom blinked, his eyes coming back into focus. Sweat tickled his collar. It seemed like he had entered a sauna and had forgotten to disrobe. His face was flush, and his mind was empty.

"Did you say something, love?"

Jaclyn simply grinned and replied, "What was the second thing you came here for?"

"Second thing?"

Jaclyn couldn't help but giggle. She had never had this type of control over a man before. She had to admit: she liked it and wanted to explore the possibilities of such power. Her parents, good people though they were before their deaths, had been rather strict with her dating in her early teens. The CIA had been as strict, and even more so.

"Yes, you said you came here for two things: retrieving your weapon was one. I was of the belief that it was of some importance. Instead you're drooling on the floor."

Tom's eyes flew open wide with fear at this social faux pas, bringing his hand to his mouth immediately. There was nothing there.

Jaclyn doubled over with laughter. Tom had to chuckle despite the egg on his face.

"Alright you muppet, knock it off."

"Hey," Jaclyn said, feigning hurt. "That's what you called that terrorist."

"I meant it in a derogatory manner then; this is playful, now."

"Tom?"

"Yes?"

"For the third time: What was the second reason you came here for?"

"Oh, that. Yeah." Tom lifted the collar of his jacket and said, "Scouser to M1, area is secure. Send her up."

As soon as Tom lowered the collar, Jaclyn asked, "Who is coming up?"

The sounds of footsteps coming up the wooden steps reverberated in the old building.

Jaclyn looked at Tom curiously as he walked toward the doorway again. The footsteps changed in pitch; no longer were they climbing.

They were on the landing now. The shadows, through her HUD, Jaclyn could tell were growing.

Tom turned to her and said, "She wanted to see you. I couldn't refuse her. No one will know of the visit, okay? My guys on the street won't say a thing."

Jaclyn nodded.

Tom extended his arm out the door, his palm facing out, when the shadows grew deeper. A woman turned into the room.

Jaclyn's breath left her.

It was Jane Messingham. Tom led her into the room.

"Mum," Tom said, "this is Jaclyn Johnson, CIA. Jaclyn, this is my mum."

Jaclyn smiled at her and held out her hand. Tom's mother shook it with the grace of a woman who had been through so much heartache in so little time. She looked to be a strong woman walking into church, but to hear the priest tell of Nigel's death and to see the subsequent destruction of Nigel's casket and remains must have been too much for the poor woman to bear.

Jaclyn understood why she was frail now. She would be, too, if that had been her husband. She saw that Jane's eyes were red from crying; the eyelids looked like they wanted to slam shut and never open again.

She wondered if Jane was going to be able to sleep at all ever again, or if her dreams would be a nightmarish missile coming toward her in perpetuity.

"I'll leave you two alone," Tom said softly, before he turned to his mother. "Mum, I'll be downstairs with the guys. We'll bring you home when you're done."

"Thank you, Tommy," she said. She kissed his cheek, before Tom gave Jaclyn a soft look. He turned and left, leaving them to talk.

"Would you like to sit down, Mrs. Messingham? A cup of tea, perhaps?"

"Please, call me Jane, dear. And yes, a cup of tea would be lovely, thank you."

As Jane sat down, Jaclyn walked to the nearby pantry. She opened the cabinet doors and looked for some decaffeinated tea — she didn't think Jane could use any more caffeine, or else her blood pressure would shoot through the roof of the safe house — only to find a small box of coffee K Cups in the back.

The box reminded her of the trip from Heathrow to Wembley, when Nigel had made her a cup of tea.

It was only four days ago.

It felt like another lifetime.

She put the K Cups down and continued to rummage for tea. She soon found a full box of Celestial Seasonings Sleepytime.

She brought two steaming mugs of the pale green tea to the couch as soft tendrils of chamomile and mint wafted to the ceiling. Jane took little sips of her tea, holding her mug in both hands. The warmth seemed to comfort her in a way Jaclyn never knew possible.

Jaclyn sat down and looked at Jane, waiting for the reason why she came to see her so late at night to come forth.

"I met Nigel when I was in Sixth form," she said. Jaclyn's minute knowledge of England's educational system translated to Jane being 16 or 17 years old when she met her future husband. "He was a year older than I was, and he was about to go to Oxford. He looked so handsome in his black commoners robe over his suit coat that first day." Jaclyn noticed that Jane's eyes grew distant as she pulled those memories back to her. Jane took a sip of tea. "I knew he was going to be something special even back then."

Jaclyn smiled. Her tea sat untouched on the coffee table.

"He entered the military right out of Oxford, and he rose quickly through the ranks and received the rank of commander when our last child was born. He transferred into the SIS shortly after that because I was concerned he would be killed in action." Jane's voice trembled. Jaclyn reached over and soothed her, rubbing her back. "I didn't want our young family to be without a father. We took out life insurance policies to make sure we were protected in case one of us were to... well, you get the idea."

Jaclyn simply nodded, even though she had no idea what this woman was truly going through. She had experienced her parents' deaths, but this was something completely different.

Jane let out a long breath.

"When he was assigned to the Olympics case at Wembley, I had a feeling something was going to happen. Little did I know," she said, before heavy sobs racked her body. They lasted for several minutes before she was able to compose herself. "I'm so glad you were there, Jaclyn. You were able to kill that creep, and you were able to kill the one who... who..."

She couldn't say it. Jaclyn knew she meant about what happened this morning.

Jaclyn's eyes, hidden from the woman, became wet again.

"Nigel had called me that afternoon," Jane said after she composed herself once again. "He had told me he was working with you, and he believed you were a top-notch operative. He had so much respect for you on a professional level: when he told me of what you did at Wembley, trying to save that man's life, they way he spoke in amazement of what you tried to do made me glad he was serving alongside you."

Jane turned her gaze upon Jaclyn.

"Tom has told me what you plan to do, Jaclyn. Please," she pleaded, "honor Nigel. Honor him the way you would want him to honor you.

"Find him. Find this son of a bitch and kill him."

Hearing her ask her to do what she was considering only cemented her plans. It was as if Jane's plea gave her a license to kill. Jaclyn firmed her lips and nodded her promise.

Jane's tear-streak face tried to make a smile come to it, but it could not. She only whispered "Thank you" to Jaclyn several times. She hugged the American.

Jaclyn showed Jane out of the safe house, bringing her downstairs and out to where Tom and the other MI5 agents stood. There were only a few of them, but she was rather sure there were several others in unmarked cars nearby.

After what happened this morning, she wouldn't have bet against Willows putting Jane Messingham under 24-hour protection so the terrorists wouldn't come anywhere near her.

August's warm evening air hit the two women hard. They walked down the stairs as agents came forward and escorted Jane to the car. Jane thanked Jaclyn for the tea before the door closed.

"Is everything okay?" Tom asked.

Jaclyn nodded.

"Yeah," she said, wrapping her arms around herself, as if she had caught a chill in the air. "It was just a little girl talk. That's all."

Tom sniffed his amusement. He turned and walked toward the car.

"Tom?"

He turned back and looked at her.

"Take care of your mom. Please."

He just smiled.

"That's what dad would have wanted me to do."

Jaclyn breathed easier as she watched Tom walk to the lead car and slide into the passenger side. As they drove away, Jaclyn stood on the sidewalk for a few moments, watching the red tail lights disappear. Her thoughts turned to what she promised Jane Messingham only a few minutes ago.

I'm not going to wait until he finds me, she thought as she walked up the stairs, securing herself inside the safe house proper. *I'm going to find him and fulfill what I came to England to do.*

It's time for the hunted to become the huntress.

Chapter 34
The West End, London, England
3 August 2012 — 22.15 GMT/5:15 p.m. ET

Jafar sat on the couch, his prayers completed, *Iftar* safe in his belly. He was deep in thought over what happened that day.

He truly did not know what to do next. His Imam back in Afghanistan did not explain this to him thoroughly. Winning was the only objective, and how a field general achieved that goal was up to the field general himself. There was no calling home for reinforcements: You used what you had. If, by some stroke of luck or Allah's blessing, that other young men of the same beliefs heard of you and sought you out, then by all means, use them in Allah's service.

His thoughts — another operative dead, killed in Allah's wonderful service — made *Iftar* nearly come back up again.

Jafar did see a bright side to the day's events, however: one of his operatives, an agent of the martyred Yusuf, came to him, pledging his allegiance and wishing to continue in Yusuf's stead.

Jafar welcomed him with open arms.

There was another thing on his mind: How did the rogue American know about the attack? She couldn't have just simply attended the funeral. She was a wanted woman. She should not have been out in the open. It was stupid, and it was insane. If she had been a man and in the service of Osama bin Laden, he would have taught her the benefits of staying hidden while on the run from authorities.

Then it hit him: there was, however slim, the possibility of the captured operative talking about his plans. That operative was to have participated if the original shooter — the one who killed the Briton in the first place — could not handle the job. He could have let it slip so the Britons would show him mercy.

The realization caused him to swear loudly.

He launched himself off the couch, cell phone in hand. He began to dial numbers, holding the phone to his ear. He paced the length of the room, staring at the approaching wall.

As soon as the other party answered, he began to speak rapidly in Farsi, moving his free hand around as he verbally castrated the operative. Jafar spoke in this manner for several minutes, not letting his contact speak until it was time.

When the operative did speak, it was in the affirmative and quick to the point. Jafar did not allow for a question-and-answer period. He had said long before this that Allah did not tolerate such subversive activity from underlings.

Jafar hung up the phone and paced once more. He thought it all through. It was a hastily created plan, he admitted, but he had to make sure.

He had to be positive.

If the captured operative had said something, anything, he wanted to know.

If the operative said anything, Jafar wanted to kill the operative himself.

Chapter 35
Thames House, Millbank, London, England
4 August 2012 — 03.00 GMT/3 August 2012, 10:00 p.m. ET

A slight tremor on her chest alerted Jaclyn to the incoming text message. Her eyes immediately opened as she grabbed her BlackBerry and her HUD, sliding the latter onto her face and letting her thumbs dance on the former.

The message from Dupuis was clear as day:

He is still there. Happy hunting. AD

Jaclyn didn't grin or show any mirth at knowing her quarry was where she last left him two days ago. A lot had happened in that amount of time. She was surprised he hadn't been moved to Vauxhall Cross on the other side of the river.

Her lip curled when she recalled she had threatened to drown him in the river.

That won't happen tonight.

I need him alive.

Jaclyn put on the one-piece Lycra jumpsuit when she walked back into the safe house, sliding the form-fitting tool up her body within seconds. She waited until now to arm herself for her mission of revenge.

She filled her utility belt with darkness bombs and other incendiary devices, storing spare magazines in the rear sleeves. She dropped her Walthers into their respective holsters, but the one for her right hip, she screwed a silencer onto the barrel.

"I don't want to make too much noise while I'm in there, now do I?" she whispered as she held up the gun. She checked the magazine inside and noticed she had plenty of ammunition stored. It had been a few days since she used this gun.

It will be enough, she thought, as she snapped the clip back into the handgun.

Jaclyn grabbed her once again vibrating BlackBerry — "I can check that later," she said as she slid it into a side pouch — and her iPad, then slipped her black body-length trench coat over her shoulders. She pulled her hair back and attached a hair clip to keep her straight blonde tresses out of her face during this operation. She grabbed the keys and left the safe house.

She doubted she would return.

The streets of Islington were quiet at that time of the day. Streetlights flickered on and off periodically. A stray tabby cat had nestled itself between the Carlton Cinema's pillars. A light breeze, rare in early August, tickled the kitten's fur and cooled the pavement.

Jaclyn made the trip from the safe house to Thames House in just a little over 25 minutes. With no one on the streets except her, the traffic signals along the bus route went her way, and she drove without drawing attention to herself.

The thrum of the engine echoed through Whitehall as she drove south along Parliament Street, crossing the intersection with the Westminster Bridge before she flipped open the center console. She slowed down and pulled over across the street from Westminster Abbey.

Jaclyn looked around. She saw no one walking about or running along the Victoria Embankment. Not even a constable swinging his nightstick about was out this early. She hoped any of the Queen's Scholars inside the abbey did not forget to say their prayers before going to sleep.

She hit a switch in the console and immediately felt a lurch as the Citroën rose by its lonesome. Servomotors churned and buzzed as the car's tires folded in and tucked under the chassis. Jaclyn also felt the steering column collapse by an inch. She pulled it toward her and immediately the Citroën soared upward. By the time she realized how high up she had climbed, she came even with the clock on the left side of the abbey façade.

She slowly dragged the steering wheel toward the dashboard and felt the Citroën soar south on Abingdon Street until it brought her onto Millbank. Jaclyn passed the glass-topped buildings on the right-hand side of the road. The glass-topped River Thames looked calm to the left.

Jaclyn brought the car upward as she approached Thames House. She dragged the wheel to the right as she hovered over Page Street, then set the Citroën down on top of the roof.

She held her breath. If her luck held, no one from MI5 would know she was near the place. Tom didn't know she was coming. This was something she decided about after he and Jane departed the safe house.

Tom couldn't have tipped anyone off. No one rushed to the roof to fend off the unwanted visitor.

Jaclyn let the breath out slowly, then slipped out of the Citroën and set the security code.

It was time to interrogate the prisoner her way.

Two days ago, Jaclyn wanted to get a little rough with him to see if he would divulge anything tangible about his benefactor, but Dupuis and Willows forbade it. Now, she was officially off the books, and he would give her anything she asked tonight. She knew it would happen.

It was only a matter of how many bullets it would take.

She readied her silenced Walther.

Using her iPad in the same method that she used to get into the FA a couple of days ago, she managed to break MI5's security without breaking a sweat. She let her fingers dance across the screen as she found a way down to the cells before making the journey. She quickly disabled the cameras and caused them to run the past half an hour in a loop.

She drew her gun, entered Thames House and found no obstacles as she walked down the stairs.

She did find two obstacles in the form of hulking guards in front of Maqil Gnosh's cell, however. They looked to be asleep. Jaclyn figured they were bored guarding a prisoner who wouldn't talk to them, nor had any chance of escaping.

Even though they were asleep, she couldn't take the chance of them waking up until after she was done giving Maqil the once, the twice, and the thrice over. That meant she needed to take them out of the game.

She moved her left hand into one of the pouches on her utility belt and grabbed three ether balls. Each ball contained a very high amount of ether, enough to knock a man out for a good 45 minutes.

Three of them would keep the two of them out long enough to get what she needed and get out of there.

She tossed the balls toward the guards, hearing them crack as they landed just next to their chairs. The ether poured out, the fumes rising to the ceiling, tickling their noses and massaging their subconscious. They fell to the floor.

Jaclyn slid nose plugs into her nostrils and stepped into the hallway. She took out the thin device Parkerhurst gave her last night.

She unlocked the door and entered the dim-lit cell. The device immediately scrambled the signal and looped the darkness over again. She hit the lights and felt her HUD darken to compensate for the glare.

Maqil was asleep. Smirking, Jaclyn closed the cell door quietly and walked to the table, where a glass of water sat, full and untouched.

She grabbed the glass and threw it at him, soaking his face and shattering against his nose. A trickle of blood came to the surface almost immediately.

"Don't even think about shitting yourself. I know you're already scared," Jaclyn said as she brought the Walther up and kept it trained on him. "Get over to the table."

Maqil's eyes squinted as he tried to get used to the light, but he wasn't moving fast enough for Jaclyn's tastes. She grabbed him by the t-shirt and tossed him the five feet to the table where they sat some 60 hours ago. The force of her throw knocked the table askew and sent Maqil tumbling to the floor.

I hope this cell is sound proof, she thought.

She power walked to him and stepped on his throat, causing him to gag as she applied pressure. She yanked his sock off, then turned around and stuffed it into his mouth. Wide-eyed, she lifted Maqil off the ground. He found himself in the chair quicker than he could blink.

"Now," Jaclyn said, bringing the cold steel of the silenced Walther up to his right temple. "Let's try this again, shall we? Let's discuss Mr. Mohammed."

By now, Maqil's eyes had somewhat recovered from the shock of being roused from his slumber at 4:30 a.m., only to find a woman dressed in tight black Lycra holding a gun to his head. Only when he heard Mohammed's name did he look into Jaclyn's face and saw the dark Foster Grants staring back at him did he recognize the voice.

"You bitch," he tried to say through the gag.

She twirled the Walther as she brought it back toward the left. The handle flew at Mach speed, the resulting crack echoed throughout the cell. The blood on the bridge of his nose was the least of his worries right now. Blood and mucus streamed from his nostrils. He was groaning, but the smelly gag muffled the sound.

"Manners, Maqil," Jaclyn taunted. "Manners will get you everywhere in the West."

She grabbed his sockless leg and swung it onto the table.

"Now, I will shoot off one of your toes every minute until you tell me something I haven't heard before," she said. "What size shoe do you take, Maqil? A 10? A 10 1/2? Something tells me you're going to have to play mix and match before the night is out."

"You're bluffing," he said through the gag.

A feral grin danced along Jaclyn's face.

She turned and blew off his big toe.

The screams didn't make it past the gag. She saw the tears falling from his widened, panicked eyes, though. She felt strengthened by the terrorist's pain.

"I don't bluff, big boy."

The prisoner shook his head wildly. He tried to move his arms, but MI5 kept him restrained, his hands behind his back. He bit down hard on the sock, but it was so thin that he bit his tongue. He tasted his own blood.

"Want to try again? You keep delaying, I'll keep shooting."

Maqil, in incredible amounts of pain, managed to calm himself to heaving breaths.

"Your government will never allow this! They have condemned torture!"

Jaclyn grabbed him by the t-shirt again, but this time, pulled him close to her face. She could feel his fear on his breath.

"I don't give a shit what the United States government says I can do or not do," she said through her teeth. "I've gone rogue. I'm outside of their control. My country will never hear of this, the British will never hear of this, and your countrymen will never hear of this."

The words registered in Maqil's brain, but it took a second for the signals to process and send directions to his eyes.

When his eyes finally got the memo, Jaclyn could have watched a movie on them.

"You're mine to do with as I please until the British come and rescue you — which won't be for a few hours," she said teasingly. "Can you hold out that long, Maqil? Should I call Vegas and see if Caesars will put odds on you talking before then? If not, I bet the new hotel down the Strip will do it."

Maqil closed his eyes tight in defiance.

She pulled his head back by the hair. He whimpered.

"Tell me what I want to hear, Maqil, or I'm going to shoot a finger off this time."

He chewed on the sock as he scrunched his face up, as if he were waiting for the pain to come.

Jaclyn shrugged. She brought her Walther down level with the back of Maqil's chair and pulled the trigger.

His right thumb vanished. Blood spurted from around the knuckle.

Maqil's eyes flew open. He tried to scream. He pleaded for one of the Brits to come and stop her.

No one came. The tears flowed from both eyes. He bent his head down so Jaclyn could not see how much he was suffering at her hands.

"You're such a stubborn little camel, Maqil. You're lucky I'm a very patient girl, and I have plenty of bullets and plenty of guns. I came ready for a standoff with you, because I knew how much you just love talking to me and giving me information.

"You're going to spill your guts before I'm through though." She leaned over and whispered into his ear. "You're going to go to hell. One of the seven gates of hell are going to open for you, and there will be no virgins waiting there; instead, it'll be *Jahanam* for you, bucko."

Maqil wailed through the sock.

"Are you going to talk?"

He shook his head vigorously. He braced for the pain.

A look of evil passed over Jaclyn's face.

"Oh well."

She pulled the trigger again. His index finger fell to the floor.

If he didn't have the sock in his mouth, he would have woken the Queen with his blood-curdling screech.

She shot his middle finger off. He started banging his head off the table until the pain in his forehead matched the pain in his foot and in his hand.

"Had enough yet?"

He nodded just as vigorous as he did when he shook his head not two minutes prior.

Jaclyn removed the saliva and blood stained sock from his mouth. She put the Walther against his already broken nose.

"Give me something concrete or you'll be sniffing through your ears for the rest of your pathetic life."

"His name is Jafar," Maqil breathed. He face looked like he was vomiting the name. "Jafar Abdul Mohammed."

Jaclyn kept her grin to herself. It was the exact name — the first name, at least — that Lavi Witz had shown her on the dead terrorist's cell phone earlier in the day deep in the tunnels of Islington.

"Where is he? Where can I find him?"

"I don't know."

Jaclyn didn't like that answer. She kicked the chair out from under him, her right foot coming across and booting it left. Maqil came down the center, his chin hitting flush with the table edge.

She shoved the barrel of the silenced Walther inside his mouth.

"This is the last chance to save your pathetic life."

"I don't know!" he screamed around the metal. The tears were dripping off his chin.

Jaclyn became incensed.

"You're lying, Maqil! You took a call from him, so you have his number. Give me the number and I'll keep the fucker on long enough to trace the call."

Maqil spat the barrel out and looked at her.

"Okay, I'll give you the number. Please, don't shoot me again."

Jaclyn sent a mental command to record the number Maqil gave her and cross-referenced it against the number Witz gave her.

They were exact matches.

Jaclyn breathed a sigh of relief. Maqil didn't notice it, though, as his head was down on the table. Jaclyn could hear him asking Allah for forgiveness.

An explosion caused the building to shake. Alarms sounded throughout Thames House. Jaclyn turned her HUD toward the cell door and ran a scan. No one ran toward the cell block, which allowed her several extra minutes of time to spare.

"Al-Qaeda operatives are in the building," the voice over the loud speaker announced. "All available armed hands report to the GMW Arch."

Jaclyn was shocked. *Al-Qaeda in Thames House? Impossible*, she thought. *The security here is much too good.*

She looked to Maqil. Her HUD saw that he looked to be on cloud nine. His rescuers were in the building, and he thought he was getting out of here.

She leveled the Walther upon him.

His look of glee vanished in a heartbeat.

"Thanks for the information, Maqil," she said as if they were old friends. "It's been nice knowing you."

She pulled the trigger. The bullet tore Maqil's head from between the eyes backward away. The terrorist's body slumped to the side and fell out of the chair, coming to rest face down in front of his killer. What was left of his brains slipped out and coated the concrete floor.

Jaclyn slapped the button on her utility belt and felt the Kevlar lining form up.

She didn't holster her Walther, just in case the terrorists were anywhere near the Citroën.

Chapter 36
Driver's Seat, Citroën C6, Hovering above London, England
4 August 2012 — 04.45 GMT/3 August 2012, 11:45 p.m. ET

Dawn slowly broke over Millbank as Jaclyn stormed out the rooftop door. She heard the echoes of shooting on the lower levels of Thames House, but that was not her concern right now.

She had the Citroën's security system disabled and her BlackBerry out the second she stepped onto the roof.

"Dial Chief," Jaclyn told her HUD. As soon as she shut the door, the BlackBerry began to ring. She had the Citroën up in the air by the third ring.

"She must be dead asleep," Jaclyn surmised. She turned the wheel and steered herself toward Hyde Park. She figured she would have plenty of landing room there without attracting a lot of attention.

Alex picked up on the fifth ring, saving the call from going to voice mail.

"Hello." The Director of the CIA sounded half asleep through the car's speakers.

"Chief, we got a name," Jaclyn announced as she soared northwest over Buckingham Palace.

"Jaclyn? How did you get it?"

"I thought you wanted to have deniability?"

"The president does, Snapshot, not me."

"I don't think you should ask."

"Keep it to yourself then."

"I planned on it."

"What's his name?"

"Jafar Mohammed."

"Any idea where he is?"

"Not a bleeding clue."

"You're not supposed to hanging around Tom, Jaclyn. That was in our agreement."

"I know, but if I didn't run into him, I wouldn't have gotten the information in the first place. My operation this morning that you have absolutely no idea about confirmed his name." Jaclyn went into her narrative of the day, meeting Lavi Witz and the information he gave her.

"I need to get in touch with Salt and run a trace, Chief. Are you still on the island?"

"For the foreseeable future, yes. Parkerhurst, however, has chosen to swim home."

Jaclyn grinned. She began to descend into Hyde Park.

"I'll call Salt. Keep the phone close. You may want to put the coffee on, Chief."

"Why? Are you coming over?"

"Not yet, but a cup of coffee would be pretty good right now."

She disconnected the call and quickly called Washington. She spoke briefly with Salt.

"I need you to trace the call I'm about to make. Give me the location via the SIM card."

"You got it."

Jaclyn switched lines and had her HUD began to dial the number Witz gave her.

I wonder how long this will take, she thought. *He must be going through his morning prayers right now. God, I hope I throw his day into complete disorder.*

He picked up on the second ring.

"Hello?" the tired voice said.

Even though she had heard it on his broadcasts, Jaclyn was not impressed with the man's voice now. There was a hint of a British accent in it, which she did not take by surprise. He sounded utterly exhausted, as if he did not have much sleep recently.

Of course, he's trying to ruin the world in less than a week, Jaclyn thought.

"Hello?" Jafar said when she didn't answer at first.

"I am coming for you, Jafar," she said. She kept her tone measured, as if not letting any emotion into her voice. "I am coming for you and there is nowhere to run."

There was a slight pause on the other end.

"Who is this? Who dares disturb Allah's most loyal servant?"

Jaclyn rolled her eyes under her HUD.

"I'll give you three guesses, bitch. Ask Allah who I am; He always knows, doesn't he?"

"How did you get my number?" Jafar began to panic. "You are that damned Johnson bitch!"

"Ding, ding, ding! It took you long enough. I just wanted to call and tell you the operative you sent to kill me, the one I took out in Regent's Park, is now dead. He is burning in hell as we speak, Jafar. He died for nothing."

"He gave his life for Allah!" Jafar protested.

Jaclyn laughed. She had taken it, and had done so with as much force as she possibly could.

She still felt the still smoking Walther resting against her hip.

"He's not getting his virgins, Jafar. It's going to be the worst form of hell: it was *Jahanam* for him, and it'll be *Jahanam* for you."

Jafar howled his outrage into the phone, his words switching between Farsi and English and back again.

"I will get you, bitch! Allah will have his revenge! *Allahu Akbar!*"

He quickly hung up.

Jaclyn switched lines.

"Did you get it?" she asked Salt.

"Barely. We couldn't pinpoint his location; the best we could get was that he's near Soho. He had to know we were tracing him. Sending your iPad the approximate coordinates now."

Jaclyn swore. Jafar had been so close this whole time!

"Thanks, Salt."

She hung up and quickly re-dialed Dupuis' phone. Dupuis answered on the first ring.

"That was fast," they chorused.

"We got a partial, Chief. The muppet hung up on me before we could get an accurate trace through his cell." She explained Salt's prior explanation.

"You know I hate it when you get uber technical."

"You can blame Salt for that one, Chief. He uses it to get the girls."

Alex chuckled.

"He just sent me the approximate coordinates."

"What good are approximate coordinates, Snapshot? We need exact. Direct. Right on the money. Approximate and almost don't count. This isn't horseshoes, Snapshot. This is international security."

"Right, I forgot." Jaclyn looked at her iPad. She saw the possible blanket area and figured it would take more than just her hovering over Soho to find one Muslim male walking about at 5 a.m. There had to be plenty of Muslim men going to their mosques for early morning prayer services. It would be like trying to find Waldo in a painting.

She just had a radical idea strike her, though.

What would it hurt?

"Chief," she said, "forward that picture you sent me of Mohammed to Metropolitan Police. Ask them to send patrols over to the Soho and West End areas. Tell them to look for someone making a quick getaway or someone making a ruckus in a flat. He's panicky, Alex. He's going to make a major mistake. I just know it."

"I'll do that right now. I just don't see how that's going to help; if we had the exact coordinates, we could bust his ass in 10 minutes."

"If we had them, we could, but we can't, so we'll do the best we can."

"Very true," Dupuis said following a lengthy sigh. "Don't break the sound barrier getting there."

"I won't, and I'll check back in soon."

Jaclyn ended the call and stowed the BlackBerry into her utility belt. She did some quick calculations: it was going to take Dupuis some time to convince Metropolitan Police to get over there, maybe five minutes, at the most. MI5 will, of course, get wind of it within a minute later, and they'll send over a fleet of agents and take command of the site.

And while I can't actually be anywhere near MI5, Jaclyn thought, *I can be just on the peripheral edges of the target area, picking up gossip and learning what I can, before I start the next phase of my operation — taking this son of a bitch out.*

She smiled as she turned the key, feeling the Citroën purr under her touch.

Chapter 37
The West End, London, England
4 August 2012 — 05.01 GMT/12:01 a.m. ET

Jafar stared at the cell phone for several minutes after he hung up with the American.

Anger welled deep within him. She had contacted him. He felt dirty. She dared to call him out!

He didn't even notice the popping of his knee joints as he jumped off the couch. He walked to his prayer window, knowing that he should be kneeling right now and giving his morning offerings to Allah.

Johnson had thrown him off with her call. His daily routine was now out of whack. His mind was churning now.

He growled as he thought of the call.

How dare she not know her place in society! Women are not to disturb men while they are meditating, or preparing to meditate. The bitch must pay for this! Allah will destroy her!

Jafar breathed in through his nose and expelled the bad air from his system seconds later. Knowing his god would take care of the situation left the Afghani at peace. He smiled as he pictured slaughtering the American on an altar of Islam, sacrificed to Allah in exchange for great blessings.

Coming to his senses, he realized why the American had called him, and more specifically, called his cell phone. He knew governments could trace a person's location through the SIM card in the phone. Anyone with a rudimentary knowledge of wireless signals could pinpoint one's precise location in a matter of seconds once they engaged a call.

He recalled the American's words:

I am coming for you, Jafar, she had said.

It means only one thing: *she was trying to trace my location. She kept me on just long enough to get an idea of where I am. I ended the call just in time: if we spoke longer, I would already be in custody. Police work quickly when they had all their camels lined in a row.*

I must leave this place now, Jafar thought. *Thankfully, I've been ready for this moment.*

He turned from the window and walked to his room, where a small bag waited for him. It held his netbook computer that held all the same web sites and information his laptop had saved. He had emailed every site he visited in relation to his ongoing mission of terror to himself, so that in the event his laptop crashed or he had to make his getaway, he would be able to have everything at his fingertips. There would be no delays.

All except one delay, he thought. *I must ride that insufferable Tube in order to get to my safe house.*

Or it will be my safe house, as soon as I take care of a few Muslims who have gone astray.

An evil grin came to him.

You cannot run from her, Jafar, the voice said.

"Yes I can, and yes I will," Jafar replied calmly. He reached into his dresser and pulled out a gun. He checked to make sure it was loaded, and he found another magazine with it. He shoved that into his pants pocket. He put a sport coat on and slid the gun into a side pocket. He hoped it would not bulge, but thankfully, the gun was small.

That won't be enough to stop her.

"It will. I have an entire arsenal at my beck and call. You'll see."

The voice simply chuckled at Jafar's bold pronouncement.

Jafar ignored it and walked back into his common room. He sat down at his laptop and began to wipe the computer's memory in the event that authorities found it. He wouldn't take the chance of the Britons coming up with a warrant.

Jafar rose from his couch. He could not take anything of relative comfort, for that would have been a sure sign of his permanent departure from Cavendish Square. He couldn't even take a bag of clothes, even though he knew he would need something to change in to, especially if a stand-off occurred. He grabbed the netbook bag and slung it over his shoulder. He would need that, he knew. It was the most important part of his operation: if the terror attacks were to continue, he would need to be able to control the operation through his netbook while at the safe house.

He departed the flat without a second look. It wasn't important to him, nor did he have an attachment to it. It was only a short stay in the Grand Scheme of Allah.

It was time to move on to bigger and better things.

Jafar stepped outside and felt the early morning warmth. The sound of police sirens froze him, but he resumed his walk a second later.

I have nothing to fear from them, he thought. *I am a simple Muslim going to my mosque for prayer. They have no reason to accost me. I will make my way to the Tube, and I will look like I am traveling. Not even the American bitch will stop me.*

He walked down the alleyway separating Cavendish Square from Oxford Street. It was early enough that none of those disgusting Western women would walk into the college. He walked with purpose, much like any other person during rush hour. He came to Oxford Street within two minutes. He prepared to cross over to Oxford Circus Station, but he caught a glimpse of a black Citroën C6 slowing to a halt several blocks away to the west. Police officers were there. MI5 were nowhere near him.

Jafar didn't see any reason to panic. He breathed evenly as he crossed Oxford Street and then Regent Street. He made his way down the stairs and into the vast Tube station.

He was as good as home free.

Chapter 38
Oxford Street, London, England
4 August 2012 — 05.19 GMT/12:19 a.m. ET

Jaclyn didn't waste any time in getting over to the command site. She stayed over to the side and tried to blend into the shadows. Instead of talking to the officers, she listened to whatever conversation she could pick up with her ears — and even some she couldn't from normal procedures.

She activated a small switch in the center console. A panel in the grille slid open, and from within a small parabolic microphone emerged. Despite its size, the parabola was able to pick up conversations from up to 500 feet away. Her iPad was able to discern and tune to which frequency and distance away she wanted to hear.

She expertly fiddled the attenuator and began to hear various British voices and until she was able to match voices to the moving lips. Her HUD centered on a group of three officers standing at the corner of Oxford and Holles Streets. One had the uniform of a higher-ranking officer, and Jaclyn could tell, just from his body language, that the end of his shift was approaching and that he wanted to go home.

No one is going home until I get to go home, Jaclyn thought.

She listened.

"Sir, we received word from one of the residents in Cavendish Square that they had heard a man shouting in what sounded like Arabic this morning. They knocked on his door about five minutes ago, and there was no answer. They entered the premises and found it empty."

Jaclyn cursed.

Shit, he's gone, she thought, smacking her head off the steering wheel.

She lifted her head back at the trio.

"He won't get far," the officer in charge said. "Let's blanket the area. The Americans have sent over a picture of the suspect; how the devil they got the information first, I'll never know."

"There is that rogue agent, maybe she —"

The officer in charge cut him off.

"Think, Jameson. If she's rogue, why would she call the Americans? That just doesn't make sense, and it's beyond human thought."

Jaclyn tried to stifle a grin.

Then she gasped.

Tom walked toward the officer in charge and the two flatfoots. He showed them his badge, and they immediately differed to his. Except the officer in charge, though.

"Why is Five sending over a bleeding wet-behind-the-ears kid when they have plenty of agents with experience?" he said.

"Because if it has to do with this case and the terrorism against the Olympics as well as the attack on my father's funeral yesterday," Tom responded, "then I'm the one they send. You got that?"

Jaclyn's mouth twitched. *Touché, you fat bastard.*

"What do we have?" Tom asked.

Jaclyn immediately called him on her BlackBerry before he got the question out. She watched as he grabbed his phone and told the officers to wait a minute. He brought the phone to his ear.

"Hello?"

"He's not there any longer," Jaclyn said.

"Snapshot? Where are you?" he said, turning his back and lowering his voice to a conspiratorial whisper.

"I'm about two blocks away, I can hear every word you say, and I can see every move you make."

"Those are some bloody fantastic ears you have," Tom replied. "Your eyes, too. Which direction are you?" He began to search toward the Tube.

"I'm behind you now, silly."

Tom immediately turned, startling the officers. He began to look fervently for Jaclyn, until he finally saw the black Citroën off to the side of Woodstock Street.

"I see you. I'll be there in a few moments."

"I'm not moving any time soon."

They hung up and she heard him say "I'll be right back; I have to discuss something with my associate," before walking past them and across Oxford Street. Jaclyn switched the feed from the parabola to 94.9 FM. She watched as he walked the three blocks to where Jaclyn sat. He didn't look like he was happy.

He walked around the bonnet and slid into the passenger side.

"What in the devil are you doing here?" he asked. "You know you're not supposed to be anywhere near here. It's an MI5 operation."

"I'm far enough away that I can do my own investigation and follow any leads that I come up with."

"You're sitting in your bloody car listening to the BBC."

Jaclyn smiled.

"Yes, to the untrained eye that looks like what I'm doing, but in all actuality, Mr. Messingham, I'm doing serious rogue agent-type stuff."

"I say it again," Tom said, not believing her, "you're sitting in your car —" Jaclyn flipped the switch again, this time with a tight grin. She adjusted the volume. The voices of the cops Tom just spoke with streamed over the speaker, "— listening to every word those blokes are saying."

Tom sank into the seat. His cheek twitched.

"Believe me now?" she asked.

He nodded.

"Pretty boy Jafar is no longer in his flat, which means he had to have left as soon as he hung up with me. The police want a cordon of the immediate area and —"

"Don't tell me you've talked with the bastard?" Tom said, amazed as he sat up.

"I did, about half an hour or so ago, which means he is long gone from here by now. And if he was smart, he would have either hopped into his car or onto the Tube. The police are not going to find him around here."

Tom couldn't see a flaw in the logic.

"I thought he was going to panic and make a mistake. I underestimated him," Jaclyn said. She breathed through her nose. "He was quick and decisive. And somehow he escaped before I got here. I was only in freaking Hyde Park!"

"Alright, keep your knickers on," Tom said. "It was a setback." He paused. "What's our next move?"

"You're asking me?"

"Of course I am. This is your mission still, unofficially. I'll follow your lead."

Jaclyn gave him a soft smile.

"Thanks, Tom."

"You're welcome."

"I would think he would try to find a place to stay and regroup," Jaclyn said. "I would think mosques would be his first choice: They don't let non-Muslims in, and it would be a perfect place for him to find sanctuary."

A light bulb went off in Tom's mind.

"Right, and if you or me or any Western agency barged in, the Muslims would cite religious prejudice and would file a complaint all the way to Her Majesty, if they wanted."

"Exactly, so it's going to have to be done in a very stealthy manner."

Tom began grinning like a Cheshire cat.

"So you're saying you have to wait until the cover of darkness in order to apprehend him."

"That would be the wisest course of action, I think."

Tom leaned over, his head positioned right over the console.

"What do you need in the way of surveillance and materiel?"

Jaclyn turned her head away and looked toward Oxford Circus.

"We need to see if he actually took the Underground," she deduced. "How quick can you get the tapes from the past half an hour for Oxford Circus?"

Tom had his cell phone in his hand before Jaclyn finished.

"Great minds think alike, I guess," Jaclyn said.

Tom simply grinned as he put the phone to his ear. It took a few seconds, but he was able to connect with Thames House. Jaclyn kept her HUD trained on the street.

"Get in touch with the Underground; I need the tapes of Oxford Circus for the past half an hour analyzed and every face run through the facial recognition system. Our target escaped the area, and we have reason to believe he took the Tube out of there."

"We're going to need to know which train he took and in which direction, and then a look at every stop's cameras in relation to the time he left Oxford Circus."

Tom lowered the phone and covered the receiver.

"Blimey, that can take all morning, and we have a dead terrorist back at headquarters," he said. He blinked. "You wouldn't happen to know anything about that, would you?"

"You have twenty-two hundred workers at MI5, I'm sure you can spare a few techs to review those tapes after you confirm he entered the Tube," Jaclyn said, ignoring his question.

"Right," he said, bringing the phone back to his ear. "We're also going to have to get all the techs we can to locate this bastard, especially if we have him on the run. This may take all morning and well into the afternoon."

Tom paused as he listened.

"Right, I want to know immediately when you find something. We don't need every bloody agent looking for the terrorist's killer. We need to know where this muppet ran off to. Just give me a call when something unusual pops up."

He closed the phone and looked to Jaclyn. Jaclyn stared off into space. Her finger traced a line down Oxford Street.

"Well, that was fun. It may be a while before we get anything."

"Question: What mosques are near the Tube lines out of Oxford Circus? That may narrow our search down a bit."

"True enough, let's see," Tom replied. "There's the one on Baker Street, that's not too far away."

"That's close enough for him to keep an eye on the proceedings here."

"There's one near Whitechapel."

"Where is that?"

"A pretty fair distance; only a couple of miles, but it's one or two stops away off the Tube, but it involves a transfer from any one of six lines."

"That would be a good way to throw us off the trail."

"True. There was supposed to be a mosque built near the Olympic Park."

"Supposed to be?"

"Yeah, but they didn't build it. There's a mosque in Morden, and that's all the way south of Wimbledon. Gorgeous building, too. There's a mosque in East London that serves the Bangladeshi people, there's one in Brixton on the Victoria Line."

"That's a possibility, since the Victoria comes through Oxford Circus."

"There's also one in Southfields, but it's quite a bit of a walk from the Tube. I would think that Mohammed would want some place rather close to the Tube, within a minute or two's walk away —"

Tom's eyes widened. Jaclyn looked curiously at him.

"What is it, Tom?"

"Spank my arse and call me Harriet! That's it!"

"What's it?"

"The North London Central Mosque, and it's on the Victoria Line, to boot. It's not even a two-minute walk from the Finsbury Park Station."

Jaclyn could see two acceptable reasons why Tom would bring this up: one, it was a mosque, and two it was on the Victoria Line. The fact that Tom was excited about it to the point of bursting had her interest piqued.

She waited for Tom to explain, but when he didn't, Jaclyn had to prompt him.

"So tell me why he would pick this mosque in North London? Why wouldn't he pick one of the others to go to?" she asked.

Tom nearly gave her a look of astonishment, but he held it: he suddenly remembered she wasn't British.

"In a nutshell, the North London Mosque had, at one point in the 1990s, developed into what many consider the center of radical Islam in the capital. Extremist Islamic preachers came into North London and took it over, and several al-Qaeda operatives, like Richard Reid and Zacarias Moussaoui, attended it."

The name Moussaoui caused Jaclyn to shiver. Moussaoui was an al-Qaeda operative who had knowledge of not only the September 11 attacks, but of another attack that was to occur after that fateful day.

If Mohammed chose North London as his next base of operations, the fact the mosque had trained al-Qaeda operatives made Jaclyn press her irony button.

"In 2003," Tom continued, "the mosque was taken over by mainstream Muslims — ones not intent on killing every God-fearing person on Earth — after a hundred police officers raided it and arrested the radical Imam Abu Hamza al-Masri. It was in all the papers; I'm shocked it didn't make the *New York Times* or the *Washington Post*."

"It probably did, but I wasn't keeping up to breast on England at the time," Jaclyn replied sarcastically.

Tom ignored it.

"I would bet that is where he is," he said.

"Or where he will be," Jaclyn countered. "How long does it take to get from here to Finsbury Park?"

"About 15 minutes with the crowds getting on at King's Cross."

"So if he's there, he would have already gotten off the Tube then."

Tom looked at his watch. It was nearing 5:30 a.m.

"That would be my guess, yes."

"We need to find out if he's there."

"Yes, and we should try to safeguard these other mosques, too. We have absolutely no idea where he's hiding out. We need to figure out where he is, then come up with a plan of attack."

Jaclyn turned her head and looked right at him with a smile.

"I already have one. Just let me know where he is. I can't make a move until tonight."

Tom looked at her and nodded.

Jaclyn noticed that they became quiet, wondering what to say next. Jaclyn felt Tom's eyes on her, and she felt herself shudder. It wasn't a bad shudder either. She suddenly had the urge to change into something a little less restricting than the Lycra jumpsuit.

"It's going to be a while for us to gather every little bit of information we can get. And since you're not going to go after him until tonight, what are you going to do in the meantime?" he said, a light smile coming to his lips.

"I have no idea," she replied innocently. She saw where he was leading this. Her mother didn't raise a fool, and the CIA didn't train one, either. "Do you have any suggestions?"

He inched closer.

"How about you go back to Islington and get a little sleep? I know you were busy this morning, breaking into Thames House and torturing a prisoner, putting a bullet not only in his head, but blowing his toes and fingers off, too. It has to be hard work not to follow the rules and I'm sure you're tired."

Jaclyn sniffed her amusement. She somehow knew he would never tell anyone her involvement. She leaned in a little closer to him. Tom's face was just inches away. She just noticed her heart was beating so rapidly that it was bouncing off her breastbone like a paddleball.

She didn't let it distract her. She continued to play the game.

"And how, Agent Scouser, are you going to prove that I was there? And may I remind you," she said, inching closer, lowering her voice so that he didn't have to strain to hear her over honking cars on Oxford Street, "that I am above the rules, since, you know, I'm not officially affiliated with any countries."

Tom moved his face closer. Jaclyn could feel his breath on her cheek, and when he brushed the backside of his fingers down her other cheek, she exhaled, her breath quivering. She was suddenly more nervous than she had ever been before, and she was relishing every moment of it. Intense, potent desire charged the air between them.

"I know that," he said, tilting his head.

Jaclyn tilted hers.

"Are you going to arrest me for breaking international law?"

Her voice shook.

"Only if you don't kiss me this second," he whispered.

"I thought you'd never ask," she said before their lips finally met, the tension finally broken. Jaclyn felt her heart blossom as their first peck turned into a slightly longer kiss. Her arms slinked about the back of his neck as his reached around her waist.

Their kiss lengthened. Jaclyn's fingers laced through the back of Tom's hair, the nails dragging down the back of his scalp.

Her cell phone's ringer broke the moment.

Both broke away with intense remorse.

"Damn phone is going to go in the Thames the first chance I get," Jaclyn muttered as she pulled out her BlackBerry from her utility belt.

Tom rubbed his lips absent-mindedly. She accepted the call without checking the caller ID. "This better be fucking good."

"Did I interrupt something, Snapshot?" Dupuis said. "I've never heard that tone out of you. You've never sounded so, what's the word I'm looking for, distraught?" The director of the CIA paused for the briefest of moments before adding, "Are you being a naughty secret agent?"

Jaclyn knew Dupuis was gently teasing the younger operative, but she wasn't in the mood for it.

"What's up, Chief." Jaclyn was officially irritated.

"That means you *are* being a naughty secret agent."

"Alex, what's going on?"

"Fine, tell me later. What is new with the investigation?"

Jaclyn leaned her head against Tom's shoulder.

"The target flew the coop. Box 500 is conducting video surveillance of the Tube from the past half an hour or so — time suddenly stopped for me," Jaclyn said, causing Dupuis to chuckle, "so that may be off by a few minutes or a few hours."

"He was that good of a kisser?"

Jaclyn sighed. She picked herself off Tom's side.

"That would be affirmative, Alex," she said through gritted teeth.

"Alright, I'll stop. Let me know when something pops up – with the mission."

"You are fucking incorrigible, Alex. This is sexual harassment and I don't have to take it," Jaclyn said before turning to her right, away from Tom, and lowering her voice. "If anything happens, you'll be the first to know."

"Girls' night out? I'm up for that. But Jaclyn?"

"Yes, Alex?"

"Survive the mission first, then have fun."

Jaclyn couldn't help but smile. She had finally broken through Dupuis' rigid shell — even though Alex had warned her about that sort of fun.

"I will, Chief. I'll call you when we learn anything from the surveillance."

Dupuis, like normal, did not give a closing salutation. Jaclyn pressed end and put her BlackBerry back into the utility belt.

"Where were we?" Jaclyn said with a sly grin.

Tom leaned in and kissed her lips tenderly.

"I was just getting back to investigating whatever we were called here to investigate." Jaclyn groaned. "I'm sorry. I've been gone too long, and those cops are probably wondering what I'm up to."

"Tell them the truth."

"What, that I was snogging a sultry foreign secret agent in a Citroën? They'd never believe me."

Tom winked at her.

Jaclyn smirked.

"Are you going back to Islington?" Tom asked.

"Yeah, I think that's where I'm going. If my plans change, you'll be the first to know."

"I'll call you the moment I find anything out about Mohammed," Tom said as he opened the door.

"Alright, but I warn you I may be kissing someone when you call, so if I sound pissed, don't be alarmed."

Tom caught the sarcasm, leaned back over the dash and kissed Jaclyn one last time.

Jaclyn moaned into his kiss.

"Alright, get out of my car before I shag you, you sexy British man."

Tom laughed as he departed. He shut the door and walked around the bonnet one more time, giving it a pat as he walked back toward the police officers, a smile as wide as a football goalmouth on his face.

Jaclyn watched him walk away.

She, too, smiled as she started the Citroën's engine and drove off to Islington, the memories of the kiss not able to distract her from paying attention to the road.

No one paid any attention to Jafar when he stepped into Oxford Circus. He was just another passenger to them, he saw, and it seemed as if they were in their own little worlds as they headed to the Victoria, Bakerloo and Central Line terminals. They read their respective newspapers — the funeral attack was plastered as the headline story in the *Daily Mail*, the *Mirror*, the *Telegraph* and the *Guardian* — while drinking coffee, and none flashed furtive looks at him. He expected more, especially after a masked Muslim man had ravaged London recently. No one would have been able to recognize him, at any rate. He left the cloth in Cavendish Square.

He doubted he would need it any longer.

The next time he spoke to the world, he would fully reveal himself. He thought of his plan and his next message he would broadcast as the train rocked through the Victoria Line tunnels, surging through Warren Street and up into King's Cross. Passengers departed and passengers jumped aboard. Several Muslim men came aboard here and nodded to their brother in Islam.

Respectfully, he nodded back.

The train rolled out of King's Cross and headed for North London. Jafar found the sound of the train soothing.

The feel of his silenced gun against the side of his chest comforted him even more so. He breathed easier knowing that it had not slipped out of his pocket when he walked across Oxford Street. With police running about, that would have been a disaster, especially if the gun discharged.

He banished those thoughts from his mind. He was away from that circus, and the American was far from him.

I will call her out, though, Jafar thought. *I want her to come to me so I can kill her. I want to make an example of her.*

He grinned much too wide. The Muslim men looked at him, wondering just what would make him smile. He quickly made the smile vanish.

A few minutes later, the train rumbled through Highbury & Islington Station before continuing on to Finsbury Park. At one point, he heard the rumbling of the Piccadilly Line train in another tunnel headed for its next stop, Arsenal Station. The Emirates Stadium was above him.

Soon the train began to slow down as it entered Finsbury Park Station. A clamor began as many people — the Muslim men included —

263

hopped off the train and made their way upstairs to the bright sunshine above.

Jafar followed slowly.

He drew his cell phone from his pocket and began to dial the number of Yusuf's old cell. He pressed send as soon as he stepped onto Seven Sisters Road. It rang as he crossed to Rock Road.

"Hello?" the voice of his agent, Achmed, answered.

"Brother Achmed, where are you now?"

"I am holed up near the Muslim Welfare House in North London. Where are you?"

Jafar was stunned. He spun and looked to the west. The Muslim Welfare House was less than 300 feet away.

"I am not that far from you. Do you have any of Yusuf's agents with you?"

"Yes, brother Jafar. I have two of them. We are enjoying *Suhoor* before we begin our fast for the day."

"You do know you are supposed to have *Suhoor* before the sun comes up, correct?" Jafar looked to the sky. The sun was rising, but a cloud cover was moving in from the west. The clouds were not dark, but he knew that could change at any moment: It was England, after all.

There was an awkward pause on the other end.

"Yes, brother Jafar, we know. We will offer ourselves to Allah in reparation —"

"Quiet, Achmed. You will be able to make up for this, and Allah will gladly honor you for it. Are you and your operatives armed?"

"Yes, of course we are."

"Good," Jafar said, smiling as he heard this. He looked down the road and saw the Muslim men from the Tube walking down the street. "Come now and meet me. I'm at the corner of St. Thomas's Road and Rock Road. Keep your weapons hidden and we will make the world fear us."

"It will be as Allah commands."

Jafar hung up and waited a few minutes. The three men, with Achmed at the head, walked to their leader and bowed.

"What is Allah's wish, brother Jafar?" they chorused.

Jafar stood tall in front of them.

"It is time to take back one of Allah's houses of worship. Those Muslims who want to play nice with the West will pay for their double-dealing and backstabbing of their own faith. Allah has deemed this necessary in our war against the infidels."

Jafar turned and led them down St. Thomas's Road only a few feet, as the North London Central Mosque practically sat at the head of the road. They walked through the steel gates and up the stairs. They barged inside, the four of them.

Morning prayers were underway. A man, the mosque's Imam, came to them with a smile on his face.

"Welcome, my brothers in Allah! Welcome to our humble sanctuary. Is this your first time here?"

Jafar leveled a feral grin upon him.

"Yes, and your last," he said, drawing his gun and squeezing a round off. The bullet impacted the Imam's chest. He dropped hard.

The gunshot caused the fifty worshippers to scream and turn toward Jafar, still holding the smoking gun. Achmed and his two cronies held guns of a more advanced yet older type: they appeared to have been American made. Jafar knew they were the weapons the Americans gave the Afghani *muhajadeen* in 1979.

"Do not be alarmed," he said, raising his voice as he stepped over the dead Imam's body. "We are not here to insult Allah; we are here to glorify Him. Who of you are true Muslims, Muslims who wish to see the infidel West exposed as frauds and godless fools?"

None raised their hands, despite looking at the guns for several seconds. A wave of fear passed over their faces. Those who were already kneeling toward Mecca began to pray feverishly.

Jafar frowned at them all. He shook his head and tsked a few times as he paced the floor.

"It is a shame. It truly is. You are all going to hell for your disobedience." Jafar stepped behind Achmed's men before he pronounced the worshippers' doom.

"Kill them all."

The three men, including Achmed — he brought his rifle up a second slower than the others, though — responded as ordered, pulling triggers and spraying the chapel with bullets, rapid-fire. They blasted those worshippers that tried to get up and run for their lives.

After two minutes, the terrorists were the only ones alive inside the mosque. They barricaded themselves inside, locking the doors immediately.

Jafar figured it would only be a matter of time before the American showed her face. He began to prepare his next broadcast to the world.

Chapter 40
Islington Safe House, London, England
4 August 2012 — 20.00 GMT/3:00 p.m. ET

As soon as she returned to Essex Road, Jaclyn fell asleep. Her exhaustion carried a heavy toll. She had gotten little sleep over the past few days and had been running on fumes — the price to pay for a counterterrorism operative when there is a psycho blowing up Olympic venues and hearses on the loose.

She slept deeply. Nothing entered her mind. Tom's command to her was to sleep and not worry about anything. She didn't know that as she pulled back into the small lot behind Carlton Cinema that Mohammed had entered the mosque and took it for his own.

It would be a worry for another hour — when she woke up.

It turned out Jaclyn slept nearly 13 hours; removing and storing her guns as well as removing her jumpsuit took a few minutes before she slid into bed. When she awoke, twilight had descended upon London. The thrumming, chopping sounds of helicopter propellers were heard somewhere nearby. She showered and ate, then called Tom's cell phone.

He picked up on the second ring.

"Hello, Sleeping Beauty."

Jaclyn smiled and said, "Good evening, Prince Charming. What's up?"

"A bloody situation is up, and that's not just the saying: Apparently our friend the terrorist has upped the ante a bit, and just where we thought he would go, too."

Alarms rang throughout Jaclyn's body. Her arms jerked taut.

"Where is he?"

"He's in Finsbury Park, in the mosque as we suspected. Fucking wanker shot up the prayer service and barricaded himself inside. We only heard about it a couple of hours ago; some Muslims tried to get in for midday services, only to find the doors locked. They left, not thinking of anything out of the ordinary happening.

"But when they returned for evening services, they found the doors still locked. They knocked on the door, it opened half a minute later, and the person who knocked was shot in the head."

Jaclyn cringed.

"People panicked, ran home, and some managed to call 999 and 112 and calmed down long enough for emergency services to figure out what the bloody hell was wrong. The police called us and informed us of the situation."

"How did you know it was Mohammed and not another jihadist flunky?" she asked.

"He sent another blooming broadcast to the BBC, they sent it to us; I don't know if they are going to broadcast it or not."

"I wouldn't place bets on them not broadcasting it, them being the bastion of journalism here and all."

"You just sounded like dad for a second," Tom said, after a pause.

Jaclyn smirked into the phone.

"He said that to the president before we fortified Olympic Park."

Tom became silent for a moment. Jaclyn knew what he was thinking.

"Tom," she said, "I'm going to get that bastard. Don't worry about that. Where are you now?"

"I'm on scene. I'm not too far away; I can come get you."

"Don't worry about it, I'll be there in a few minutes. I have to get dressed anyway."

That perked Tom up.

"Why, what are you wearing now?"

Jaclyn giggled softly.

"Don't you wish you knew?"

Tom laughed.

"Of course, that's why I asked."

"You are a naughty boy."

"You know it. I'll see you when you get here."

"Can you send that message to my iPad?"

"Of course I can. It's on its way."

Jaclyn pressed end, then tapped off a message to Dupuis.

Things are about to get hot here. Will advise. JJ

She sent the message, then looked to her jumpsuit. It was hanging on the door, unzipped, empty, and beckoning to her.

Jaclyn got up and walked to the door.

It was time to bring this son of a bitch down.

***

Once Jaclyn was dressed and armed — she slid a barrette into her hair with a crooked grin as soon as she had her Walthers stored — she grabbed her iPad and played the recording Tom sent her.

The first thing Jaclyn noticed was Mohammed's lack of a balaclava to hide the lower half of his face. She saw he had a thin goatee lining his chin and upper lip, and a rather large nose in the middle of his face. His hair receded quicker than the tide pulled out.

268

The eyes, though, remained unchanged: they had a darkness about them that only told Jaclyn he did not have an ounce of humanity inside him: He was a monster, plain and simple.

The recording played.

"Citizens of the world," Mohammed said, staring into the web cam on his laptop. The décor, Jaclyn noticed, had changed significantly; she figured he was broadcasting from inside the mosque. Candles burned on wall sconces, flickering light shadows off the red wallpaper. "I come before you to apologize for disturbing your celebration of sport."

Nice try, Jafar, she thought. *The people aren't going to buy your apology. A second after the explosion in Wembley would have been too late.*

"I will make it up to you."

Jaclyn's eyebrows, hidden by her HUD, rose a sliver. This ought to be good, she thought.

"I will take away the worst part of your society in exchange for a peaceful Olympic Games over the next week: Give me Jaclyn Johnson, the rogue American, to do as I wish to her."

Jaclyn breathed so hard through her nose that it seemed fire would have been the least worrisome thing to emerge.

"This bastard is desperate."

"If you give her to me," Mohammed continued, "I promise that I shall leave not only the Olympics alone, but the world at large, as well. Jaclyn Johnson is what is wrong with the Western world today: you allow women to dress scantily and provocative, not needing the help of men, not appearing to be weak."

Mohammed leaned closer, his eyes seeming to penetrate the camera, as if searching for Jaclyn.

"Give me Johnson, and I shall give you your freedom!"

The image winked out. Jaclyn tossed the iPad onto the bed and made a dash for the door.

No one bargains for my life, she thought as she leaped into the Citroën. *I'll take his before he swaps for mine.*

North London Central Mosque, Finsbury Park, London, England
4 August 2012 — 20.35 GMT/3:35 p.m. ET

"When will she come, brother Achmed?" Jafar asked in Farsi. "I expected her long before now."

The imposter Islamic operative leaned against the wall, his arms crossed in front of him as he stared at Jafar, a surly look in his eye. He continued to play this role as well as he could. It was simple enough to Witz: pretend to despise the West, say *Allahu Akbar* a few times, not eat pork. He made it appear that he was doing this all his life. The not eating pork part, he had. It was easy.

Inside, though, he seethed. These jihadists disgusted him. If he could break his cover and shoot all three of them before one of them raised their gun, he would have done so in a heartbeat.

"I do not know, brother Jafar. The Americans are predictable, though. She will come," Witz said.

"But when will she arrive? I want to kill her quickly so I can get on with Allah's noble work." Jafar began to pace. Witz noticed he looked over his left shoulder occasionally, as if looking for someone that was not there.

"Will you honor your promise, my brother?"

Jafar looked at him as if he were crazy.

"What promise? The one where I said I would leave the Olympics and the world alone?" Jafar laughed. "I had my fingers crossed when I said it. The camera didn't see it.

"As soon as I kill the American, I will send out a signal, where the final attack will take place. I may even do it before I kill the bitch; I haven't decided yet. The West underestimates me because they are a trusting lot. They do not believe we wouldn't dream to go back on our word: it's why negotiation and peace treaties never work. The Americans believe we want democracy in our nations. Their presidents and armies force-feed us their bull shit. It is the farthest thing from the truth. We want to be left alone, to mind our affairs, and to take back Gaza from the damned Israelis and give it to the Palestinians."

Witz's training prevented him from reacting. He simply raised his eyebrows, nodded his head, and smiled at the jihadist.

Inside, he wanted to ring Jafar's neck.

"She will come soon, brother Jafar," he said. "It is only a matter of when and how."

"The front door is out," Jafar was quick to point out. "She won't try the windows. American burglars would not want to let the occupants know they were trying to break in. When she does come, she'll try the rooftop method."

"You believe so?"

Jafar sneered. Witz could tell the terrorist was starting to lose what little patience he had.

"I know so. When she comes, I will be there waiting, and I will get the drop on the little bitch."

Jafar smiled as he walked away from Witz, motioning for the two goons to follow him. He turned and saw Witz standing there.

"Brother Achmed, come. We need to give Miss Johnson a welcome she will never forget."

"Give me a moment, brother Jafar. I must use the facilities. I feel like I have been carrying a large weight in my bladder since midday."

"You should have taken care of it long before now. Be quick about it. We shall be upstairs."

Jafar turned and walked away, the goons trailing him. Witz walked as quickly as he could without giving Jafar reason to believe he was being duplicitous.

He walked into the bathroom and leaned against the wall. He took out his phone and began to move his thumbs quickly against the standard phone keypad. It took him about a minute, but he was able to get a message off to the American's cell phone before flushing the toilet.

***

Jaclyn used the Citroën's GPS device to get her from the safe house to Finsbury Park. She meandered through Highbury, getting off Highbury Grove and slowly driving through the neighborhoods surrounding the old Arsenal Stadium — now a residential development called Highbury Square — and the new home of the Gunners located less than 700 feet apart from each other.

She didn't want to alert these good English people that death was approaching, a Grim Reaper on four wheels.

She drove down Avenell Road, the old East Stand of Highbury sliding by on her left. She turned left onto Gillespie Road. The Arsenal Tube station loomed at the western end of the street.

Jaclyn signaled to turn onto St. Thomas's Road.

Her HUD darkened as the mosque was under a group of floodlights, located at the far end of St. Thomas's.

An MI5 cordon waited near the bend where St. Thomas's Road met Pimsoll Road. Numerous residents stood near the barricade, all anxious for a glimpse of the doings up the street; red and blue strobe lights flashed away from the hood and fenders of various government vehicles.

The agents had seen the missile in black before, and this time framed by what had been the North Stand. They waved for it to stop. They knew who was in the driver's seat.

Jaclyn thumbed the window down. The sound of helicopters drowned out the servos driving the glass, reverberating off the pavement. The choppers were like the echoes of a broken record slamming her ears.

"Hello, lads." She smiled.

"Hello, Agent Snapshot. Agent Scouser said you may be making an appearance. Hold here, we'll go get lover boy for you."

Jaclyn blushed as the Britons smirked and walked away.

Moments later, Tom walked up and leaned over the Citroën, flashing a roguish grin Jaclyn's way.

"Hello, beautiful. What's a gorgeous secret agent like you doing in a place like this?"

Jaclyn's smirk was infectious.

"I'm here because you sent for me. What's the sit-rep?"

"Same as before," Tom replied, leaning closer. "We haven't gotten a dicky bird out of the mosque, and no one can get in."

"I haven't tried yet," Jaclyn said, before driving around the MI5 cordon. She pulled to the side and turned the engine off, before throwing the door open. She stepped out. A chorus of male voices sang in awe of the American; their eyes met the Lycra and became lost in it.

She was oblivious to their attention.

"What's your plan?" Tom asked as he and a few other agents walked up to her on the other side of the barrier.

"Right now, I don't have one. Do we have detailed blueprints of the building?" Jaclyn looked to the mosque and saw the tower spotlights weaving back and forth across its façade.

"Not yet, but we can get them for you," one of the agents said before sprinting off like a track star.

"What do you know about this building?" Jaclyn said as she walked to the middle of St. Thomas's with Tom. She looked up toward it, letting her HUD move across the upper levels.

"There's not much to know. There's one gate on the left-hand side, if you're looking at the building from the street."

"What about back entrances?"

"Only if you want to be run over by a train; the place is sealed up."

"That dome on the roof," Jaclyn said. "Is there a panel that can be moved so I can get in?"

"I think we should wait for the blueprints to get here," Tom said.

Jaclyn bristled.

"You're not being much help right now."

"I'm trying to be as much help as I possibly can. You need a plan before you go barging in there like a cock-a-whoop."

The agent with the blueprints returned, out of breath but holding the tube like a relay race baton. Tom grabbed the tube and unfurled the blueprints, laying them as flat as can be on the Citroën's hood.

Jaclyn rubbed her side against Tom's as her HUD scanned every inch of the paper. She was trying to see where the rooftop entrances were located.

She wanted to invade this building using stealth; there was no way to pull off a stunt like Waco without infuriating millions of Muslims around the world.

Her HUD scanned the southwestern part of the roof. It outlined a small door and flashed through her limited vision.

"Here we go," she said, pointing at the door. "Right there. That's the only way in from the roof that I can see."

Tom looked at it with raised eyebrows.

"How the bloody hell are you going to get up there, though?"

"I have a crossbow and —" Jaclyn said before she paused. She felt at her utility belt. "Shit!"

"What?"

"I don't have my crossbow and grappler line. Fuck my life."

"So that's going to put us in a bit of a bind, right? Do we bring in ladders? Give you a boost? I'm sure a few of these blokes would love to help you up if they got to run their hands on your arse."

Jaclyn shook her head in disbelief.

He was right, though: *we're in a bind*, she thought. Without her crossbow, she would be unable to get to the roof without a sound.

She stared into the dark North London sky. Three helicopters shone their spotlights upon the mosque, circling the building counterclockwise. The heavy whirr of the propeller blades met her ears once again.

A slight smile touched her face.

An idea had struck her. It was a moment of brilliance she hoped would last long enough to work.

"Tom," she said, keeping her Foster Grants trained on the metal birds. "Does MI5 or the SIS have helicopters?"

"Yes," he replied quickly. "Those are three of ours."

"Have any more in service?"

Another grin made its way across Tom's face.

"What do you have planned, Snapshot?"

Jaclyn's smile matched that of the Briton.

"I just think I can meet Mohammed a little easier if I can get the drop on him."

A landing zone was set up for Jaclyn inside the Emirates Stadium.

Tom and Jaclyn rode in a government car to the stadium, lights flashing despite no traffic on Gillespie Road or Drayton Park. The car turned onto the bridge over the Drayton Park Rail Station and came to a stop on the other side. The couple stepped out and looked out upon the southeastern façade of the Emirates for the briefest of seconds. They rushed forward as soon as security guards wearing red vests popped their heads out the doors.

"MI5," Tom said as he blew past the security guards. "Chopper is incoming."

Jaclyn kept on his heels as they ran through the bowels of the stadium, a blur of black Lycra. They turned into the lower bowl and trotted down the steps of the Clock End, surrounded by a sea of red. For half a moment, the seats reminded her of the lower bowl at Wembley.

The helicopter began its descent into the stadium, its blades sweeping around as they displaced air.

Jaclyn and Tom waited at the wall separating the seats from the pitch until the bird touched down on the midway line. They felt the powerful surge of wind come at them as the helicopter landed.

Without prompting, Jaclyn leaped over the wall, Tom following. They rushed forward. A door on the side of the chopper slid open, the cargo bay's maw ever welcoming.

"You better not get hurt," Tom said. "I have no idea how you're going to manage this."

"Why? Think you're going to come in and save my ass? I think not." Jaclyn winked. "And don't worry about how I'm going to do it; I was in gymnastics and ballet when I was a girl. This will be nothing compared to that experience."

"Just take care of yourself. Don't underestimate this guy."

"He underestimates me, Tom."

Tom stared at her for the longest time before he nodded. He raised his hand and stroked her cheek. He bent in and gave her a soft kiss upon the lips.

"For luck."

Jaclyn's grin was mischievous.

"I hope there's more of that for when I get out of there."

"You bet your arse there is."

"My BlackBerry is on. If it doesn't ring and goes to voice mail, I'm in trouble: I've set it to self-destruct if someone can't input the password."

"If it goes to voice mail, I'm coming in with both guns blazing."

Jaclyn smiled as she stepped onto the chopper. The door slid closed. Tom backed away from the helicopter as Jaclyn began to belt in.

Tom was on the pitch drop as the helicopter's engines purred, the pilot giving it the gas. The bird began to rise.

"Good luck, Jaclyn," he whispered.

***

Jaclyn looked through her HUD and watched as the helicopter rose through the rectangular opening in the Emirates' roof. The steelwork arches seemed to drop away as the bird lifted into the darkness, and as soon as it was clear, they departed Ashburton Grove and headed just to the right of north.

"Do you have any idea how you're going to do this?" the pilot asked Jaclyn without turning his head.

"I do," she replied. "You guys have rope?"

"In the back, near the hatch."

Jaclyn turned her head to the left and saw the coils of rope sitting there, waiting for her. A crane-like device sat near it, which would help lower her to the roof.

"Good. Once you get near the mosque, file in and follow until I tell you otherwise. We'll take a few rotations around the mosque while I get ready. Then we'll play hardball with this psycho."

"Roger that."

The chopper passed over the row of houses that lined Quill Street and fell into line with the three other helicopters as soon as they came to the mosque. The pilot radioed to the others as the searchlights danced from street level.

Jaclyn unbuckled and made her way to the back of the helicopter and immediately wrapped the rope around her waist. It was a thick strand. Jaclyn managed to make a thick knot.

"Now would be a great time to forget my crossbow," she said to herself. "Alright, open the hatch and hover over the mosque until I untie this knot."

"Roger that, Snapshot. Beginning to hover in five."

The pilot counted off the seconds until the helicopter hovered directly over the holy Muslim building. The hatch opened and Jaclyn sat on the edge. One of the MI5 agents in the chopper kicked the crane into motion, and Jaclyn pushed off as soon as there was plenty of slack.

She began to repel as the rope loosened. Jaclyn slowly dropped the 50 feet from the rear of the copter. The small dome on the roof was directly under her, a pillar to the right.

Less than a minute later, Jaclyn's feet touched the dome's roof. She quickly untied the rope and flung it to the side. The helicopter tilted to the side, then took off toward the southeast.

Jaclyn slid down the dome on her backside. She grabbed her right hip Walther and walked slowly to the door, creeping along as the other three helicopters continued their circular vigil over the mosque. She slapped the button on her utility belt and felt the Kevlar form up.

She slowly opened the door and eased herself in. A circular stairway led down into the building. She tried not to make any noise as she walked downward.

Her HUD scanned the hallway for threats. Her breathing was even, her heart rate normal. She kept her steps lively, ready for anything to come at her. Her Walther was up by her head, right hand on the handle, her left providing support.

A ladder lay upon the landing. Jaclyn looked at it and thought it out of place inside a mosque. She wondered what it was doing there.

"*Allahu Akbar!*" sounded through the small landing. Jaclyn's eyes widened. The HUD wailed in her ears. The alarm was too late.

Instead of Jaclyn getting the drop on Mohammed, the terrorist, one of Yusuf's goons, got the drop on her, leaping from the hidden alcove above, knocking her to the floor. The impact caused Jaclyn's Walther to discharge. The smell of gunpowder hung in the air. She kept a firm grip upon the gun, though.

Jaclyn and the terrorist began a slight tussle on the landing, but the terrorist had the advantage. Jaclyn tried to elbow the bastard hard from the right side, but only caught the muscle on his arm instead of his head. The terrorist felt it, though, and fell off to the left.

Jaclyn pounced.

She landed on the terrorist's broad torso, the Kevlar cushion causing his breath to rush out of his lungs. Jaclyn brought the gun up and over her right shoulder, ready to pistol-whip him like she did to the bastard in Regent's Park.

Her HUD rang out in surprise as the foot came out of nowhere.

She didn't react fast enough.

She heard a crack against the back of her skull. The Walther fell from her grasp. She crumpled to the floor just as everything in her HUD's field of vision went dark.

Jafar stood over her, looking down at the American as if he wanted to put her lights out permanently. His sneer was contemptuous, full of loathing.

His foot stung, the force of the kick tingling his toes.

"Bring her to the altar," he ordered Achmed and the other agent, before turning to the other one, a look of hatred in his eyes. The others grabbed Jaclyn and pulled her away, her knees dragging on the floor.

"You let a woman best you," he said to the other. "She nearly beat you, and if it wasn't for me, she would have taken you out of the game."

The agent labored to breathe. The force of the American's pressure to his chest caused him to gulp huge chunks of air.

"I'm sorry, brother Jafar," he gasped, each word separated by a breath. "I won't let it happen again."

"No," Jafar said. "It definitely won't happen again. Say hello to Allah for me."

The gun went up.

The agent's eyes went wide in sheer terror, in sheer disbelief. The blood rushed out of his face. He tried to get his arms up, as if he could ward the bullet away.

"No, brother Ja—"

Jafar ruthlessly pulled the trigger before the agent uttered the second syllable.

The blood rushed out of his agent's body from the wound between the eyes. Jafar turned and left him there.

He followed the others, who dragged Jaclyn into the Muslim sanctuary. His quick gait allowed him to overtake them.

He began to feel slightly weak. The hour for *Iftar* had long passed, and he had not had the chance to eat anything since the last *Iftar*. He cursed himself for letting this American get his goat. He missed *Suhoor* this morning because of her interference. It had now been well over 24 hours since he last ate anything.

Jafar looked on as the two others dumped Jaclyn onto the altar, securing her arms and legs. They removed her utility belt and took her guns away. They slipped her Foster Grants away from her face, her eyes closed.

They tipped it onto its side. Soon, they had the altar top facing away from the wall.

To Jafar's eye, the American looked ready to be sacrificed to Allah, almost in the same manner the Romans killed the Christian god: Jaclyn's arms were stretched out to her sides, bound to the edge. Jesus had been the King of the Jews, their great hope. They cast the American in the same light, the only hope for the West against the wave of Islam that crested above them.

Jafar knew Allah would vanquish the Americans, the Britons, and anyone who stood in the way.

It was how he believed.

North London Central Mosque, Finsbury Park, London, England
4 August 2012 — 22.45 GMT/5:45 p.m. ET

Jaclyn stirred. A soft moan escaped as she came to.

Her head throbbed.

She tried to move her arms, but couldn't. The throbbing grew as she became fully conscious.

"Did you have a good nap?"

The voice was eerily familiar to her ears. She didn't have to strain her memory that far to find it. She had heard the voice in her head every waking minute since she came to England.

Jafar.

She kept her eyes closed. She noticed the weight upon her face had left, which immediately told her she was without her HUD.

Oh boy, she thought. *This is going to be just a tad difficult.*

She also felt light around the waist. The utility belt, she realized, was gone. So were her guns, and so was her BlackBerry.

She grinned.

Jaclyn grinned because she knew the terrorists would try to find out what was on the device; terrorists were a curious lot. It meant that Tom would come in with the RAF when he tried to get in touch with her and couldn't.

For now, she awaited the torture that was sure to come.

She could withstand torture. She had to. It was the only way of making it out of this situation alive.

Jaclyn opened her eyes.

She wished she hadn't.

The lighting, to normal eyes, was of candles and soft light bulbs illuminating the small room. To Jaclyn's eyes, it was the worst form of hell. Light shone brighter than the sun to her eyes. It was visual overload to the point that it impeded her limited vision.

She slammed her eyelids shut.

Without her HUD, in these lighting conditions, she was extremely handicapped.

She heard footsteps rapidly approach. The left side of her face stung half a second after the steps stopped.

The stinging lingered.

"Wake up, you bitch," Jafar said. It sounded as if his face was centimeters away. "Open those eyes. I know you are awake."

She kept her eyes closed.

He slapped her again, this time harder. Her head turned with the slap, absorbing the impact. Her mouth opened. Her tongue slid out and licked at the blood trickling out of the corner of her mouth.

"Open your eyes or I'll knock your head clean off!" Jafar threatened.

Jaclyn forced her eyes open, a sliver at a time.

The pain was overwhelming.

She kept them open, regardless of the pain. She inhaled and fought the pain away.

"Do you know who I am, bitch?"

"Jafar." Jaclyn said it as if uttering a disgusting swear word.

She tilted her head as he snickered deep in his throat. The terrorist came into somewhat clearer focus. Jaclyn could only see shadows, as if the terrorist was only vapor without form. If he didn't have a voice, she wouldn't even know the shadow represented anything.

"Yes, I am Jafar." He began to pace in front of her. "And you, Jaclyn Johnson, are my prisoner, my bargaining chip, and as soon as the West bows down to me, my ultimate sacrifice to Allah."

The sound of his voice ground upon her ears.

"What makes you think the West would ever bow down to a lunatic like yourself?" she asked.

This time, the right side of her face stung.

This time, Jafar didn't hold back.

Jaclyn didn't allow the pain to affect her. She turned her head and stared down the terrorist.

What surprised her was the terrorist did not recoil under her white-eyed stare. It was if he accepted it blindly.

She grinned inwardly at the pun.

"The West will bow down to me," Jafar said. "The West has seen that I have the power to destroy one influential city; I have brought London to its knees."

"Really?" Jaclyn replied sarcastically. "People are walking about outside. The Tube continues to run. No one is waving a white flag. The

Queen continues to rule. Apparently you're taking a page out of Osama's playbook: He may have hit New York and Washington hard, but they were able to withstand the blow. They are rebuilding the towers, Jafar. He did not win."

"He won!" Jafar screamed. "The defeat of the West on September 11 was only the first! More are coming! The West will fall, and I'll be praised for helping to bring about their downfall!"

"You're absolutely delusional!"

"You're a filthy woman!"

"Let my hands free and I'll show you filthy," Jaclyn sneered.

"Brother Jafar," one of the other men said, causing Jaclyn's spine to straighten.

That voice, Jaclyn thought, *belongs to Witz. He got in.*

She kept her relief to herself.

"The bitch is unarmed, she is blind, and she's just a woman. What would it hurt to let her down? She can't hurt you at all."

Silence ensued.

"Take her down," Jafar said, "but keep your weapons on her. The bitch may be unarmed, but she's still dangerous. I know what she is capable of."

Witz pulled his gun out and set the chamber while the other terrorist untied her. As soon as she was loose, she began to rub her wrists to get the circulation going again. She was soon standing on her own. The second terrorist brought his gun to bear.

Jaclyn was unconcerned. The guns, as far as she knew, did not point at her skull. They did not know that her jumpsuit contained a Kevlar lining.

She smiled as she felt the body protection against her skin.

"So," she said to Jafar, "what are you going to do to me now? Have me wash your dishes? How about you make me sweep out your hut? How about brushing your camel for you?"

Jafar sneered. Jaclyn didn't see it.

Her eyes burned.

"You are an insolent woman, and exactly the reason the West must be brought to its knees."

"Why, because I speak my mind?"

"Yes! Women are beneath Muslim men; we are the powerful gender in the Middle East!"

Jaclyn huffed.

"No wonder you're losing the war."

Jafar held in his temper. His hands clenched several times, his fingernails digging into his palms. If Jaclyn wore her HUD, she would have seen blue flames surging from the terrorist's nose.

Where that device was, she did not know.

In this light, she would be able to see its shadow.

"Enough of this," Jafar said. "I will show you exactly how the West will bow to me. Follow me."

The terrorist turned and walked away. Witz stuck a gun lightly into Jaclyn's back, feeling the resistance to the Kevlar. They led her into a small anteroom near the sanctuary, where Jafar had his netbook set up. The terrorist maximized a window on the toolbar.

"Can you see this, Miss Johnson?" he asked as he turned toward Jaclyn.

"Not at all. I can't see a thing without my glasses," she replied. "I can see shadows, though. All I can see is one big blur."

Jafar seemed to smile.

"Very well. That means you won't be able to see what I'm doing right now." He raised his hand. A gun was in it, and he pointed it right at the American. The other terrorist eased his gun down.

"You just lifted your arm," she replied. "Like I said, I can see shadows. If you're holding something, I wouldn't be able to know without my glasses."

"Achmed, give her the glasses."

Witz was not so light this time, especially under Jafar's harsh glare. He took the HUD out of a pocket and slapped them into Jaclyn's hand.

Jaclyn put them on, and the terrorist — and his netbook — came into view.

She now saw a countdown clock, which had already begun. The netbook display indicated that 3:26 remained until whatever the countdown was for was set off.

I need to know what this sociopath has in mind, she thought.

"So what is the clock for? Your birthday? Your kid's birthday? I know it's not New Year's Eve yet; boy, did I have fun last year..."

"It is not for something as uninteresting as that," Jafar said impatiently. "You see, Miss Johnson, I have said that the West shall bow to both myself and Allah. This will prove the Middle East's dominance over the rest of the world. This will be the start of more strikes: we shall get our revenge against the United States for its sins, the sin of turning its back upon my homeland in the '80s.

"But first, we will focus our attack upon England, and it shall be the greatest attack of them all."

Jaclyn defiantly crossed her arms across her body.

"You've already destroyed Wembley and a part of Olympic Park. What's next? Heathrow? Big Ben? The O2? London Bridge? Am I missing anything?"

"How about Buckingham Palace?"

The way Jafar said it made Jaclyn pause, as if she were giving it consideration. She turned her head thoughtfully.

Then she realized he was being serious. Shock registered immediately.

"You're absolutely insane," she said.

"I'm actually a Taurus," Jafar said in an off-handed way. "I'm glad you've realized what I'm going to do; it would have taken the Briton I had killed ages to discover, even if he went to Eton. My people have taken over a farm on the Iberian Peninsula. I control the warheads. I have received an email from my people, and they informed me they armed the weapons. Our plans, the Grand Scheme of Allah, is about to reach a fevered climax."

Jafar turned and began to input commands. Jaclyn stared at the back of his head and wished her HUD came equipped with poisoned darts. She felt a sudden weight come upon her right side. She knew exactly what it was.

Witz stepped behind her. He, too, wore black. He stuck his gun into her waist.

"Now," Jafar said, "All it is now is a waiting game. I've set the warheads, and now the plans are to be carried out. We might as well get comfortable."

"Tell me, Jafar: What kind of warheads are you using?"

"Why is that important?" the terrorist asked.

"You just told me to get comfortable," Jaclyn replied, reaching for the barrette holding her blonde hair back. She pulled it out and shook her hair free. "If they are just bombs, then I want to watch them hit. If they are nuclear, then I want to relax until I'm incinerated."

Jafar simply chuckled.

"We will not be killed; no, I'm not ready to sacrifice myself. I've had plenty of time to be killed, and I haven't been. Even during the Afghanistan Civil War, during the Soviet Invasion, I endured. Allah had big things for me to accomplish. I touched off the London bombings in 2005. I prepared the Olympic attacks, which you tried to stop. And now, I'm going to take out the British monarchy in," he turned and looked at the netbook's timer, "30 seconds."

"Well," Jaclyn said with a slight laugh, "that's a relief. I thought you were going to turn London into a ghost town."

Jafar laughed, too.

"That's my next attack on the city. And then Washington, D.C. will be next after that. Of course, I'll be long gone from here, and I will receive plenty of virgins when I meet Allah."

Jaclyn smirked. She pressed down on the barrette until it clicked. Her HUD told her that the jihadist fool to her left had lowered his weapon.

"I hope you brought plenty of condoms, since the only virgins you're going to get are males."

Jafar looked quizzically at Jaclyn, but the American smiled at her prey. She raised her right hand and flicked her wrist at Jafar's neck. The terrorist's eyes widened as the *shiruken*, a modified ninja star, spun toward him.

He ducked and felt the breeze go over her head. The star became stuck in the wall behind him.

The goon to Jaclyn's left was dumbfounded, but she spun and kicked the gun from his hand, rendering him out of action. Witz covered Jafar, leveling his gun upon the terrorist. Jaclyn snapped her Walther from its holster and squeezed the trigger once, burying a bullet into the first. He dropped like a stone.

Jaclyn quickly turned her gun toward the terrorist.

She found Jafar holding the gun, aimed right at her.

It was two on one: Jaclyn and Witz were holding Jafar at gunpoint, while Jafar had his weapon trained steadily upon Jaclyn. If Jafar shot at Jaclyn, Witz would pop the terrorist. But if Jafar moved the gun over and shot the Israeli Intelligence officer, Jaclyn would be free to put a bullet in his head.

The seconds on the counter ticked down with every heartbeat and breath. Time descended rapidly. There were 11 seconds left.

"Stop the launch and you'll walk out of here alive," Witz said quickly, his disguise and cover thrown away.

Nine seconds.

"And if I refuse?"

Seven seconds.

"You roll out of here on a gurney," Jaclyn said.

Five seconds.

Jafar didn't move for the netbook. He stood there and grinned, holding the gun upon Jaclyn. Jaclyn looked past the gun and saw the countdown at 00:01.

Jaclyn's HUD toned before a gunshot ripped through the small anteroom.

Witz yelled. Blood poured from the wound in his left leg. He fell to the floor, distracting the other combatants. He grabbed at the wound with his left hand, dropping his gun as he writhed in agony.

Jaclyn saw the one she had shot holding a smoking gun from the floor. The terrorist laughed before he died. He dropped his gun in front of him.

Jaclyn looked back to Jafar. Jafar looked back to Jaclyn. They weren't far apart; two feet separated the guns. A nervous tension filled the room.

It was too late now, though: the weapon Jafar set off had already blasted off some somewhere in Spain. Jaclyn only had one option.

"It's down to us now, Jafar," Jaclyn said softly. "Us alone. Who's quicker on the draw? You or me?"

Jafar sneered at the American.

"You think it's going to come down to a gun fight." It wasn't a question.

"I know it's going to come down to that."

Jaclyn breathed deep. Jafar's shoulders rose and fell with each breath, too. Jaclyn's HUD saw Jafar's eyes did not blink as they stared at her. The left corner of Jaclyn's mouth twitched in anticipation.

Jaclyn's left hand was a blur. It came around, grasped the barrel and turned it up, wrenching it from the terrorist's grasp. She pulled away with a gun in each hand.

Jafar looked in shock. He was in awe that a woman would best him in anything, and here he was, looking down the barrel of his own gun and the American's remaining Walther.

Jaclyn, however, enjoyed her triumph.

"Enjoy your nap," she said darkly, before pulling the trigger of her Walther and the swiped gun at the same time. Jafar shrieked as the first bullet shattered his heart. The other burrowed into his brain. He fell hard and never moved again.

Even though the death of Jafar should have ended the mission at last, there was more work to be done now. Jaclyn tossed the other gun as far away from the dead terrorists as possible, holstered her Walther and located her utility belt. It had been right next to Jafar's netbook that she didn't even notice it until she took a good glimpse at the computer. She dug out her BlackBerry and quickly dialed it.

Her HUD said it was closing in on 11:30 p.m.

The phone rang twice before Tom picked up.

"Where the devil have you been?" he said.

"Right here, like I said I would be. I only took a little bit of a nap. Tom, he's dead, but not before setting off a warhead. It's set to target Buckingham Palace."

"What?! A warhead? How?"

"Computerized controls. I can see the path of the rocket. It's headed north. I need to try to stop it."

"And how the devil do you think you're going to do that?"

"I have no idea."

"Great, I'm glad you have a plan, Jaclyn."

"I don't give a shit about the plan right now, Tom. You need to get a hold of Willows and let him know he needs to evacuate the Royal Family."

"I'll call him right now."

"Good. I'm going to see how to stop this blasted rocket."

The pairing hung up before Jaclyn took a good look at the netbook display. She moved the mouse over the abort button. She clicked it.

Abort overridden, it flashed twice.

"Shit!" she said. She took a deep breath after she cursed and thought up a new plan of attack. "Alright, let's try to alter this bad boy."

She found the coordinates tab and pulled them down. She quickly changed the coordinates only a few degrees to the north and east before pressing the redirect key.

Redirect confirmed.

Jaclyn took a deep breath as the command was accepted. She swooned as the pressure was felt falling off her shoulders. She leaned against the counter.

"Jaclyn," Witz whimpered.

"Lavi," Jaclyn breathed. She pushed herself off the edge and kneeled in front of the Israeli.

"I need a doctor," Witz said.

"I'll get one. Keep your gun handy. Hopefully these guys are really dead and not playing."

"Jaclyn?"

"Yes?"

"You see that red stuff on the floor over there?"

Jaclyn looked at the Mossad agent and snickered.

"You have red stuff pouring out of you, too."

"Don't remind me, please."

"I'll get EMS in here, double quick."

Jaclyn grabbed her utility belt and ran for the door. She drew her Walther and blasted the padlock away. She yanked the chain and tossed it aside before throwing the doors open.

Exclamations of "She's alive!" met her ears before she yelled for medics to rush in to tend to Witz's injuries. She ran down the stairs as the medics rushed up. Jaclyn saw Tom coming toward her just as a rather large missile roared off to the side.

"What the blooming hell was that?" one older man shouted.

"I take it that was the missile?"

"That would be the missile."

"Where did you send it?"

"To tell you the truth, I have no idea. I just typed in some numbers and clicked redirect."

"We'll know soon enough," Tom said, just before they heard a booming echo coming from the northeast of their current position.

Within five minutes, radios all over St. Thomas's Road squealed: "Large building on Love Lane, N17, fully engulfed."

Jaclyn heard that and saw Tom's eyes shift back and forth. Then they widened a bit as he looked to Jaclyn.

"You don't happen to be an Arsenal supporter, are you?"

Jaclyn gave a quizzical look.

"No, why?"

"You just torched White Hart Lane."

The pair laughed for several minutes while the news of the bomb detonating at The Lane, went through the crowd. At first there was disbelief, but the skepticism soon turned into cheers.

They all happened to be Arsenal supporters.

Chapter 42
West Ham Park, Stratford, London, England
18 August 2012 — 10.00 GMT/5:00 a.m. ET

The Closing Ceremonies went off without a hitch on August 12, the Olympic flag handed over to Rio de Janeiro. The IOC president, who was close to collapse only a week before, looked dignified as he stood in the middle of the Olympic Stadium. He declared that the Games, marred by tragedy early, withstood the hatred that the Olympics oppose.

The crowd roared its approval of the president, who introduced his successor to the world.

The 2012 Summer Olympics were over.

Jaclyn watched the ceremony from a side tunnel. She did not want to receive any accolades from an adoring crowd. She did not want to receive their thanks. That wasn't in the job description: clandestine officers were supposed to be undercover. Even though Bennett had outed her in the papers, she still maintained a strict no pictures policy — at least when she wasn't modeling, that is.

At that point, though, she wasn't worried about modeling; she didn't even know if she would have any contracts coming toward her due to her rogue status.

The next Saturday was cloudy. Tom picked Jaclyn up from Islington and brought her past the Olympic Stadium to nearby West Ham Park.

"I know you're going to enjoy this," he said from the driver's seat. Jaclyn had returned the Citroën earlier in the week and had done so in near mint condition. Other agents couldn't say the same.

"Where are you taking me?"

"A little park in Stratford. It's not that far away."

They drove.

By the time 10 a.m. rolled around, they were nearing the park. Tom had timed their drive just right: It if had been a few minutes earlier, they would have caught the traffic headed to nearby Upton Park for the West Ham United-Barnsley football match. The Hammers could not avoid relegation a year ago and dropped from the Premier League. It was the opening weekend for the Football League.

Tom drove them up the Portway and took a left onto Upton Lane. A parking lot awaited them.

Jaclyn jumped out of the car as soon as it stopped. Warm air hit her face. Tom popped the trunk before he dug out several pairs of pads, a helmet and a long, flat paddle.

"Are those —"

"Yes, they are. It's cricket equipment. I'm going to teach you how to play the game."

"I thought you liked soc—"

Tom glared.

"Football?"

He nodded.

"I played cricket during Sixth Form, but I always was a footballer. Dad was the cricketer in the family. The girls played rounders."

They walked hand in hand toward the cricket pitch on the northern side of the park. He showed her how to strap the pads on to her legs as well as how to stand; Jaclyn quickly learned that a batsman must stand in front of the stumps, unlike on opposite sides of the plate like in baseball or softball.

"Remember that you have 360-degree hitting; you can send the ball in any direction. It's much better than baseball."

"If you say so," Jaclyn replied.

Tom smirked and walked back about 25 yards from the end of the pitch.

"You need to keep the ball away from the stumps," he yelled. "When the ball gets close, you whack it away, even if it hits the ground. Okay?"

Jaclyn nodded.

Tom began to run forward, his feet churning the grass. He picked up speed and, as he got within five feet of the opposite edge of the pitch began a quick, windmill wind up. His arm never crossed 15 degrees.

He released the ball.

Jaclyn's HUD was able to pick up the ball's rotation as it sped toward her. It began to dip and bounced off the ground some five feet away, kicking up a light bit of dirt off the pitch. It went toward her legs.

She swung heavily to the left. The bat made contact and sent the ball flying away. It went right over midwicket, just as the sun pierced the clouds and sent its warm rays below.

Nigel, Jaclyn knew, smiled down upon her and Tom at that moment.

She couldn't help but smile, too.

THE END

Like what you read? Check out more books and stories by Sean Sweeney

Model Agent: A Thriller
Rogue Agent: A Thriller

Royal Switch
Zombie Showdown (Coming August 2011)

The Obloeron Prequel Series
The Rise Of The Dark Falcon
The Shadow Looms (Coming soon)

As John Fitch V

The Obloeron Trilogy
The Quest For The Chalice
The Return To Labergator
The Fall Of Myrindar

One Hero, A Savior
Turning Back The Clock
A Galaxy At War
The Mastermind: A novella

Short stories
Sidetracked
Vuvuzombie
Refugees (in David Dalglish's A Land of Ash anthology)

About the Author

Sean Sweeney's love of reading began in 1988, when he was handed J.R.R. Tolkien's classic *The Hobbit*. His passion for writing began in 1993, as a sophomore in high school, when he began writing sports for his local newspaper. Born and raised in North Central Massachusetts, Sweeney has written for several newspapers. When he is not writing, he enjoys playing golf, reading, watching movies, enjoying the Boston Red Sox, the New England Revolution, Arsenal F.C., Gold Coast F.C., and playing with Caramel The Wonder Cat.

Web site: http://www.johnfitchv.com
E-mail: johnfitchv@yahoo.com

A fan of Jaclyn Johnson? Find her fan page on Facebook (Jaclyn Johnson, a.k.a. Snapshot)

Made in the USA
Middletown, DE
18 May 2020